# PILGRIMS IN PARADISE

# PILGRIMS
# IN PARADISE

## A Novel

### FRANK G. SLAUGHTER

Doubleday & Company, Inc.
Garden City, New York

# BRISTOL

THE pane of the cupboard-washroom window was thick with frost. When he pushed back the casement to let out the steam from his morning tub, Dr. Paul Sutton saw there was a fresh blanket of snow on Bristol Quay—but the breath from the harbor was sweet with a promise of spring. Scanning the morning bustle at the gangways while he toweled himself, he wondered again at his strange sense of withdrawal.

True, the salt tang in his lungs was a familiar elixir; the chantey drifting across the water (from the capstan bars of an outbound coaster) struck the same chord from his heartstrings—but he felt none of the usual urge to board his own ship forthwith and put to sea. After a scant week in England, it seemed, the hug of the tight little island was strong as ever. It was impossible to believe that a year ago today he had still enjoyed shipwreck on an unnamed island deep in the Indian Ocean—where the amber-skinned natives (especially the females) had proved as hospitable as their climate.

Even there—he saw it clearly now—he had been destined to make this inevitable rendezvous with Silas.

He had returned from that last long voyage, via a Portuguese Indiaman from Goa. In due course, he had put into the Thames, with the vague thought of hanging out his shingle in either London or Edinburgh. Silas' letter had awaited him in the former capital. It had announced the fruition of his brother's lifelong dream: the mustering of the company of Eleutherian Adventurers, and his urgent need of a ship's doctor to make the roster complete. It had never occurred to Paul to refuse the order (all his brother's missives were orders of a sort). Once he had reached Bristol, and grasped the extent of Silas' vision, he had wished the letter had miscarried. Without the promise he had given, and Silas' obvious need, he would have long since resigned the post thrust so hastily upon him.

The urge to withdraw was not due to age: he had not yet turned thirty. Nor was it fear of peril ahead: his whole life had been passed in danger's presence—a calculated risk to milk the last drop from experience, no matter what language his friends or enemies might be speaking. Nor was it blind desire to settle in England after his wandering: in the late winter of 1647, this was no place for a wise traveler to linger. Torn by years of religious dissension, England was a land whose king and Parliament were now at armed loggerheads, with the booming voice of Cromwell in the wings, like an absurd villian who had muffed his first entrance cue and was already rehearsing his second.

The prophets of doom had said that universal civil war must wrack England tomorrow: for once, Dr. Paul Sutton concluded, the prophets were accurate. Footloose as he was, he should rejoice at a chance to put an ocean between himself and this time of troubles. He could still wish for another ship—and other companions than the Eleutherian Adventurers. Silas' colonists were a mixed bag indeed.

Leaning on the washroom sill, he had an unimpeded view of the slab-sided vessel that would soon bear him to the New World. In her mooring across from the Feathers Inn, she seemed a poor relation at a royal levee—yet she was entirely at ease in the company of sleek argosies from the Orient, purse-proud merchantmen from Antwerp and Hamburg, exotic traders (bold of sterncastle, proud of banner) from other European marts. Paul admitted the *Adventurer* was seaworthy, in her lumpish way: it was right that her stubby bowsprit should be pointed toward new horizons, rather than ports across the Channel. He judged her not too much larger than her famous counterpart—another tub called the *Mayflower*.

Twenty-seven years before, the *Mayflower* had helped to make
history in what was now the Massachusetts Bay Colony, the first
Puritan settlement in America. If she reached the Lucayas safely,
the *Adventurer* might add another, no less important page to the
record.

More than one hundred and fifty colonists had pledged their
names to the voyage. Thanks to Silas' missionary zeal, and the
contribution from the estate of Geoffrey Trevor (the great Puritan
divine), there were ample stores aboard for the conquest of a
tropical paradise. As ship's doctor, he had checked those stores
thoroughly: he knew that his brother's courage was infinite. Why
should his doubts persist?

On Captain Sperry's chart, the island they sought was called
Eleuthera: the tongue-twister was more melodious in the original
Greek, where *eleutheros* was a synonym for liberty. Explorers
had marked down its location (not too precisely) in the Lucayas
—a sprawling archipelago off the Florida coast, which some car-
tographers called the Bahamas. Sperry himself had sighted it on
a previous voyage to the New World, so there was no reason to
doubt his ability to fetch another landfall.

It was still hard for Paul to vision Eleuthera clearly. Sperry
had said it was ringed by coral shoals—but Paul was certain it bore
no resemblance to the atoll where he had lived through six months
of agreeable (and intensely pagan) shipwreck. Nor did it resem-
ble the jungle-choked volcanos he had seen rising from the sea
below Java Head, swarming with kinky-headed cannibals. The
Bahamas, from all reports, were largely uninhabited, save for a
pirates' nest or two.

If Eleuthera found its niche in history—the ship's doctor faced
the conviction on the eve of his sailing date—it would be another
island outpost of England, on the doorstep of New Spain. This,
he felt sure, had been his brother's true motive when the colony
was first organized, though Silas had yet to state his plans clearly.
The Puritan sect had fought hard for recognition in the mother
country: if Cromwell triumphed in the next (and final) clash
with the House of Stuart, his lieutenants beyond the seas would
share the glory. Silas Sutton (a Puritan in the classic mold and

the great Geoffrey Trevor's most brilliant disciple) had been the
natural bellwether for this newest enterprise—whether Eleuthera
remained a peaceful colony, or a steppingstone in England's war
with popery.

At Massachusetts Bay, those same Puritans were sometimes
dubbed Pilgrims—or Pilgrim Fathers. Silas' band of pioneers
would wear the same mantle in the Lucayas. Pilgrims in paradise,
thought Dr. Paul Sutton, was a contradiction in terms—but history
had been founded ere now on paradox. As the leader's brother, he
could hardly question the purity of Silas' motives, or the eternal
rightness of his cause.

After he had shaved and donned nankeen drawers, Paul
rubbed his body with a snow-soaked cloth until the blood danced.
Toweling a second time, he turned into his bedroom to select a
special wardrobe. This, after all, was a banner day in the lives of
the Sutton brothers. He had agreed to ride to Salisbury to escort
Silas' promised bride to Bristol for her farewell visit. Today, a
dandy's toilette seemed in order, if only for contrast to the dun-
dreary garb so many of his fellow voyagers affected. The morning
tub had been part of his preparation: the glow of health that
suffused him was worth an early rising. Cleanliness (as he knew
too well) was not a cardinal virtue among English gentlemen—
but he had acquired the habit of daily ablutions in the East
and saw no reason for discarding so good a custom.

The room had grown chill while the cupboard window stood
open. Once he had closed it, the brazier he had lighted on rising
made the air snug again. Paul was careful to walk on tiptoe after
he had lifted his favorite cambric shirt from its portmanteau.
Lili still slept behind the curtains of the alcove bed they had
shared last night: he was reluctant to disturb her while he donned
the fine white chemise, with its prodigal puffs of lace at sleeves
and bosom, and tucked the tails into apple-green riding breeches.
. . . More than once, Silas had damned such finery as sinful. He
would dress more simply, once the Adventurers were at sea. This
might be his last chance to play the popinjay: he refused to be
cheated of the drama.

His stockings, Paul noted with satisfaction, were as artfully wrinkled as any courtier's in Whitehall. The shoes (they had cost him dear in Bootmakers' Row) were high of heel and flaring of toe. The coat, with an overlay of embroidered silk, was the same color as the breeches, and the silver-handled dagger at his waist was both ornament and razor-sharp weapon.

Were it not for the voyage, he could be displaying his finery in London at this very moment—following the scent of a dozen escapades whose endings were far more predictable than the destiny awaiting him in the Bahamas. *Damn Silas,* he thought—but without real rancor.

Today, he was glad his brother was deep in slumber in a bedroom below. Last night, Silas had been struck by one of the violent headaches that had plagued him since boyhood—and Paul had prescribed a posset to ease the pain. Knowing the attack had come from overwork, he had added a heavy opiate to the cup, without informing Silas of its exact content. With luck, the leader might sleep until midday, while the preparations for departure ground on without him . . . Silas (whose passion for detail was infinite, who demanded perfection in others as well as in himself) could do with those hours of rest. His doctor-brother would be happy to slip away—for one morning, at least—without argument. Since he and Silas' bride-to-be were strangers, he had both anticipated and dreaded his ride to Salisbury.

Surveying himself in the cheval glass, Paul felt he was a worthy escort for Mistress Anne Trevor, regardless of her approval. The dark, richly curled hair that swept back from a deeply sunburned forehead was his own. (He had quarreled with Silas on that subject too: once they sailed, he would crop as closely as any Roundhead aboard, as a sensible comfort in the tropics.)

He set his hat at a rakish angle. It was of the finest Spanish felt, flat-crowned, with its left brim caught up in a gay burst of feathers—a world removed from the solemn-shovel headgear the Puritans favored. . . . It was only when he stood in the door that he saw the curtains of the alcove bed had parted.

"For shame, Dr. Sutton!" said the innkeeper's daughter. "Are peacocks prouder? I doubt it."

Turning to meet her eyes in the cheval glass, he made a deep bow. Lili was a child of nature—and, like the earth goddess who was her near-namesake, quite unspoiled by an extensive contact with the world. Since his arrival at the Feathers, they had shared the alcove bed quite frequently, to the complete satisfaction of both. Paul considered a change in his immediate plans, remembered that Silas might waken early after all, and dismissed all thought of dalliance.

"Don't forget I'm meeting a prospective sister-in-law at Salisbury," he said. "I must look my best."

"Sure you aren't planning to court her, *mon brave?*"

"One doesn't court a brother's betrothed."

"Then why did you try to slip out on tiptoe? And why are you looking at me so strangely? You've seen me before in my pelt."

"You remind me of an island girl I knew once. Only your skin's a bit paler."

"The sun in the New World will remedy that," said the innkeeper's daughter. She stepped calmly from the bed, to dive into her dress.

"Don't think you'll go naked on Eleuthera. It's hardly that kind of Eden."

"Why shouldn't I, if the climate's warm enough?"

"Silas will forbid it, my dear." It was still hard to believe that both Lili Porter and her father had decided to join the colonists. In a way, it was a tribute to Silas' missionary fire—but Paul suspected that Giles Porter had more mundane reasons for establishing the first tavern in the Bahamas.

"Let's hope your brother's still napping downstairs," said Lili. "I'm sure he's guessed who warms your bed these winter nights."

"There's no cause for alarm today. However, I'll look in on him to make sure. Drugged though he was, I could have sworn he was praying in his sleep."

Lili had completed her dressing in short order. Since she was averse to undergarments of any sort, it had consisted of a series of expert hip-weavings to settle the skirt of her gown—and what appeared to be a single pass of a comb before the cheval glass. An air of *déshabillé* (as the girl's French mother would have called it, had she lived) was part of her hoyden grace. Lili herself was far less ingenuous than she seemed.

"How can two kinsmen be so unlike, Paul?"

"Don't forget we have different mothers," he said. "Silas is almost ten years my senior: he's tried hard to be my second father, since we lost the real one. I can't pretend he's relished the burden."

"That I well believe," said the girl, with another practiced toss of the comb through jet-black curls. "Why did he invite you to join this venture, since he disapproves of you—and the life you lead?"

"Silas knows I've visited the tropics often. Sinner though I am, he needs my knowledge badly."

"Why did you come, then—since you two are always at sword's point?"

"I'm hoping a new existence, and a good marriage, will improve even Silas."

"So blood's thicker than water—even in the Sutton veins," said Lili. "You couldn't let him take the risks alone—"

"Risks?"

"The New World *and* a bride," said the innkeeper's daughter. "Since you're sure he's asleep, let's see how he's faring."

Silas' bedchamber, on the landing below, was a replica of the one they had quitted. During the night, Paul had left both doors ajar: from time to time, he had listened to his brother's heavy breathing, lest the headache prove a harbinger of something worse. As he had hoped, the leader of the Adventurers was sleeping quietly under the opiate—but it was evident that he had wrestled with the devil, even in repose. The bedclothes were tangled round his massive frame, and his nightshirt was drenched in sweat —yet even in that undignified posture there was no mistaking his strength. Silas Sutton was a towering figure in any company: at the moment, his silent figure had a medallion quality, suggesting a crusader carved in marble on his own tomb.

"He needs fresh linen and a bath," said Paul.

"Call down for hot water," said Lili. She had already rolled back her sleeves. "I'll change the bedclothes now."

"I can't leave such tasks to you."

"Nonsense. I'm not just a barmaid, *chéri*—I'm also a first-rate nurse."

When Paul returned from the stairwell, the girl had stripped the bed and unbuttoned Silas' nightshirt, revealing two huge fists still locked in tension and superbly muscled arms. "He's well fleshed for a pulpit-pounder," she said admiringly. "How do you explain it?"

"My brother was Geoffrey Trevor's disciple in every way. From the first, he knew he'd be a colonist: during his religious training, he built his body to fill out the dream. I'm a fair boxer—but he's my master in the ring, and at single-staff. Each day of his life, he walks ten miles. I've seen him plunge into a snowbank to cool his blood after an hour on the crossbars."

"I heard Geoffrey Trevor preach just once," said the innkeeper's daughter. "It was at a Puritan service here, the last year of his life. He seemed a great man, Paul. If he trained his pupils thus, he must have been a fanatic too."

"Most great men are, my dear. You're sure you'd like to perform this chore?"

"Why not? Someone must help him to face the day when he wakens."

"Silas wouldn't thank you, if he knew."

"I expect no thanks from such as him," said Lili. "Get down to your breakfast before I splash your finery."

Standing aside to admit the two scullery maids who had just brought steaming ewers into the bedchamber, Paul saw the girl was firmly in control: a talent of this sort, he knew, would be beyond price in a pioneer settlement. When he sat down to ale and bread in the ordinary, he knew that Silas would waken refreshed, thanks to the ministrations of these handmaidens: perhaps it was not too much to hope that he would also waken in a good humor. . . .

Lili, he told himself, had spoken truly when she said that no two brothers could seem more different. Their father had been a gentle Welshman, a country physician by trade who had brought back a bride from Edinburgh after completing his medical studies there. Paul, of course, had never known the first Mistress Sutton, but he could picture her easily enough—a Scotswoman as devout as she was dour, a dutiful wife who brought little earthly love to her marriage bed. She had raised Silas as strictly as she herself had been reared . . . Paul had been told that her house was both bleak and spotless: he assumed his father's marriage had followed the same uncompromising pattern. It was both fitting and ironic that the good woman should die of a fever—perhaps the only true warmth that had ever invaded her body.

No one was surprised at Dr. Sutton's second marriage. Paul's mother had been a dark-haired Irish lass, as pretty as the first Mistress Sutton had been plain. His memory of her was tenuous but touching: when he thought of her now, it was as an illumination of the spirit rather than a woman. . . . Though no clear image remained, he was sure he had loved her as much as his father did. Silas had hated her from the first, since she was the opposite of all he had been taught to revere. He had called it a judgment of the Almighty when she had persuaded their father to take a holiday in Ireland—and the vessel on which they were crossing the Bay of Galway went down in a storm.

Silas had breathed a short prayer for his father's soul—and turned to the task of rearing Paul, then a child of nine. He had discharged the task with scrupulous care. Disapproving of his half-brother's Irish blood, he had borne the boy's waywardness with fortitude—and had flogged him soundly after each misdeed. Already in training for the ministry, he had tried to persuade him to the same course. He could hardly object when Paul turned to medicine (it had been their father's calling). But he had prayed for his salvation, when Paul set forth on the first of several voyages to the Orient as a ship's surgeon: the temptation of the Eastern fleshpots—he had thundered—were manifold, and his brother's resistance to sin all but negligible.

In those years, Silas had already become a disciple of Geoffrey Trevor—committed, heart and soul, to the advancement of the Puritan faith. The great man had always hoped to found a colony

of Puritans in the New World (to rival, if not surpass, the settlement on Massachusetts Bay). Aware that he would not live to
make the voyage himself, he had made Silas his deputy—and,
like all true preachers of the Word, had fired the younger man
with his missionary zeal.

Silas, who rarely confided in his half-brother, had given Paul
few particulars of that association. Geoffrey Trevor had been in
failing health when they met. Silas had once said that he had
sworn at Trevor's deathbed to carry through the New World venture. Paul could not help wondering if he had promised to marry
Anne Trevor on the same occasion.

There was no mistaking the depth of Silas' devotion to his betrothed. Nor could Paul doubt that Anne—as her father's daughter—would be a model wife, as perfect in her fashion as the image
Silas cherished of a long-dead Scottish mother.

Guy Lebret (a friend of long standing who had signed for the
voyage) had planned to meet Paul for breakfast at the inn. He
had not yet arrived when the ship's doctor finished his own repast.
Paul lingered at the bar a moment more to chat with Giles Porter's
nephew, who had agreed to look after the Feathers in Giles' absence—and would buy it outright in a year's time, if Giles decided to settle in the Bahamas. The innkeeper himself, Paul
learned, was aboard the *Adventurer,* taking a final inventory of
his stores. Knowing he should make his own check of the lazaret
(which housed his materia medica) Paul crossed the quay to seek
him out.

The ship was deep-laden, but a stream of boxes and bales still
flowed across the gangways. A coxswain named Marco (a grin-
ning Italian who had made friends with the doctor from the first)
saluted smartly as Paul came overside. Captain Sperry, he observed, was overseeing the stowage from the foredeck: the mate
(a sullen Norseman called Lars Brack) was bawling orders in
the waist: since the *Adventurer* was sailing with a minimum crew
to accommodate its bumper cargo of colonists, Brack also doubled
as bosun.

"Welcome aboard, Doctor," said the captain. "I see you're dressed to the nines."

"I've a mission to perform."

"Aye, in Salisbury. Your brother told me last night that you'd be fetching his promised lass to see him off. It should be a good omen."

"And one we'll be needing," observed the mate.

"Stow your gab, Master Brack," said Sperry. "You'll grow used to our passengers in time. So will we all, God willing."

His eye strayed to the afterdeck as he spoke: his face (colored like old leather by wind and sun) was set in a bland mask, but his eyes were twinkling. A half-dozen Puritans were storing the last of their belongings in the cramped 'tween-deck area—and, though they seemed no more lubberly than the average landsman, it was easy to understand the Norseman's ill humor. Crowded as the ship was, Paul found little in the bearing of these sobersided folk to inspire confidence. Garbed in the rusty black that was almost a uniform of their sect, with strips of white cloth at neck and wrist in place of the lace affected by the Cavaliers, they seemed dowdy as jackdaws.

Captain Sperry took snuff, exploding his muffled laughter in a sneeze. "I daresay you've never sailed with stranger shipmates, Doctor."

"Let's hope they find their sea legs," said Paul. "They don't seem too happy at the prospects ahead. Is cargo space holding up?"

"Well enough—once I've discouraged 'em from bringing all their worldly goods aboard."

"I've come to check my own supplies, and have a word with Giles Porter. Where do I find him?"

"Counting hogsheads below," growled the mate. "Where else?"

Paul moved toward the afterhatch, nodding to his fellow voyagers and ignoring the black glances at his finery. The reek of bilge water, familiar wherever ships sail, greeted his nostrils as he descended the ladder to the cargo hold. Even in the semidark, there was no mistaking the ponderous shape of the innkeeper.

Giles was holding a candle-lantern in one hand and a bit of chalk in the other. At the moment, he was in the act of examining the tuns of wine and spirit ranged beneath the deck timbers, and numbering each cask. In that light, he bore a remarkable resemblance to one of his own hogsheads. It was only when he lifted the candle and greeted Paul with his familiar, near-toothless grin, that he assumed natural attributes. Giles Porter might be a somewhat moldy Falstaff, but Paul had met few shrewder men in his travels. The fact that the innkeeper had chosen to make this voyage was one of the few points in its favor.

"All shipshape, as you see, Doctor," he said. "I had to be sure."

"You've brought quite a stock aboard."

"No more than I'll be needing. There's nothing like a drop of spirit to comfort a man in a far-off place."

"You've many a drop in there. How did you get those tuns past my brother?"

The innkeeper's vast frame rumbled with mirth. "'Twas you who arranged that, when you put him to bed. We've been rolling kegs aboard since midnight."

"Didn't you have a quota agreement?"

"You're a seafarer, Doctor. I needn't tell you that liquor's wife, sweetheart, and mother to a sailor, afloat or ashore. Aren't we all sailors now, in a manner of speaking—including the bluenoses?"

"You haven't answered my question."

"Captain Sperry knows what we're carrying, to the last bung starter. He'll endorse what I've just told you. And Lars Brack has ballasted his other cargo round my casks. It's too late to hoist them now."

"Do you really plan to set up a tavern on the island?"

"Why not, if the Lord's willing? It's my trade."

"Was that part of your agreement with my brother?"

"Of course. He needed one hundred and fifty colonists in this first boatload. No more than half are Puritans—the rest are plain farmers who want a better life, and the usual assortment of rascals who always flock to such a venture. *Those* folk, at least, will want a drinking place after dark. The colony can't prosper without."

"You plan to stay on, then?"

"If it's the land of Canaan that Master Sutton claims—and it shows a profit."

"Why bring Lili?"

"A tavern's not a tavern without a pretty barmaid."

"D'you think she'll be happy, Giles?"

"Lili's happy anywhere. You know that yourself, Doctor."

Paul felt himself blush, and stepped out of the circle of light. "I hope you're right on all counts," he said. "It still seems a risky business."

"Why are you one of us, then?"

"I'm used to risks. And I can't desert my brother."

"To me, the gamble's worthwhile," said the innkeeper. "If I'm wrong, I'll cut my losses and return. One thing's certain: the future's in those lands across the Atlantic. It isn't here—unless you're highborn, and pick the right side when the fighting starts." He moved on, to chalk a number on yet another keg. "I've seen too many good companions sail from Bristol Quay without me, Doctor. It's time I went exploring on my own—and staked out a corner that's all mine."

When Paul climbed to the deck again, his melancholy had departed; as always, the innkeeper's bluff courage had found an echo in his own spirit. It was true that the *Adventurer*'s passengers were a motley crew. It was also true that a happy voyage could mold them into a band of brothers: a land where all men were equal, could work the same miracle. . . . Silas could be right in the end, he told himself. It might be God's will that the Eleutherians should prosper—even though Paul suspected that Silas' special God had been created in the image of Silas himself.

He shook off the cynical thought, and breathed deep of the salt breeze from the harbor, to drive the noisome odor of bilge from his lungs. He would have preferred the ship to be less odorous—believing, as he did, that a foul bilge meant disease, and certain that the *Adventurer* carried more than the usual complement of rats and other vermin. So far, he had limited himself to a solemn warning. The passengers themselves must keep clean, even if it meant public scrubbing. His whole experience told him that cleanliness and health went hand in hand on long voyages—though he could not have said why.

Crossing the deck to the gangway, after a brief look at his own cramped quarters, Paul paused when the captain spoke his name through the open chartroom door.

"I'm having my first tot of the day, Doctor. Will you join me?"

The bottle on the table held rum, a drink that was beginning to displace aqua vitae in many a captain's cellar. Sperry poured out two liberal portions, and lifted his glass to the sunlight streaming through an open port.

"To a safe voyage, and a speedy one," he said. "We'll get neither, of course, on a winter crossing. I'm damned glad you're with us, Doctor. We're going to need you badly."

"Let's hope you're wrong on that score," said Paul. "My brother's already prayed we'll cross with no loss of life. He's accustomed to having such requests answered."

"Master Silas Sutton is a remarkable man," said the captain. "He's a fair one too—despite the company he keeps. I trust he'll lead his flock into pasture. It's too much to hope we'll fetch Eleuthera without losing lives."

Again, his glance turned to the open door. Another group of Puritans had just mounted the gangway. A tar at the capstan hoist, sweating at his work, released a blue stream of curses that caused one man in the group to redden and clench his fists—though he managed to bite back the reproof he so obviously yearned to utter.

"There'll be trouble of many sorts," said Sperry. "Perhaps your brother can keep his folk in line. It's a touchy task when you're chockablock full—especially with females aboard."

"If you can call them that."

"Don't forget I've carried more than one shipload of these people to Massachusetts Bay. They're still two-legged animals, no matter how they try to conceal it."

"Let's not be too hard on our human cargo, Captain."

"Don't pretend to miss my meaning," Sperry said. "Passions always get out of hand on a long haul, if men and women are berthed too snugly. *I'm* praying for a fast crossing, a minimum of burials at sea, and no more pregnancies than the law allows. And I'm thanking God we needn't beat up the coast of America. The Lucayas should be an easy landfall, once we've raised Bermuda."

Long before he could cross the quay, Paul heard Silas shouting in the taproom. He stifled a groan as he saw he must arbitrate yet another quarrel. This time, it seemed, the innkeeper was the object of his brother's wrath: it was easy to guess the reason. Seventy-odd Puritans were quartered in Bristol to await the departure of the *Adventurer*. Most of these pious folk were tireless in their spying.

When he was truly aroused, it was Silas' custom to pace the floor until the worst of his rage had abated. Today, he was quartering the ordinary, and windmilling his words. Giles Porter, Paul noted, continued to stand his ground: his arguments were no less vehement, though his voice was a poor match for his leader's. It was only when Paul shouted for attention that the war of voices was silenced.

"Didn't I tell you to stay in bed?"

Silas ignored the question. "How long have you known our hold was packed with spirits?"

"I'm fresh off the ship—"

"Why didn't you order the kegs removed?"

"The captain approved the loading," said Paul. "We've more than enough space—"

"When the devil can't come, he sends rum," Silas cried. "'Tis well known the Indians are crazed by it."

"There are no Indians in the Bahamas," said Giles.

"What's your purpose, then? To tempt my settlers?"

"Man's thirst is never quenched, Master Sutton," said the innkeeper. "You can't found a colony on loblolly and water."

"Take care, Porter! There's still time to strike your name from the list."

"If I leave the ship," said Giles, "forty English yeomen leave with me—all of 'em farmers or artisans. You'll die without us, Master Sutton. Ask your brother."

"Giles can sell to passing ships, if he's overstocked," said Paul soothingly. "The colony has the right to tax each barrel."

"Captain Sperry is putting in at Virginia on his return," Giles added. "I've marked twenty tuns for sale in Jamestown. He tells me they pay top prices for good English grog."

When his brother fell silent, Paul saw the battle of wits was ended. Despite Geoffrey Trevor's bequest (and the sale of shares through factors in London) the colony was still pressed for cash. "*We'll* need extra spirits for my sick bay," he said. "Rum and Jesuits' bark make a sovereign remedy for most fevers."

The leader of the Eleutherians raised his eyes to heaven. "Thanks to my brother, Master Porter," he said, "you may leave your tuns aboard. But no more, mind you. We're overburdened now."

"Not another flagon," said Giles. "You can wager on that."

The innkeeper, moving nimbly despite his bulk, had already whisked into his kitchen. Deprived of a target Silas turned again on Paul. Worsted in this duel of wits, he had not yet emptied his reservoir of wrath.

"So much for our Boniface," he said. "The man's a scoundrel: we'll never rescue *him* from the pit. I haven't despaired of you."

"Where have I erred this time?" Paul asked.

"I've just spent twelve hours abed. Why was I drugged last night?"

"I mixed the potion myself. You were near collapse."

"I can judge my own strength."

"Not while I'm ship's doctor. Sometimes, I believe you take pleasure in driving yourself beyond endurance."

"When I wakened just now, my bedclothes had been changed. I was new-washed, and clad in a fresh shift. Was that your doing too?"

"Giles Porter's daughter was your angel of mercy. Two scullery wenches helped her scrub."

"You let that woman touch me?"

"Lili's an experienced nurse: I was glad to discover her talents. We can use her in the colony."

"From what I've heard," said Silas, "you've used her in other ways."

Paul shrugged. "We enjoy each other's company. I won't deny it."

"I'll have no sinning at sea—or in Eleuthera!"

"Sin's a word of many meanings," said Paul. "I don't grasp your definition."

"I say this relationship must end. As your leader, I demand it."

"I agreed to serve as ship's doctor, not to be made over," said Paul. "Flog your own spirit, if you must. You've flogged *me* for the last time. We'll agree on that much, or I resign now."

The brothers faced each other a moment more, while the claret flush in Silas' cheeks subsided. His voice seemed drained of choler when he spoke again.

"The devil can take you then, along with Porter," he said. "I've done my duty." There was a note of near-despair in his tone that contrasted oddly with his words—but his eyes were bright as dagger points when he strode from the taproom. Like all their quarrels, the point at issue remained unsolved. With each of Silas' explosions, the gulf that divided them seemed deeper.

Paul turned with relief to the clatter of hoofs in the courtyard. Guy Lebret, he saw, had arrived at last.

The Frenchman swept into the ordinary with his saddlebags across one shoulder, and called for drink before he held out his hand. They had been friends since their student days at Edinburgh. At the time, Lebret had planned to become a Paris apothecary, a trade that had flourished in his family for generations. Instead, he had opened another of his father's chemist's shops in London, which had flourished under his management—enough, in the end, to permit Guy to follow his true avocation, the study of nature. He had written tomes on the flora and fauna of the Orient (where he had voyaged with Paul). Now he was sailing on the *Adventurer,* to prepare a companion volume on the Bahamas.

"Here's your Jesuits' bark, my friend," he said. "I had to scour London to get the quantity you demanded. It explains my tardiness."

"Silas will pay your price, Guy. When it comes to medicines, he accepts my orders."

Lili came into view with three mugs of ale, and sat down between the friends. "Father would join you," she said, "but he's keeping busy in the kitchen, rather than run afoul of Master Silas."

Lebret drank deep. "How's that indomitable brother of yours, Paul? I heard his bellow when I rode in."

"As indomitable as ever, I'm afraid," Paul admitted. "We've just knocked our heads together to no purpose—except to remind him I'm leading my own life henceforth."

"Not if you're riding into Salisbury as his deputy. Have you time to enjoy this stirrup cup?"

"Yes, since Lili's brought it."

"Shall we drink to the mysterious Anne, who is godmother to our colony?"

"I'd hardly call her a mystery, Guy. These Puritan females are as alike as the stays in their corsets."

"Why do they truss themselves like fowls?" asked Lili. "God meant women to have proper curves. How else could you tell them from men?"

"In your case, *mignonne*," said the Frenchman, "that difficulty is not likely to arise."

"Nor do I think this Mistress Trevor will be mistaken for a man," said Lili, with a laughing glance at Paul. "Let's withhold our judgment, until we've seen her in the flesh."

"Never mind her charms, or lack of them," said Paul. "Speaking plainly, I think Silas should wed her now—stays and all."

"Do you feel that marriage will change his views?"

"This expedition could destroy itself—unless someone tames him a little."

"Have you suggested it?"

"I'd have tried today, if he hadn't flown into a passion with Giles. So far, he's determined to keep his betrothed in England until the colony's established. Perhaps he'd listen to you."

"I fear not, Paul," said the Frenchman. "Sometimes, I believe he's a block of marble, not a man."

"He's a man, all right," said Lili. "I learned that much today, in his bedchamber."

Guy Lebret's brows lifted. "Are you implying—?"

"Of course not," said the girl. "He was dead to the world, and I was bathing him—with help from Nell and Jennie. But I could make him want me quite easily, if I wished it."

"Don't talk nonsense, Lili." Paul had cut in sharply: his voice, he knew, was harsher than he intended. "If my brother desired a woman not his wife, he'd flog his own back in penance."

"Not even Master Sutton could accomplish that feat of contortion," said Lebret. "As for you, Mademoiselle Porter, I doubt that your lures, potent though they are, could accomplish the improbable. I hope I'm not being ungallant."

Lili shrugged, and drank down her ale. "You're merely proving you don't know much about men."

"I'll admit you've the advantage there."

Paul rose to take his leave. The raillery, though only meant to tease, had made him vaguely uneasy. "It's possible we're all mistaken about Silas," he said. "I'll agree that he's intolerant—even bigoted. But he's a completely honest man, a rarity in any century. Maybe he's even the stuff of which saints are made."

"Or martyrs to lost causes?" Lebret asked.

"Be that as it may. When this business is over, I'll wager he makes history for both God and king."

"Spoken like a loyal kinsman," said the Frenchman. "What's more, I think you mean it."

"How else could I follow him to the New World?" Paul bent to give Lili a good-by kiss: forthright though their talk had been, he could not resent his friends' candor. "Try to keep him tranquil while I'm gone. I'll return day after tomorrow."

"Salisbury's only a day's riding," said Lebret.

"Mistress Trevor will be with me. I doubt if she can ride the distance without rest."

"If she rides at all," put in Lili. "Can you picture a Puritan lady on horseback?"

The King's Highway led to Bath—and thence, by rolling moors, to Salisbury Plain. Paul had changed mounts at a posting house: while a red sunset painted the clouds, he circled the town itself, to approach by way of the great broken ring of Stonehenge. The sight of the druidic riddle had never failed to lift his spirits—symbolic, as it was, of an immortality that defied all labels. So (for another reason) did the soaring spires of Salisbury Cathedral, when he paused in its shadow to study the written directions that would lead him to the Trevor abode.

It had been a long, hard ride. He had not spared the horse he had hired at the Bear and Key—but he was pleasantly tired rather than weary as he approached the end of the fifty-mile journey. The home of the late Geoffrey Trevor, he discovered, stood on a low knoll at the northern side of town, in a grove of firs. The low-eaved stone dwelling had once served as a parsonage for the church across the way: the graveyard that lay between was ancient too, its worn stones askew in the snow-streaked earth and still gleaming faintly in the last rays of twilight. Paul chuckled as he dismounted and lifted the knocker of the plain oaken door. The timing of his arrival, like the solemn background, suited his errand.

The manservant who admitted him wore the rusty black of a Puritan. So did the girl—she was little more than that—who emerged from a book-lined study. Anne Trevor, he observed, was precisely what he expected—but there were overtones that defied analysis. Neither the tight bun into which her russet-colored hair was drawn, the mobcap that covered it, nor the full skirt of her severely plain housedress could hide the fact that she was as lovely as she was wholesome.

"You are welcome, Paul," she said—and gave him a hand that was as cool as her manner.

"Don't commit yourself too soon," he said. "Not unless Silas has told you everything about me—and you're still determined to be charitable."

"Silas has told me a great deal," she said. "In the circumstances, he'd hardly keep you a secret."

"Then you are charitable indeed," he said, doffing his cloak and handing it to the gray-haired maid who had appeared behind her mistress. "My esteemed brother doesn't regard me too highly. In fact, I was sent as your escort only because no one better could be spared."

A ghost of a smile hovered for a moment on Anne Trevor's lips. For the first time, he noticed how pleasingly full they were. "Why speak ill of yourself so soon?"

"That was hardly my intention," he said. "But I'll not be vexed if your opinion coincides with his. I've observed that members of your sect are usually birds of a feather."

He knew he was forcing a quarrel deliberately, driven by a feeling of truculence he could not explain. Now that he was in Anne Trevor's presence, he felt he was on trial—and that his conviction was mandatory, no matter how spirited his defense. Her glance at his apparel was part of that unreasonable opinion— and the fact she had refused to be impressed had only fanned his anger. Catching a glimpse of himself in a dim hall mirror, he realized that he had overdone his self-imposed role of popinjay, that he had meant to dazzle (perhaps even to startle) a woman he had never even seen. Now they were face to face, the effort seemed absurd.

Anne Trevor led the way to the study, and the fire on the hearth. For a moment, he was sure she would refuse to pick up his challenge. Then, as she turned from poking the blaze, he saw that her lips were curved in that same smile.

"Speaking of birds, Dr. Sutton," she murmured, "one could hardly accuse *you* of dowdy plumage."

"Is that meant as a compliment?"

"Only as a statement of fact. You wished to shock me, I take it. Have you forgotten I've always lived in London? My father preached there: this was only his country retreat."

Paul stood with his back to the hearth. The chill in the room had nothing to do with the tiny blaze, or the fact that the carpets were rolled to the wall, the books shrouded in cheesecloth.

"*Touché*, Mistress Sutton," he said. "I deserved that thrust."

"Won't you call me Anne?"

"I'm not convinced I should—now I've fulfilled your worst expectations."

"Believe me, I've formed no judgments, so far. Silas tells me you're an excellent doctor—I accept his estimate."

"You disagree with the Bard of Avon, then? The apparel doesn't always proclaim the man?"

"Not in your case," she said. "You're a free soul, with the seven seas as your playground. Why shouldn't you dress as you see fit? And you *are* a good doctor—aren't you, Paul?"

"I won't deny I've fought most of the world's diseases, Anne. Though I can't pretend to understand them all."

"You're the man for our task then," she said. "We'll find you beyond price in the New World. Health is our first concern, of course."

"*We?* Silas isn't planning to take you on the first ship."

"I've just sold this place outright, so there's nothing to keep me here. I intend to join your company."

"There isn't an inch of extra room aboard."

"Silas is the leader," said Anne Trevor. "I'll be his wife, won't I? Surely I've the right to share his quarters."

"I'm afraid he intends to break ground on Eleuthera before you join him. He'll need a year's time at least."

"As a ship's doctor, would you say I'm too frail to suffer the hardships of this voyage?"

"Most of our female passengers are the wives or daughters of yeomen," said Paul. "It's been my experience that white women, if they're wellborn, don't thrive in hot countries."

"Not so well as brown ones, perhaps?"

He felt his cheeks burn, and knew he was yielding to a mood of truculence he could not justify. (The teasing reference to his shipwreck had been only natural.)

"You don't seem to like the truth about yourself," he said. "And it's evident you like me still less. I'll put up at the Red Lion, and call for you in the morning."

"Did you come here spoiling for a quarrel, Paul? I'll not have you lying at an inn tonight. Will you stay—if I ask pardon for questioning your medical views . . . and your tastes in women?"

A duchess in Whitehall could not have countered his bad manners more neatly. He bowed a silent acknowledgment of her skill before he spoke: it was the last thing he had expected of a blue-nose's daughter.

"*I'm* the one to ask pardon, Anne," he said—and even now, he found it difficult to meet this enigmatic girl halfway. "Naturally, we must be under one roof to make an early start. But I think Silas is right. You should stay in England, until we've staked out the frontiers of our new kingdom."

"Eleuthera is God's kingdom," said Anne quietly. "I mean to share in its founding."

"It's your quarrel—and my brother's. I refuse to intervene."

A clock chimed in the hall, and Anne rose briskly. "Meg will show you to your room," she said—with the air of a well-trained hostess skirting a difficult subject. "We dine in a half-hour. Our table's simple: I hope it sustains you."

"I've lived on land crab and coconut, with rain water to drink," he said. "I'll last until morning."

It was only when he stood in the guest room that Paul realized he had yet to speak a civil word to his hostess: even his sneer at her food had been a form of baiting. He was still damning his lack of finesse when the maid spoke from the doorway. Wat, the manservant, had already brought up his portmanteau.

"I trust you'll be comfortable here, sir. We've sold the house: all of us move out tomorrow."

"You're joining Mistress Trevor in Bristol?"

"Wat and me would never leave her. We'll follow you by cart, so she'll have her trunks and bags in time."

Paul smiled inwardly. If Anne meant to take servants and a wardrobe to the Bahamas, she had reckoned without the size of the *Adventurer*.

"How will she travel tomorrow? By coach?"

"Not Mistress Anne. She's as good a rider as any man, and she's anxious to make a fast journey. Her father trained her for this new life, sir, ever since she turned twelve. Taught her to make camp on the moors, with only tinder and a clasp knife. She can handle a ship's tiller and swim a stream, if need be. Tomorrow, she'll wear boy's clothes and ride with you."

It was yet another side to Anne Trevor. Paul was not too surprised at the revelation. He could even suspect that Anne had sent her maid with this report, to prepare him for the morrow.

"Do you all expect to sail on the *Adventurer?*"

"Indeed not, Doctor. Mistress Anne realizes you're much too deeply laden. *She'll* be aboard, if she can make your brother marry her at once. Me and Wat will stop at Bristol to help outfit the second ship. We'll join her then—and bring such things as she'll be needing."

At dinner, as he had expected, his hostess wore the same dark gown, and the grace she offered was on the solemn side. Once they were at table, however, she spoke with ease on a variety of topics, as befitted a great man's daughter. Had he been able to ignore his rather gloomy surroundings, Paul could have sworn he was dining in one of the world's capitals. This girl's education, he felt sure, had more than matched his own—not only in social usage, but on the burning questions of the day.

"I forgot to ask after Silas' health," she remarked, during a pause in the service.

"He's overworked, as usual. And driving himself to sail on time. Even when I order him to rest, he refuses to keep to his bed."

"Silas resembles Father in that," she said. "Once he's settled on an objective, he feels the slightest pause is sinful, until the goal's in view. This colony is his life. Nothing's more important than its success."

"Not even your marriage?"

Anne's eyes were lowered, her lips unsmiling. "I'm only his help-mate, Paul—and proud of my part. Naturally, I've given all I possess to the enterprise. That, too, was Father's wish. I think it would kill Silas if he failed."

"So do I," said Paul. "It's the only reason I agreed to sail with him. Will you accept that as a motive?"

"By all means. You're kinsmen."

"It's hard to remember sometimes."

"I can understand that too," said Anne. "Like my father, he finds it hard to forgive those who are—shall we say, less good than he?"

"Especially an unrepentant brother?"

"Do you quarrel frequently?"

"And to no real purpose. Aside from my medical knowledge, I wonder how much I'll really help him. He can still fail, you know. I've never seen the Bahamas, but I doubt if they're really an earthly Eden. Even in the New World, heaven will take a deal of planning."

"You forgot one thing, Paul. The Lord's on our side."

"You believe that, don't you?"

"How else could I justify my faith?"

"The papists think He's on theirs," Paul reminded her. "And the Established Church has its own beliefs. Must the Almighty favor only a small sect that's quarreled with all the others?"

"But we're God's elect," said Anne. "Why else did Massachusetts prosper?"

"Perhaps it was luck—and courage."

"Do you question our fortitude?"

"You'll have sturdy folk in the colony," he admitted. "I'd be happier if we had more such yeomen, and fewer theologians."

"Do you question our *faith*, Paul?"

"By no means. I'm only reminding you that God helps those who help themselves."

"You believe in God, then?"

"Of course. Just don't ask me to define Him as precisely as Silas. To my mind, He's everywhere—"

"You're a pantheist, then. I'd hardly call that a religion."

"Can't a man believe in God, and not be religious, in the formal sense? Isn't it possible to love God, rather than fear him?"

"Do you deny that God is stronger? Or that we must obey His commandments?"

"So we're back to those commandments," said Paul. "It's my opinion that most good men follow them, regardless of creed. I also believe a little faith in one's own strength is worth more than membership in any sect, however noble."

"Including mine?"

"Forgive me if I'm rude, Anne—yours most of all."

"Why?"

"Because too many of you are eternally convinced of your own righteousness. To me, it's one's own courage that matters. Not blind belief in an avenging God, who'll punish every heretic that dares to think differently."

"Perhaps that's the way of all young religions, Paul. They might not survive without such a belief."

Once again, he saw that he was losing ground in an argument— that Anne Trevor could plead her cause as smoothly as any divine. He was thankful, in a way, that she had risen with her last question, now that their simple meal had ended. There had been no spiritual nourishment to match the excellent food. Try as he might, he sensed that he had made no impression on her whatever.

"I won't deny that faith can move mountains," he said. "As I just remarked, contact with adversity can help as much. Silas has trained his body for the task ahead—and he's a natural leader. But can he handle a small boat in a storm, or make a fire in the rain? How many of our Bible-backs could build a wilderness hut, or live off the land in case of shipwreck?"

"You're looking at one who can," said Anne.

"So your maid informed me," he said drily.

"Meaning, of course, that you've yet to be convinced."

"Let's say I'll keep an open mind when you reach Eleuthera."

Color stained her cheek for the first time, but she had regained her composure instantly. "That's charitable of you, Paul," she said. "I hope I'll be worthy of the opportunity. Perhaps we should say good night now—since we'll be up with the sun tomorrow."

"There's no need to leave so early."

"There's every need," said Anne crisply. "We must reach Bristol before dark. In these times, the roads aren't safe at night."

"I'd planned on a two-day journey."

"And I on one," said Anne. "You rode here in just six hours, I believe?"

"With a change of horses."

"We'll do the same tomorrow, then," said Anne. "If only to prove Meg wasn't fibbing." She held out her hand—and again, the pressure of her fingers was coolly reserved. "Perhaps we'll be friends in the New World, Paul. I'll grant you, it will take doing."

"Is this, by any chance, an olive branch you're offering?"

"Of course. Haven't you heard we Puritans are a peaceful folk, once we've had our way?"

He bowed over the hand and kissed it lightly: the pantomime of Roundhead and Cavalier, he felt, must be played out to the end.

"Good night, Mistress Trevor," he said. "Thank you again for your hospitality."

"I hope you sleep well, Dr. Sutton."

"I intend to," he said—and stood aside to let her precede him up the stair.

When he heard her bedroom door shut above, he took up the rushlight and climbed in turn to his own chill couch. (The bed-warmer, as he had learned to his sorrow, was an unheard-of luxury in Puritan households.) He was bone-weary now—but the weariness in his soul went deeper. Hanging between sleep and waking for a long time, he fought for the repose he so badly needed—while his conscious mind informed him, in no uncertain terms, that he had behaved like a boor. It was only when true oblivion submerged that nagging certainty that his tormented brain found solace.

In a twinkling, he was sporting with a festive Lili on a palm-fringed shore. Then (as is the way with dreams) the picture changed—and the naked girl who swam just beyond his reach in the jade-green lagoon was no longer Lili Porter, but his brother's betrothed.

Lowering clouds hung above the house when he awoke, and the air smelled of snow. He found his breakfast laid for him in the dining room, and Meg bustling in the kitchen.

"Mistress Anne has already eaten and gone to the stable, Doctor," she said. "You may leave when you're ready."

He made a hasty repast at this news, angry at himself for having slept so late. There was no mistaking Anne Trevor's eagerness for this reunion with Silas, and the realization put a further damper on his spirits.

In his room, donning the knee-length boots of Spanish leather he used for riding, he could hear the horses stamping in the court below. A glance through the window told him that Wat (the manservant who doubled as groom) and a boy assistant had already prepared both mounts for the road. The second horse was a skittish mare, already dancing in her haste to be away. She was a vivid contrast to the sturdy gelding he had ridden from the Bear and Key.

When he carried his portmanteau downstairs he was not too surprised to find that the figure he had taken for a boy was his hostess. Anne wore dark breeches and boots and a thick leather jerkin. Her russet locks were concealed in a kerchief—and a slouch hat and cloak made the masquerade perfect. She gave Paul a smiling nod of greeting while she adjusted her stirrups. He could see that she was bubbling over with excitement at the prospect before her.

"As soon as you've strapped on your bundle, we can be off," she told him.

"Is that mare your own?"

"We'll leave her at the Bear and Key, and ride what they offer us into Bristol. Wat can collect her, when they go through in the cart."

"Perhaps we should change," he said doubtfully. "She's on the spirited side."

"I've handled this girl for years," said Anne. She was in the saddle in a bound: when Wat released the reins, she slapped the mount's flank. Obviously, it was a game both horse and rider enjoyed. First, they danced once round the gelding, as formally as though this were a royal *dressage*. Then, with a spurt of gravel, they left the courtyard. Paul, struggling with his own stirrups, had not had time to mount. When he followed Anne through the courtyard arch, she was already crossing Salisbury Plain at a hand gallop, riding with the easy, swinging poise of a born horsewoman and apparently oblivious of his pursuit.

Urging his own mount, he followed at his best speed—but soon realized that he stood no chance of catching up until she was so minded. They were far beyond the town, and well on the highroad to Bath, when she reined in at last and waited serenely for the hard-pressed gelding to overtake her.

"Diana always likes a morning run," she explained. "We didn't mean to be discourteous."

"You took me by surprise," he said. "Else I'd have been with you all the way."

"Don't be too sure of that, Paul. We've yet to meet our match here."

"Do you ride like this often?"

"Whenever I can find company that isn't shocked by my attire."

Her slender body, he noted, was a taut extension of the horse she controlled. Remembering certain details of his dream, he pulled his hatbrim low and pretended to consult the map on his pommel, to hide the flush at his cheeks.

"Which way do we go?" he asked.

"The road to Bath is the safest."

"Even so, we must keep a sharp eye for footpads."

"Surely they'd be more apt to molest a gentleman riding with his lady than one with his groom."

He closed the map case—unwilling to grant her the last word. "I'll accept your masquerade," he told her. "If you accept mine as gentleman."

"You *are* a gentleman, Paul," she said. "I discovered as much last night. No one else could have controlled his dislike of me so manfully."

"Believe me, Anne, I don't dislike you—"

"Mistrust, then," she said quickly. "I don't blame you for that—since I'm so foreign to your experience. Nor do I blame you for that costume. After all, Joseph wore the coat of many colors, and he ended up next to Pharaoh."

It was midafternoon when they reached the Bear and Key: thanks to a steady downfall of snow since noon, they had been forced to proceed at a cautious trot. Paul had suggested they pass the night here, but Anne had insisted they push on after a light repast, in hope that the storm would lift before they reached Bath. If need be, she was resigned to stopping in that ancient town, at the famous Weavers' Inn. From that point, it would be only a short journey to Bristol.

Her new mount was a plodding hackney that seemed more suited to cart than saddle: Paul was glad that the mare had been spared the rigors of the next hour. His own horse was a fugitive from the plow who seemed to understand the snowy highway well enough, even when the fall grew fetlock-deep. Anne's prayer for better weather, it seemed, was destined to go unanswered. Though it was still late afternoon, the winter's day had begun to grow dark as midnight, with only the ghostly snowfall to reflect what light remained. A keening wind from the east, lashing their faces with the cold, swirling flakes, suggested a near-blizzard in the making.

The horses' cautious trot had long since been slowed to a walk. Bath, to judge by the last road marker, was a good five miles' distant when they reined in. Only a blur of trees showed at the fork in the whitened highway. It was impossible to guess which turning to follow.

"At this rate," said Paul, "we'll never sleep at the Weavers'. Let's trust there's a shelter nearby: it's no night to camp in the open."

"Which road do we take?"

"I'd guess the left. There are no more landmarks to follow."

A quarter-mile beyond, a barn stood beside the road. Paul led his mount through the door, with Anne close behind: the wind was keening now, and it was impossible to see more than a few feet beyond the horses' ears. After the buffeting of the elements, the hay-scented interior seemed drowsily warm.

They had been fortunate in their choice, Paul saw. This was a work barn, with a forge and bellows, and a flue to convey the smoke. In the cleared space, a number of iron-shod wheels awaited repair: there were horse stalls below the haymow, none of them tenanted at the moment. He guessed there were farm buildings nearby, but he dared not risk exploring until the driving snow abated.

"Let's hope your servants aren't in trouble," he said, as he unsaddled both mounts and led them to separate stalls.

"Wat's a farmer born and raised," said Anne. "He'll be wiser than I, and stop his journey sooner."

Paul turned from the haymow, at the sound of striking tinder. Anne had already laid a charcoal fire in the mouth of the forge, and was teasing it alive with expert blasts of the bellows.

"We can sleep here without frostbite," she said. "The storm is sure to lift by morning."

"I'll find the farmhouse, once I can see to navigate," he promised. "They'll sell us food—even if they can't bed us."

With a half-dozen blankets from the stalls, a pair of sawhorses that served as a trestle-table, and an arrangement of baled hay that made two armchairs of sorts, Anne Trevor quickly gave their shelter an air of human habitation. Settling beside the forge with a grateful sigh, Paul found himself responding to that instinctive homemaking. Letting his eyelids droop, he slipped into a half-dream—imagining that he was back in the taproom at the Feathers, with thick frost on the windows and Lili en route from the bar with a pint of mulled wine. . . . The contentment remained when he risked a direct glance at Anne Trevor, across the cheerful dance of the flames. Already, their day-long ride, and this lucky finale, were part of a shared experience.

"The wind's dying down," Anne said. "These late-winter storms often blow themselves out across the Severn."

"I'll find the farmhouse in another moment. What do you suggest for supper?"

"A dozen bacon rashers," said Anne. "Chives and allspice—and as many eggs as they can spare. All I'll need is a saucepan and your clasp knife to prove I can fashion a camp omelet."

"Why not let me cook and rest awhile?"

Anne shook her head firmly. "I don't expect you to believe I could stay alive in a wilderness. At least you'll see I'm not entirely unfitted to become Silas' wife. Once you've tasted my cooking, you may dislike me a trifle less."

"How often must I insist that's a false impression?"

"What's between us, then?" she asked, with a smile that belied the heat of the question. "Does it shock you to learn I've a mind—and that I'm not ashamed to use it? Am I too independent of spirit to suit you?"

"By no means. My brother's far luckier than he deserves." Paul wondered at the sudden huskiness in his voice. Moving to the doorway, he saw that the snow was mixed with sleet—and that the wind had veered to the west. In England, he recalled, a west wind often promised fair weather on the morrow. . . . Already, he could see the bulk of the farmhouse on a hill above the barn, and the wink of candles at the windows.

"I can risk a run for that kitchen now," he said.

"Stay a moment more," she begged. "We can't move until morning. Our supper will wait."

He studied her at a distance, troubled by the urgency in her tone. "Have we left something unsaid, Anne?"

"I want you to answer one more question honestly. If I'm to believe Silas, you've led what we'd both call an ungodly life . . ." She lifted both hands appealingly before he could speak. "I know godliness is a matter of definition: you've every right to reject mine. I'm only wondering how you can remain a spiritual nomad and be satisfied."

"I've always managed," he said, with his eyes on the storm.

"What's your future, Paul? What is your true purpose?"

Even then, he refused to face her directly, though he could not suppress a grin at the answer that sprang to mind. At this moment, his greatest wish was to take Anne Trevor in his arms—to prove that a woman existed beneath that boyish disguise.

"What do *you* expect from tomorrow?" he countered.

"To be a good wife to Silas. To make his hopes come true."

"Isn't that too easy an answer?"

"Do you doubt me?"

"By no means. It's still true that your course has always been charted: the mold was formed from the beginning. I've lived for the moment, with no fear of tomorrow, and still less of hell-fire. I'll grant it's no existence for a lady of your persuasion. You might still find it rewarding."

"Not so rewarding as God," she said. "Can't you learn to love Him a little—even if you've no fear of hell?"

"Are you planning to take a convert back to Bristol? It's a task beyond your powers."

Anne made a patient gesture of dismissal. "Bring me what food you can," she said. "I'll see you sup well, even if I can't minister to your soul."

Struggling up the path to the farm kitchen, he told himself he had fought Anne Trevor long enough: it was worse than churlish to rebuff her offer of friendship, as coldly as he had refused the invitation to join her faith. Resolved to resist her no longer, he was calm enough when he returned with a capacious wicker basket. The farmer's wife had sold him the food Anne desired, along with two bottles of fair wine. There were no spare beds in the house—but he had paid for enough charcoal to insure a comfortable night beside the forge.

"Did you tell her the truth about us?" Anne asked.

"I explained I was riding to Bristol with my groom. She took it for granted we'd spend the night here."

Anne colored faintly at the declaration—but her smile was still oddly un-Puritan while she prepared the omelet.

"I hope Silas will understand, when we recount our adventures."

"Perhaps we should leave out this part of our journey," said Paul—and turned deliberately to fetch a fresh bag of charcoal. "After all, he expected us to stop on the road. Must we explain we slept in a barn?"

The sleet had changed to rain while they supped on the doorframe, with the strong heat of the forge behind them. Already, there was a smell of thaw in the air; the blizzard that had howled so ominously at the day's end seemed ready to depart like a spring lamb before morning. Expecting their argument to continue, Paul sat a little apart—and contented himself with praising the excellence of Anne's camp omelet, the expert way she handled such matters as washing-up and tidying their impromptu dwelling.

While these chores were in progress, she had refused all aid. It was only when he had poured their second cup of wine, and she had settled comfortably before the banked embers, that he ventured to return to more personal topics.

"I'd already guessed my brother was rarely fortunate," he said. "Now I've observed your housekeeping firsthand, I'm sure of it."

Anne tossed her head at the teasing. "Does our example inspire you to do likewise?"

"If you mean marry—"

"What else? I firmly intend to settle in the Bahama Islands, when Silas becomes their first governor. You could do worse than follow our example."

This time, he was careful to hide his irritation—now that he was beginning to perceive the cause.

"Why are all women convinced that marriage is the only normal state of man?"

"You've refused to turn to God," said Anne. "Don't tell me you're against marriage too?"

"It's a partnership I've refused to risk so far. Perhaps I never will."

The girl colored faintly, but she did not pursue the argument as she went about her tasks before the fire. Watching her, Paul could envy Silas his luck. Here (by one of those strokes of fate that lift some men to the stars) was the perfect helpmate for a wilderness, a wife who could face down hurricane and pestilence with the proper husband beside her. This was no time to question his half-brother's fitness for the role. Nor did he dare to ask himself how different his own life might have been, had Anne Trevor —or her counterpart—crossed his path in time. He was glad of the dying firelight when he put down his wine and rose to make a bed of horse blankets, at one side of the barn.

"You'd best sleep here," he said. "I'll bed down beside the forge, and keep the coals alive. With luck, we'll be at Bristol by early afternoon."

As Anne left the forge she held out a hand. It was a gesture of peace—and there was no trace of coquetry in her unsmiling eyes.

"We're friends now, Paul—in spite of everything?"

"Friends, Anne. No matter what befalls us."

"And shipmates too?"

"I'll make no promises where Silas is concerned," he told her. "Try to sleep well. You'll find me a good watchdog."

When she had gone to her makeshift bed in the horse stall, he listened tensely for a while—fearful, even now, that she would rejoin him at the fire to resume the battle for his soul. When her even breathing told him that she slept at last, he reached for the second wine bottle, and drank deeply before he prepared his own shakedown couch beside the forge. In the past, an extra bottle had cleared his head, when he faced a hard problem on the morrow. Tonight, he could feel his brain whirl in a vortex of indecision while he sought to plot his course. . . . One fact was clear, and he could avoid it no longer: he was in love with Anne Trevor, as deeply and as disastrously as a schoolboy.

Loving her (and knowing his own nature all too well) he swore an oath he would surely break tomorrow: he must protect her from that discovery by any means at hand.

Late the next afternoon, the coach they had hired in Bath rolled up to the doorway of the Feathers.

They had paused at the Weavers' Inn, just long enough for Anne to change to proper feminine garb. Now (helping the porter with their boxes, insisting that she go at once to the room that Silas had reserved for her) he found Paul could hold thought at arm's length without too great an effort. It was easy to plead an engagement with friends in the taproom—and easier still to stand back as she mounted the stair for her meeting with Silas.

Today, at least, there had been no flaws in his armor: his performance as an escort had been flawless. Tomorrow (he clung to the certainty, in quiet desperation) their paths would divide forever. The sundering would be bearable, if he could continue to stand apart.

His withdrawal was short-lived. He had barely settled with a flagon in the empty ordinary when the porter informed him he was wanted in his brother's room.

To his surprise, he found Silas alone. The leader of the Adventurers was pacing the carpet of his chamber: he still wore a rain-wet cloak, and his eyes were cold as the dusk that had begun to close in outside. Paul surmised that his brother, busy with some task on the quay, had hurried to the Feathers when told of Anne's presence. It was also evident the reunion had been short. Silas' first words confirmed that judgment.

"I've asked Anne to rest in her room while I talked with you," he said. "Did you inspire her mad wish to sail with us tomorrow?"

Paul was careful to keep his temper. "The idea was hers, not mine," he said. "Knowing you'd refuse, I didn't argue the question."

"She's still unhappy at my firmness," said Silas. "Even when I told her my word was final, she wouldn't accept it. That's when she asked I discuss the matter with you. I agreed, rather than appear unreasonable."

Knowing he must proceed warily, Paul settled in the one chair the bedroom boasted. "I'm flattered by your summons," he said. "And a bit puzzled too. Why should my opinion be important to either of you?"

His brother's frown was still thunder-dark. "I've already gathered that Anne values you above your deserts. I'm not surprised—now you've had the chance to display your celebrated charm. Just what passed between you on your journey?"

"If you're suggesting I cosseted your fiancée, the answer's negative," said Paul. "I won't deny I found her a far more spirited lass than I'd expected—and far more resourceful. As I've just told you, I refused to discuss her wish to accompany us—though it's my opinion she'd make the best of shipmates."

"You take her side, then?"

"You asked for my views: you have them. May I hear your reasons for excluding her?"

"I won't expose Geoffrey Trevor's daughter to unknown dangers. Until I've measured the risks we're taking, I'll suffer them alone."

"Other colonists are taking their wives. Why not the leader?"

"I've no right to her company now. What if we fail?"

"Surely you don't admit that possibility."

"This is no time for levity, Paul. I consider our task of settling the Bahamas a sacred trust. Anne's father devoted his life to planning it; when the plan's a reality, his daughter's hand will be my reward. I won't claim her prematurely."

"Surely you know she's been trained for this venture, as rigorously as a man?"

"A year from today will be soon enough to test her training. Geoffrey Trevor was a great man—but some of his ideas were too advanced for my taste. The position of women in our society was one of them."

"Does that mean you won't permit Anne to help realize her father's vision?"

"Don't twist my meaning," said Silas heavily. "Anne will join us, once our colony has prospered. Until then, she'll be needed in Bristol to help outfit our next ship. Someone must serve as a rallying point, if we're to have other settlers."

"Surely you can assign a different deputy to that task. Wouldn't it mean far more to the cause to have Geoffrey Trevor's daughter at your side—to prove her courage matches yours?"

Silas turned to the door, with a flailing gesture of the right arm: it was a move Paul recognized as a final dismissal. "The subject's closed," he said. "Your argument's ingenious, but it's failed to impress me. Anne remains in England."

"In your place, I'd marry her tomorrow," said Paul. "You may have cause to regret this self-denial."

His brother's eyes narrowed—and there was a sudden, feral gleam beneath the lids, a reminder (however fleeting) that this man of God could burn as ardently as lesser mortals. "I won't deny it's cost me some effort to refuse her," he said. "There can be no compromise between love and duty. Is that too much for you to grasp?"

"Not if the distinction's clear-cut," said Paul. "In this case, the boundaries of duty seem a trifle blurred."

"A man of destiny must choose the course God wills, then follow it."

"Have you consulted God on your marriage, too?"

Silas stalked from the room with a last, hot-eyed glare. He had made no attempt to answer the mocking question: in its way, that silent departure was an admission of defeat. It had been a hard-fought contest, and Paul had chosen his weapons carefully. Had he used softer words, he might well have persuaded Silas to alter his stern ruling. Instead, he had offered the one argument that would make his brother refuse Anne's request—the reminder that Silas (like other men) could not live alone forever with his desires. . . . The attack had been deliberate, the result fore-ordained: had Anne Trevor's name been added to the passenger list on the *Adventurer*, the result would have been tragic for them all.

Brooding on these certainties, he did not stir from the chair when a side door opened and Anne herself stood before him. He had forgotten that the bedroom Silas had chosen for her adjoined his brother's own monkish quarters.

"Thank you, Paul," she said quietly. "I'm aware it was a lost cause."

"Were you listening?"

"I heard every word. Don't tell me it's a sin to eavesdrop: I *had* to know what passed between you."

"You heard my arguments," he said. "Perhaps I could have been more eloquent in your behalf. I felt it was unwise to push him too far."

"Why does Silas wish me to stay in England, Paul? I still don't understand."

"You're Geoffrey Trevor's daughter," he said. "You're my brother's promised bride, and a statue on a pedestal. You must play both parts, for his sake."

He had risen as he spoke, shaking off the lethargy that gripped him. *For his sake and mine,* he thought. *For your own sake as well.*

"I don't enjoy pedestals," said Anne. "I belong at my husband's side, now his real lifework's beginning."

"You'll finish that work together," said Paul. "Silas will send for you in time."

Hearing her quick sob, he did not dare to speak a word of comfort. Merely by turning to face her, he knew he could have told her of his love—and his fear of the ruin that love might cause. It was safer to continue the deception until the *Adventurer* sailed.

"I'll stay, of course," said Anne. "I'm going down the Severn with you tomorrow: I made Silas promise to take me that far—until he dropped the pilot. Was it too much to ask?"

"He'll survive the concession, I'm sure."

"Are *you* sorry I'm to stay behind, Paul? I hope you'll say yes—it's only gallant."

It was a perilous moment, and he forced himself to answer calmly. "Of course I'm sorry you're to remain. In another sense, I'm glad Silas stood by his decision. I'll sling my hammock with a lighter heart tomorrow, knowing you're safe in Bristol."

"Even if I *want* to share your perils?"

"I also prefer you on a pedestal, Anne. Shall we leave it at that?"

"Perhaps you're right, Paul," she said. "I won't argue any longer —with Silas, or with you."

Hearing the door close, he dared to turn at last: had she questioned him a moment more, he knew his last defense would have fallen. He stood for a while in the cheerless room, while he waited for the first shock of his desolation to subside. Then, flinging one of Silas' coats about him, he left the Feathers by the side door, to walk for hours on the quay—only half-aware of the fresh snow that had swept in with the changing wind.

Because of Paul's absence, chores had piled up aboard the *Adventurer*. Dividing his time between the inn and the lazaret he had chosen as his sick bay, he found it easy enough to avoid both Silas and Anne until the actual moment of departure.

Guy Lebret had helped him inventory his slender stock of drugs: they had made sure that the instrument cases were snugly stowed in the ship's locker beneath the rough operating table he had built in his quarters. Before donning the work clothes of a sailor (and offering his hair to the barber's shears) he had made a small ceremony of locking his finery in his sea chest, which he consigned to the cargo hold along with Guy's own specimen cases. He would have small use for a Cavalier's garb in the Bahamas: until he chose to stay on Eleuthera (or leave it) he would be under Silas' command, a Puritan in outward guise if not in name.

The day of the colonists' departure dawned clear and cold, with a brisk shore wind that promised a fair passage down the Severn. Aware that Anne might come aboard at any time, Paul had planned to remain in his surgery until the lines were cleared. At the last moment (admitting he had hidden too long below) he volunteered to join Lebret in tallying the arrival of the passengers. Since he had been asked to serve as historian of the voyage, it was time he learned their names—hard though it was, so far, to give this dun-colored assembly the dignity of individual characters.

He would remember that tally later (when each face in the company was as familiar as his own). He would damn the intolerance that had dismissed them as bigots—or incurable romantics fleeing a troubled England in search of the rainbow. The voyagers who thronged the waist of the *Adventurer* that winter afternoon were a motley lot—but even then, he was conscious of the enigmas behind those faces, the unspoken hopes and fears that had brought them here, the stubborn courage that would see them through.

Few of the faces were pleasing at first glance—and too many suggested the fanatic. He remembered one ultra-pious couple in particular, named Ralph and Charity Welles, with a twelve-year-old daughter called Patricia—a mincing creature who had proved herself a born troublemaker during her short stay at the inn. The elder Welles had quarreled over their billeting when informed that men and women must occupy separate quarters due to the crowded conditions amidships. On the duplicate passenger list he would include in his medical log, Paul marked down the Welleses as a family unit that would bear watching.

Similar notations were made for others in the Puritan contingent. By the same token (though for far different reasons) more than one name among the non-Puritans was ticked with a question mark. Not all of these were yeomen: the charter of the Eleutherian Adventurers had called for an original ship's complement of one hundred and eighty colonists, and Silas' recruiting agents had been forced to look into some odd corners to round out the list. Here, cheek by jowl with Kentish farmers and rawboned plowboys from Lancashire, were more than one weedy vagabond whose face seemed a stranger to the sunlight, whose twitching

fingers suggested the cut-purse rather than the pioneer. Others
had the stamp of failure that marks the desperate everywhere,
regardless of race or creed. These Paul judged to be fugitives
from some debtors' prison—or men with prices on their heads who
were quitting England under assumed names.

Still others were merely victims of the pall of poverty that had
settled over so many Englishmen in these parlous times—stunned
oxen in life's great procession who had stumbled too often along
the way and now groped blindly for the nearest haven. Such men
could hardly be said to follow a dream, since the struggle to keep
alive (in the London stews, in fishermen's villages, on hard-
scrabble Yorkshire farms) had allowed no such luxuries as dream-
ing. Most of them had signed the Adventurers' roll on the simple
premise that any change in their status must be an improvement.

It was hard to picture such men as successful colonists, no matter how bounteous existence might be in the Bahamas—and yet
(if he could believe reports from the New World) similiar miracles had occurred in both Massachusetts and Virginia. Freedom's
breath, Paul heard, had a special healing power. Could he believe
that these poor creatures could find true liberty of action under
governors like Silas Sutton? Enough, at any rate, to shake off their
bovine air of hopelessness, and remember they were men?

It was a relief to shake off his doubts, and turn to such couples
as the Halls—both of them sturdy farmer-folk, who had sold their
Suffolk freehold and brought their nineteen-year-old daughter
Deborah aboard as confidently as though they had planned this
voyage from the first day of their marriage. Young Jack Sikes,
the Halls' broad-shouldered farm manager (who had elected to
make the voyage with them rather than serve a new master)
had already gone exploring with Deborah. At the moment, they
stood among the rope coils on the foredeck, watching the last of
the colonists come aboard. From his vantage point, Paul noted
that their fingers were interlaced, and guessed that the first, inevitable romance had begun its blooming, even before the *Adventurer* could spread its sails. . . . In England, he reflected,
near-gentry like the Halls would never have countenanced the

marriage of an only daughter to their overseer. In that other world (where each man, at least in theory, was his brother's equal) other codes might well prevail.

Paul pulled his scattered thoughts together, and raised his eyes to the afterdeck rail, where two gaunt figures towered against the winter sky. Seen thus, they might have been twins, dressed in suits of identical black: their craggy profiles, and their ice-cold stares, seemed cast from the same die. Paul needed a second glance to remind himself that the taller of those two silent observers was his brother. The second man was Obadiah Lambert, a crusading Puritan divine and the spiritual leader of Silas' flock: he was waiting until the gangway was lifted to pronounce his blessing on the voyagers. It was hard to believe that his words would prove warmer than the stiff wind knifing the deck.

The last stragglers had begun to cross the quay, carrying their boxes on their shoulders. They had emerged from the ordinary of the Feathers, with Lili in the lead. She wore a bright peasant scarf about her shoulders and a skirt of flaring red. When she saw Paul at the gangway, she lifted one hand in a saucy salute, ignoring the stares of the women on deck.

Old Giles was the focal point of the small procession that followed her. He seemed to waddle rather than walk, thanks to a crushing burden of sacks and portmanteaus. Most of them (Paul guessed) were loaded with bottles rather than clothing. The innkeeper was followed by Elmo and Denis, his two black freedmen, who had served as waiters at the inn, and by a nondescript female known only as the Duchess, one of the rag-bag kitchen slaveys who (at the last moment) had elected to emigrate with her former employer. The little procession struck a raffish note as it filed aboard and disappeared into the makeshift living quarters in the ship's waist—and Paul chuckled at its impact as he exchanged a look with Guy.

He closed his tally as he lifted his hand to assist the Duchess' ponderous body down to the deck. It was appropriate, he thought, that the last foot to tread the gangway should be Anne Trevor's: knowing that she had gone into Bristol on some errands, Paul

had even hoped she would not reach the ship in time. Now, as
he saw her coach come rattling up the cobbles of the quay, he
stifled an impulse to run for cover. It had been one thing to ignore her presence while he bustled in a world of sailormen to
batten down the hatches. It was quite another to face her now,
in the sure knowledge that he must not look upon her face again,
after the short run down the Severn.

Anne came aboard in a rush—and only the glow of her cheeks
betrayed her when their eyes met across the high coaming. It
was Guy Lebret who stepped forward to hand her from gangway
to deck. Sailors had already leaped down to the quay to bring
her boxes aboard: Paul knew they contained sweetmeats for the
young aboard, and bolts of cloth for each woman passenger. He
saw at once that Anne's own presence was gift enough at that
precarious moment, when many of the voyagers were close to
tears at the thought of leaving England.

He stood a little aside as she moved from group to group, letting
his eyes feast upon her one last time. On that gloomy deck, she was
like another sun, lighting each face she touched in passing. Her
disappointment at her exclusion from the passenger list was wiped
clean away: Paul found time to curse Silas as he deserved before
he bolted into the companionway.

In the murk of the passage that led aft to his quarters, Paul
paused as a hand fell on his arm. He found himself staring into
Guy Lebret's mocking eyes. The Frenchman had followed him
below, to lock the door that separated the men's and women's
quarters.

"When did this begin, *mon vieux?*" he whispered.

"I don't know what you mean—"

"You are a poor liar, Paul. Not that I blame you for your interest. In your place, I would not restrain it."

"If you refer to Mistress Trevor—"

"Who else would I have in mind, among these blackbirds? For
your sake, it is well we sail without her, *n'est-ce pas?*"

Paul broke free without answering, and closed the lazaret door.
The gesture, he knew, was childish—but he was in no mood for

Guy's teasing. He could only hope that his absence would be over-looked in the bustle that always attends a sailing.

From the deck he could hear the pontifical booming of Obadiah Lambert as the spiritual leader of the colonists exhorted God's blessing on their venture—and warned those same voyagers, no less solemnly, of the eternal torment that awaited them if they ignored His holy commandments. (The Reverend Obadiah, Paul gathered, was prepared to itemize those commandments at daily prayer meetings during the voyage.) The harsh, metallic voice seemed to go on endlessly. Aware that there was no escaping its strident message, Paul opened the door to his quarters and went on deck to join the now thoroughly chilled audience in the waist.

Lambert had just launched into his peroration when he ar-rived—and, though he was careful to stand in the ambush of a water cask, Paul had the uncomfortable conviction that the par-son's final diatribes were aimed directly at his head. The ship's company was well aware (said the Reverend Obadiah) that there was a division of faith among them—but it was explicitly stated in the articles of colonization that the disciplines of the Puritans would prevail, both at sea and shore. Until the *Adventurer* touched land, men and women would live apart, even those who were lawfully wed. Carnality would be dealt with sternly at all times, and man's natural predilection to sin would be countered by an extensive program of good works, sea-water baths each day regardless of weather, and the sovereign therapy of prayer.

Lambert paused on that note—but he had not quite finished his harangue. The Eleutherian Adventurers, he proclaimed, were rarely fortunate in Silas Sutton, their secular leader—a man whose authority, as stated in the articles, was final in all matters. Now that the last tie to the Old World was about to be severed, it was appropriate that Silas lead the closing prayer. . . . The minister stepped back at last, as Paul's brother moved to the after deck rail, with both hands extended in solemn benediction.

By contrast to the sulphurous rhetoric of the minister, Silas' prayer was short, almost stark—but even the lowliest cutpurse on the deck below him could not mistake its sincerity. Here, one saw instantly, was a man whose belief in his own rightness was absolute: Silas had been born to lead, whatever his shortcomings, and regardless of his goal. The Amen that rang out from the *Adventurer* was genuine. So was the cheer that rose from the quay as the lines were cast off and the half-hundred relatives, who had assembled to wish the vessel Godspeed, surged forward to wave hats and scarves.

It was quite in character for Silas to seem oblivious of the cheering, even as he ignored the fateful parting of the vessel from the quay. He had already turned into the chartroom, where Captain Sperry was plotting the first leg of the voyage. At his nod, Anne followed him to the same shelter. At the wheel, Lars Brack was bawling orders to the sailors, scrambling in the yards like so many monkeys to sheet the sails home as the kedging skiffs fell astern. The pilot who would con the ship down the Severn stood beside him, ready with soft-voiced directions—but Paul could already see that the man's help was needless. Long before the *Adventurer* had lifted her bowsprit in the following wind (with such stubborn grace as a vintage beldam possessed) he realized that the mate, like the casehardened men in the shrouds, was a natural ship handler.

Paul's heart had never failed to lift in this solemn moment— when a brave vessel stood free of land with canvas taut. Today, the thrill was strangely absent. He felt no emotion beyond a deep melancholy when he turned to re-enter the lazaret. Most of the passengers, he noted, had remained on deck to witness the ship's entrance into the Severn. Now that Silas' compelling eyes were no longer upon them, some were frankly weeping as the full implications of their departure sank home.

He closed the door against the contagion of those tears, determined to stay below until the pilot's departure: he had no wish to observe the farewell between Silas and Anne. He sat for a while at the open stern window, careless of the biting cold as he watched the shape of England merge with afternoon mist in the fast-widening estuary. Late afternoon had stained the seas a rich wine-red, and a shifting wind had forced the *Adventurer* into a series of long tacks to set her course for the Irish Sea, when the pilot boat put out from the shore at last. Paul slammed his window on the sight and turned to his work table, to busy himself with pills and mortar.

He was still hard at his task (and taking perverse comfort from it) when the lazaret door opened. There was no need to turn; he realized that Anne stood on the threshold.

"You've been avoiding me, Paul," she said.

He raised his glance to hers: with the pilot boat on its way, it was safe to speak his mind. "Don't you know why?"

Their eyes held for a moment. "I do know." Her voice was not quite steady, but she had gained control when she spoke again. "I only came to say good-by—and ask a favor."

"If it's in my power."

"You know what the success of this colony would have meant to my father. It means quite as much to me. I hadn't been long in Bristol before I saw that Silas' leadership leaves something to be desired."

"Like understanding—and tolerance?"

"Our venture could easily fail without them, Paul." Her eyes dropped. At that moment, she seemed entirely forlorn—and he would have given the world to comfort her. "He's going to need help badly in the months to come."

"I'm sorry *you* can't give such help, Anne."

"You mustn't say that," she told him quickly. "It was wrong of me to ask to join you—I can see that clearly now. Not when Silas wished otherwise. All of us must fight temptation at times. I'm glad you helped me conquer mine."

He managed the travesty of a grin. "It's true, then? Even a Puritan can be tempted? You as well as Silas?"

"Silas has the strength to resist temptation," she said quietly. "I'm sure of that."

"So do you, Anne."

"Don't give me too much credit. What I'm feeling at this moment isn't too important. It's the others I'm worried about, both Puritans and Anglicans. They'll need a buffer between them and

Silas—especially at first, when he's feeling his way. Will you be that buffer, Paul?"

"I'm here," he reminded her. "Does that reassure you?"

"Forgive me for prying into your affairs—but Captain Sperry tells me you're thinking of going on to Virginia."

"I've considered it, Anne. I won't leave Eleuthera until the colony's established."

Her face cleared. "I'm glad you said that without prompting. The whole company needs you—and I don't mean just as a doctor."

"There was a time when you didn't value me so highly."

Even in the bad light, he saw that she had flushed. "That was before I really knew you."

"Well enough to see why I must go to Virginia?"

"Yes, Paul. Perhaps that will be the best course in the end."

"I'll have no choice, Anne."

"You'll stay with the colony for the time being? That's a bargain?"

"Until you come, at least." He managed another smile. "If I know Silas, the buffer will be rather battered by then. You can take over the chore."

A rasp of wood against the hull shook the vessel slightly. Anne turned toward the sound.

"Is that the pilot boat?"

"If you don't leave at once, you may go to the New World in spite of yourself."

"Good-by, Paul." She did not give him her hand, and he made no move to touch her. "God bless you."

"Good-by, Anne. I'll go on deck to see you off."

Two sailors, lashed to belaying pins at the rail, lowered Anne in a bosun's chair, until she could settle in the thwarts of the tiny vessel bobbing in the waves below. Silas, Paul observed, had emerged from the chartroom. He stood on the after deck, his arm raised in a gesture of farewell—a gesture Paul duplicated numbly. Seated beside the helmsman, wrapped to the eyes in a boat cloak against the bitter cold, Anne waved in return. Driven by the thrust of the following wind, the smaller boat heeled sharply in its run for the land, and the sail hid the slight, proud figure from view.

Silas spoke from the deck as Paul stepped into the ship's waist. "Did she find you in time to say good-by?"

Paul nodded, with his eyes on the angry sea: for once he could bless Silas' obtuseness. Already, with the sunset behind it, the little boat seemed no more than a speck in the vast estuary of the Severn. In another moment, he knew, the shadow of England would claim it.

Weather was making with a vengeance before the *Adventurer* could set her first course in the Irish Sea—and the passengers, their spirits thoroughly dampened, had long since retired to their crowded quarters to face the threat of seasickness. Ignoring the supper bell, Paul continued to pace the empty decks until the near-freezing wind drove him below. There, still wrapped in his boat cloak, he flung himself on his hammock (slung athwart the surgery, to save space) and tried hard to compose himself, though the uneasy doze could hardly be called slumber.

When he heard the knock at his door, he saw it was hard on midnight. The ancient vessel, creaking in every stem, was fighting a wind of gale force in the open sea and the smoking tallow in the lantern overhead had guttered close to extinction. Knowing who was waiting outside (and the risk she had run to join him thus) he hastened to unbolt the portal. Lili, clad only in a quilted wrapper and the flimsiest of shifts, whisked inside.

"Don't look so surprised," she whispered. "You knew I'd come, the moment I could manage."

"You're supposed to be under lock and key, in the women's quarters."

Lili drew down her left eyebrow: the grimace was Giles Porter, to the life—including the innkeeper's acceptance of life's dodges. Paul could feel the protest die on his lips, and knew he was chuckling instead.

"We've nothing to fear," she said. "Guy saw to that."

"Don't tell me he arranged to put you elsewhere. He knows it's forbidden."

His visitor moved to the hammock, and tested it gingerly. "Guy's made his own bed in the companionway, on orders from the captain," she said. "My father was told to sleep between decks, at the main hatchway. Between them, they're to keep order in the dormitories, from darkness 'till dawn—"

"It seems they've failed with you."

Lili, finding the hammock to her liking, had already stretched full length in its folds, adjusting to the ship's roll like a born sailor. "My pallet's at the door of the women's room," she said demurely. "I arranged *that,* the moment I came aboard. Guy gave me a special key—"

"He was hardly wise."

"How else could I come and go freely? I can always slip back before dawn."

Again, he found that a reproof had gone unuttered: from the moment Lebret had guessed his secret, he had expected him to arrange matters thus. In the cynical Frenchman's book, one nail could drive out another, in love as well as life.

"Have you any idea of the risk you're running?" he asked— aware, even as he uttered them, how lame the words had sounded.

"I'm used to risks," said Lili. "So were you, before you came aboard this tub. Don't tell me you're ready to pattern your behavior on the Reverend Obadiah's."

"What can I say, if he or Silas should find you here?"

Lili continued to sway comfortably in the hammock. "If we're surprised, you can always say I came for treatment. Guy will back the story."

He took her hand and pressed it warmly. As always, it was impossible to resist this child of nature for long. "I'm honored by your visit," he said carefully. "That goes without saying. But we must think of the future too—"

"Must we tonight, Paul? Why should I go back to that hen coop before morning? Aren't you just as lonesome as I?"

"Believe me, my dear, I've never felt more alone—"

"I was right to come then. You want me to stay, don't you?"

He bent to kiss her lightly, intending the caress as a prelude to a gentle dismissal. Instead, he found himself involved in an embrace that could have but one meaning—and admitted, even then, that his response was no less ardent than her own. Love, he thought sadly, was a word of many meanings—and desire, after all, was one side of the coin. The bitter fact remained that he had been perishing of melancholy when Lili entered: while the warmth of her presence surrounded him, the sense of emptiness was, at least, endurable.

"You're glad *now*, aren't you, Paul?"

"Of course I'm glad—and you're quite right. We needn't turn Puritan until tomorrow."

"I'll never turn Puritan—nor will you. Don't try to be like Silas, just because you've joined the Adventurers. You're a doctor: you've the right to make your own rules."

"Even tonight, when I'm under his orders?"

"Tonight most of all," said Lili serenely. "You aren't your brother's keeper, *chéri*—as you said in Bristol."

"What's that supposed to mean?"

"I don't think you need a translation, Paul."

What she said was true enough—and he made no effort to defend his false morality further. Only a few hours ago, he had bidden Anne Trevor good-by in this cabin. Life remained, along with the insistent demands of the flesh: he would go on existing as best he could. In a way, it was an ironic joke that he should be kissing the innkeeper's daughter now, in the same setting—and that he had long admitted these kisses could have but one ending. He knew that Anne would have forgiven him in advance, since her own future was charted just as firmly. Man was not born to lie in the dark alone, to surrender to his sadness and his fears. Not on a night like this, with the last gale of winter howling outside the ports, and a tomorrow of unknown perils waiting down the horizon.

The keening of the wind died briefly outside when he took Lili in his arms again—only to be replaced by another, stranger wailing. For a moment, he could not identify the sound. Then he knew it was his brother's voice, from the cabin above them, raised in frenzied prayer.

An hour later, when he dropped into slumber, he was aware that the harsh voice still droned on. It was odd, he reflected, that Silas Sutton (whose belief in his own cause was absolute) should ask God for strength as he lay alone in darkness.

# THE *ADVENTURER*

NAKED to the waist, his arms and shoulders streaked with dirt, Paul crawled the length of the bilges one more time. On the catwalk beside him, young Jack Sikes held a bull's-eye lantern above his head, to give what help he could on this final inspection tour.

Thanks to the subtropic heat that pressed down on a windless sea, the hold of the *Adventurer* was stifling; because of the sulphur that smoldered in pots at each of its four corners, it might have passed for an antechamber in hell. Yet the shout of joy the ship's doctor gave when his crawl ended was anything but despairing. Today (for the first time since the vessel had left the Severn, six weeks ago) the bilges were free of rats. There was no longer a trace of their noisome presence, now that the pumps had been at work below—and the heavy air, despite the breath of the smudge pots, promised life rather than death.

"I think we've won this fight, Jack," he said. "Pray God the plague is ended too."

Young Sikes, his honest country face creased in a frown, followed Paul without comment, helping him to douse each sulphur fire in turn before they ascended the ladder to the deck. All during the previous day, Jack had stood with a dozen volunteers along the edges of the main hatch, to club down the starveling rodents that had scuttled topside to escape the heavy fumes of sulphur. The day before, he had led a similar hunt through the cabins—to make sure the vermin had not sought refuge elsewhere. Now, bone-weary though he was, he had insisted on helping Paul in this final check. Jack Sikes, the ship's doctor perceived, was another proof of the Englishman's ability to stand firm in the face of crisis. He deserved an explanation this April dawn—if it was possible to explain the reasoning behind their chore.

"It's only a hope," Paul said, while they stood at the salt-water cask in the waist, washing the grime from their bodies. "Tomorrow death may strike again. The fact remains: I've sailed to most of the world's ports—and Sir Rat and the plague have always been shipmates."

Jack's frown had not yet lifted. "Some say it's crowding and bad air, Doctor—"

"They may be causes too. That's why we're ordered all ports left open—and clothing boiled in lye to kill the fleas."

"Others say the Spaniard brought the evil thing aboard. He was the first to fall sick—remember?"

"All too well—it was the day after we left the Bermudas. I still think it was the vermin, and not Lopez."

"Your brother makes small choice between the two, Doctor."

"Silas engaged the Spaniard as a guide," said Paul. "Why invite him aboard, if we can't trust him?" He broke off with a shrug. He could afford to speak his mind to Jack, but this was no time to rail against the leader, bad though Silas' luck had been so far—to say nothing of his judgment. "What do *you* think caused the sickness?"

The yeoman scratched his head—but his grin was broader now. "'Tis not for me to say, Doctor. Who knows what keeps one man well, and strikes another low? But I'll tell you this. I'd rather chase death with fire than ask God to send it away. So would most of us."

"The ship's behind me on smoking out the rats, then?"

"The ship's behind any decision you make, Doctor. Fair wind or foul, you can lay to that."

Paul could not help flushing with pleasure, though he had expected the endorsement. Since the plague had struck, he had been in charge in fact if not in name. It was hardly news that the ship preferred his stern but understanding discipline to the orders that issued from Silas' cabin. He took refuge in gruffness, since he could not afford to challenge their leader, even by implication. With their goal only a few days' sail down the horizon, Silas still had the right to prove himself.

"Get to the captain's cabin, and report we're free of vermin," he said. "Then go to your hammock and stay there until the next watch. You've earned some rest, Jack."

When Sikes had climbed the quarter-deck ladder, Paul moved wearily toward the men's dormitory to make his morning sick call. As he had hoped, there were no new signs that the plague had spread: seven deaths, he reflected, had been a fair price to pay before the scourge had run its course. Of the cases that remained, only one was still too sick to rise. This was Ralph Welles, whom the ship's doctor had ticketed as the most pious (and the most troublesome) of all the seventy-odd Puritans aboard. Paul's other patient was the Spaniard—whom everyone called Lopez, since it was the simplest of his names on the English tongue. The first to be stricken, he was now almost recovered, though he still kept to his hammock.

Lopez had come aboard under mysterious auspices during their ill-starred pause at the Bermudas: most of his fellow passengers would have continued to look at him askance, even had he not been the first victim of the plague. This morning, Paul made it a point to pause and exchange civilities in the man's native tongue. It was appropriate, he thought, that Lopez's hammock had been slung apart from the others, in a far corner of that cramped mid-deck area. It was also fitting that Ralph Welles' sickbed should be made on the cabin floor itself—and that it had been a focal point for the general discontent among the Puritans.

Today, Welles was resting quietly, with only the glitter of his ferret-sharp eyes to betray his dislike. Once he had assured himself his patient was out of danger, Paul found it easy enough to ignore the man's complaints, while he administered an opiate that would keep Welles mute until nightfall.

Back in the companionway, he saw that Guy Lebret was still asleep on his pallet: knowing that his friend had stood a night watch, he was careful not to waken him when he lifted the key from his belt and unlocked the door to the women's quarters. He was greeted by a universal shriek of dismay—and remembered, too late, that he had forgotten to don a shirt for this tour of duty. So far, none of the Pilgrim contingent had made the slightest concession to the heat that had enveloped the *Adventurer* since her departure from the Bermudas. Though they scrubbed at his orders, and sent their drab garments to the lye pots to kill off the fleas, they had refused, so far, to discard so much as a jerkin or a petticoat.

This morning, Paul observed that most of the women had even continued to sleep in their bonnets—yielding to the universal belief that they offered some protection from deadly night vapors. He saw (with a grim nod of approval) that Lili—serving one more stretch as night nurse—had stripped the cloth blinds from the ports while the others slept. Lecture though he might, he could not convince these fearful females that they were not observed in their cautious disrobings between landfalls.

There had been three deaths in this section of the ship—and Paul had all but despaired of several others, when the danger was at its height. Accustomed as they were to the hard routines of the hearth, most of these women had moped through the long voyage, refusing to show their faces on deck save in the best of weather. As a result, they had had little reserves of strength when the plague stalked among them. Again, the ship's doctor could tell himself that only his Draconian insistence on baths and fresh air had averted a real calamity.

This morning, Paul had only a few convalescents to attend, most of whom would be up and about tomorrow. Patricia, the vixen daughter of Ralph and Charity Welles, had suffered a mild attack of the disease. She still babbled from fever on her cot—but he saw at once that the crisis had moved on, even as he stared the girl's acid-tongued mother into silence. Patricia, as he had feared, had proved herself an accomplished toady during the voyage—and a born eavesdropper. He was sure that she had given Silas a complete account of Lili's visits to his quarters. He was equally certain that a child with Patricia's capacity for evil was far too sturdy to die.

Deborah Hall was the last female patient on his list, and he was still at a loss for words when he paused to examine her. Both the girl's parents had been victims of the plague—and Jack Sikes had been her only consolation since their bodies had been committed to the sea. At first, Paul had thought that this plucky English lass had merely asserted the privileges of her sex and yielded to melancholia. Today (after a whispered consultation with Lili) he confirmed another guess: Deborah Hall was merely pregnant, and suffering from the morning sickness that troubled so many expectant mothers.

It was the third such diagnosis he had made in the women's quarters since the long voyage began. Captain Sperry, a cynic to the end, had called the score absurdly low, and predicted still other prostrations of the sort before they reached Eleuthera.

One look at Deborah was all Paul needed to reassure him. He had seen from the first day that the girl and Jack Sikes were deeply in love: he could hardly blame them for proving that love by the oldest of means, in the few moments they had stolen together. Winking at Lili behind Charity Welles' ramrod-stiff back, Paul knew the girl had no cause for alarm. Her parents' deaths had made her the best-dowered woman aboard—and Silas would be forced to ask Obadiah Lambert to marry her to Jack, thunder though he might at fleshly lures.

In a way, now the threat of plague was ebbing, this newest conception was an affirmation of the life force. As such, it might even be called an augury for the success of this venture into the unknown.

Paul's inspection of the crew's quarters, the last item in his morning sick call, was soon ended. Significantly, there had not been a single case of plague in the forecastle area. Lars Brack was not only a hard-driving first officer, but a fanatic for cleanliness. Sluiced with daily sea baths, his seamen had long since learned to strip to the bare essentials of clothing; they slept on deck, in high-slung canvas hammocks, whenever the occasion offered. The regime had proved its worth. Paul could hardly call the *Adventurer* a happy ship (the freight she bore was too grim for such labels). Thanks to Brack, the hands on watch were sharp as seamen on a man-of-war.

Giles Porter was taking the air on the afterhatch while he chatted with the helmsman. Paul was careful to pass close enough to make sure the innkeeper was sober. It was an open secret that Giles (restless as a brood hen after long weeks at sea, and missing the easy companionship of his Bristol bar) was in the habit of tapping his kegs at odd hours. He had also secured the captain's permission to supply the off watch with rum or whisky at stated hours. It was one of Paul's duties to see the privilege was not abused. (Silas had railed enough at the British custom of grog at stand-down, regardless of a seaman's rank.)

Today, the innkeeper was but mildly redolent of his wares. Continuing to his own quarters, Paul poured a tot of his own, and downed it neat before he settled at his worktable and cradled his head in his arms. It was one of the few intervals when he was really alone. Since that moment of parting in the Severn, he had learned to dread loneliness more than any peril of the voyage.

In the weeks between, Lili had filled many nights with her presence (the long, blank hours would have been intolerable without her). His days had been fully occupied, since he had insisted on standing one watch in three, to learn the temper of Sperry's crew. Between that duty, he had found his physician's chores arduous. There had been scurvy before they could reach the Azores and take on enough fresh fruit to fight it down. The land-lubber passengers (poor sailors all) had sustained their share of bruises and shattered bones when the North Atlantic gales threatened to stand their ancient ark on its beam-ends.

Paul had welcomed the tasks his calling imposed. As the historian of the voyage, he had taken pride in the notation—made just before the *Adventurer* reached the Bermudas—that Captain Sperry had brought his charges within striking distance of the New World, without the loss of a single life. It was a rare occurrence during a crossing of the Ocean Sea.

His mind dozed on that memory: while he hovered on the edge

of sleep, Anne Trevor whispered (as she always did) from the void, luring him with a promise she could never fulfill. If only to shake off the vision, he lifted his head from the table and opened his log, to set down the details of that call at the last English port they would see on this voyage. . . .

It had been a long, rough crossing from the Azores, with constant head winds and a sky that streamed rain. The colonists had raised a cheer when the veil of cloud lifted that spring evening, to give them their first glimpse of the low, gray-green hills of the Somers Islands—now known as the Bermoothes, or, more simply, Bermuda. Gleaming in the late sunlight, those hills had welcomed them in advance—and Silas had argued hotly with Sperry when the latter refused to press on into the gathering night. The islands, said the captain, were treacherous with reefs. It was common knowledge that they had been settled by chance, when colonists bound for Virginia, had driven their ship on coral outcrop—and stayed to make the Bermudas a kind of outpost in Britain's New World pioneering.

They had sailed off and on that night in deep water, making a cautious approach with the dawn, to drop anchor just outside the harbor bar, where England's standard hung above a wooden fort, and a cluster of cabins proclaimed a town of sorts. Rain descended in torrents during the mooring. When it ceased at noon, a warning gun from the fort had restrained them from proceeding farther. Already, it seemed the *Adventurer* was an object of suspicion. The explanation came when a longboat put out from shore, bristling with men in armor. The boat officer explained that the story of the Eleutherian Adventurers had preceded them. It was his duty to inform the colonists that the governor (a stanch Royalist, to whom Puritans were little better than heretics) refused them permission to land.

Captain Sperry had left in his own gig to plead the colonists' cause, stressing the rigors of the voyage and their need for provision. In the end, he had been permitted to land for a conference with the governor. When that august personage had read through the king's own charter, he yielded to a point. No one was allowed ashore—but he convoyed provisions to the anchored vessel, along with a map of the Bahamas (drawn by one William Sayle, who had explored them from this same starting point, twenty years ago).

Later, he had relented still further, and sent the Spaniard to the *Adventurer*, along with a last, grudging gift of food. Lopez, he said, was a guide Captain Sperry could trust—a man who had jumped ship to escape the tyranny of the dons, an explorer familiar with every reef and roadstead in the Lucayas.

Lopez had no English, and only Paul and Lars Brack could speak Spanish at their first conference. Some of the colonists had questioned the wisdom of accepting his advice too readily: it was pointed out that Lopez was an enemy alien on British soil, and that the governor of the Bermudas might have delivered him thus to rid his islands of an unwelcome visitor. Paul himself was convinced the man was an honest renegade, and might prove valuable. Surprisingly enough, Silas concurred in this judgment—though the leader of the Eleutherians could hardly make head or tail of Lopez's jargon.

The interrogation lasted through their departure from the precarious anchorage off the Bermudas, with much conning of maps and papers. Silas made copious notes, crouched over a knee desk on the after deck, oblivious of the green islands gliding past the starboard bow. The *Adventurer* sailed warily down the coral reef that fringed the southern shore: he scarcely raised his eyes when a hidden battery on that coast belched a final warning.

It was a fitting dismissal from the English—and, to Paul, an ominous one.

An hour later, the *Adventurer* had sailed into the unknown waters to the south, with no speck of land to spoil the ocean's perfect round. Silas was still crouched over his notes. Reading the meaning of that avid look, Paul held his tongue when the Spaniard had gone to his hammock. He had always suspected that his brother had planned to occupy Eleuthera from mixed motives. Once the outpost was established, it could serve as a springboard for a holy war against the Spanish Indies. Insane though the project might seem to the historian of tomorrow, the appeal to Silas was irresistible.

It had been quite like Silas to keep his own counsel in the matter, so far as Paul himself was concerned. Thanks to the nearness of his cabin, the younger brother could hardly avoid overhearing his communions with the Almighty. Ever since the Spaniard had come aboard, Silas had closed his nightly prayers with a request for the speedy conquest of both Cuba and the Floridas.

Paul looked up from his musings, and closed his log of the voyage. The ship had shivered faintly, responding to a puff of wind that had just teased the sails. When he stepped on deck, he saw that the calm had lifted, though there was barely enough breeze to put the *Adventurer* in motion.

Thinking of Silas, he lifted his eyes to the crow's-nest on the foremast. As he had expected, the leader had gone there with the first light: for several days, it had been his custom to sit in that lofty perch, immovable as the ship's own figurehead, his eyes on the southern horizon. Today, there was no clear-cut division between sea and sky—but Silas had insisted on relieving a sailor of the chore. The Bermudas were many days' sailing to the north, and the ship was rife with rumors that a landfall was imminent. Though he would have shrugged off the superstition as an invention of the devil, Silas firmly believed he must be the first to glimpse his future domain.

Paul ran halfway up the mizzen shrouds for a survey of his own. The mist lay like cotton batting along the horizon. It showed no sign of lifting in the freshening breeze—and the sun was only a pale phantom in the cloud rack overhead. For the last two days, bad weather had prevented Captain Sperry from taking a noontime shot—not that this still-primitive aid to navigation would have revealed much more than his traverse tables and dead reckoning.

The master of the *Adventurer* sat at his chart table, comparing his own map of the Lucayas with the counterpart he had brought aboard at Bermuda. He welcomed Paul with a grunted good morning, and jerked a thumb at the demijohn suspended on a gimbal at the bulkhead. Neither of them spoke until Paul had poured out two pannikins. During the voyage, Sperry and his doctor had learned to accept crises without words.

Paul studied both maps while he sipped the fiery blackstrap liquor. Sayle's drawing, he saw, was much more detailed than the captain's rather sketchy chart. There was no mistaking such elements as the dark ocean tongues that thrust into the midst of the Bahama Islands, the shape of such landmarks as New Providence (said to be a favorite careening ground of the corsairs who preyed on Spanish shipping), the great complex of reefs and shoals that lay between that island and Cuba, and the elongated shape of Eleuthera itself. Sayle had placed the latter island twenty leagues to the east of New Providence. Other, still larger islands lay to the west, along the edge of the Bahama Passage, the channel that separated the archipelago from the Florida peninsula.

The Sayle chart seemed complete. There was no doubt that the explorer from Bermuda had touched at Eleuthera and mapped it as thoroughly as his resources permitted. Sperry himself had cruised in these waters before: he could rely on his bump of direction, once he had raised his first landmark. The fact remained that his ship might pile on coral at any moment, thanks to this spell of murky weather and the guesswork as to her true position. Silas had been inexorable in his demand that they crowd on sail—and Paul knew that Sperry blessed the dead calm that had held them under idle canvas until daybreak.

"What's our last entry in the log, Captain?"

"I'm leaving the page blank until there's another show of sun," said Sperry. "Meanwhile, I wish you'd lure your brother from that crow's-nest. Don't tell me he can see better than Marco or Brack. I'll want a sailor aloft when we raise Corncob Key."

Paul bent closer to study the captain's own chart. Corncob Key was his name for the minute island he had sketched in the upper corner of the chart, with precise notations of its longitude and latitude. Paul had sailed with other masters who did not hesitate to improve their official maps with additions of their own. The islet (named after those ears of Indian maize the first explorers had brought back from the New World) had been Sperry's first view of the Bahamas—and his good-luck charm. Sailing blindly as he was, he could still rely on his dead reckoning, if the weather cleared by noon. Even in that wilderness of sea, he could hardly miss Corncob, and other markers he had jotted down beyond.

"Did you point this out to Silas?"

"Of course. If you'll pardon the observation, your leader is looking far beyond such matters as a safe passage to the east of New Providence. In *his* mind's eye, he's already ruler of all the islands, with a thousand armed men to take his orders, and a fleet to deliver them on Spain's doorstep."

"Even Silas must realize that's worse than a dream."

"Not since Lopez told him there's only a thinly held fort at the Havana, and another on the Florida coast at St. Augustine. I'll lay odds he asks for those troops, when I take his report to Bristol."

"Surely the king will ignore such requests. We've come to plant the British flag, not to make war on Cuba."

"Cromwell might think differently," said Sperry. "He's giving orders now—and he's itching to spill papist blood. Thank God *I'll* have no part in that quarrel. The *Adventurer*'s a ferryboat, not a man-of-war."

"Be honest, Captain. You've seen these islands, with your own eyes. Wouldn't you like to put down roots there?"

"Life's hard enough at sea," said Sperry. "I can't abide the land —even when it's at peace. Take my word, this island paradise won't keep its status overlong. Not when your brother takes marching orders from Jehovah himself."

"Aren't you judging Silas a little harshly? He's said nothing of fighting to either of us."

"I can hear his prayers as well as you," said Sperry. "I'll grant you he'll walk warily, until he's sure of his ground. Once he's established his island base, he'll burn to move on—unless you're prepared to stop him."

"I promised I'd stay until he was safely established; then I'm moving on myself."

"Perhaps you'll have no choice but to remain," said Sperry. "Let's not argue that for the present: I want that foremast lookout for a crewman. It's making the whole ship nervous, having Master Sutton perched on the crossyards. From the deck, he's the image of a black-winged albatross—and that's bad luck in any language."

"I'm flattered by your metaphor, Captain," said a new voice from the doorway. "Perhaps I deserve the description. In any event, you'll find your crow's-nest free. I've business below with the doctor."

Silas had crossed the deck without a sound: he could walk softly when it suited him. Paul moved toward his brother deliberately, making himself a shield between Silas and the captain. This morning, the spots on the leader's cheeks were a deeper red than usual: he could not believe the flush was due wholly to rage. At all costs, he felt he must prevent an open battle.

"I've made my report to the captain," he said. "I'm sure he'll excuse me."

"It's a bit late to explain I've first call on your services," said Silas. "Why didn't you rouse me at dawn, as I ordered?"

"I did come to waken you," said Paul steadily. "For the first time in weeks, I found you deep in slumber. I felt you needed rest—"

"Will you come to my cabin—now?"

Sperry, lolling in the captain's chair, had already bellowed an order to the quarter-deck, sending Brack himself to the crow's-nest on the double. He got up now, with a lazy good humor that was more ominous than open contempt, and faced Silas across the chart table. "Can *I* be of service, Master Sutton?" he asked.

"Your service will end when you've dropped anchor at Eleuthera, Captain," said Silas. "This is hardly the time or place to complain of insubordination. I'll do that when I report to London."

"Complain and be damned, sir," said the captain. "I'll deliver you safely—and I'll stay on, till I've made sure you can scratch a living. Until then, don't say we've treated you badly. Thanks to your brother, you've lost just seven souls on this voyage—a fine record for any crossing, with sickness aboard. To balance that, your rutting males have started three lives. Not a half-bad score—when you consider both sexes were under padlocks."

"Have you no shame, man?"

"'Tis not a question of shame, Master Sutton. I'm merely reminding you we've been fortunate as voyages go. Don't crowd your luck—"

"When I wish your advice, I'll ask for it."

"You'll do well to listen to this warning," said Sperry. "Take your brother's orders, and rest while you can. You'll need all the strength you can muster when you set foot on land. So will the seasick Bible-backs you call your flock. It's no secret that you've only a month's food under hatches—and barely enough powder to defend yourselves, once you've raised a fort. I'd build those breastworks before I looked beyond."

"What does that imply?"

"You know my opinion of self-appointed crusaders," said the captain. "May I wish you good day—and good resting?"

Silas' hand lifted: had he possessed the power, Paul knew he would have blasted Sperry in his tracks. Again he took a step forward—but there was no need to restrain his brother after all.

"Don't remind me you're in charge, Captain," said Silas. "It's a cross I can bear, now we're near our journey's end. Just try to avoid me until you're spoken to. Will you come to my cabin, Paul?"

Expecting a fresh outburst as they descended the ladder, Paul was troubled by his brother's brooding silence. Silas seemed to reel a little while he fumbled for the door catch: he moved to steady his elbow, only to have his hand shaken violently aside.

The leader's cabin (in the sterncastle below the captain's) was low-ceilinged—and, like all Silas' abodes, bare as some anchorite's cell. Paul frowned at the whiff of stale air that greeted him. He had opened the stern window when he found his brother sleeping in the murky light of dawn—and guessed that Silas had slammed it shut when he arose. Like other members of his flock, he was convinced that the night air teemed with evil spirits.

"Did you bathe with the men, as I ordered?" Paul asked sternly. "Did your clothes go to the lye pot?"

Silas settled behind the table that served as his dresser, brushing aside a heap of sea-damp clothing as he did so. As always, the desk was transformed instantly to a pulpit.

"I've no time for indulgence of the flesh—"

"One's health is hardly a matter for indulgence. I needn't remind you there's been plague aboard. We've gone two days without a new case—and those in the sick bay are mending. It'll be a bad omen if you spoil that record."

"I'm here to make records for God," said Silas.

"Would you have preferred to conquer the plague with prayer?"

"Surely there was no need to expose a whole ship to temptation—with communal baths, and wholesale washing of garments?"

"All that is behind us now, I hope."

"I didn't call you here to discuss the ills of the body," said Silas. "Today your soul is my concern. Yours—and a woman's. Will you help me to save both?"

"I thought my soul was already lost."

"No man's soul is beyond help."

"You said as much in Bristol."

"So I did—when I was too ill to control my temper. I've long since asked God's pardon for my lapse. Now we're about to become fellow colonists, I can't have that defeat on my conscience. Will you try answering my question?"

"How can I, if you won't supply the lady's name?"

"I'd hardly call the innkeeper's daughter a *lady*. Her soul is still worth saving."

Paul felt anger grow within him, like a fire that has run beyond control. Expecting just this attack since the beginning of the voyage, aware that he must cover his feelings at all costs, he found himself speaking his mind without reserve.

"Lili Porter may not be a lady by your standards. She's one of the gentlest and finest persons I've ever known. She'll preserve her soul with no help from you. So, for that matter, will I."

"I feared that answer, Paul," said Silas. "Remember you can't defy me forever."

"Is this a threat?"

"Call it a reminder that I rule our colony. The moment we go ashore, Sperry's authority ends. He can't go on shielding you from God's wrath—"

"Meaning *your* wrath—because I was lucky enough to have a hammock mate on this voyage?"

"So you admit your sin freely?"

"I admit I found a woman to solace my loneliness—like others on this ship."

"Do you deny she shared your cabin the first night out from Bristol?"

"Of course I don't. She visited me many nights thereafter."

"With the connivance of your friend Lebret?"

"Guy was a willing accomplice."

"Against my express orders?" Silas was on his feet by now, and his voice had regained all its lost resonance.

"As ship's doctor, I make my own rules—and my own hours of employment." Surprisingly (now the issue was joined) Paul found he was enjoying the contest. "That includes the use of my free time."

"Were you with her today, when you were supposed to waken me?"

"Only until midnight, Silas. Lili rose then to help minister to the sick. You must know she's the best nurse we have aboard."

"Spare me her virtues for now. Were you lying, when you say you came to my cabin at dawn?"

"Jack Sikes will bear that out," said Paul. "We found you asleep, just before we went to clean the bilges."

"I'll accept the evidence," said Silas. He flung into his desk chair again, and stared up at his younger brother with burning eyes. "I'll do more: I believe you've worked hard to save lives on this voyage. If you'll mend your ways, I'm willing to keep you on Eleuthera. Will you take your first order now?"

"Try me."

"I'm ready to marry you to this girl who's shared your quarters. Today, if she too is willing."

Despite his good resolves, Paul burst into a roar of mirth. It was a relief to let his choler explode into laughter—though he saw the sound was tinder to Silas' rage.

"Your zeal does you credit," he said. "But I'd advise you to leave matchmaking to others. Lili and I are the kind who seldom marry."

"Levity won't save you, Paul."

"Suppose I don't wish to be saved?"

"Think of the girl, then. Make what amends you can."

"I've done no harm to Lili."

"Young Sikes has the choice of marrying the Hall girl, or returning home in irons. *He's* remaining with the colony."

"Deborah and Jack are in love—"

"The sailor who sinned with Mistress Morrow's daughter has also agreed to marriage. Sperry will let him join the colonists. There's no help for the widow Emmett: her paramour's a married man, and he must remain nameless. She'll take her sin's fruit back to England, along with her brand of shame."

"My sinning, as you call it, has been without fruit."

"So I gathered. As a doctor, you're wise in the devil's stratagems. It doesn't lessen the transgression."

"Will you brand me too, and ship me home?"

"The others met their fate. Why should you be an exception?"

The challenge was thundered, and Paul was tempted to accept it outright. His brother meant every word: of that he was positive. Once they were ashore, the leader's power was absolute in such matters. A point-blank refusal would earn him a trip home with Sperry: in two months' time, he might be in Bristol with Anne. Since all was fair in love, he would be a free agent thereafter. . . . He put down the image of Anne's surrender to a whirlwind courtship—his bargain with her was still valid. Had he not been aboard the *Adventurer,* death might have ruled on the quarterdeck: there would be other crises tomorrow. His place was at his brother's side, until the colony was firmly rooted.

"I'll think your offer over," he said. "Will that do for now?"

"I'm going to marry you to that slut today," Silas shouted. "Bring her to my cabin. I'll call Obadiah and witnesses—" His voice choked on the rest, as Paul's fist closed on his shirt collar, shaking him into silence.

"Leave Lili out of this," he said. "I'm only staying with this boatload of bigots because it can't live without me—and I'm doing as I please meanwhile. You'll agree to that, when you've regained your senses."

"Have you no regard for your immortal soul?"

"Not if I must make you its custodian."

Silas reeled across the cabin when Paul released him: had his arm failed to brace against the sill of the stern window, he would have fallen to his knees. Certain that he was about to raise his voice in prayer, Paul had already turned away. He froze in his tracks when he realized that Silas, after a strangled sob, had tumbled unconscious to the floor.

When he turned to give what help he could, Paul saw—too late—that his brother's face was claret red, the skin at neck and wrists brown-spotted. His diagnosis was already made when his hands, running swiftly beneath Silas' clothing, detected the dread buboes of the plague, already swollen to nightmare size. Driving himself to the limit, the leader of the Eleutherans had proved, in his own iron person, that it was possible to rise above fleshly ills—even to ignore them for a while, in his search for souls. The effort was beyond him now.

A half-hour later, with the help of Lili and Giles, Paul had stripped his brother to the skin, sluiced his fevered body in sea water, and clothed him in a clean shirt. Two sailors, working on the doctor's orders, had scrubbed the bulkheads, stripped the bunk of its mattress and flung Silas' sea-soaked clothes overside, to rid the cabin of its last flea. (Obeying an instinct he could not define exactly, Paul was still positive that there was some evil connection between these vermin and the plague.)

Now, with Silas lying on a fresh mattress—and beginning to moan faintly with returning consciousness—Paul lifted his eyes to meet the innkeeper's. Lili, who had gone to fetch clean blankets, had just returned to make her last gesture toward their new patient's comfort.

"Does this mean a new outbreak, Doctor?" Giles asked.

"I hope not. Heaven only knows how long he's been carrying the sickness in his body—"

"Will he recover?"

"That's a second question we'll leave to fate. Judging by the other cases, he'll be in delirium for a day or so. If the buboes come to a head in that time, we'll use the lancet." In most cases, the sickness produced large abscesses of the groin which a surgeon's scalpel could open, releasing evidence of the disease in the form of a purulent discharge. Both Ralph Welles and Lopez owed their lives to the healing knife.

"Then there's nothing more you can do?"

"We must keep him quiet, if his delirium drives him mad." Paul glanced sharply at Lili, who had already taken a place beside the bed. "It may be work beyond your powers."

"I'll see to it he stays in this cabin," said Lili calmly. "Father can spell me at night." So far, no nursing problem had proved too formidable for Lili Porter. It was ironic that she should take on this task as well, in view of the insults Silas had just been mouthing.

"Call me if you need help. He's very strong."

"The girl can manage, Doctor," said Giles. "This won't be her first plague patient—though I'll admit he's bigger than most. It's time you went on deck, and announced you're the new leader."

"My brother gave me no such endorsement."

"He would—if he'd been in his right mind."

"Believe me, nothing was further from his thoughts—"

"What your brother was thinking isn't important now," said Lili quickly. "Who else can hold this company together until we're safely ashore?"

Despite his doubts, Paul could not repress a grin—though the sight of Silas (waxen pale, now the faint was upon him, and writhing in his bunk like a man possessed of devils) was hardly reassuring.

"Would you call this a sign from above?"

"I've seen stranger portents in my day," Giles murmured. "I'll say this as shouldn't, Doctor—but your brother's a harrier, not a leader. There isn't a yeoman aboard who isn't rubbed raw by his counsel of perfection—to say nothing of Brother Obadiah Lambert's Bible-pounding. The same goes for the bluenoses themselves. At least, for the ones who haven't let their religion get in the way of their own interests—"

"We can say Silas is resting; there's no need to announce his true condition."

Giles shook his massive head. "This old tub is too small for secrets."

"Obadiah Lambert will never take orders from me. Nor will fellows like Welles—"

"They will if the captain backs you. If need be, we'll put it to a vote."

"Your brother will take command again when he's on his feet," said Lili. "You've no choice, Paul."

"Perhaps he'll be kinder, if he *does* come back from the grave," said Giles. "We'll give him a second chance, Doctor, rely on that."

Paul glanced again at Lili, who nodded pointedly at the door: he went out with a shrug, realizing that he must yield to such hard common-sense. It was a relief to leave his brother's side, secure in the knowledge that he would be cared for.

Paul found Captain Sperry beside the helmsman, and recounted the scene in the cabin. The master of the *Adventurer* smote the rail with his fist, and nodded a vigorous endorsement.

"Porter's right," he said. "Saving your presence, this is a rare bit of luck for us all." He barked an order to the sailor on duty to pipe all hands on deck. When the ship's company had assembled in the waist, he gave the news in clipped sentences, fixing each would-be ringleader with a steely eye as he did so.

"Your shepherd's down with the plague," he said. "We've every hope he'll recover. Meanwhile, the doctor's your leader and mine —in all matters that don't concern the handling of the ship. Anyone who differs is courting a leg iron. Is that clear?"

No one spoke for a moment. Obadiah Lambert voiced the only protest.

"By whose order does Dr. Sutton take command?"

"Does it matter, since *I* endorse him?" asked Sperry.

He was answered by an uncertain babble of voices from the lower deck—and Paul caught more than one black look leveled in his direction before a ragged cheer was raised. Led at first by the yeoman, it was echoed by more than one Puritan—until such islands of resistance as the Reverend Obadiah (who continued to stand with folded arms and refused to meet Sperry's eyes) were swallowed in the sigh of relief that rose like an all but visible breath.

It was hardly a tribute to Silas in his affliction, thought Paul. He moved to the after deck rail to stress the temporary nature of his command—only to have his voice drowned in a long-drawn hail from aloft.

"Sail-ho! Dead on the starboard beam!"

The rush to the starboard rail was universal—and so precipitate that the ancient vessel canted dangerously for an instant before she righted herself, in a blare of orders from the captain. The breeze that had just swept the horizon clean of cloud rack had forced the *Adventurer* into a long tack to hold her course. Only when she came about and began to run toward the tiny blur of white against the sky could Paul be sure this was indeed another ship.

He glanced at Sperry—but the captain, his eyes shaded against the glare of noon, shrugged off the implied question as he gave his order to hold course.

"Friend or foe, we've no choice but to speak her," he said quietly. "She's already marked us—and if I can judge her by those topsails, she has enough canvas to run us down at will."

A sailor had already rushed to the chartroom, to bring out the leather-bound Dutch telescope that was Sperry's proudest possession. He studied the strange ship carefully before passing the spyglass to Paul.

"What d'you think, Doctor?"

"You're right about her canvas. I don't doubt she can outsail us."

"Can you see a flag?"

"No, Captain. Is that a bad sign?"

"We'll soon learn," said Sperry—and bellowed an order at the passengers in the waist. "Clear decks—all of you! He's studying *us*, I'm sure. We mustn't look anxious."

The assembly went below with considerable muttering, to watch as best they could. Marco, the Genoese seaman who had the best sight aboard, ascended the foremast to call out the new-comer's course. Guy Lebret (who had remained topside at a nod from Sperry) now came forward to take the spyglass. The French naturalist had sailed under most of the world's flags.

"I don't think she's a Spaniard," he said. "Her sterncastle's much too low."

Sperry nodded in agreement. "What d'you call her, then?"

"English—or perhaps French. It's hard to be sure."

It was now obvious that the strange ship was spreading every sail to overtake the *Adventurer*. Within the hour, when she was less than a half-mile distant, there was a puff of smoke from her foredeck, followed by the dull, thudding bark of a swivel gun. The round shot, intended as a warning, fell a safe hundred yards from Sperry's bow. Lars Brack, watching from the anchor chains, swore in two languages and shook his fists across the narrowing strip of sea.

"She wants us to heave to, Captain."

Sperry nodded. "We'd best take the hint. Pass the order, Master Brack."

Standing at the captain's side—and trying hard to match his granite calm—Paul spoke quickly. "Is there a black pennon in the flag locker?"

"I think so—why?"

"I suggest we fly it above our standard. In most navies, it's a sign there's plague aboard."

Brack hurried to the locker, without awaiting the order. The black pennon went fluttering aloft just before the deck crew dropped the sails. In a matter of seconds (or so it seemed to Paul) the rush of white water at the bows diminished to a ripple. Sperry barked a final command to the helmsman, who backed the rudder sharply. In another moment, the *Adventurer* had ground to a halt, less than two hundred yards from the other vessel.

It was evident that Sperry had been wise to heed the warning. The black snouts of a dozen cannon at the starboard gun ports, and the swarm of men that had moved to serve them, proved that the newcomer's intentions were anything but peaceful. At that distance, it seemed obvious that she intended to bear down on the *Adventurer* under full weigh. Then, at a shouted warning, the helmsman backed his rudder in turn, and her own sails came billowing to the deck. The black flag it seemed, spoke a universal language.

"That square of cloth just saved our lives, Doctor," said Sperry. "Here comes a longboat. Be ready with your story. I think they're in the mood to listen."

The sturdy boat, with a dozen men at the oars, bore down upon the *Adventurer* in silence. The oarsmen were naked to the waist, and burned so dark by the sun that it was hard to tell if they were white or Negro. By contrast, the officer who lolled in the stern sheets, seemed a dandy born to the purple: his long frogged coat was rich with cloth-of-gold, and a lace hat shaded his eyes from the glare. When he lifted it in a mock salute to the *Adventurer*'s quarter-deck, Paul saw that he was tanned as deeply as any of his sailors. His handsome, wolf-thin face bore the stamp of command, and the gold ring that glistened in one ear suggested his calling in advance.

"Ahoy, there—what ship are you?" The voice was English, but it did nothing to relax the fear aboard, as the officer signaled the oarsmen. A dozen blades, backing water as one, stopped the longboat dead, just outside the shadow of the deck.

Captain Sperry raised his speaking trumpet—a stratagem that permitted him to address the salty popinjay in normal tones.

"The *Adventurer* out of Bristol," he said. "Bound for the Bahama Isles with colonists."

"Are you now?" cried the other. "And who, pray, invited you?"

"We come with our king's charter," said Sperry. "And we come in peace."

"That I'll believe. How else could you arrive—in a tub like that? What's the meaning of that black pennon you're flying?"

Paul spoke up, at Sperry's nod. "It means we've plague aboard."

"D'you have a doctor?"

"*I'm* the doctor. We've fought the sickness since we left the Bermudas."

An uneasy murmur rose from the longboat, which the officer

stilled with a look. "How do I know your flag isn't a trick—to keep us from boarding you?"

The captain cut in quickly: his voice was still calm. "Are you pirates?"

The lace hat lifted in a second ironic bow. "Forgive my bad manners. I'm Captain Jeremy Hood, of the *Falcon*. My trade is harrying Spanish commerce—and I do well at it."

"I'm Jonathan Sperry—and I've sailed these waters before, without let or hindrance. As you'll observe, I fly my sovereign's colors, and I'll see you in hell before I'll accept boarders."

The battle of looks continued for a long moment across the strip of gently rolling sea. The dandy in the longboat, fingering his earring with slender brown fingers, seemed a far call from the usual buccaneer. Somehow, the aristocrat's air made him even more menacing—and Paul liked his air of mocking lassitude least of all. Under it, he was sure, lay a brute strength that could destroy at will.

"So you've sailed these waters before, Captain Sperry," Hood said at last. "Believe me, you were lucky to escape our notice. I trust you gave New Providence a wide berth."

"The island's a name on my chart, nothing more."

"We've made it our home port," said Hood. "If you've been sent to settle the Bahamas, one of us must give way. I can assure you *we've* no intention of moving on."

"Surely you'll recognize your king's charter," said Sperry. "We knew nothing of your settlement on New Providence. I can assure you we've no intention of sharing it."

A guffaw rose from the longboat, in which Captain Jeremy Hood joined heartily. Paul saw that Sperry had flushed deep-red —but even now, he was too shrewd to antagonize the enemy further.

"I'm touched by your consideration," said Hood. "However, I still intend to board you—if only to see how strong a threat you are to my future."

Again, Paul spoke at his captain's nod. "You'd take that risk, with plague aboard?"

Hood shrugged. "Even if you aren't lying, it hardly matters.

We can still consign you to perdition. Since dead men don't bite, it might be simpler. If King Charles hears you're lost at sea, he'll hardly send more colonists."

"We don't question your power to do just that," said Paul. "However, it's my duty to warn you that such action could doom you as well."

"In what way?"

"We *do* have plague on board, Captain Hood: the black flag means what it says. You can hardly sink us without exploding our magazine—and the disease will surely be blown over to your ship. I've seen it happen often."

A gasp of surprise rose from the deck, where every man on duty—frozen at the ropes like so many waxwork dummies—had grasped Paul's stratagem; from below, he could hear an echo of that same surprise, and guessed that Puritan and yeoman alike were listening intently at the ports. In the longboat, Paul saw that more than one oarsman had tightened his grip. All eyes turned to Hood, who continued to twirl his earring. The wolf-grin remained on his handsome lips—but it seemed a trifle strained.

"I still think you're lying, Doctor," he shouted. "Nor do I believe the plague can be blown through the air. I'll return to my ship and sink you with round shot."

Paul watched the hand on the earring—and guessed that the corsair, despite his brave words, was still hesitant to prove them. A final ruse remained, and he knew he must employ it promptly. Pretending to ponder Hood's threat, he addressed the Genoese in Italian.

"Can you swim, Marco?"

The seaman smiled broadly. "*Si, dottore.* Like a fish."

"Whip out of sight, and roll up in one of the spare jibs. I'll join you directly."

Marco did not question the order, but ducked promptly beneath the deck ladder, to lift a sheet from the sail locker. Lars Brack, who had caught Paul's import, also faded from view to help wrap the Genoese in that impromptu shroud. Hood and Sperry were still trading black glances when the last quick knot

had been tied in the eyelets of the sail. Paul descended to the
waist, and held up a hand for attention before he turned the
corner of the charthouse. He returned instantly, with Marco's
ramrod-stiff form in his arms, covered from head to toe in the
canvas jib. At his nod, Brack came forward to help steady the
burden on the rail.

"Here's a man who died of plague this morning," said Paul.
"I was about to give him Christian burial—but he'll float over to
you if we don't weigh down the canvas. See for yourself if I'm
lying."

Before Hood could object, he let the shrouded figure drop
overside. Longboat and ship had drifted somewhat closer during
the captains' exchange. Before the sound of the splash had died,
the twelve oarsmen leaned on their blades as one, without awaiting an order from their officer. Steering a prudent arc, and
careful to hold his position to windward of the *Adventurer*, Hood
set out full speed for his own ship. The longboat was still close
enough for Paul to note that the sardonic face was now a frozen
mask of fear.

The mate, anxious for the fate of his seaman, still leaned out
from the rail to mark the progress of the canvas sack. Moving
like a log in the pulse of the sea, it seemed to follow in the longboat's wake, as though it were attached to the pirates by an invisible cord: Paul choked down a laugh when he realized that
Marco (swimming, after a fashion, in his canvas jacket) was
helping that malevolent illusion as best he could. The oarsmen,
rowing as though the devils of hell were dogging them, managed
to widen the gap before they reached the *Falcon*. The corsair's
sails were already raised. Before the longboat could be hoisted to
its chocks, she had set a southeast course and begun to make a
hasty retreat.

Marco now dared to swim free, though he was careful to keep
the ballooning shroud between him and the buccaneers. Moving
underwater with amazing ease, he gained the anchor chain of
the *Adventurer* and mounted to the deck on the far side, to the
cheers of his shipmates.

Sperry lifted his telescope and studied the *Falcon* carefully.

"She'll be hull-under within the hour, Doctor," he said. "That was a near thing, but it was neatly ended—thanks to you."

"Don't praise me," said Paul. "Marco deserves the credit."

"I'll order extra grog tonight. We've two things to celebrate."

"Two, Captain?"

"Our escape from Hood, first of all. In my opinion, he'll give Eleuthera a wide berth in future. After all, there's sea room to spare between that island and New Providence."

"Let's hope that's an accurate judgment," said Paul. "What's the second cause for rejoicing?"

"The fact that these babes in the woods have a new leader. For their sakes, I hope your rule's a long one."

That night, with fair winds and a moonlit sea, Captain Sperry risked holding a southerly course into the dawn. An hour before sunrise, his daring was rewarded by a shout from the foremast. Corncob Key had just risen from the blue plain, in the precise spot the chart had indicated.

The reef (a barrel-like amalgam of coral and sand, with a tuft of green at its center to justify its name) was far too tiny to qualify as a proper landfall—and there was no smudge on the horizon's perfect round to suggest islands beyond. Still, that speck of land was proof positive that the *Adventurer* was on course. Joined with balmy weather, and the conviction they were near their journey's end, it was enough to raise the colonists' spirits for the first time since they had left the Bermudas.

In his shuttered cabin, Silas continued to fight for his life, as Lili and Giles spelled each other at the task of nursing. Aware that death might come at any moment, the whole ship's company seemed to move on tiptoe around the sickroom. Though there were daily prayers for his soul, it was a measure of Silas' popularity that no calls were paid to that sickroom while the dread pattern of the disease moved toward its climax. Convinced though the colonists were that the plague had run its course, none was certain enough of immortality to venture inside the cabin door. Even such stalwarts as Ralph Welles (who was now sufficiently recovered to hobble on deck each morning) contented themselves with discreet inquires at the threshold.

On the fourth evening after Silas' collapse, the two buboes attained maximum distention, and Paul risked a stroke of the lancet in the center of each. The gush of bright-yellow fluid that followed, and the patient's gasp of relief (even though he remained sunk in delirium) proved the crisis had been surmounted, though it was too soon to pronounce him out of danger.

When the cabin had been tidied once again, and Giles arrived for his stint of nursing, Lili followed Paul to the deck.

"You were right about his madness—and his strength," she said. "At times, they were beyond belief. They should see him through."

Paul nodded. From the first, he had expected Silas to win his wrestle with the plague, as handily as he had won each fall with the devil.

"Has he been conscious recently?"

"For a few moments, now and then. But he seems terribly aware of his surroundings. I'm sure he hates the fact I'm there. I can feel his eyes on me, even when my back is turned."

"Don't think he hates you, Lili. He's burning to save your soul, as well as mine. You might call it unfinished business on his conscience."

The innkeeper's daughter kept her eyes on the moonlit sea. "Your brother hates me for several reasons, Paul. Mostly it's because I trouble him as a woman."

"So you said in Bristol. You've yet to prove it."

"Wait and see," said Lili calmly. "Some day you'll admit I'm right. Does he really mean to wed this Anne Trevor?"

"Their troth is plighted. She'll join him within the year."

"'Tis a pity she isn't here now. Perhaps she could save him from himself."

"What does *that* imply?" Paul moved to the ship's rail, aware of the anger in his voice.

"Your brother spoke of Mistress Trevor often in his delirium," said Lili. "It seems he worships her—as one worships a saint. Often he'd damn himself for wanting her—as a husband wants a wife.

Then he'd forget all he'd said before, and damn *her* too, as the devil's agent."

"Call that the war of flesh and soul," said Paul. "It's never-ending, in someone like my brother. Delirium has merely brought it to the surface."

"How can a man hate his own desires? Doesn't it mean he's sick—in heart and soul?"

"Do you mean hate, or fear?" asked Paul.

"Both, I suppose." Lili's eyes were troubled when she faced him. "Would you believe me if I said he won't admit life can be a pleasure? Or that he might dare to enjoy it with a wife?"

"The Puritan mind can't believe it's in error," said Paul. "Not where sin is concerned. It's a cardinal principle of the dissenting faith that man was born evil. That's why Silas can't permit himself to dwell on the pleasures of the marriage bed—far less speak of them, until he's in delirium. It's the reason he means to separate us, even if it means banishing me from the colony."

"He's right about us, Paul. I can't go on sharing your hammock, now you're our leader."

"I refuse to accept that ruling."

"As your brother's deputy, you must set a good example. How else can you lead your flock to the promised land?" Lili chuckled warmly, as she moved into his arms for a lingering kiss. "Don't you think I'll enjoy the sacrifice: it's one we must both make."

"Can't we begin this new regime tomorrow?"

She fended him off expertly, dodging his attempted embrace in the shadow of the mainsail. "That kiss must content you, Dr. Sutton—until we've some notion of the future. May I wish you good night?"

He made no effort to detain her as she ran nimbly toward the companionway, and the nunlike seclusion of the women's cabin. Admitting her attitude was justified, he turned again to the rail, to stare at the ladder of moonlight without seeing it at all. At such a moment, the weight of his loneliness seemed too great to endure. Knowing he could never love Anne had been a near-mortal blow—but the long voyage had dulled the worst of that agony. Lili Porter had done her robust best to make that loss endurable. It was hard to lose her now.

He scarcely lifted his head when the long-awaited cry of *Land-ho!* rang out from the foremast. This time, he could not doubt that the cloudlike shape on the southern horizon marked their journey's end.

Sperry did not venture to sail on, once the dark cloud to the south had changed to a definite land mass. Instead, he set a prudent triangular course to the north, until daylight assured him that the sea was empty of shoals. Most of the ship's company (save for the convalescents and the chronic invalids who had not yet recovered from their last bout of seasickness) had lined the rails throughout the night, to await this first real glimpse of their destination. Now, as the sun rose in a cloudless sky, they raised a cheer at what they saw.

Viewed from the north, the island was long and low, with a jutting headland to mark its tip, and dazzling sweeps of beach, arched by coconut palms and backed by a gray-green mass of sea grape and wind-twisted mangrove. At that distance, it seemed untouched by the hand of man. After the long weeks at sea, and the chilling repulse in Bermuda, Paul could understand the cries of delight that surrounded him, the babble of demands for an instant landing.

He signaled a plea to the quarter-deck, and the captain's stentorian voice shouted the colonists into silence. When he was sure of their attention, Paul mounted the ladder to address them.

"Two points should be settled before we touch land," he said. "First, we must be sure this island is as deserted as it appears: for all we know, Captain Hood has baited a trap there. Second— and more important—we must find a safe harbor before we can leave the ship untended. The chart indicates there's an approach from the northwest, into a deep bight, with an anchorage at its end —but we can't vouch for its accuracy. Until we verify the soundings, Captain Sperry intends to sail clear around our future home, and select the best spot to put down roots. I'd call that common sense. Do you agree?"

There were only isolated murmurs of protest at the question—most of them from younger members of the company. The others nodded approval: Paul could see that his reference to the pirates had struck a responsive chord.

"Lopez is too sick to walk," he said. "We'll carry him topside the moment there's a real landmark to identify. Meanwhile, I'd suggest you breakfast—and don't neglect to police your quarters afterward. We want no more sickness, now we're about to turn pioneers."

Thanks to a brisk breeze from the west, it was a simple matter to follow the shoreline. Paul noted that the Sayle chart and the actual shape of the island coincided, with the sweep of beaches trending roughly from northeast to southwest. Here and there, whitish patches of rock lifted in low bluffs above the dense, wind-beaten forests. These (said Guy Lebret) were patches of coral limestone, the foundation on which the Bahamas had been based, long before the dawn of history.

At intervals, the shore was broken by small bays, protected from the Atlantic ground swell by clusters of islets. At one point, where the beach narrowed to expose another coral outcrop, the porous, weather-blackened stone formed a natural bridge, as though the backbone of the island had been scooped out by a massive trowel. This, said Guy, was a phenomenon of the coral islands; it was known as a natural window, the result of endless erosion of the waves. At deck level, it was possible to look through this high archway and see the western shore—where the action of those same waves had formed a moon-shaped bight. Here, the water was milk-green and riffled by the wind, a sure sign that it was filled with shoals and could hardly serve as an anchorage.

Carried by two sailors, the Spaniard came on deck at last. Weak though he still was, he could raise his head enough to scan the shoreline. The natural bridge was the only landmark he needed to identify Eleuthera—though it was called Long Island in his own tongue. The chart, he added, was more accurate than Paul had dared hope. The whole island was perhaps forty miles in length—and the *Adventurer* could reach the southern channel by dark, if the wind held.

All that afternoon, the ship continued to skirt the low coastline. The sweep of beach seemed endless, with a mangrove lowland here and there to break the view—and, on occasion, more of those low, sandy cliffs crowned by fine stands of trees which Lebret identified as cedar or yellow pines. The cocoa palms, he said, had been a legacy from the Spaniards, when they had swept up from the Indies in the last century to make up their slave coffles among the Lucayan Indians.

Already, it was evident that the dons had made a clean sweep: from end to end of Eleuthera, there was no sign of human habitation. Long before day's end, Paul was regretting his decision to put off exploring until the morrow—but it still seemed prudent to verify the last contour of the Sayle chart before venturing ashore.

An hour before sunset, the wind died to a series of cat's-paws, making further inshore sailing hazardous. By this time, the ship had reached well down toward the southern extremity of Eleuthera—revealing the fact that a wide channel separated it from another (and much smaller) island to the southeast. A closer inspection suggested that the channel was navigable, though both islands broke away in a series of treacherous shoals, and it was impossible, in that uncertain light, to estimate the extent of deep water between them. A session in the chartroom convinced both Paul and the captain that they must stand off-shore until morning before risking the passage. It was now obvious that no practical anchorage existed on the eastern face of Eleuthera.

All through the day, the passengers had thronged the decks, only to be ordered below repeatedly, when their presence made ship-handling impossible. They were now sent to their supper and their hammocks with the cheerless news that another day must elapse before the captain would risk a landing. During the night, the *Adventurer* lay well offshore in a near-calm, her canvas straining at the blocks as helmsman and lookouts whistled for a breeze. When the second morning broke hot and clear, with a hoped-for dance of whitecaps, it was decided that one of the two shallops should be lowered away, to act as escort vessel in the hazardous navigation between the two islands.

At the captain's orders, Lars Brack was stationed at the shallop's tiller: Paul and Lebret took their places in the bow, with a spare chart and Sperry's prized spyglass. Marco and another sailor were assigned to handle the two triangular sails that gave the little boat the look of a cruising archangel once she was underway. Two days' provisions were put aboard, along with sculling oars, in case the wind should die.

A heavy sea was creaming the shoals when the shallop cast off. Looking back at the row of heads along the rail, Paul was happy to be part of the pilot group—and happier still that he had escaped from the *Adventurer* without an interview in Silas' cabin. Lili had reported that his brother had seemed almost coherent during the night watch. Knowing Silas' amazing powers of recovery, he sensed that it would be impossible to postpone their next head-on collision. When he returned to the ship, he hoped to report the discovery of a safe anchorage: Silas could hardly damn him afresh, if he could really write finis to their journey.

From the quarter-deck, Captain Sperry waved Godspeed. The shallop, catching the full brunt of the wind on the matching sails, danced into the wash of the current that churned round the rocky terminus of Eleuthera. Light as a swallow on the flood, she had soon drawn away from the ship. The mate (handling the braces on his own, with the tiller anchored between his knees) was forced to sail off wind to keep in sight. The procedure soon demonstrated its advantages. At this near view, it was apparent that the channel between Eleuthera and the smaller island (which lay like an extended cat's claw in the glare of morning) was wide enough to accommodate a man-of-war. There was no need to take soundings as they squared their course at last, and began to slip past the sheltered western face.

Here, a series of apparently endless islets (or *cayos*, as the Spaniards called them) stood between the shoreline and deep water—some of them thick with cocoa palms, others little more than sand bars. Twice in the next hour Brack risked a starboard tack among them, only to return to blue water in an explosion of curses when a hoped-for anchorage changed to a mass of shoals, rainbow-tinted under the sun.

It was their closest view of land so far, and Paul found it hard to share the mate's mood. Fish were everywhere in the shallows (Lebret had already sketched a dozen edible varieties in his notebook). At each sand bar clouds of birds rose in alarm at their first sight of the sails. Others, sailing in precise formation overhead, broke surface in dives for fish, like so many falling arrows. On closer inspection, Paul saw that they were ungainly at water level—gray-black of feather, with grotesquely distorted beaks, and pouches beneath that served as storehouses for their catch.

"Pelicans," said the naturalist. "*Pelecanus erythrorhynchos.* It's a bird one must see to believe."

The shallop was skirting a mangrove thicket at the moment. The serpentine roots were thick with shellfish. On a sandbank, a giant sea turtle, caught in the act of crawling from the spot where it had deposited its eggs, entered the lagoon with a prodigious splash, shooting a wary look at the invaders from hooded eyes.

"At least there's food enough," said Paul.

"It's an ideal world for man and beast alike," Guy agreed. "A primeval innocence, unspoiled by time. It was worth risking death to find it."

"Not if we can't locate our anchorage," grumbled the mate.

"The Sayle chart tells us it's a good distance from here," Paul said.

"What if the fellow was romancing? He says it's on the western shore of the island. We should have sighted it, at least."

"Couldn't we moor in this lagoon?" asked Lebret. "There's a patch of deep water."

"Not with shoals about," said Brack. "You gentlemen are both sailors: you know the sort of hellbroth they can raise in bad weather. If you mean to plant the flag here, you must find a true harbor, with enough landlock to keep off the gales. Otherwise, you'd best call quits to the whole venture."

"With only three weeks' provisions aboard?" asked Paul.

"We can drop you in Virginia, for a price," said the mate. "That's our next port of call—to take on tobacco and naval stores. You'll do nicely as ballast meanwhile."

In the open sea again, the shallop leaned into a long tack, with a firm bead drawn on a kind of rounded hummock that marked the first headland noted on the chart. Because of its height, it was impossible to guess at the shape of the land beyond. Close inshore, the coral seemed thicker than ever. Some of the reefs foamed with surf, others were barely awash, and still others (sprouting in convoluted clusters) seemed to rise from the ocean's floor like giant flowers. Guy explained that these odd formations were known as brain coral.

Hard though it was to believe (until the lead line had been dropped to prove it) some of those giant buds were a good fifty feet below the keel. Here, the water was vividly green, so crystalline that both fish and coral appeared as reflections in a mirror: elsewhere, the colors varied with the depth. Sometimes it was as deeply blue as the English sky in spring; again, when they skirted a covered reef, it seemed brown as the coral itself; along the bars, it was a sulphur-yellow echo of the sandy floor beneath. Yet nowhere in this prism did the clarity change. It was only at the shoreline, where the mangrove lowlands lay like blots, that the faintest stain appeared.

It was still evident that this section of Eleuthera, for all the marine wonders that fringed it, would be suitable neither as harbor or settlement. Once again, the *Adventurer* was signaled to lay well out in the ocean tongue while the shallop drew its final bead on the headland. By running straight before the wind (and resisting the temptation to make time-consuming tacks among the coral gardens) they fetched the point before noon. Once it was turned, the accuracy of the Sayle chart was plain to every eye aboard. Dead ahead, the ocean tongue ended in a sand-bar maze: much of it was navigable in the light-draft boat, but the whole area would be a graveyard for the *Adventurer*. Far beyond, another wide bight opened to a crooked but entirely navigable channel that joined with blue water at the northwestern extremity of the island. To starboard, where the bight touched the land, was the contour of the natural harbor noted on the map.

Paul lifted the spyglass to study the anchorage in detail. It was bounded at its southern edge by a fairly large islet or cay, separated from the main island by a narrow channel. Curving in the shape of a rough rectangle, and boxed by gently rolling hills, it seemed an ideal haven. True, it could be reached only from the west, after the dog-leg channel had been navigated: the *Adventurer* would be forced to retrace her course, skirt the Atlantic face of Eleuthera a second time, and make her final approach from the northwest.

Since each bearing on the Sayle chart had coincided with reality, it was agreed that the shallop must report at once to the mother ship, and advise Sperry to begin his somewhat roundabout voyage. A groan rose from the rail when these tidings were conveyed, but the captain approved the explorers' suggestion without argument. Since the shallop carried a duplicate of the Sayle chart, it would be an easy matter to trace the channel. White buoy markers were taken aboard to make the *Adventurer's* approach easier on the narrows—and Brack cast off a second time for his run to the anchorage.

The mate risked a direct approach across the sand-bar maze, with Marco in the bow to call soundings. Once they had gained the bight, it was apparent that their first impression of the anchorage had been accurate. The ticklish approach might even be to the colonists' advantage. With a stockade on the cay, and ample stores, they could live in safety from a surprise attack mounted in New Providence. Such an attack, if made by water, could approach only from the island's northwest corner.

Within the harbor, the water was millpond-still. When the canvas was furled, and the sailors put out their oars, the little vessel followed the shoreline closely to take soundings. A dense growth of trees (not too different from the English cedar) covered the surrounding hills and grew down almost to the water's edge, where the narrow, tan-colored beach sloped sharply to meet the bay. Along the cay, the water was deep right up to the shore, with a narrow channel between islet and main. The shallop ran through it with ease. Here and there, Marco reported, the bottom was covered with grass, but there was no sign of coral heads.

"Shall I mark the chart correct, Lars?" asked Paul.

"What are your readings?"

"Two fathoms off the cay. Three to five fathoms in the harbor proper. The lead line agrees at all points."

"That's water to spare," said the mate. "In the captain's place, I'd drop my hook there. Providing he can work his way through those shoals to the north."

"There's a clear route on the chart—and it's yet to fail us."

"We'd best make a final check, before we go ashore. That breeze may not last forever."

For the next hour, they sailed the channel leading into the broad sound that washed much of Eleuthera's western shore— proving, for the last time, that Captain William Sayle was a sound navigator. For much of the approach, there was ample room for maneuver. At three points, thanks to the dog-leg turns, sea- manship of a high order would be needed to avoid the reefs. These points were identified with the white markers. Marco, stripped to the buff, dived boldly to the coral heads below, and secured the ropes with iron spikes, while Paul noted their positions on the chart.

They had made good use of the day—but the final buoy was anchored none too soon. The wind had shifted to the east, leaving the bight glassy-calm. The oars came out again for the return journey, and sweat was pouring from every back when the harbor was entered for the second time.

The shallop grounded easily on the steep pitch of beach. Paul (taking wordless command, now they had made contact with the land) stepped out boldly from his station in the bow. It was impossible to suppress a deep thrill of accomplishment while he waited for the boat to be made fast. The perils of the deep had been avoided: another colony had been brought to the verge of a snug haven. Somehow, the moment called for a gesture. He wished they had brought a flag ashore, so they could plant the British colors at the water's edge.

"Do you claim all this for England, *mon vieux?*" asked Lebret. "Speak the thought aloud, if it'll help."

Paul smiled in some confusion while the mate and Marco joined them, leaving the sailor to guard the boat. Already the precaution seemed needless: it was impossible to believe that this beach had been touched by a human foot.

"I feel we're intruders," he said. "Let's trust we're worthy of the occasion."

To Paul's ears, the crunch of their boots in the sand seemed loud in that windless afternoon. Moving into the shade of the cedars, he breathed deep of their fragrance as he improvised a path among their stout brown trunks: the pitch of the hill was steeper than it had appeared from the harbor, and he was panting when he gained the summit. He found he had chosen the highest of the wooded crests that boxed the anchorage: the view from that summit repaid his long climb.

Eastward, in the middle distance, he could see the vast plain of the Atlantic, confirming his belief that the waist of Eleuthera was on the narrow side. To the south, the land rolled gently, covered for most of its extent with stands of yellow pine: there were gullies choked with cabbage palms and patches of dense, saw-toothed growth that Lebret identified as palmetto scrub. Spotting that green-gray vista were dozens of small blue ponds, like fragments of ocean prisoned by the land. Some of these, the naturalist said, were probably caches of rain water, held by the ancient coral outcrop that formed the backbone of the islands. Others were salt-water tarns, fed through hidden passages by the sea itself.

To the north and northwest, the coastline dissolved into the miragelike heat haze. The telescope, passed from hand to hand, proved that the upper reaches of the island, save for the wedge of cape that had been yesterday's landfall, were on the barren side—a series of gull-haunted beaches, relieved by the green smudge of sea grape, and an occasional lowland thick with mangrove. Guided by the Sayle chart, they had touched at the section of Eleuthera most suited to human habitation. The promise (at this first, wide-eyed view) seemed limitless. Here, Paul rejoiced, was plantation land in abundance—and, though soil might be on the thin side where the coral substructure was near the surface,

there would be enough fertile pockets to support colonists by the
thousand. Supplemented by catches from the teeming sea, the
fruits of the coco palms and the other exotics Lebret had not yet
had time to classify, the ordinary hazards of existence seemed
solved in advance.

"Well, Lars," said Paul. "Isn't this a spot to put down roots?"

"I haven't quite decided, Doctor," replied the mate. "No man
could ask for finer."

"The captain will give you leave to settle: it's in your articles.
We can use you here, this next month or so—"

"That I can believe," said Brack drily. "The question is, can
I use you? The *Adventurer* will be rare peaceful, once we've
dumped our human cargo."

"Wouldn't you like to grow with this colony? Be part of it from
the first?"

"It doesn't take too many men to spoil good land, Doctor.
Maybe this sun will thaw out your bluenoses. I doubt it. In any
event, I'll try to visit you when the first supply ship drops anchor
in that bight. Perhaps I'll change my mind about Puritans, once
they're settled in. If anyone can keep this colony in line, you're
that man."

"I'm only staying long enough to give my brother a start. That's
in *my* articles."

The exchange, Paul thought, had been a needed corrective.
This first contact with Eleuthera had been a heady experience.
It had been all too easy to yield to the tyranny of a vision, to
picture a plantation house on one of these rolling hills (built of
coral blocks, and gay with tropic vines), a thriving port where
the shallop was now beached, and Anne Trevor awaiting him at
day's end. The vision faded when he reminded himself that Anne
was promised to another. Such hopeless fancies belonged to the
night, when there is no defense against dreams. . . .

Captain Sperry had given the explorers overnight shore leave,
in case the expedition took them far afield. Paul made no attempt
to probe the interior in depth, once he had convinced himself
that these pine-scented groves were barren of habitation. After
Lebret had briefly sketched the features of the terrain (and made

a few tests of the soil to assure himself that it was arable) he led his company to the harbor. Until darkness fell, they skimmed the shoreline, tending north and west, until the triangular horn of land that marked the northern terminus of Eleuthera was in clear view from sea level.

On this voyage, they discovered new wonders of the deep. At intervals, where clusters of cays made backwaters against the tides, they looked down on coral gardens, tinted in pastel hues no artist's palette could imitate. At the meeting of sand and sea, they counted shells by the thousands, including a species of whelk (some of them monstrously large) which the naturalist said could be eaten in extremity.

Fathoms deep in the same cove, where no current stirred, the voyagers could see specimens of outsize jellyfish, dead-white on their outer surface and pink as the dawn within: sailors called them Portuguese men-of-war, and their long, trailing filaments could impart a painful sting. Here, too, was the shadow of a large ray, whose long, prehensile tail, Lebret warned, could inflict a fatal wound if the creature were disturbed in its usual resting place on the bottom. At the backwater's end, Lebret pointed out what was perhaps the strangest animal they had met today. Shaped like the sausage one finds hanging in a French kitchen, yellow-brown in color and larger than a man's upper arm, it did not stir in its sandy bed as the shallop approached—and showed no sign of life, save for the gentle pulsation of its circular, puckered mouth, through which the sea water flowed.

"We call them sea slugs," said the Frenchman. "As you see, they're well named. Even Eleuthera must have ugliness and danger to highlight its beauty: the loathsome jellyfish, the deadly sting ray, the barracuda that hunt in packs inside the reefs and strike at the first show of blood. Now we observe the repulsive sea slug, who refuses to leave his bed of ease, even to obtain food."

"What's the moral, Guy?" asked Paul. "That happiness must be earned?"

"Exactly. We've a half hour of daylight left to fish for our supper. If Lars will head for the next offshore reef, we should find a school there. They'll be more apt to take the hook, now the sun is fading."

The naturalist's prediction proved accurate. Moments after a line had dropped in the shadow of the coral, a fish struck at the hook. Paul was able to bring the catch aboard in short order, though he needed all his strength to hold it. The fish was huge and moon-shaped, with an underslung jaw that gave it a strange affinity with the English bulldog: the flesh, said Lebret, could be cut and broiled as steaks, and was sweeter than halibut. The single fish was large enough to provide supper for the five voyagers—and there was still daylight enough to permit a visit to the next stand of mangroves, where a pail of oysters was scraped from the roots.

After the long, sun-steeped day, it was a pleasant task to gather firewood on the beach of the next cove—and pleasanter still to lie in the shade of a budding oleander, sipping a cup of wine while the sailors broiled fish steaks above the embers of the driftwood fire. A full moon, lifting from a palm grove across the island's spine, bathed the sea and shore in its placid rays. Holding the thought of tomorrow at arm's length, Paul found he was almost happy—filled, as he was, with the sense of accomplishment. While the high moment endured, he could even hope Anne Trevor would find her future home unspoiled when she became his brother's wife—that he could leave her here (when that moment of dedication came) with an untroubled mind.

Guy Lebret, smiling at Paul over the last of the wine when their repast ended, put his unformed thoughts into words in a way only a Frenchman could. Brack had gone to check the mooring of the shallop, and they had just spread their blankets for the night; though the naturalist spoke in a whisper, his words were more a philosophy than a confidence.

"Suppose we're murdered in our sleep by bloodthirsty aborigines?"

"The island's deserted, Guy."

"Everything we've seen today would confirm that view. As of tonight, Eleuthera is ours, to do with as we like. It's a stirring challenge. Can we rise to it?"

"We can try."

"Are you familiar with the words of the psalm?—

> *Who can understand his errors?*
> *Cleanse thou me from secret faults!*"

"Silas has chanted them often enough."

"Will he remember them, now he's facing his greatest test?"

"Can he do less, as a servant of the Almighty?"

"The important thing is this, Paul: Will he realize he needs your help to win out here? The success of your colony will depend on the answer."

"It's hardly *my* colony, Guy."

"You're wrong there. Now you've come this far, it's a responsibility you can't escape."

"My contribution's already made. As ship's doctor, I've brought these people here with the loss of only a few lives. They should flourish once they're ashore—"

"Your work has scarcely begun, Paul."

"You know why I can't linger."

The Frenchman sighed, and let his hand rest lightly on Paul's shoulder. "So you love *la petite Anne:* there's no helping that. You, too, must take the psalm to heart. Doesn't she deserve your best efforts here?"

That night, the five explorers slept deeply on their makeshift beds beneath the stars.

Paul was the first to waken, just after dawn. Profound though his slumber was, he had been dimly aware that a breeze was stirring the oleander leaves above him. When he saw the wind was offshore, he seized the telescope and hastened to the nearest coco palm to check the position of the *Adventurer*. Captain Sperry had said he might wait for the return of the shallop, to pilot his approach to their chosen harbor. With the buoys in place, a proven chart and a favoring wind, he might have decided to run for the anchorage.

His stay on the tropic atoll had made Paul adept in scaling the gently sloping bole of the coconut palm. Using his belt as an anchor, and his body as a counterweight, he ran up the smooth stalk barefoot—and, in a matter of minutes, was seated in the bushy crown. The sun was just above the horizon when he swept the sea with the telescope. As he had expected, there was no sign of the vessel: it seemed fair to assume that Sperry had come in from the northwest with the first light, and was now snug in harbor.

Reluctant to waken his sleeping companions, Paul let his eyes feast on the vista to the south. Once more, he forced himself to remember this was Silas' domain—that he must work with his brother to make that domain secure. Knowing him as he did, he was sure that Silas had long since risen from his sickbed to take back the reins; he would be needed aboard today when the unloading began, if only to make sure that Silas husbanded his strength. . . . Yet it was a long time before he slipped down the palm bole to the beach. Even then, he did not disturb his fellow explorers until he had fished their breakfast from the sea and cooked it to a turn above a fresh bed of coals, along with bread and bacon.

The party set forth in good spirits, on a sea gay with whitecaps. It was soon apparent that Captain Sperry had been wise to follow the difficult channel with the dawn; as the sun rose higher, the breeze shifted to the south, forcing the shallop to beat along the coast in a series of short tacks. At noon, the wind died to a zephyr, and the oars came out again. The five men in the boat were stripped to the waist and sweating like troopers when the last marker was turned and the landlocked harbor opened before them.

Paul's heart lifted when he saw the *Adventurer* riding at anchor as serenely as though she had berthed there a score of times. The cheer that rose in every throat was loud enough to send the gulls wheeling.

There was no answering cheer from the ship, and no sign of life, save for the port lookout at the stern. Paul understood why, after the oars had driven the shallop nearer—and a confused murmur from the waist translated into robust voices, tolling out responses of a divine service. It was only fitting, he reflected, that the colonists should offer up a prayer, now their voyage was really ended. He found he was smiling, after he had caught a snatch of the verses they were chanting, in solemn chorus:

> Enter into his gates with thanksgiving
> And into his courts with praise.
> Be thankful unto him and bless his name.
> For the Lord is good, his mercy is everlasting.
> And his truth endureth to all generations.

It was the ending of the Hundredth Psalm. Silas and the Reverend Obadiah had added it to Sunday services during the voyage, at the request of non-Puritans among the pilgrims. The addition had been made reluctantly. Both men had insisted the words be spoken, not sung, since they were a too-potent reminder of an English evensong—and, by extension, of the hated Anglican service these Puritans had crossed half a world to escape.

The speaking of the psalm, it seemed, had ended the service: there was a murmur of voices amidships, and a great scraping of feet, as the congregation dispersed. In another moment, the decks were thick with sailors, who appeared to wander aimlessly, as such men will in port when liberty is denied them. Only a handful of passengers were in evidence, and few of these were Puritans. The mystery was still unexplained when the lookout hailed the shallop.

Paul ran up the Jacob's ladder while the boat was brought alongside and hastened to the captain's cabin. He found Sperry in the act of pouring himself a noggin of rum—and the scowl he gave the returning explorer proclaimed his ill humor in advance.

"Too bad you didn't return sooner," he said. "You could have joined the service."

"When did you drop anchor?"

"Just after sunup. Your brother called us together at nine."

"Don't tell me Silas is up against my orders."

"He spoke *his* sermon from a chair," said Sperry. "The Reverend Obadiah harangued us for two hours more, on the theme of God's mercy. The prayer for strength that followed was nearly as long." He tossed down his rum in a swallow. "Why are you staring, Doctor? Didn't you take a calendar on the shallop?"

"So this is the Sabbath. I might have guessed."

"Your brother feels it'd be an affront to Heaven to go ashore on such a day. He's given strict orders: no one's to stir from quarters until tomorrow. Seamen are allowed to trim ship—and that's the limit of our activities."

"Is Silas giving orders too?"

"He's been in command since yesterday," said Sperry. "Lambert and Welles were his deputies, until he was strong enough to come on deck. At first he raged at me for refusing to find an anchorage on my own. When I sent back word that ship-handling was my business, and not his, he suffered a slight relapse. Enough, at any rate, to put him out of action for the afternoon—"

"I'll go to him at once," said Paul. "It was wrong of me to leave the ship."

The captain held up a detaining hand. "Don't reproach yourself, Doctor. You know as well as I that your brother would have refused medical help, the moment he was well enough to speak. And don't blame him too much for misdirected piety. According to his lights, it *is* a sin to work on the Sabbath—even to enjoy an outing ashore. I've given in to his reasoning. You must do the same."

"How can you keep your men out of the boats?"

Sperry touched the straw-covered bottle in his hand, and winked broadly. "Our friend the innkeeper has assisted me in that respect. He's tapped a keg in the main hold, and we're serving grog to all comers. If my crew's asleep in the scuppers tomorrow, so much the worse for the Bible-backs. They can unload their own gear—"

Paul found himself joining in the laughter; the situation had its comic side, regardless of the inhuman nature of Silas' order. He could even understand the captain's yielding. Back in England, Cromwell's fortunes were riding high—and the Puritans, to a man, were in the Roundhead camp. A shipmaster whose life depended on government business could hardly afford a bad report from Silas Sutton—a firebrand whose fortunes would rise with Cromwell's, once the colony was launched.

"In your place, Captain," he said, "I'd put a strict limit on that grog ration. We've had troubles enough at sea. I want no broken heads before we go ashore."

"I'll keep peace on my ship," Sperry growled. "Rely on that, Dr. Sutton. Just advise your brother he can't deny sailormen their fling forever. For my part, I'd say the same rule applied to Puritans—but I won't poach in his bailiwick."

It was a cogent warning, and Paul pondered it on his way to the leader's cabin. En route, he was careful to avoid the knots of seamen who loitered on deck with their eyes fixed longingly on the shore. Nor did he pause to investigate the clink of tankards in the hold, the muted explosions of mirth and ribald song. This, after all, was Giles Porter's first real chance to ply his trade.

Silas lay in his bunk, propped in a nest of pillows, with a mass of papers on the counterpane. Welles and Lambert (the two assistants he trusted most) were beside him, conferring in earnest tones. Welles was still waxen-pale from his own illness: he stood his ground when Paul entered the cabin, letting his thin lips curve in a deliberate sneer of dislike. The Reverend Obadiah Lambert, his arms folded into the flowing sleeves of his churchman's coat, gave the arrival the barest of nods. As always, he had chosen a corner where the shadows were deepest: because of his commanding height, he loomed there like a visible portent of disaster.

Despite the heat, both visitors were dressed in their heaviest Sabbath garb, and wore their high-crowned hats pulled low on their brows. The cabin was stifling since the ports were closed, but Silas seemed unaware of the discomfort. His concentration was absolute as he continued to read the chart on his knee: he seemed to ignore his brother entirely. It was only when the voices of his two lieutenants sank to whispers that he looked up from his work.

Ignoring the sick man's visitors, Paul moved to both ports and flung them wide. "I won't censure you for leaving your bed," he told Silas. "If we can't worship God ashore on our first Sunday at Eleuthera, at least you can breathe its airs. You'll find them salubrious."

Silas put down his chart, and motioned to Ralph Welles to stand aside. The leader was also dressed in black—and, to a casual eye, seemed recovered from his bout with death. But Paul had already noted his flushed cheeks, his trembling hands that could not quite still the rattle of papers on the counterpane. The fact that Silas had permitted himself the luxury of partial repose at this hour showed he had already regretted his appearance on deck.

"I don't recall sending for you," he said. "By what right do you interrupt this meeting?"

"I'm here as your physician. Obviously, you're in need of me."

"I've recovered with God's aid," said Silas, in the same dead-level tone. "So, as you'll observe, has Brother Ralph. "We'll no longer require your services."

"Prove it," said Paul—and this time, he let his temper flare. "Rise from that sickbed, and walk to the deck unaided. I'll wager a hundred pounds you'll faint on the threshold."

Silas pushed the papers aside, as though to take up the dare. The effort, Paul saw, was beyond him. When his brother sank back with a stifled groan, he felt he had won the first round of their battle. He pressed the advantage, throwing the cabin door wide and nodding curtly to the visitors.

"Leave us, while I minister to my patient," he told them. "I'll tell you when he's strong enough to hold meetings again."

Both lieutenants bridled at the dismissal—until they observed their leader, who had gone ashen-pale after his futile effort to rise. Even then, they did not budge until Silas addressed them.

"I must talk to Paul alone, since he insists," he said in a faint whisper. "You may return later."

"You promised he'd interfere no more—" Lambert began.

"We'll settle this in our own fashion, Brother Obadiah. Go, please."

Paul was careful to hold his tongue after the door had shut on the two crestfallen pilgrims. Making the most of the gesture, he poured brandy from a carafe, and held the cup to his brother's lips.

"I'll take no spirits on the Sabbath, Paul."

"This is medicine you need badly. Can't you even realize you're standing with a foot in the grave?"

Silas gave a long shudder as he drank, but made no further protest. Now he had admitted his weakness, he seemed strangely subdued. When the ship's doctor began clearing away the litter on the bunk, he lifted his hands dutifully from the maps and closed his eyes.

The papers, Paul observed, were lists of ordnance the colonists had brought to the New World: a musket and *pistola* for each man, a score of cutlasses and the brassbound cannon for the stockade that would be one of their first projects on landing. The maps were of the Floridas and Cuba—with insets showing the defenses of St. Augustine, and the *castillo* protecting the Havana, the island's principal harbor. Paul stowed the papers in a wall cupboard, letting the silence build to mark his anger.

Incredible as it was, these men of God still clung to the dream of conquest in Cuba. Ignoring the fact they were not yet prepared to resist an attack in force (whether it was launched by the pirates or the dons), wrapped in visions of glory, they were capable of wrecking this fledgling colony before it could put down its first taproot.

Such visions, Paul knew, must be scotched today, while Silas (with the fear of death upon him) would still harken to a voice other than his own.

"Are you well enough to listen to a few home truths?" he asked quietly.

"I'm well enough to talk myself," said Silas. "*You're* the one to listen."

"I'll be the judge of your strength," said Paul. He pulled up a stool beside the bed, and took his brother's wrist between his fingers to test the thready pulse. "Keep your voice low—and above all, don't waste it on anger."

"Is it true you dared assume the leadership when I was stricken?"

"Yes, Silas. On the captain's orders."

"Without consulting Lambert? He's my deputy."

"In matters of the spirit, perhaps. This was an emergency that required action."

"You should never have pretended you had my mandate."

"I made no such pretense."

"Brother Welles tells a different story."

"Brother Welles lies in his teeth."

"You've no right to slander a man of God."

"I've every right—if he undermines my work."

"Just what have you accomplished during my illness?" Silas had yet to open his eyes: his voice, though it was clear enough, seemed to come from a vast distance.

"The day I took charge, I saved the ship from pirates. With the help of others, I've explored Eleuthera from end to end, and marked down a dozen ways we can prosper here. We found this harbor and brought you to a safe anchorage—"

"The Lord has led us here."

"Did He send the plague, too?" Paul demanded.

"Yes. To test our fortitude."

"Did He drive off the pirates, mark down a harbor on Sayle's chart, and lead the *Adventurer* through the shoals?"

"Of course—once we'd proved ourselves worthy. Why should *you* claim the credit?"

"Then we're no more than pawns in the Almighty's hands—is that the end of your philosophy?"

"There's no need to sneer, Paul."

"Man was born in sin, and spends his life in atonement?"

"Look about you: Can you say otherwise?"

"I'll endorse your theology, to a point," said Paul. "It's obvious it suits your purpose at the moment. A few practical realities remain—and I'll mention them in order. Accept them, and we can strike a bargain. Insist they're God's doing—as a special favor to you—and I'll return with Sperry to England."

It was a calculated ruse: when he felt the sick man's fingers close on his wrist, Paul knew it had succeeded. For the first time, his brother was afraid. Not for his soul, but for Eleuthera.

"Speak your mind," said Silas. "I'll hear you out."

"First, there's my deputy leadership. Have you another man aboard who could have kept this ragtag group together?"

The query was a cruel one—but Paul had good reason for making it. From the start of this venture, Silas had clung to the fiction that his colonists were united in the same religious faith. Last minute defections in Bristol had reduced the Puritans' roll: so had the plague. Today, if they had voted as one (and even here, Silas could not count on universal backing) they were not a clear-cut majority. It was true that each man was pledged to obey the Articles of Settlement, under which the Adventurers had obtained their charter. But other charters no less binding had been repudiated by rebellious pioneers.

"When the plague struck," said Paul, "there were faint hearts that longed to turn back to England. There'll be others here—if you don't grant us some measure of freedom ashore. Give me my own freedom from Welles and Lambert: I'll keep those faint hearts in line. Believe me, you'll need the help of every man aboard if we're to prosper."

"I won't dispute that," said Silas.

"Can you deny you'd be at the bottom now, if I hadn't out-guessed Captain Jeremy Hood?"

"Claim the credit, if you must. It was a trick worthy of the devil."

"Can you deny we'll perish, if Hood decides to attack us—before we've built a stockade? Do you still hope to conquer Cuba before you've proved that Eleuthera can support us?"

Silas' eyelids drooped—and his mouth twisted into a bitter mold. A martyr at the stake, thought Paul, might have pursed his lips in this fashion at the first lick of the flames.

"Are you asking me to admit failure in advance?"

"By no means. Our chances are excellent, if we don't overreach."

There was a long silence in the cabin—so long, that Paul leaned forward sharply, convinced that Silas had fainted. When his brother spoke, his eyes turned to the ceiling, and both hands were clasped on his chest.

"Don't think you'll take advantage of my weakness," he said.

"It's true that I've overextended my strength. I'll grant we may need you awhile longer, if I must keep to my sickbed—"

"You'll go on using me, then—as you always have?"

"Isn't that my duty?"

"This goes deeper than the plague, Silas. It's a blindness that won't let you separate Caesar and God."

"Don't speak in riddles."

"You're a man of the cloth, with a mission. Pursue it if you must: it's your right. But don't try to be Caesar too—"

"Are you asking me to divide my authority?"

"I'm offering to serve as a link between your factions, to prevent open warfare. Conduct your mission by your rules—but don't expect others to join overnight. Let us find what Eleuthera offers, in our own fashion."

"With you as ringleader?"

"Call me the artisan who builds your home—and makes sure the walls are firm. I won't abuse the trust. The moment the task is finished, I'll leave the island. Surely you mean to give Anne the best—"

"Just what do you propose?"

With victory in his grasp, Paul forced himself to speak gently. "Tomorrow I'll go ashore with Lebret and plot our settlement. I'd advise you to establish your headquarters on the cay, and raise cabins there for your people. It'll give you privacy from the others, and a minimum of friction—"

"The suggestion is sound. I endorse it."

"We'll build a fortress there of palmetto logs, large enough to protect the whole colony. Until those ramparts are ready, we must live in tents, and forage as best we can."

"Surely our church house comes first."

"Not with pirates on New Providence, and the dons just down the horizon. Until we've a safe refuge, you can worship in the open air, like the early Christians."

"What comes next?"

Paul hesitated, aware that the bargain he was sketching must include a spirit of give-and-take, yet reluctant to surrender the initiative.

"You're determined on this crusade against Spain?"

"Like iron," said Silas. "Of course we must scout the ground before I launch it."

"With or without help from Cromwell?"

"I'll await word from London before I move," said Silas.

Paul checked a sigh of relief: he had not expected this flash of common sense. "Lebret can visit the Havana in the meantime. He carries a Spanish passport, and speaks the language like a native. If we decide Lopez is trustworthy, they can go together—"

"Can the Frenchman visit Cuba without arousing suspicion?"

"Guy's a citizen of the world: he has many friends in the Havana. He can pretend he's a victim of shipwreck."

"How will he make the journey?"

"Marco has decided to join the colony. He's a first-rate seaman. Using the shallop, they'll have no trouble fetching the Cuban coast and hiding their tracks."

Silas' hand made a fist on the counterpane, then relaxed slowly, as though the fingers were releasing an invisible sword.

"I've set great store in this blow for Cromwell," he said. "I needn't tell you he burns to destroy all papists, no less than I. Suppose we learn from Lebret that the dons are weak as water— and the Havana an open city? He'll think me remiss in my duty."

Paul controlled his impatience. The objection, he realized, was only the peevish complaint of a sick man, determined to cling to his illusion.

"The Havana's a hundred-year-old city," he said patiently. "It's known as the Pearl of the Antilles. The Spaniard has his faults— and all the world knows it takes ten of him to match one English-man. But I'm sure he guards his jewels, as carefully as most mi-sers."

"I'm aware I must have trained troops before I can strike," Silas admitted. "I still can't help feeling that Noll would have been less cautious."

Again, Paul let the objection pass. Oliver Cromwell (called Noll by his intimates) had been a crusader without peer in the Roundhead cause: most observers agreed he would be ruling England tomorrow, in name as well as fact. It was easy to understand Silas' hunger for the great man's approval, as crusader no less than colonist. His half-brother and Cromwell, Paul decided, were birds of a feather—avenging eagles who must wither and die unless they are winging into battle.

"Perhaps you're right, Silas," he said. "God may have sent the sickness after all—if only to humble your ambition."

"I've asked you once not to blaspheme."

"Will you promise to take your medicine—and my orders—until you're truly well? And let *me* decide how far you can push your strength?"

Silas' lips moved in silent prayer: Paul would never know if it was a benediction or a curse. There was no gratitude in his brother's eyes when he raised them at last. The look he threw at Paul was too weary to be called malevolent, but there was no resignation in his yielding. This, after all, was an uneasy truce between kinsmen, never the ending of their war.

"I'll permit you to found my colony," he said. "You give me little option, since I'm too weak to take my part. I can't pretend I'm happy that an unbeliever should do work in my stead. I'll hold you accountable if my cure isn't speeded."

"We'll manage that, I think—if you'll keep to your bed, and send your lieutenants to me for orders."

"You may give orders pro tem," said Silas. "In the circumstances, I suppose that's only fair."

"I've one more condition," said Paul. "If Lebret reports the dons are too strong to attack, you must accept his verdict."

"Even if England sends me troops?"

"Even then—if the odds are on the enemy side. You've a kingdom of your own to secure: promise you'll make it safe for Anne, before you look beyond."

"You drive a hard bargain, Paul."

"Too many lives are at stake: I can't consider this task otherwise. Promise me now. Or I go straight to Bristol—and advise Anne to remain in England."

Silas kept his martyr's mask—but Paul knew the challenge had found its target.

"Anne believes in our cause. She'll be on the next ship, no matter how we fare."

"She'll wait for Captain Sperry's report in Bristol. *You* arranged that, when we put to sea. Would you have her risk her life, because you refused to make haste slowly?"

"Very well, Paul." Silas' voice was choked: he seemed to float between sleep and waking. "I'll endorse Lebret's report on Cuba. But I ask one promise in return."

"Name it."

"Swear to me you'll stay clear of your tavern harlot. I'll not entrust my settlers to a fornicator."

"That promise is easily made. Lili herself has refused me her favors while I'm in charge."

"See that you hold her to that resolve. Remember, I've the power to condemn you both if you transgress. To the stake, if need be."

"Would you burn your half-brother for his failings?" The threat, Paul knew, was in deadly earnest. According to the charter, the leader of the Adventurers was also a supreme magistrate. Responsible only to a council of church elders, he had the authority to sentence any erring colonist at will, choosing the punishment he thought most fitting.

"I would never condemn a kinsman," said Silas, "unless he condemned himself in the sight of God."

Paul turned numbly to the door. The task he had assumed was heavy as lead on his shoulders—yet his step was oddly light when he paused on the sill.

"I'll send Lili with food," he said. "You could do with some hot broth."

"Not now."

"You promised to take your medicine, Silas."

"Send someone else, then. I don't want that creature about me."

"Whether you like it or not," said Paul, "Lili Porter did her part to save your life."

"Don't ask me to thank her."

"I wouldn't expect that act of grace," said Paul. "You've surprised me enough today."

When Paul tiptoed from the room, Silas appeared to be sleeping—but the clenching of the fists on the counterpane betrayed him. Giving orders in the galley, Paul could hardly believe he had left his brother with the last word. Nothing in that head-on encounter had been more revealing than the sick man's refusal to face the innkeeper's daughter alone, even in the role of ministering angel.

Lili was right, thought Paul. Silas hated her for many reasons—most of all for her power to trouble him as a woman.

# CUPID'S CAY

RAIN had fallen in the night, a drenching downpour that might spell the ending of the wet season and the threat of storms. Stirring drowsily in the cabin that adjoined his surgery, Dr. Paul Sutton had rejoiced in the sound of sluicing water on his palm-thatched roof. It was twelve weeks since the maize had arrived from England on the *Dolphin,* just three months since the last kernel had been planted in the Potholes, the colonist's communal farm. Already, the lush green shoots were waist-high. When the month ended—since cold was unknown in this fabulous clime—there would be sacks of grain in the fortress larder, a final proof that Eleuthera was self-sustaining. It was a good thought to cling to before he sank once again into well-earned repose. . . .

He wakened (as he always did) in the first pearl-gray promise of morning—certain, long before he rose from his rough-hewn bed, that the day would be flawless. As always, he needed a moment to adjust to the demands of a new day. At times, it was still hard to believe that this pine-log cabin was his home. Or that the truce he had struck with Silas (that long-ago afternoon on the *Adventurer*) had still endured.

Now, seven months to the day since the closing of that bargain, the colonists' doctor rose from his bed and moved to the porch of his cabin. Yawning contentedly, he looked out across the land-locked harbor that had been, from the first, the focal point of the settlement he had pushed through to completion. Dawn mist still muffled the wooded shore. It lay knee-deep along the beach of Cupid's Cay, at whose southern extremity the colony's hospital stood. Behind that diaphanous screen, the buildings of Eleuthera loomed darkly. To the untrained eye, they would have seemed unreal as the shadows of retreating night—but Paul could have traced their contours from memory. There, on his right, beyond the swift-flowing channel that separated cay and island, was the looming shape of Giles Porter's tavern—with a score of palm-thatched dwellings behind it, climbing (in cheerful helter-skelter) on the slope of the hill. Here, on his left, were the thick palmetto palisades of the Puritan fortress—set in the geometrical center of the cay, and bristling with gun ports. It was symbolically proper that his own small domain should lie between.

Thanks to the uneasy truce with his brother, he had laid down the foundations of this colony as precisely as some latter-day Euclid; when the colony itself had risen magically in this green wilderness, when each plan he had offered for its sustenance had borne its special fruit, not even Silas (or the hard-core group that advised him) had risked an objection. In the months that followed, the prosperity had been shared by Puritan and Anglican alike; with few lapses, the spirit of live-and-let-live had prevailed. The colonists' doctor, taking the pulses of both worlds, knew the tolerance was but skin-deep. The schism that divided those worlds was as visible as the channel that murmured just beyond his doorstep.

It was still too soon to call Eleuthera a success. Secure against the storms of nature, armored to hold its own against threats from without, it was still the creation of two warring camps. A common need to survive had united those camps at the outset. The need had now been satisfied, in full measure. It was too much to hope the armistice would continue.

Meanwhile, the creator of this abundance could look upon his work and call it good.

Almost from the beginning, the dawn hour had been Paul's favorite time of day. He had fallen into the habit of a morning inspection of the colony—before the inhabitants were awake, when not even a cock-crow disturbed their well-earned repose. At that time, Eleuthera was indeed a proof of what man could accomplish, when man's urge to do battle with his neighbor had been set aside.

He turned first into his surgery, and the sick bay that adjoined it. (This was another custom he followed at the day's beginning, even when there were no patients in the compact hospital.) Like other buildings on the cay, the structure rested on a foundation of pine logs: the walls, of good English oak, came from the hold of the *Adventurer*. The roof was of hand-split pine shingles, weighed at the corners with coral blocks as a protection against the gales that swept these latitudes each fall.

Unlike the cabins within the fort, it had wide windows beneath the eaves—protected by grass mats in bad weather and open at all other seasons to the sun and wind. Silas had disliked the pavilion-like plan of the hospital: to his mind, a sick bay should be shut off from the poison breath of night, no less than a private dwelling. But Paul's wishes had prevailed—based, as they were, on experience in the East. The speedy recovery of the patients he had quartered here (fever cases, for the most part, a broken bone or two, and the pregnancies that had come to term since the colonists landed) had proved his wisdom.

This morning, Paul was faintly startled to hear the snores of two sleepers in the row of cots. His head cleared of the last wisps of night when he remembered the return of Guy Lebret from his travels, with a sea-caked crew of one. (Lopez had been lost in a storm during the crossing of the Florida Straits.) Marco had handled the sheets as the shallop came into the harbor at midnight, by the light of a waning moon. The Frenchman, half-fainting from weariness at the tiller, had been in no condition to recount his travels when the bowsprit had bumped land at last, on the southern shoulder of the cay.

The sound had wakened Paul before the sentinel on the stockade had taken note of the arrivals. He had moored the shallop at his own dock, and led its occupants into the sick bay. By a happy stroke of providence, Silas had left the settlement only yesterday, to put the final touches on a map of Eleuthera, his special labor of love in the past month. As his acknowledged second in command, Paul had been within his rights to bed his friends down, assuring them that he would hear their story in the morning.

Obadiah Lambert would rant when he heard the news—but Paul had grown adept at shouting Obadiah down. Lebret and Marco had risked their skins in his behalf. Their visit to Cuba had been a daring stroke that could prove vital to the colony's future. They would tell a better story after a night's sleep.

It was a proof of his own weariness last midnight that he had resumed his interrupted slumbers with no emotion beyond a sense of relief at Guy's safe return. The Frenchman, like the Gascon cat he resembled, had always landed on his feet: Paul had dispatched him in his dangerous errand last month with a clear conscience—knowing the risk must be taken at the earliest moment, if only to keep Silas in hand.

The loss of the Spaniard was an unforeseen blow: he had proved invaluable during the colony's founding—and Paul had long since convinced himself that Lopez was honest. Now that the colony was firmly established, the man's usefulness was ended: of the trio who had made the voyage to Cuba, he could be most easily spared. . . . It was a brutal comment on the situation—but Paul had made it candidly. In a struggle for survival, casualties were the expected rule. The colony's luck so far had been far too good to last.

Paul took his breakfast from the shelf in the dispensary—a glass of Giles' best sherry, with a beaten egg as its base. The egg was fresh from the poultry house he had helped build inside the stockade. It was still hard to believe that a score of brood hens had come out from England on the *Dolphin*. So had the sow in the pen behind Giles' tavern, and the geese that were fattening in an adjacent coop. In just six weeks they would be part of the Christmas feast the innkeeper had promised to serve for the whole island—with or without the approval of the elders in the stockade. . . .

The *Dolphin*'s bill of lading was still on the dispensary desk, awaiting a final check with Silas. Since the arrival of the supply ship (and the riches her hold had disgorged) the colonists had been far too busy rejoicing in their new gains to make a precise count. Glass in hand, Paul leafed through the listings one more time, if only to convince himself that their good fortune was real.

The supply ship had brought flour out of Bristol, and enough powder and shot to service a regiment (these items had been added on orders from the Proprietors in London.) There had been pig iron and a forge; there had been cloth and beads, for barter with nonexistent aborigines. Besides the maize, Anne Trevor had sent cuttings for shrubs and fruit trees. In addition to the poultry and the sow, there had been goats and a small family of hunting dogs.

A pair of heifers, penned on deck, had been casualties of a mid-Atlantic storm—but the three plow horses stabled in the forward hold had arrived in excellent health. (Anne could hardly know that plows were almost useless on Eleuthera.) There were tobacco seedlings from Virginia and bins of potatoes from Ireland. There was even a hand press to spread the word of God, and a cider press, sent at the request of Giles Porter, who was determined to ferment the juice of the small island apples that grew in profusion around the harbor.

So deep-laden was the *Dolphin* she had carried only a score of passengers. As before, these were divided almost equally as to sects (the Puritans, Paul gathered, had been free with their contributions, but were not overeager to risk their lives until the success of the colony was assured). A fast-sailing vessel, she had been outfitted in record time and dispatched from Bristol at Cromwell's own order: the *Adventurer*, with Captain Sperry again in command, was to sail two months behind her, laden with other necessaries and a full complement of colonists. Anne, busy with a hundred details, had written that she would be aboard.

The letter (which had been read to cheers from the pulpit of the church house on Cupid's Cay) had stressed London's growing interest in Eleuthera, but there had been no mention of London's attitude toward a possible conquest of Cuba—and Silas had been bitter at the omission when he spoke to his brother in private. It was then that Paul had insisted that Guy Lebret and his two companions make their hazardous visit to the Havana, to measure the dons' true strength—and, if possible, to determine the enemy's own attitude toward this English outpost on his flank.

Silas had kept his bargain, contenting himself with a second, even more urgent missive to the Proprietors in London, asking their permission for the attack if he could be sure of its success. Once it was written, Silas had awaited his betrothed's arrival with a kind of brooding calm. It was like the man, Paul reflected, to shrug off the fact that Captain Sperry was now almost a fortnight behind the schedule of his original voyage. The same beneficent Deity who had smiled on Eleuthera from the first (in Silas' opinion) would bring Anne and her colonists safe to harbor.

Matters had rested thus when the leader of the Eleutherians (now completely restored in health, mahogany-dark from his long labors in the sun, and lean as the shepherd-King he resembled) had embarked in one of the light-draft sailing skiffs that had come out of England on the *Dolphin*. The business of charting the capes and shoals of Eleuthera had been his favorite task from the moment he had left his sickbed. It had also been his pleasure to add detail maps of each colonial project Paul had brought to completion—and to sketch a dozen dream plantations in the areas that remained unexplored. . . . Paul was certain that his brother in all sincerity, would assume full credit for these enterprises when the charts were forwarded to London.

Silas had been a hard taskmaster from the beginning. There was no questioning his high-minded resolve to work as hard as any three colonists combined. Yet, like all zealots, he could tolerate no work that fell short of his own, no urge (however natural) to pause in that labor. Nor could he abandon the stubborn belief that each soul on Eleuthera, regardless of its own faith, was his to mold at will.

So far, his orders had been obeyed with only routine murmurs of protest. At Giles' ramshackle tavern, an eight-o'clock curfew was at least loosely honored. Even in the hottest days of summer, each woman in the settlement (regardless of creed) had worn a minimum of two petticoats when Silas or his watchdogs were nearby. Each Sunday, when the brass ship's bell in the stockade clanged out its summons, the entire colony had trooped into the stifling clapboard church house (windowless as the rectangular prison it suggested) to doze under the tongue-lashings of the Reverend Obadiah.

It was Silas who set the hours of labor in the field; it was he who assigned certain men to the fish nets, others to the logging crews, and still others to the digging and planting or the search for ambergris along the beaches. The fact that the charter of the Adventurers provided for regular legislative assemblies on Eleuthera went unmentioned. If Silas was aware that the Anglicans among the colonists were in a majority (and that his commands had been pushed through without once asking their approval) he gave no sign of that awareness. In his book, the prosperity of his venture was only an illustration of his rightness: he was content to give humble thanks to God.

Cupid's Cay, in his view, was the abode of the elect—and even here, there was no appeal from his stern-voiced rulings. The barbarian settlement beyond the channel, while it was not beyond redemption, had been created to serve his holy mission. There was no other reason for its existence.

Anne Trevor had known better of course—and her letter to Paul had proved it, beyond all question.

Sealed in Bristol and sent to him in secret (thanks to the good offices of the *Dolphin*'s captain) it was now under lock in the dispensary desk. Paul had not dared mention its existence, even to his intimates. This morning, aware of the growing day outside, he put down the need to read that missive through again. Pausing just long enough to make sure that Guy and Marco were still deep in slumber, he left the sick bay on tiptoe and stepped into the fulfilled promise of the dawn.

The mist had begun to lift as a breeze stirred the waters of the harbor. Behind him, the stockade was still wrapped in shadows, its silence broken only by the footfall of the lookout on the seaward-facing ramparts. The stout log fortress, with its double palisade, its blockhouse, and its heavy wooden portcullis above the moated entrance, was a stern reminder of enemies just down the horizon. The palisades had been raised two weeks after the colonists came ashore—and Paul had not breathed easily until the last cannon mount was in place, the powder and shot safely stowed, and the entire settlement gathered (in temporary canvas shelters) behind the nine-foot palmetto palings. Once again, he studied the placing of the guns, the sweep of open beach and harbor those ramparts commanded, and found his handiwork good. When Anne walked beneath that portcullis as a bride, she would be well guarded.

Would she be happy too?

It was a question he dared not answer, as he faced the row of solemn abodes within the enclosure, laid out like the spokes of a wheel to converge on the hub of the meetinghouse. Low-eaved, innocent of paint or other adornment, the pilgrims' cabins were locked tight as alms boxes, and shuttered against the treacheries of the tropic night. At that slight distance, they seemed empty of life. Silas' own dwelling, as befitted the colony's leader, was larger than the others, but it seemed no less forlorn in the first blush of morning. With Anne's presence to light it (thought Paul), it could not fail to take on radiance. The image refused to take shape when he turned his back on the stockade and descended the slope of beach to the channel separating Cupid's Cay from Eleuthera itself.

The sun had barely cleared the horizon to the east. Because of the shape of the hills that rimmed the harbor, it had yet to reach the fifty-odd houses that clustered on the slopes. Sparks of brilliance had just begun to show on the farthest hill, where the colonists had carved out a series of water catches in the coral outcrop. The reflected glow, bathing the palm-thatched roofs with a promise of daylight, gave the scene a kind of pastel charm that softened its rawness, making the small settlement an integral part of the earth to which it clung. Here, in contrast to the harsh lines of the Puritan stronghold on the adjacent cay, the haphazard dwellings blended naturally with the cedar grove that shaded them. In the half-light, it was hard to tell where house left off and tree began.

Perhaps it was the rakish slant of the green roofs, or the high-stilted palmetto logs that supported the floors. Or was it the open, pavilion-like structure of the homes themselves that suggested so many tree-houses floating in space? . . . The design had been Paul's—and, though the men of the stockade had sneered at the airy frames, he had insisted they were far more practical than the Puritan's airless cabins. Obadiah Lambert had preached a sermon on the immorality of the sleeping arrangements—which exposed whole families to the common gaze, as well as the sea breeze. The colonists themselves had learned to enjoy their homes—and listened to the sermon in tolerant silence.

There had been much rude joking last month, when the first high wind struck Eleuthera. The tree-house platforms, offering no resistance to the storm, had ridden out the blow without damage, save for a few easily replaced roofs. The stockade cabins—standing grimly in the teeth of the blast—had rocked on their foundations throughout. The wail of the wind had been topped (for hours on end) by the keening of pilgrim voices, as Silas' flock had prayed in terror for their lives.

The narrow channel between cay and main was spanned by a ship's cable lashed to palm boles. Beneath it, a raft of palmetto logs, floated on a dozen well-caulked kegs and anchored to the cable by a hand line, made the crossing a matter of seconds. On the far side, the land sloped gently to the steps of Giles' tavern— a primitive hut with a porch on three sides, a roof like an old hat clapped on carelessly, and a bar built of halved pine logs, discreetly screened from observation in the stockade.

The innkeeper's bed was concealed by the screen. This morning, the proprietor himself slept blissfully in a basket chair on his side veranda, with an empty tankard at his side. The resemblance to an outsized Falstaff persisted, despite the fact that Giles was naked save for a knee-length singlet. The white beard he had cultivated as a protection against insects spread fan-wise on his chest, lifted gently in rhythm with his snores. Judging by the benches and cane-backed chairs that surrounded him, he had played host to goodly company last night. The curfew had been observed so far as lights were concerned, since tankards could be filled easily enough by moonlight.

The wattled cabin at the veranda's end, which served as Lili's quarters, stood wide to the morning: Lili, who slept as easily as a kitten between her tasks (and her pleasures) was a habitual early riser. Guessing where she had gone at that hour, Paul skirted the tavern to inspect the pigsty that stood behind it, then moved down a path among the cedars to check the fruit trees he had planted last spring, in a hollow between the two nearest hills.

The sight of the green rows reminded him of Lopez—and the expedition he had led down the length of Eleuthera to search out edible specimens, before the colony was a month old. Again, he felt a sharp stab of regret at the Spaniard's passing, though the man had remained a withdrawn entity to the moment of his departure in the shallop. It was ironic, he told himself, that Lopez should take on human attributes now, when he was lost beyond recall. . . .

With Lebret to check their findings, they had brought back cuttings of each tree to the settlement; under the naturalist's supervision, they had set out their orchard in this sheltered dell. Giles, working with a dowsing rod to which he attributed occult powers, had already been assigned the task of sinking the first well. The evident lack of water on Eleuthera had seemed (at first) to be the gravest problem the colonists faced, but the innkeeper had insisted there were rifts in the coral to hold the rainfall. Working from the contours of the hills, he had made his boring in short order.

Using a series of stove-in casks to line the excavation, he had struck water at fifteen feet, revealing the first fresh-water source on the island. The result was a well that had yet to run dry. The water, though brackish, was drinkable—and the overflow, channeled among the roots of the new-planted fruit trees, had kept the little orchard green through the summer. A second well had been sunk on the cay, within the stockade. With the catches on the hills, it had solved the settlement's water problem, long before the casks from the *Adventurer* could go dry.

Jack Sikes (whose thumb was greenest of all the settlers) was already hard at work with his pruning shears, and Paul paused to chat a moment before moving on. A bridegroom of seven months'

standing, the yeoman had made history of a sort when he stood
before the improvised altar the Reverend Obadiah had erected
on the islet, and pledged his troth to Deborah Hall, less than an
hour after the pilgrims set foot there. It had been the first of
several marriages on that same beach—and there had been need
for haste, since the bride was already two months with child. Even
Silas had smiled when Guy Lebret had suggested that the site of
the stockade be named Cupid's Cay, in the Sikes' honor. . . .

Today, most of the trees had already borne their first fruit. One,
which Lebret had called an avocado, still showed a few of the
pear-shaped clusters that had repelled Paul by their strangeness,
though both the Frenchman and Lopez had insisted they were a
true delicacy unknown as yet in the Old World. This morning
(as a kind of silent tribute to the Spaniard) he plucked one of the
ripest specimens and slit it with his clasp knife, to reveal the
enormous seed within, and the custardlike fruit itself—almost
tasteless at first, but with an aftermath all its own.

The next fruit he remembered was the mango—a reddish-green
shape that recalled the avocado, though the pulp was far more
tangy. Mingled with this row were trees that were not too different from the English cherry. Yet another (whose branches had
long since been stripped of their last sweet freight) was a species
of apple, slightly smaller than the English crab, which Lopez had
endorsed highly, though neither he nor Lebret could give it a
name. Giles had been one of the first colonists to sample this fruit
—and, since it grew in profusion, he had sent out his own group of
harvesters to bring in apples by the bushel. Run through the press,
they had yielded a dozen barrels of hard cider, a beverage even
more potent than the innkeeper's fast-dwindling stock of English
ale.

Most of the trees in the orchard had been transplanted too late
to bear in season. In these warm latitudes, where all growing
things produced so abundantly, the settlers could look forward
to a constant yield from their branches, once the short winter had
turned into the new year. Concentrated in this vale, a few
minutes' walk from the harbor, the fruit trees would supply the
whole colony: women and children could help in the picking and

sorting, at a vast saving in time and labor. Lebret and Paul had planned the project between them, with Jack Sikes and two full-time helpers assigned as custodians. It was a refreshment of the spirit to walk in its green shade—and Paul moved on reluctantly, to take the path that led across the ridge to the communal farm.

Known as the Potholes, this area was perhaps ten acres in extent, and consisted of a series of breaks in the coral base that lay beneath so much of Eleuthera's soil—making the land unsuitable for conventional farming, since a plow would splinter on its first contact with the hardpan. The so-called potholes (of which there were many) were of varying depth and filled with a rich deposit of soil and decayed vegetable matter accumulated over the centuries.

Exploring the area on the eastern slope of the harbor hills, Lebret had soon learned to distinguish these breaks, since the underbrush and trees that grew there were always greener. It had been tiring work to clear way this dense growth and expose the soil for farming. Once it was accomplished, the naturalist found not one but a series of potholes—most of them on level ground, and ideally suited to the cultivation of vegetables of all kinds.

This fortunate discovery had been exploited to the utmost. Lebret had warned that even this rich soil would soon be depleted if it were farmed without some form of natural renewal. When Marco and a group of woodcutters, exploring the northern reaches of the island in search of firewood, had reported the discovery of vast quantities of bird droppings, the Frenchmen had pronounced the specter of hunger banished from Eleuthera.

Most of the droppings had been found in a broad-mouthed cave, several hundred feet in depth, which had apparently served as a rookery for generations of seafowl. Deposited in amazing quantities on the cave's floor, and reeking like the sulphur it resembled, it had seemed precious ore to the Genoese sea monkey and knew its value as a soil enricher.

The cave was not far from the natural coral window the colonists had observed on sighting the island, and at first, the problem of transporting an adequate supply of this fertilizing agent had seemed insoluble. However, since the *Adventurer* had not yet weighed anchor, she was pressed into service as a transport and moved to a reasonably safe berth outside the lazy surf. All day long, the ship's boats had plied between ship and land, each with its complement of palm-frond baskets filled with their odorous cargo. Storage sheds had been built on the borders of the farmsite. Yeoman and Puritan, their differences forgotten in this solution of a common need, had formed a human chain to move the baskets from the harbor to the Potholes. It had been a calculated gamble (and Sperry had entered it grudgingly, since a sudden wind could have piled his ship on coral). Once the storehouses were filled, Lebret had said that the fields were assured a two-years' supply. The longboats the *Adventurer* had left behind would replenish the bins thereafter.

Because of their irregular shape, and the occasional upthrust of rock spurs, the potholes could not be plowed in the usual manner. At first, the would-be farmers had mixed earth and droppings with boarding cutlasses, cane knives, and other strips of metal salvaged from bales and crates that had been dismembered for building material. Later, when the *Dolphin* arrived with its forge, plowshares had been melted down, and converted into long-handled half-moons, which could be used to turn the soil and shape the first furrows to receive the seed. Rakes were constructed from saplings that grew nearby, a tough wood which the naturalist called *lignum vitae.* Rough harrows were made of the same material, permitting teams of laborers to complete the cultivation of these vital truck gardens, as precisely as though they were turning the soil of Sussex.

After the rainy season, the plantation's yield had surpassed Lebret's best hopes. Besides the maize patch, and the acre-wide pothole he had seeded for potatoes, there were fields of bean squash and lettuce, melon vines, and frames for the climbing shoots of a plump, blood-red vegetable known in England as a love apple and deemed poisonous by generations of housewives. The Frenchman, consulting his botanical dictionary, gave it the resounding Latin label of *Lycopersicon esculentum,* insisted it was edible in both its red and yellow form, and advised the colonists to use it freely, in both *salade* and stew, along with the juicy palm hearts (a kind of tropic cabbage) that grew everywhere.

Of all the seeds brought ashore from the *Adventurer,* only such English staples as wheat, rye, and barley refused to flourish here —a sore disappointment to Giles, who had planned to use the mash for the distillation of a Bahamian whiskey far superior to Scotland's. The innkeeper had cursed again, even more eloquently, when the vineyard he had planted on the hillside behind his tavern burned brown in the heat of summer. A grape arbor, put down in open shade in the Sikes' yard, had suffered a like fate. Lebret, however, was not too troubled by these failures. The Indian corn meal, he pointed out, could be used for bread. It was equally nutritious when baked in flat loaves or pones— and the flour sacks delivered by the *Dolphin* would serve the settlers amply until the next ship arrived.

The matter of food had been a burning question since the colony's founding. When one excepted the endless debates over such topics as predestination and originial sin, it had become a cause for argument surpassed only by Silas' edicts regarding clothing— which Lili, in a moment of inspired irreverence, had dubbed the battle of the petticoats.

Lebret had drawn many lessons from his botanist's storehouse. Among the more revolutionary was his belief that man's diet (like man's clothing) should vary with the climate. Pastries and puddings, he argued, might serve as fuel during an English winter. In the Bahamas (where winter was heralded only by an occasional chill morning, and yielded to spring without a struggle) these same foods could bring on a distemper of the blood, an upset digestion, and a general lethargy that might herald serious illness. The same was true of such foods as dried apples—and doubly true of salt meats and hardtack that had been the backbone of each meal at sea.

Since the Puritan dwellings were grouped within the stockade (and since the sand of Cupid's Cay grew no living thing besides a few sparse coco palms and clumps of sea grape) the wives of the Bible-backs had continued to serve the familiar staples during the first months of roof-raising. Fresh fish abounded at their doorstep—and there was a turtle crawl on a sandbank within wading distance of the cay. Without exception, the housewives turned their backs on the sea's bounty, to serve their husbands breakfasts of fried salt pork, and pancakes made of hardtack pounded in dripping. Their one luxury (baked in secrecy on the eve of the Sabbath) was apple tart, made of dry fruit and the heaviest of flour doughs, since their open hearths made true baking impossible.

When workmen from Silas' domain turned bilious, Paul dosed them with physic, scolded them roundly for their refusal to take the Frenchman's advice, and offered them sample (and easily prepared) menus to take back to their kitchens. Later, when these workmen came down with fever, he forced the same diets upon them while they lay in his sick bay. Almost without exception, they returned to their former meals the moment they recovered. Their wives (who suspected Lebret of papist leanings) considered his *salades* an invention of the devil. The love apples he offered them as food were symbols of Eve's first temptation: after a diligent search in Scriptures, Obadiah Lambert had proscribed their use from his pulpit.

Less than two months after the landing, Paul's records showed that Cupid's Cay had sent nearly a score of patients to his hospital, as compared to four from the main island. He had argued endlessly with Silas, in an effort to improve the eating habits of the cay's inhabitants—though he could understand his brother's inability to grasp the true cause of that sick list. The mixtures of raw vegetables which Lebret championed so ardently were virtually unknown on English tables. So were his fish chowders and turtle stews, as well as such doubtful delicacies as conch meat, and the flesh of the giant lizards (called iguanas) which Marco snared in the palmettos. Variety of this sort, said the Frenchman, could spell health in the tropics—but such advice was beyond his time.

Traditional in their choice of food, the men of the stockade were even more rigid in their dress. Day and night, regardless of season, they wore the same coat and breeches of thick black worsted; disdaining to walk barefoot when they fished, they trudged heavily through the sands of Eleuthera in the same

square-toed boots they had worn in English snow. Their one concession to the climate was a hat of woven straw (with the same
black band) adopted as the official male headgear after an earnest
consultation among the elders. When several of their number
were felled by sunstroke, coats were shucked at last during their
heavier labors—but no Puritan, regardless of sex, exposed an inch
of unnecessary flesh.

Now, after seven full months in one of the world's balmiest
climates, their faces and bodies (save for a few sunburned necks
and noses) remained dead-white. Nor did they neglect to don
still heavier garments with the onset of autumn, as they had always done in England, ignoring the fact that the climate on their
island, if anything, was even warmer than before.

Again, Paul had argued with Silas to no avail, even when the
combination of heated bodies and airless cabins had doubled the
cases of ague. A suit of solemn black (said Silas) was the Puritan's
badge of merit. From a start, he had worn it as a knight his
armor—as a shield against the temptations of the world. It scarcely
mattered that the same thick coat was a hair shirt on Eleuthera—
since it was worn for God's glory, not for the comfort of the wearer.

Curiously enough, the Puritan women had been—for a time, at
least—more overt rebels. Left to themselves by day, once the settlement was built, they had more than enough tasks to occupy
them. Even so, they could not help glancing across the narrow
channel at the doings of their less trammeled sisters. It was soon
common knowledge that the wives and daughters of the Anglicans, whether their men were gentlemen or yeoman, could dress
largely as they pleased, within the bounds of decorum. All the
women of Eleuthera (in contrast to the women of Cupid's Cay)
wore gowns of the lightest fabrics. Some had laid aside their bonnets altogether; a few even dared to go barefoot when they took
their children to play in the harbor shallows. Soon it was whispered that none of the Eleutherians wore more than a single petticoat—and that some, like the firm-breasted wife of Jack Sikes and
the hussy daughter of the innkeeper, wore nothing at all beneath
their dress.

There was little chance to verify these rumors, since visits between cay and island were frowned on by the elders. The after-dark doings in Giles' tavern could only be imagined by the lady-Puritans; the outdoor feast Giles Porter served to all his neighbors, to celebrate the raising of his roof-tree, could only be glimpsed from afar. True, the innkeeper had invited the entire colony to join the festivities—but Silas had closed the stockade gate at sun-down to muffle the sounds of revelry and ordered each pilgrim to seek his couch. . . . Wine was said to flow freely that night, and there was no escaping the music of Marco's guitar, the shouted songs, and the knowledge that men and their wives were dancing openly beneath the stars.

Ralph and Charity Welles were among the few Puritans who dwelt on the mainland: Welles had been appointed official sur-veyor for the colony, and his map-making forced him to spend long hours abroad, making residence in the stockade inconvenient. Gossip insisted that Silas and Obadiah had placed him deliber-ately in the Anglicans' midst, to spy on their wickedness: there was no doubt that his wife (forbidden though she was to consort openly with the women around her) had done what she could to smell out sin. In this, she was aided by her long-nosed daugh-ter, the *enfant terrible* named Patricia, who was not above creep-ing on hands and knees beneath the innkeeper's veranda, to see and hear what she could.

Matters had rested in an uneasy state of truce when Charity Welles had come to the cay to pay a duty call on the wife of Obadiah Lambert, accompanied by her daughter. When Patricia stood in the doorframe with the light behind her, it was discov-ered that she wore but a single petticoat—and further investiga-tion revealed that she had forgotten her shift as well.

Cornered by the outraged minister's wife, Patricia had talked herself out of her dilemma nimbly enough. Half the ladies on Cupid's Cay, she declared, wore but a single petticoat during their husbands' absence at work: she had not realized it was a sin to do likewise. A check of the stockade cabins, conducted with the Reverend Obadiah's full approval, had revealed there was at least a modicum of truth in the child's statement.

Obadiah had preached one of his best jeremiads on the subject that Sunday, and Silas had issued his now-famous decree. Any Puritan, male or female, who was guilty of a major infringement of dress would be punished hereafter by a day in the stocks, without food or water. That evening, the dread outdoor prison frame was brought into view for the first time, and placed on the porch of the church house. There was no need of a further warning—and, when the same order was repeated on the main, most of the ladies took heed, without too much grumbling.

Lili Porter had shrugged off the command with a jest; Deborah Sikes and a few other hardy souls had done likewise. The Anglicans were well aware that neither Silas nor Obadiah would risk enforcing such an edict on Eleuthera, however sternly they might act among their own sect. (The stocks, after all, were used only for such major crimes as blasphemy, stealing, or open adultery.) But those same Anglicans still quailed before the wrath of men like Silas Sutton—preferring to walk softly in his presence, rather than risk the full weight of his displeasure. Lightweight dresses had gone into the trunk again, to be replaced by sterner garb—and for a week at least the rustle of starched undergarments, on cay and mainland alike, had rivaled the whisper of the wind in the coco palms.

Brooding, not too unhappily, on these clashes (and admitting the wave of shock that had swept Cupid's Cay had its comic side) Paul left the plantation and climbed the gentle slope that led eastward from the Potholes. The sun had just cleared the dense stand of cabbage palms that crowned the rise. He knew he must make haste, if he meant to enjoy his morning swim in the surf.

Even though most of the island still slept, and the Puritans shunned the seaward beaches at all hours, there was a certain risk in those swims. Silas would thunder his displeasure if he knew, and insist that the colony's one doctor, of all men, should adjure so dangerous a practice. It was part of the leader's tenet that salt water corroded both the skin and the brain, that swimming itself (on excellent Scriptural authority) was an unnatural act for man.

Before he could climb the slope that led in turn to the dunes, Paul knew Lili was already in the surf. A flash of black broadcloth in the tangle of underbrush between two sandhills, the hasty crunch of boots, told him Eleuthera was not without its Peeping Toms, that some man in the settlement had followed the innkeeper's daughter here, aware of her love for sea-bathing and eager to feast his eyes on her near-nudity. Once he had cleared the gully (alarmed at the doctor's approach) the voyeur moved with dispatch; because of the distance that separated them, Paul could not be sure of the man's identity, but the hunched shoulders and the ferret thrust of the head bore a strong resemblance to Ralph Welles. Furious though he was, Paul could not suppress a sardonic grin. Knowing he could damn Welles as a satyr, he felt sure the colony's surveyor would hold his own tongue for the nonce. Welles could hardly denounce him for swimming here without admitting he had first been watching the girl from ambush.

On the summit of the dune, Paul looked down on the vast sweep of beach and sea and breathed deep of the light offshore breeze. From this vantage point, the scene was empty as the day Columbus came, a century and a half in the past: the dark dot that was Lili's head, just beyond the curl of the last lazy wave, did nothing to spoil the perfect solitude. Moving down a seaward slope of the dune, he cursed aloud when he saw that Lili's shift hung like a white pennon on a strip of driftwood, along with the peignoir she wore on these sunrise excursions. It was her usual custom to wear the former garment while she swam. Today, it seemed, she had gone into the surf with no more costume than Aphrodite—and with the same casual unconcern.

Ralph Welles, Paul decided, had seen more than enough. It was obvious he had waited in the gully, hoping for a second look when Lili emerged from the waves. Oddly enough, Paul felt little real resentment at the discovery. Lili, he knew, could defend herself in any situation. Being what she was, she could hardly avoid the hot-eyed stares of every man on Eleuthera.

Obeying a wise impulse, he did not join Lili in the sea, but settled on the driftwood beside her clothes, waving a greeting across the crash of the waves and waiting patiently for her to join him. The problem of Lili Porter, he told himself, would remain unsolvable, since it had existed in every civilization worthy of the name. In Silas Sutton's book, the girl was no more than a prostitute—and by his code, she deserved the name. Yet (from the first day) she had been vital to the colony's survival.

Paul knew her favors had not been bestowed lightly. Watching from a distance (careful to keep his bargain with Silas) he had seen how easily she had stilled the turbulence of these men without women—soothing their loneliness, making the long nights endurable while these honest Englishmen awaited the arrival of wives and sweethearts on the *Adventurer*. To call such ministrations evil was to borrow a leaf from a code which had no basis in reality. Hoping against hope that Silas had not yet guessed the truth, Paul had held his tongue and waited.

Evenings at Giles' had grown even more agreeable after the arrival of the *Dolphin*. Introduced to the colony as the innkeeper's nieces from London, the three young females who tripped ashore so lightly became part of the tavern staff—helping Lili at the bar, serving the score of bachelors who dined there nightly, and joining wholeheartedly in the Saturday galas (the one night when Silas had grudgingly relaxed his curfew). It was hard indeed to believe that the nieces' true vocation had escaped the elders' eyes —but they were still permitted to attend Sunday services as a unit. Here, they were shepherded by Lili. Though the four girls sat alone in a side pew, they knew each response in the service. Their dark dresses were cut to smother the slightest curve—and their eyes were as downcast as vestal virgins when they knelt in prayer.

There had been the usual ribald jokes in field and tavern, and the ladies of the stockade had drawn their skirts aside and hissed like angry geese when the quartet passed. Paul himself had stood firmly apart from the gossip: in his view, Giles Porter's tavern, like its occupants, had been essential to the colony's future.

The unmarried yeomen, after all, were the backbone of the settlement. For seven weary months, they had found surcease from their labors at Giles' hospitable board—along with the occasional gnawing doubt that those labors might be in vain, and the constant fear of danger from without. With the arrival of the *Adventurer* (a score of would-be wives were aboard) those same hardy laborers could take the first long step toward domesticity. Meanwhile, Lili and her assistants had earned their page in Eleuthera's history. Who but Silas and his elders could say the page was not a bright one?

Paul tossed the peignoir on a driftwood stump and turned his back when Lili ran out of the shallows and wrapped the garment about her. For all his resolve to forswear her favors, he was still all too human to risk a direct glimpse of a body created for the act of love.

"Aren't you swimming today, *chéri?*"

"I think not, Lili. Sit and talk awhile. I've something to tell you that's past overdue."

The innkeeper's daughter listened in silence while he described his glimpse of the voyeur. She did not seem too concerned at the story.

"You didn't see his face?"

"He ran too fast. But I'd take my oath it was Ralph Welles."

Lili laughed aloud. "He's earning his keep as our surveyor. Only last week he was taking sights from the dunes with his spyglass and quadrant. Of course he pretended to ignore me entirely when I came down to bathe. When he refused to move on, I ignored *him* and took my swim just the same."

"In your pelt?"

"Just so," said Lili calmly. "With that grab-bag wife, can you blame him for spying?"

"What if he tells Silas?"

"I hardly think he'd dare, now you've caught him in the act. Put the surveyor from your mind, Paul. You didn't come here to discuss *his* form of starvation."

"Has it occurred to you that your father is playing a dangerous game—and you're abetting him?"

Lili laughed again, and began tousling her hair dry in the hood of the peignoir. "Don't tell me that *you*, of all people, resent the fact we're growing rich here?"

"You know better. I'm merely warning you that Silas has wide powers as governor, if he chooses to use them."

"We've always given honest weight, Paul."

It was hard to resist the girl's bubbling humor for long, but he felt he must make the effort.

"I'd be the last man on earth to deny your usefulness," he said carefully. "Nor do I blame Giles for charging what he can get. Is it true that he sent back enough hard cash on the *Dolphin* to pay off his whole investment here?"

"We've done better than that, Paul. He's beginning to buy up land as well."

"The colonists' shares, you mean?" According to the articles in the charter, each original settler had been granted the right to possess and develop a considerable tract of land on the island. So far, they had been too busy to stake out claims to individual plantations. If Giles had begun to acquire these rights, he was bound to run afoul of the elders—who would consider themselves the arbiters of all transfers of title.

"Father plans to clear each deed at the stockade before he accepts it. Some men are born lazier than others, Paul. The laziest are already in the tavern's debt for food—and other necessities. Naturally, they've no other way to repay us."

Paul abandoned the argument with a shrug. It was clear that Lili had reason on her side. Giles was aware he must make haste slowly. The truce between cay and tavern was still workable, despite its shaky foundation.

"Has Brother Welles forced his attentions upon you?"

"Of course not. He hasn't the courage."

Paul hesitated: it was a hard question, but he felt it must be asked.

"Would you receive him, if he did?"

Lili shook her head. "I'll have no truck with married men— here or elsewhere. It only leads to trouble. Besides, there's nothing I could do to improve Ralph Welles."

"Back in Bristol, you said you could have Silas himself—if you wanted him. You repeated the boast, not too long ago. Isn't that a contradiction?"

"Silas can be turned into a man, Paul—in the hands of the right woman. A real man, not just a skulking hypocrite."

"Please don't elect yourself for the task, Lili. We're near enough now to an explosion."

The innkeeper's daughter tossed her head proudly. "Don't lose sleep on that score," she said. "I've told you I leave the marrieds strictly to their own problems. That goes double for a man like your brother. *He'll* improve fast enough—once he's bedded with his bride. You can trust Mistress Trevor there, I'm sure."

Paul nodded, without trusting himself to speak. He had forgotten Lili's easy camaraderie—and how she could tease out a man's innermost thoughts.

"Bigots aren't reformed in a day," he said. "Right now, you're walking a hairline at the tavern. So is Giles, and those young women he calls his nieces. Don't you wonder why you haven't been the subject of one of Obadiah's sermons?"

"He wouldn't dare. Half the single men in that stockade have slipped over to our side when the moon's dark. If the preacher doesn't realize it, he's an even bigger fool than he looks."

"Has it occurred to you that they may be biding their time? Waiting for you to make a mistake you can't explain away? They've a dozen ways of striking back, you know."

"If you mean the stocks—they wouldn't dare that either. I'd be rescued before they snapped the locks. So would my father."

"They can bring you to trial before the elders. If found guilty, you could be sent back to England."

"I don't think they'll trouble, Paul. Not when they hear I'm about to return on my own account—along with the girls who came out on the *Dolphin*."

"When did you reach this decision?"

"It isn't definite yet: we've no intention of leaving while trade is brisk." Lili had spoken quite casually, but there was a twinkle in her eyes that betrayed her. "If it's true there are wives aboard the *Adventurer*—and sweethearts burning for husbands—our usefulness here will be ended. So far, Eleuthera's been a kind of frontier post. We've been the vivandières—the ladies of the campfires, whose task it was to keep the troops contented. What your brother calls fornication's one thing when a man's far from home. Adultery's quite another, once the camp becomes a town, with wives in charge. Sometimes, I'll grant you, it still pays. To me, the game isn't worth the candle."

"Perhaps your work will be done as soon as mine then," he said. "We might even sail back together."

"Stranger things have happened Paul," said Lili: for the first time, she seemed quite serious. "We enjoyed each other in Bristol. It isn't your fault—or mine—that we've failed since. We may find the password again, once we're free of this island and its rulers."

"Does that mean you'll defer to Silas, from now on?"

"Yes, if it will make you happier. I'll even give up my sea bathing —though that's the greatest sacrifice of all. And I don't think we'd better meet like this again—innocent though we are. Welles isn't the only one who can spy on us."

"Who else would take the risk?"

"Ask your brother what he was doing last Wednesday in the watchtower of the stockade."

"D'you mean that *Silas*—"

"I'd gone swimming in the harbor at dawn," said Lili. "No one else was stirring at that hour. He'd brought his spyglass and pretended to study the other shore. But he didn't miss a move I made—"

"You're inventing this."

The innkeeper's daughter shook her head vigorously as she got to her feet. "I wish I were, Paul, for his sake. I'm sure he was watching me in the hope I wasn't alone, so he could read me a lecture later—"

"Were you in your shift?"

"Fortunately yes: that was one morning I took care to keep it on. Do you say prayers for him, Paul—even now?"

"Sometimes—not that I hope they'll be heeded in Silas' heaven."

"Say one more, on the chance it's heard in time. Pray that the *Adventurer* isn't *too* late. He needs his betrothed—badly."

Lili and Paul returned to the settlement by separate routes. This time, he followed the curve of the harbor, to inspect the turtle pen the colonists had built there the week before, then followed the beach to the hand ferry. The sun had only touched the highest roof-trees in Eleuthera, though it was already blazing on the Atlantic beaches.

A group of colonists, nets slung on shoulder, were preparing to leave for the reefs. Others, with mattocks and steel-bladed poles, were assembling on the shore of Cupid's Cay, receiving their orders from Ralph Welles before taking off for a day's labor at the potholes. It was a morning like a hundred others, yet an almost visible tension seemed to fill the air. It vibrated in waves across the channel to tease Paul's nerves while he stood waiting for the hand ferry to make the crossing.

Welles, he observed, had no part in it: if the surveyor realized he had been caught peeping in the gully, he gave no indication when he favored Paul with a curt nod before stumping back to the stockade. The Puritan workmen were a different story as they made their crossing to the main, spoke a gloomy good morning, then set forth to their work with grim-jawed purpose. Their faces, without exception, were frozen masks of disapproval, but he read an identical question in each eye.

Just in time, he remembered the two sleepers in the sick bay, and realized that news of their return must have spread through the stockade. Obviously, all of Cupid's Cay was eager to hear the report they had brought back from Cuba—and fearful that it might portend an attack against that not-too-remote bastion of Spain.

Opening the door to his surgery, Paul felt his own jaw set in a hard line. With his brother absent, no action of any sort could be taken. It was true that Silas (clinging to his dream of conquest) had put each male colonist through a series of exhausting drills, including assaults on dummy breastworks and practice in the longboats. Since they lacked practical transport, matters had rested thus while the leader awaited the arrival of the *Adventurer* —but the whole colony knew of Silas' purpose, and his hope that Lebret would advise that an attack was entirely practical, given a stout ship and trained boarders.

The hope, as Paul well knew, could only be called fantastic—

but he had refused to argue that point, either with his brother or the colonists themselves. Today (with Silas map-making to the north) he was in charge on the cay. He was resolved to keep Lebret's report to himself until his brother's return.

Both men still slept deeply in the hospital when he settled at the desk in his dispensary. With the memory of Lili's last words still heavy on his mind, he unlocked the drawer and took out Anne's letter. Since its arrival on the *Dolphin*, he had read it over a hundred times.

Dear Paul:

I speak to you across the Ocean Sea, aware that this is only another form of good-by—but I could not let the *Dolphin* leave Bristol without sending you some word.

Eager though I am to see Eleuthera, I must linger here awhile longer. The welfare of the colony is Silas' first concern: it must also be mine. At your end, you will need time to consolidate your gains. Here in England, we are facing an era of great change. I need hardly to tell you that the balance is swinging fast toward Cromwell, who sends the *Dolphin* on her way with his personal blessing.

When the *Adventurer* sails, he hopes to dispatch troops as well. In any event, he will write direct to Silas, outlining his plans for the colony's future.

By now, if I know Silas, he will have made no secret of his ultimate goal—to possess the island of Cuba for England and crush the papists there, root and branch. At this writing, I cannot say if Cromwell will endorse such a project. Beset with problems at home, he may not wish to risk a war with Spain. But he is a man of vision and inflexible purpose—divinely ordained, in his view, to the task of reforming mankind. Silas and he are identical in that respect. Perhaps he will endorse your brother's plan to use Eleuthera not merely as a colony, but as a spearhead for conquest.

Regardless of Cromwell's decision, I beg you to do all in your power to dissuade Silas from this purpose now. As paymaster of this project, as the Proprietor's deputy in Bristol, I know your present resources to the last musket ball. The men Silas commands are farmers and builders, not conquerors. Even if he could persuade all of them to follow him to battle (and I doubt he could) it would only end in their destruction.

Both of us realize, I am sure, that Silas is a man of noble aims with little real knowledge of the world. Perhaps his knowledge has ripened, now you have shared the hardships and the rewards of pioneers: the warning I have sounded may be needless, after all. If so, this letter needs no answer, and I can sail to my wedding with a tranquil mind.

Before the year ends, I look forward to seeing you one more time, however briefly. If I can believe Captain Sperry's report, you have done all that one man could for our band of pilgrims. I can only assume that you plan to return with him to England. So our reunion must also be a farewell—a final one this time.

For either of us, there can be no other ending.

Anne.

*Postscriptum:* As I was about to seal this, news came from London. Cromwell is definitely sending troops to Eleuthera. But they will come on yet another ship, which will follow the *Adventurer.* At this writing, the size of the force is secret. I cannot believe it will be too large. Perhaps it is no more than a guard for the stockade on Cupid's Cay.

Regardless of its size, I have decided it is wiser to withhold such vague news from Silas. Tell him, by all means, if you differ —but I think we are of one mind there.

Tempted though he was, Paul had sent no reply to this candid missive. Because of the method of its delivery (and the confidence in his judgment that breathed from it) he felt he could not risk an answer, that he could say nothing to lighten Anne's fears. It would have been a needless cruelty to burden her with a recital of his long, hard fight to insure the colony's prosperity—or to admit (even by inference) that Silas' determination to play the crusader had only hardened with each passing month.

Rereading Anne's cryptic postscript for the hundredth time, he faced its numbing message squarely. England's future in the

Bahamas, the existence of every soul on Eleuthera, no longer rested with Silas Sutton: Oliver Cromwell (another man of destiny) would call the tune beyond the Ocean Sea. Orders were already en route. If the firebrand of the Roundhead cause had decided on a full-scale conquest of Cuba, the die was cast—and Anne Trevor had chosen a bad time indeed to join the colony. Yet Paul realized that no power under Heaven could have persuaded her to delay her sailing. Her fate, no less than Silas', was bound up in the island. If Eleuthera became a battleground tomorrow, she would take her place beside him.

Come what may, Paul concluded (and it was the bitterest admission of all) his usefulness here was ended: whether the verdict from London was peace or war, Anne's arrival would be his own signal to depart. There would soon be a doctor here to assume his duties: he had kept his bargain with Silas—and he would honor his promise to Anne with the same grim scruples. Once he had made that decision, he felt the expected calm descend upon his spirit. It was cold comfort to admit that his future would be governed by forces beyond his control—but it was better than the long torture of waiting. . . .

Hearing Guy Lebret stir in the nearer bed, he rose from the desk in his dispensary and locked the letter away. The Frenchman, he saw, was on the point of awakening, though Marco snored heavily in the next cot. Unwilling even now to disturb the two weary voyagers, Paul moved to the door of the sick bay and looked out at the harbor—as though the mere act of staring could bring Captain Sperry into the anchorage. By any count, the *Adventurer* was a full week overdue: he could not share Silas' assurance that Providence would watch over her course forever— and the fact that one hurricane had spun close to Eleuthera in the past month did nothing to lessen his fears.

Silas listened in silence while Guy Lebret retold the story of his Cuban adventure. Expecting an outburst at the first enumeration of the dons' strength, Paul found the quiet even more chilling.

Two days had gone by since Lebret's return. Silas himself had been a scant half-hour on Cupid's Cay. His summons had been deceptively mild, in view of Paul's steadfast refusal to permit either the Frenchman or Marco to be questioned before the leader's return. Lebret's account of the Cuban visit, confirming his own mental picture in every detail, had convinced him the news would keep.

When his brother broke in at last on the recital, his question seemed reasonable enough.

"Why do they call their fortress the Morro?"

"The word means a round hill in Spanish," said Lebret. "It's well named, Master Silas: from the sea, it appears to be a giant's breadloaf forgotten in the sun."

"It has but a dozen cannon?"

"The dons call them the Twelve Apostles," said Lebret. "Each of them could split the *Adventurer* to her keelson. The harbor entrance is narrow. Ships can't beat in against the tide, which brings them under the Morro's guns. It would take an armada to force an entrance to the Havana."

"You say these guns are all trained upon the sea. Can't the fort be taken from the rear?"

"Perhaps—if you could beach a thousand trained men, and approach the walls without revealing your presence. Save for the Havana, there are no good anchorages nearby. It would mean a forced march through jungle. With the best of luck, you'd be ambushed before you reached the city walls. If you fought your way out, you'd find them ready for a siege."

"Did Lopez concur with this view?"

The Frenchman sighed, and spread his hands. "He'd have told you as much off Bermuda, if you'd listened. It would have saved us a dangerous journey."

"I don't trust a papist, Lebret. The Spaniard was useful, to a point: Paul tells me he was most helpful while we settled Eleuthera. I needed my own man in Cuba, to observe things as they are today. I won't deny that you've disappointed me profoundly."

"Because I've told the truth?"

"I can't believe the picture's as black as you've painted it." Lebret glanced at Paul, and rolled helpless eyes to heaven.

He had brought maps and notebooks to Silas' house in the stockade: for the past hour, he had drawn a painstaking word picture of Cuba. From the first, Silas had appeared to give the Frenchman his undivided attention. It was only when he had begun his inevitable pacing that Paul realized his brother's mind had closed, as abruptly as though a shutter had slammed behind his eyes.

The fact that Silas had tossed both coat and shirt aside as he roamed his cabin was an added sign of his distress. Now, as he stood in the open window and beat the sill with both fists, he seemed a copper-dark image of his own wrath, cast in some heroic sculpture's mold. Strength had poured into that magnificently endowed body in a healing flood, from the day he had risen from his sickbed. . . . Watching him carefully, Paul knew he was using all his will power to keep his fingers from Lebret's throat.

"What would you have Guy say?" he asked quickly. "That a hundred men could take the Morro?"

Silas had frozen in the window frame: he seemed unaware of the interruption. "Lebret may go, Paul," he said at last. "I wish to talk with you alone."

The naturalist bristled from his chair. "If you doubt my word, Master Silas—"

"Don't ask me to meet you on the field of honor," said Silas. "I'm a warrior for the Lord—man's quarrels don't concern me."

"The Lord will be ill served if you insist on fighting the dons," said Lebret. "In your place, I'd look to my own defenses. You'll do well to hold this island, if they attack *you*."

"Allow me to fight my own battles," said Silas. "You've carried out your mission: I won't thank you for your conclusions."

The Frenchman drew his dignity about him, and stalked from the leader's quarters. Standing beside Silas in the window, Paul saw he had walked into a knot of Puritans on the church porch: they followed him eagerly as he moved toward the stockade gate—speaking in angry bursts and shaking both fists at heaven. The story of the Cuban adventure, Paul knew, would be on every tongue by nightfall: he had planned it so, when he had kept both

Lebret and Marco in the sick bay until Silas' arrival. Lebret was a popular figure on both sides of the stockade. Most of the colonists would believe his story.

"Why did Lebret lie?" asked Silas. "Did you ask it?"

"He gave you the facts. Don't take out your spleen on me, because you find them unpalatable."

"He said we'd need a thousand soldiers to take over Cuba. Doesn't that prove he's either a liar—or a madman?"

"Call in Marco. He'll tell you the same story."

"I've no time to listen to an ignorant sailor, Paul. Besides, I'm sure Lebret has coached him."

"You agreed to send these three men as observers. You said you'd accept their report."

"I was ill with fever when I made that promise. I don't consider it binding."

"Why won't you trust them to have our interests at heart?"

"Lopez was a papist. So, I'm persuaded, are both the sailor and Lebret. Naturally they'd side with their own. It was folly to send them out."

"Who else could have gone into Cuba, and returned alive? Guy Lebret is one of my best friends: I'd accept his opinion as my own. So, I'll warrant, will your colony!" Paul had shouted the last words at the open window. The knot of men on the church porch could not help hearing.

Silas strode across the room to close the shutter. "My colonists take orders from me alone," he said. "I've brought them into this wilderness, and shown them ways to tame it—"

"Do you take credit for that as well?"

"As the leader, it's my right. They'll follow me, if I choose to invade Cuba."

"Issue that order now," said Paul. "Even if you had transport, you couldn't enlist a dozen men. These people came to the New World to seek a better life: they've found what they want here. We needn't argue over who made the colony prosper. Now it exists, we must build on what we have. You've already shipped home a fortune in ambergris and brazilwood. In the new year, you can open up plantations for five hundred settlers. Why try for more—when you know in your heart you can't win a bigot's war?"

"Is that your name for Cromwell and his cause?"

"We aren't discussing your friend Noll, or his plans for England. No doubt we'll hear he's master there when Captain Sperry arrives. This is still a crown colony: you signed the articles that organized it, like all the others. I hope you haven't forgotten their content."

Silas sat down heavily at his worktable. It was not the first time they had debated the meaning of the *Articles and Orders of the Company of Eleutherian Adventurers,* the imposing document each settler had signed in Bristol. One of its most important provisions (inserted over the bitter disapproval of Obadiah Lambert and some others) assured each member of equal standing, regardless of his religion or his former station in England. It was true that Silas had been elected as leader: he and the group of elders who advised him were—in a very real sense—the rulers on Eleuthera. The historic clause remained, a milestone on mankind's long road to freedom. True, it had been inserted in the articles solely to drum up recruits for the *Adventurer's* first voyage. But Silas knew better than to flout it, even in this moment of fanatic blindness.

"There's a fortune in gold at the Havana," he said thickly. "Every man here has heard of it. Surely that's a powerful inducement."

"You'd use such bait to further God's work?" Paul asked incredulously.

"The Crusaders did."

"Don't forget how the Crusades ended."

"What would you have me do, Paul? Turn my back on duty, simply because your French friend's a coward?"

"Admit the obvious, Silas. You've no power to make war now— and no authority to quit this island until Cromwell gives you leave. I insist you stand firm here, and defend what we have."

"*Insist?* Do you realize this is sedition?"

"I call it common sense. I'm trying to save your leadership, before it's in hopeless jeopardy."

For once, Silas had been outfaced. Paul knew he had won (for a time, at least) when the leader leaned forward in his chair, and buried his face in his hands. These spells of near-hysteria were familiar: Paul knew how brief they could be.

"Why must you reach for the impossible?" he asked quickly. "Can't you trust me to defend your interests?"

"How can I trust you—when you go back on your word? You promised to stay clear of that hussy at the tavern."

"The promise has been kept, Silas."

"You've been meeting on the Atlantic beach."

So Ralph Welles had tattled after all. About to brand the surveyor as a Peeping Tom, Paul choked down the accusation when he saw that his brother had gone white to the lips. Lili had said that Silas had spied on her from the watchtower. Was it possible that he, too, had trailed her to the beach—and watched her sport naked in the surf?

"Who was your informant, Silas?"

"Does it matter—since you've resumed carnal relations?"

"I've done nothing of the sort," said Paul. "I've kept my word, hard though you're finding it to believe. I'll go on keeping it until I leave the island. Take that much on faith, or we're done."

Silas looked up with haggard eyes. "I've heard that all of Porter's wenches plan to go back on the *Adventurer*. Will you join them?"

"That's my present intention."

"What if I refuse you permission to depart? Those women have immortal souls. They're worth saving, no less than your own. I'm not this easily beaten, Paul."

Once again, Paul had the conviction that he was hearing words in a nightmare. "Why ask *us* to repent?" he demanded. "Lili's done her tour of duty here—and done it well. So have I. If repentance is in order, it's on your side. Don't force me to tell you the reason."

Silas raised his fist, and Paul braced for the blow. It was a long time since his brother had struck him in anger—and today he was glad to provoke the assault. The fist dropped, as a long-drawn call sounded from the watchtower. It was the voice of Marco, on sentry duty.

"Sail ho!"

Silas burst from the cabin to gain the ramparts in a bound. Paul was only a stride behind. From that elevation, which commanded a clear view of the sea beyond the harbor mouth, he could catch the glint of sunlight on canvas. The vessel lay well outside the last reef: there was something familiar about her rig.

"Is it the *Adventurer,* Marco?"

The Genoese, eye glued to the telescope, leaned out from his perch. "No, *dottore.* It's the vessel we met at sea. What was her name—the *Falcon?*"

A sigh of dismay swept through the stockade. For the first time, Paul realized that the cabins had emptied en masse at Marco's shout. The seaward ramparts were black with heads. Along the shore, a half-hundred colonists, their work forgotten, shaded their eyes against the sun glare and stared fearfully to the west.

"What's the man saying?" asked Silas. "Is it the corsair?"

Paul climbed the tower stair. When Marco handed over the spyglass, he saw that the lookout had spoken truly. Though she was prudent enough to show no colors, and was holding course with only a spinnaker and a foresail, there was no mistaking Captain Jeremy Hood's vessel.

"It's our friend the buccaneer, Silas."

"Is he moving closer?"

"He won't dare—without a channel marker to guide him." After the *Dolphin* had sailed, the buoys had been taken in as a precaution against the autumn storms. Lacking those vital guides, no ship of the *Falcon's* size could risk a nearer approach. The cannon that had just boomed from her stern was obviously intended as a signal of her arrival. At that distance, it was impossible to fire on the settlement, even had the shape of the shoreline permitted a clear view.

The smoke from the signal cannon had scarcely lifted when a longboat dropped from the corsair's stern davits and set out briskly for the land. Paul breathed deeply with relief when he saw the men at the oars were unarmed. Captain Hood, a glass of fashion in the stern sheets, had fixed a white pennon to a spare oar, which he was holding aloft in lieu of a flagstaff.

"Is he planning an attack?"

Silas was still on the rampart below. Curiously enough, he had made no attempt to climb the tower for a better view: he had spoken with one eye on the group of Puritans that surrounded him. It was evident that this was a warrior without a battle plan. Though he was too proud to ask advice, he seemed almost painfully eager for guidance.

"He's showing a white flag," said Paul. "At the worst, that means a parley. It'll do no harm to unlimber our cannon and prove we're prepared to repel boarders. While we're about it, we can sound a general quarters, and stand-to with muskets."

He had spoken quietly, for Silas' ears alone. His brother's bewilderment, he observed, was not caused by panic. Rather, it was the honest shock of the dreamer—immersed, but a moment ago, in a vision of empire, and now forced to descend to earth, with no interval for adjustment.

Once he had grasped Paul's strategy, Silas gave his orders in ringing tones. It was heartening to note the stockade's response, as each man hurried to his post.

Driven at top speed by six pairs of oars, the *Falcon's* longboat was soon near enough for hailing. Hood, steering with easy competence in the maze of shoals, could not have been cooler in his own roadstead. His hawk's eye, sweeping the harbor mouth and the solid palmetto blockhouse that faced it, sparkled with genuine good humor as he lifted a hand in salute.

"Let me sound him out," Paul suggested. "Remember, he doesn't know you by sight. It may be an advantage." He moved from stockade to gate, lifting his hat by way of response before he strode boldly into the cleared space before the ramparts. A small dock had been built here, to accommodate the fishing boats that served the cay. Paul reached the end in time to catch the longboat's painter. The twelve oarsmen, reversing their blades, brought the slender vessel to a stop, as smartly as though it had been a king's barge.

The maneuver had been accomplished in a silence that could

not be called threatening—but Paul could feel the tingle of goose flesh on his arms while he made the line fast. He was in no immediate danger, with the blockhouse guns behind him and the corsairs unarmed. The probe of their eyes was no less menacing when they sprang ashore, with Hood in the van. Even when the debonair captain held out a hand in greeting, Paul could hardly feel assured. The man's smile had been no less mocking in their first exchange at sea.

"So we meet again, Doctor," he said, in a voice smooth as cream. On surface, it was a salutation from friend to friend. Paul saw it would be fatal to respond otherwise.

"Do you come in peace, Captain Hood?"

"Would I fly this pennon otherwise?"

"In that case, welcome to the English colony of Eleuthera. May I ask why we're honored by this visit?"

"Shall we call it the curiosity of a neighbor, Doctor?"

"Does that mean you're still based on New Providence?"

"In my trade," said Hood, "we don't require a permanent base. New Providence happens to be an ideal careening ground. You'll generally find us at home there, however. I'm surprised *you* haven't come calling sooner."

"You broke ground in the Bahamas, Captain. Good manners would suggest you pay the first call. Besides, as you'll observe, we've been too busy founding this outpost of empire to look beyond."

"Do I gather you've outlived the plague?"

"Even before we'd landed, we'd thrown it off completely. Since then, we've enjoyed good health."

"May I compliment you on your industry—and your progress?" Hood's voice carried clearly to the ramparts. The sweeping bow he offered Paul was intended for the watchers above them—including Silas, who stood with folded arms and a face of granite.

"These islands are ideal for colonists," said Paul. "It's obvious we've prospered. You'll also observe we're prepared to defend that prosperity."

Hood's glance took in the great rectangles of brazilwood set out to dry along the shore. "You've sent cargoes of this stuff to England, I take it?"

"And a fortune in ambergris," Paul announced boldly. Already, it was evident that the buccaneers had observed the departure of both the *Adventurer* and the *Dolphin:* the decks of both vessels had been stacked high with the reddish dyewood—which, if not quite so valuable as the logwood of the Mosquito Coast to the south, was still precious enough. Neither cargo would have been of interest to a pirate—who, by the very nature of his calling, could deal in little else but gold. It was still hard to imagine why the two vessels had been allowed to depart unmolested. Or why Hood (if his designs were still hostile) had put off this visit until today.

"I take it you hope to be self-sufficient in the near-future, Doctor."

"We can make that boast now," said Paul.

"Do you expect other ships?"

"We're expecting a second group of colonists daily, with a man-of-war as escort." The risk of speaking a near-truth, Paul felt, was worth taking.

Hood's handsome eyes rolled skyward: the sensuous lips, framed so elegantly in his courtier's beard, dropped in a laughing pout. "Evidently I did well to grant you a *laissez-passer* when we met at sea," he said. "With such powerful friends in your camp, I might have fared badly otherwise. Do you still think these islands spacious enough to hold us both?"

"Of course. Eleuthera will satisfy our needs for years to come. We've no wish to extend our domain."

Again, Paul had spoken boldly, with a silent prayer that Silas (still a stone-cold observer on the ramparts) would not interrupt. The silence behind him was his reward: Hood's level look and the shrug of his velvet-clad shoulders were proof that he intended to play the game by his host's rules.

"As a model guest," he said, "I'll accept that avowal, and hope it holds true in a year's time. Perhaps you'll do as much for me, when you visit New Providence."

"You've come to declare an armistice?"

"Better than that, Doctor. Like a red Indian from Virginia, I'm offering to smoke a pipe of peace. As I say, you'll find proof of my intentions when you visit my careening ground."

There was no time to ponder the corsair's emphasis on New Providence. Paul had studied the not-too-detailed chart of the island, which lay some twenty leagues to the west of Eleuthera. The map suggested that an excellent deep-water harbor was its principal feature, accessible from both east and west. Since it was central to the whole vast archipelago of the Bahamas, it was ideal to Hood's purpose. Fishing far to the west of his home port, Paul had had occasional glimpses of the island's chunky silhouette against the horizon. He had yearned to press on and explore its coasts in detail—but prudence had dictated otherwise. Now (for whatever motive) it was evident that Hood was eager to welcome him there. With each flourish, the man's enigma deepened.

"I'd like nothing better than a glimpse of New Providence," Paul said. "Today, it's our turn to play host. Let me present you to our leader."

Marco and Lebret were waiting at the stockade gate, with a double squad of sentinels, each with his musket grounded. Paul stood aside to permit Hood a detailed inspection of the stout palmetto gates, and the crude but sharp-pointed portcullis that hung above them. At his nod, the crew of the whaleboat (who had listened open-mouthed to the exchange of civilities on the dock) shambled in their captain's wake—nut-brown giants with tarred pigtails, a rolling gait ill suited to land, and hands that seemed to fidget for the absent cutlass at their belts.

Silas had come down from the ramparts to take his stand on the church porch. Obadiah Lambert (hands folded, as usual, in the wide sleeves of his robe) loomed just behind him. The doors had been thrown wide to show the church proper—a place of bare walls, benches formed of split logs, and a raised platform in lieu of an altar, where it was the elders' customs to pour forth the endless lectures that passed for sermons. The tableau, of course, had been arranged deliberately. With the trappings of his faith as background, Silas had grown a foot in stature. When Paul stepped forward to make his presentation, his brother's frown suggested Moses on the mountaintop.

"Captain Jeremy Hood of the *Falcon*," said Paul. "This is my brother, Captain—Silas Sutton, the leader of the Eleutherians."

Hood's bow was worthy of a levee. "Your servant, Master Sutton," he said. "It's good of you to receive me so readily. As I've just told your brother, you won't regret it."

"Are you a pirate, sir?"

Hood took the stern question coolly. "As a harrier of Spanish shipping, I give myself a somewhat higher rating. In fact, I've our king's permit to follow such a trade. As an Englishman, I fly that country's colors when I do battle. Call me a privateer, please —we'll stay friends longer."

"Isn't it true that you threatened to sink us on our voyage here?"

"Only because I mistrusted your intentions. For all I knew at the time, you meant to set up as my rival. I've since seen my error. Will you accept my apology?"

"What is the purpose of this visit?"

"To prove my friendship's real."

"How can I be sure you aren't spying out ways to destroy us later?"

"My visit is a peaceful one, Master Sutton. I'll give you my word never to molest Eleuthera, if you will do as much for New Providence."

The offer, spoken in a ringing tone of sincerity that carried to the last listener in the stockade, shocked Paul into a quick re-appraisal of Silas. Never had his brother seemed more serenely assured—or more remote: the image of the prophet on Sinai per-sisted as he turned to Obadiah. The question he asked was word-less, but the spiritual leader rumbled into speech instantly.

"What is your faith, Captain Hood? Are you Established Church?"

"I lean toward the Puritan persuasion, sir. Naturally, I guaran-tee religious freedom to all who serve me—even as you do on Eleuthera."

Utterly bewildered as he was by this change of front, Paul could see that the buccaneer's barefaced espousal of the faith had impressed both Silas and Obadiah. For an instant, they withdrew to the end of the church porch, where they conferred in whispers. When Silas returned alone, Paul saw that the latter had won his point—and his audience.

"Pro tem, Captain Hood," he said, "we'll take your word as a gentleman that you've spoken truly. You may visit our settlement, and discover for yourself we're here to stay. My brother will serve as your guide."

Hood bowed from the waist. "You won't regret this decision."

"I've reached no decision, as yet, but I'll ask both of you to return here within the hour. We'll see then if we can strike a bargain." Watching Obadiah trail Silas dutifully from the church porch, aware that Ralph Welles and several other elders had detached themselves from the staring mass of pilgrims, Paul could guess his brother's purpose. Hood had declared himself an enemy of Spain—and Silas had all but accepted the claim. Hood had also offered an alliance, based on mutual hatred of the dons— and Paul knew his brother was burning to accept.

Bracing himself against that numbing certainty, Paul led the way through the stockade gates. The pirates followed in a knot. At a command from Hood, the oarsmen returned to the longboat. Then, linking arms with his guide, the buccaneer strode gaily down the beach that led to the hand ferry.

"This needn't take long, Doctor," he said. "My main purpose is to give those Bible-backs a chance to agree among themselves. All I really want is a glass of Giles Porter's best brandy while I wait. I've seen enough of your handiwork to convince me of your competence."

"Who told you of Giles Porter?"

"You'll hear that in good time, I assure you. Isn't it true that your brother dreams of storming the Havana—and hopes to use me as his battering-ram?"

"I can't read his mind, Captain."

"Forgive me if I differ. You can read him like a book—and so can I. I'll tell you this much now: where the dons are concerned, we see eye to eye. It just happens that my plan for besting them is somewhat more practical—"

"How can you know this much about Silas?"

The hand ferry, responding to Paul's tug on the cable, had crossed the channel to touch the cay. On the far shore, the Anglican colonists were clustered three deep in their eagerness to gawk at the buccaneer. Hood held up a soothing palm at Paul's question, and dropped his voice to a whisper.

"Two facts for now, Doctor: the rest will keep. The *Adventurer* is fast on a shoal just off New Providence. I'm leaving her there, and harming no one aboard—until I've made sure your brother speaks my language."

"*What are you saying?*"

"The gospel truth." Hood made another swift gesture of peace. "Don't ask me more. My time is limited, and I can't tell the same story twice. You'll have my whole thoughts when we sit down with Master Sutton—and not before."

For the next half-hour, Captain Jeremy Hood kept his word.

Strolling among the palm-thatched huts in the cedar grove, lolling in the tavern with Lili Porter to fill his glass and Giles sketching improbable adventures at his side, he remained the soul of courtesy—and a conspirator whose defenses were impregnable. After a few tentative efforts, Paul made no further move to breach them. . . . The buccaneer, he gathered, was sincere in his offer of an alliance. He could believe him when he vowed that the people aboard the stranded *Adventurer* (so far) were in no danger of their lives. It was little enough, but Paul clung to these verities while he waited for Hood to show his hand.

Most of the colonists had passed the tavern door in that half-hour to stare at the pirate. Hood took such interest as was his due, exchanging bows with all the women and signaling a man from time to time, with a shouted offer to drink his health. As glass succeeded glass, Paul waited hopefully for the pirate's tongue to loosen—but it was evident that the man had hollow legs, as well as an iron will.

Both Lili and Giles were aware of Paul's agitation, though he had not dared express it openly. They stayed close, obeying the buccaneer's whim and keeping up a running comment that was a fair substitute for conversation. Paul's own silence weighed on his brain like lead. When Hood rose at last (offering his hand to the innkeeper and thanking Lili with a resounding buss) it was hard to maintain his detachment. He spoke at last, while they stood again on the hand ferry, and his voice was an echo of his mood.

"D'you enjoy torture, Captain? Or is it a by-product of your trade?"

Hood accepted the query with a sunny smile. "Don't take my little mystery too hard, Doctor. It's only a way of testing you."

"What's your price for the salvage of the *Adventurer?* Tell me now, so I can advise Silas—"

"From what I hear, your brother usually rejects your counsel. Why bombard him with more? This time, I'll do the advising."

"Meaning, of course, that you'll give orders, and expect us to obey."

"Believe me, Doctor, I'm an easy taskmaster."

They did not speak again while they retraced the path to the stockade. Silas was seated alone on the church porch—with maps and papers before him on a desk, along with an inkpot and a sander. Two other chairs, placed at opposite sides of this table, suggesting that Paul was to be included in the meeting. The fact that the other elders were absent was proof that the leader had been given carte blanche. Silas' episcopal dignity, and the gesture that brought Paul and his companion to the porch, were part of his confidence.

"You're prompt, Captain Hood," he said. "Does that mean you're ready to strike a bargain?"

The buccaneer flung himself into one of the chairs. "Bargain is a rather large word," he said. "If I used it just now, it was to save your face. Actually, I'm here to make you an offer—with no alternative. Accept it, and we can help each other greatly. Refuse, and you're dead as mutton."

"Perhaps you'll be good enough to explain your insolence?"

"That's another word I'd advise you to forget," said Hood. "I'm here on a mission of peace, and bluster won't help you. We're both aware there's no harm in your thunderbolts."

The leader's jaw knotted, but he gave no other evidence of anger. "Leave off sparring, then, and tell us what you want."

"Perhaps we should let your brother speak," said Hood. "Tell him what you know, Doctor. It should clear the air."

Silas sat unstirring while Paul repeated the news of the *Adventurer*. The words were hammer blows, but he made no effort to soften them.

"How do we know he isn't lying?" asked Silas hoarsely.

"Sail back with me to New Providence, if you have doubts," said the buccaneer. "Speak to Captain Sperry, and convince yourself of his plight. There's still time to agree to my terms."

Silas ignored the pirate's interruption. "Answer me, Paul. Is this a trick?"

"I think not," said Paul. "I won't commit myself until I hear more."

"Your skepticism does you credit, Doctor," said Hood. "I'm prepared to tell the whole story—on one condition. Until I've done, you mustn't interrupt."

Silas' fist smote the table. "*That* offer, at least, I'll accept. Try to be brief."

Hood nodded and began to speak—easily, yet with a certain oracular flourish. The tale he told, by its very simplicity, compelled Paul's belief. A mishap of this nature (he told himself) could not be invented. Once he had grasped its import, he could hardly blame the buccaneer for exploiting the situation to the hilt.

The *Adventurer* had been caught in the high wind that had lashed the beaches of Eleuthera two days ago. At New Providence, the blow had been close to gale strength. After the storm had roared south, a pirate lookout had reported the vessel stranded on a hogback, within sight of the *Falcon*'s own careening ground, and easily accessible by longboat. When Captain Sperry hoisted a reversed standard as a signal of distress, Hood had lost no time in approaching the stranded ship. Though the seas were still high, he had sent two of his mates aboard to learn if the vessel could be floated free—and a shipwright to measure the extent of the damage.

Captain Sperry, he found, had been fighting bad weather for the last week of his voyage. When the storm struck, he had been unable to hold course: in the end, he had run before the wind, hoping to escape disaster as he entered uncharted waters. The grounding, when it came, had been a fortunate accident. The hogback was solid sand—and, though the ship's keel was wedged there, no timbers had been strained. Most of the canvas was intact, thanks to Brack's seamanship and the courage of the crew. The *Adventurer* would never float free unaided: and the task of kedging would require help from the buccaneers. So much was clear to Hood when his envoys returned.

Later, Captain Sperry had allowed Hood to come aboard: it was then that he had made his first offer. His terms were simple. First, Sperry was to write a note to Master Silas Sutton—suggesting that the colony and the pirates join forces in their common war against the dons. Once Master Sutton had accepted the suggestion, the pirates would kedge the *Adventurer* into deep water, and guarantee her a safe crossing to Eleuthera.

Sperry had answered the offer with an explosion of curses, and ordered Hood to leave his ship. The offer had been repeated next day, with similar results. This time, however, Sperry had agreed to sit behind his guns until Hood had called at Eleuthera, to make the same offer to Silas. . . .

"Your captain said he'd accept a letter, signed by you," Hood told Silas. He picked up a quill pen from the desk. "Give me that order now, and we'll begin kedging tomorrow. We can't risk waiting for another storm."

"Are you sure you've told me everything?"

"Only the essentials. You asked me to be brief."

"Was there a Mistress Trevor aboard?"

Hood's eye brightened. "A most charming lady, Master Sutton. I gather she's a kind of guardian angel for your enterprise. Captain Sperry insisted she join both our meetings."

"Did she send me any message?"

"Only that you're to use your own judgment. Like your ship's captain, she'll abide by your decision."

Silas turned again to his brother. "What do you make of this?"

"I think we should free the ship," said Paul. "No matter what the cost."

"Spoken like a man of wit, Doctor," the pirate exclaimed. "Granted, you've little choice, if you mean to save over a hundred lives. It still shows courage to admit defeat so readily."

"You may keep your opinions to yourself, Captain," said Silas. "My brother and I will decide this between us."

"You've decided now," said Hood affably. "Why trouble to deny it?"

"Suppose I write a letter to Captain Sperry, and permit you to deliver it? How do I know you won't seize our ship, once you've freed her?"

"You've my word I'll give the *Adventurer* safe-conduct here. 'Tis another thing you must take on faith."

"What will you require of us thereafter?"

"I've told you that. Peace between our camps—so we can make common cause against Spain."

"Is that all?"

"Quite all, Master Sutton."

"You'll levy no tribute, to pay for your alliance?"

"Not on fellow Englishmen."

Paul had not trusted himself to approach the conference table. Perched on the porch rail, he studied Silas across Hood's shoulder. So far, he could scarcely believe their own good fortune. If the buccaneer meant what he said (and there was no apparent cause to doubt him) his plans and Silas' own fanatic scheme had dovetailed perfectly. Fearful that his brother would betray his exultation, he was relieved to note that Silas' black-browed frown was unchanged. When it came to bargaining, Hood had met his match.

"D'you propose we fight the Spaniards together?"

"No, Master Sutton."

"I'm a soldier of the Lord, Captain Hood. If you mean to war against papists, I'll go with you into battle."

"Did you think I planned to attack the Havana? If you did, you're grossly mistaken: I'd be blown out of the water."

"Even if we joined forces?"

"Killing Spaniards is my trade. It's a way of life I can't advise you to pursue. A dead martyr's of no use to me whatever."

"How can I serve your purpose, then?"

"I want you to go on here as before—making your colony more prosperous with each ship that arrives from England." Hood turned his flashing smile on Paul. "Do our thoughts coincide so far, Doctor?"

"To the letter," said Paul. Beginning to catch a dim outline of Hood's purpose, he signaled to Silas to hold his tongue.

"As you've gathered," said the buccaneer, "I've been observing you closely. I've also learned a good deal aboard the *Adventurer*. Forgive me if I speak bluntly Master Sutton—but I consider you a misguided idealist whose luck can't endure forever. If it weren't for your hardheaded brother—and some men of good will who've aided him—you'd have foundered long since on the rock of your own obstinacy."

"Don't waste your breath on slander, Captain."

"I'm also informed that London sets great store by Eleuthera. One false move on your part, and Cromwell's bound to remove you. I can speed that removal tomorrow by seizing your ship and cutting down every soul aboard. So far, I've held my hand: I think you should appreciate my forbearance."

"I'll grant you can dispose of the *Adventurer* as you see fit," said Silas. "That's a lucky fluke. Try to take this stronghold, and you'll find the going hot."

Paul held his breath as their glances warred: this time, he was sure his brother had overplayed his hand.

"I'm trying my best to teach you a lesson in humility, Master Sutton," said Hood. "In your place, I'd admit the game is up."

"Just what do you wish of me?"

"There's no need for sackcloth and ashes," said the pirate. "All I want is a frank avowal of your limitations. If you're determined to play the crusader, you'll lose your life in Cuba. What's worse, your usefulness to me will be ended. I'm asking you to promise you'll cultivate your Eleutherian garden, and risk no outside adventures."

"What if Cromwell sends different orders?"

"I'm told Old Noll's a first-rate fighting man," said Hood. "I hardly think he'll ask you to capture the Havana with a popgun. If he does, it's still my wish that you ignore the order."

"I can't promise that."

"Not even to save your betrothed?"

Silas rose from his chair—and, for a dreadful moment, Paul feared he meant to grapple with Hood in mortal combat. When his brother sank back with a great cry of frustration, he saw the battle of wits had ended. Inevitably (since he held every card) Hood had emerged the winner.

"I'll keep to Eleuthera as you bid me," said Silas, in a choked voice. "I still can't fathom your purpose."

"Nothing could be simpler, Master Sutton. Whether you realize it or not, in your innocent fashion you're a threat to Spain. Or should I say an insult the alcalde in the Havana can't endure forever?"

"Do you mean they'd attack us?"

"It's only a question of time before the blow falls," said Hood. "If it comes in force—as I've already remarked—you'll be dead as so much mutton, unless help reaches you in time."

"You'd defend us, then?"

"Yes, Master Sutton. I'll defend you to the death, for God and country, if you'll play your own part in the meantime. Can you ask for more?"

"What must we do here, if you won't let us fight?"

"I've told you. Feather your nest, like so many doves, and wait for the Spanish cat to pounce. Meanwhile, I'll post my lookouts and bide my time. Once he's in the open, I'll engage the enemy on my own terms. I've yet to see a galleon I can't outsail—and outgun."

"What if he sends more than one?"

"I've other ships beside the *Falcon* I can call on at will. Frankly, I don't think the dons will send more than a single man-of-war to dispose of you."

"Spain wants no war with England now," Paul reminded the pirate. "They may leave us in peace."

"I'll take that gamble," said Hood. "In fact, I'll give ten to one the attack comes in the new year. If I'm right, I'll grow even richer—with at least one gold-leaf admiral to hold for ransom. If I'm wrong, I'll still have served as a watchdog. With my privateer's patent on file in Whitehall, Cromwell can hardly be indifferent to either service."

Silas leaned across his table, balancing on his fists, and studying Hood feature by feature—as though he could not quite believe what he saw. It was his final gesture of pride, and he made the most of it.

"So we're doomed without you, Captain? To survive at all, I must seal a pact with murderers?"

"Killers in the king's name, Master Sutton. Don't judge my crews too harshly. Remember, you were eager to do likewise."

"I'd give a great deal to believe you're as upright as you seem," said Silas.

"Why not make the effort?"

"Give me a moment before I answer."

The pirate nodded—and took snuff from a golden case, which he produced from a pocket in one of his lace-crusted sleeves. The gesture revealed a poniard nested there like an adder. Following his brother to the end of the church porch, Paul wondered if the gesture had been made deliberately.

"How can we be sure he'll honor his pledges?" Silas asked.

"We can't be. Instinct tells me he's on our side at the moment. It's the best we can hope for."

"In his view, we're bait to lure the Spanish north. The thought's intolerable."

"Rise above self for once, forget this blow to your pride. One hundred Englishmen are balanced on a shoal off New Providence awaiting your verdict."

"I'll do what I can to rescue them. You know that."

"Stop hedging then—and prove it. Anne's out there too—waiting for help."

"Will you go to New Providence in the shallop, and bring her back?"

Paul breathed deep: he had expected the question. "Yes—if Hood will permit it."

"How can he refuse, if he's in earnest?"

Silas turned on his heel, and returned to the conference table. In another moment, he had dashed off a brief note and sanded it. Hood, who had watched the brothers' colloquy with bored eyes, reached out his hand for the missive, but the leader of the Eleutherians withheld it a moment more.

"This will get your kedgers aboard the *Adventurer* without bloodshed," he said coldly. "My brother will deliver it to Captain Sperry as an earnest of my intentions."

"The doctor's welcome aboard the *Falcon*," said Hood. "He can visit our careening ground while we work your ship free."

"It may be a longer task than you imagine. I'd prefer to have Mistress Trevor safely in this stockade with the least delay."

"Is this a test of my intentions?" asked Hood.

"Call it a proof of devotion to a lady I'm making my wife."

"In your place, I'd go myself."

"I'm leader of this flock, Captain. I can't desert it now."

Hood offered a sweeping salute to each brother, then adjusted his hat at a rakish angle. "You're a man of stern principles, Master Sutton," he said. "I can admire such devotion to duty—even though I seldom practice it. Follow the *Falcon* by all means, Doctor, but I can't wait for you. We've barely time to fetch our own anchorage by nightfall."

Marco and a Greek sailor named Pronas (who had come to Eleuthera on the *Dolphin*) volunteered to serve as the shallop's crew. Paul crossed on the hand ferry to make his report at the tavern while the vessel was being hastily readied for sea. He knew that the close-mouthed elders, keeping their own counsel, would try to conceal the reason for his departure. It was only fair that the whole island should hear of the bargain Hood had struck with Silas.

He told his story on the porch of the inn, with Lebret, Giles, and Lili as an approving audience. Expecting their endorsement, he felt his spirits lift: strange though it had seemed at first blush, the pact was obviously to the colonists' advantage, if Hood honored it.

"For once, I think your brother's acted wisely," said the Frenchman. "Apparently our friend the buccaneer has put him in his place."

"Who knows, Guy? The dons must be aware of our strength: they may never risk an attack. We could have real peace here, now that Silas has given his word to put aside the sword—"

"Meaning that Hood's visit could be our greatest boon so far?"

"That's what I'm daring to hope at the moment. Do you share that opinion, Giles?"

"I've played the rogue myself before I turned honest," said the innkeeper. "So I'm familiar with the species. It's clear this fellow's using us for his own ends: he leads a wolf pack that's ruled by club and fang. All the same, I believe he'll honor this promise—simply because it's to his advantage."

Lili spoke without prompting. "I liked his looks, Paul—he's all man. Father's right. Even though he's a rogue, he seems an honest one."

The two sailors had brought the shallop inshore, and had begun to raise the mainsail. When he left the tavern to join them, Paul was not too surprised to hear a swish of skirts behind him. He had expected Lili to follow him, for reasons of her own.

"I wish your brother had sent someone else on this errand," she said. "Why must you always be fetching his lady?"

"Join me, if you like," he offered. "You can investigate the charms of our buccaneer ally further."

"You know that's impossible now."

"In Heaven's name why?"

Lili had already waded knee-deep in the harbor, steadying the gunwale of the shallop while Paul got aboard. Thinking she had changed her mind, he extended a hand to help her overside. On the tavern porch, she had seemed calm enough. Now, her eyes were wide with fear.

"Would Mistress Trevor welcome my presence?" she asked.

"Of course she would. It's less than a day's sail, in a craft this light. Your father can spare you for once—"

"*He'd* never let you take me," said Lili.

Paul followed the direction of her glance. Silas was standing on the palisade with folded arms: his eyes were fixed on the shallop, and the tableau of good-by at the water's edge. He was flanked by his elders, who were watching as intently. Not a man among them made a sign of Godspeed. When a ragged cheer was lifted by the watchers onshore, Silas lifted his chin angrily, as though he intended to shout for silence. . . . This, Paul reflected, was a galling moment for the leader. Forced to accept Hood's terms, obliged (by the same logic) to stand by while his brother sailed out to rescue his betrothed, Silas had good cause for the gloom that hung above him.

"Shall we put him to the test?"

Lili shook her head. "He'd stop me at the harbor mouth."

"Perhaps you're right. Keep your courage up. I'll be back tomorrow, if this wind holds."

"I've been brave enough while you were here, Paul. Once you're gone, I'll be facing him alone."

"Lebret and your father will protect you. So will every man on the island."

"Not the men on Cupid's Cay," said Lili. "Don't forget *they* make our laws."

"What can they do to you?"

"I'm not sure. But I know they're plotting something."

"In a week's time, you'll be en route to England."

"Even then, he may not let me go."

"If he doesn't, he'll have me to reckon with. We planned to be shipmates—remember?" As he spoke, Paul recalled Silas' fanatic refusal to let Lili sail until he had won the contest for her soul. The girl had sensed that threat, all too clearly.

"He'll never let us leave together, Paul. You know that."

"We'll argue that question when I return." The mainsail had swung between them and the watchers on the palisade: he bent to kiss Lili quickly, glad to note that her brief spasm of fear had subsided.

"Don't worry, *chéri*," she whispered. "I'll keep my courage up. Just come back quickly—and bring his lady with you. Maybe she'll have ways to redeem him from himself. If she does, she can't arrive too soon."

# CAT ISLAND

CAPTAIN SPERRY looked down from the bow of the *Adventurer*, to study the buoys that marked his first pair of kedge anchors. Placed at the ends of two long cables extending from the hawseholes of the stranded vessel, they would do their part in freeing her from the hogback on which her stern remained firmly wedged. A third cable, joining the *Adventurer*'s capstan to the *Falcon* (now riding at anchor two hundred feet to the east) would supply the major tug to rock the English ship free. Once the sails were spread on both vessels, the maneuver needed only a following wind to assure its success. When Paul had come aboard last evening, a half-hour before sundown, Hood's salvage crew had waited for daylight to begin their work. Now, with the sun lifting in a cloudless sky and a freshening wind from the west, it seemed evident they would succeed.

"Sure you won't sail home with us, Doctor?"

Paul moved to the weather rail to study the wind gauge. "Mistress Trevor prefers to finish this voyage by shallop," he said. "We can hardly disappoint a lady who's contributed so much to our welfare."

"We'll miss her aboard," said Sperry. "I still wish she'd elected to end her voyage with me."

"Even if you rock free today, you must put into Hood's anchorage to check your timbers. With this wind, the shallop can raise Eleuthera before nightfall."

"I'd make no predictions too readily in these waters," said Sperry. "You could find yourself becalmed by noon. Or fighting for your life in coral."

Paul studied the gauge a second time. It was true that the wind was brisk—and a line of squalls had smudged the southeast horizon since dawn. But the shallop had handled easily in near-gales off Eleuthera: both Marco and Pronas had proved their worth on the westward run. It seemed needlessly cautious to linger on the *Adventurer,* when a dozen compelling reasons urged him to depart at once.

"Tell me one thing before I leave," he said. "Is Hood acting in good faith?"

"When we first parleyed," said Sperry, "I'll admit I suspected him. Memories of our first encounter were still green. Now, it seems, he's decided your brother's flock are colonists, not rival bandits. In your place, I'd do a great deal to preserve that belief."

Paul nodded soberly. "Do you think he's right about the dons? Will an attack from the Havana come in time?"

"It's the logic of war, Doctor. These islands are mostly terra incognita—and Spain would like to keep 'em thus. Naturally, they can't police the whole archipelago and burn out the pirates' careening grounds. The best they can do is convoy their plate fleet, and hold losses down. A flourishing colony on their doorstep is quite another matter. They may not risk an open break with England to wipe it out. But I'll stake my wig against your brother's poll you'll see action of some kind before the new year ends."

"Those were Hood's sentiments too."

"Then my opinion's confirmed. He's an Englishman first and a corsair second. You can count on his help—so long as Master Silas doesn't betray his trust." The bluff old seaman hesitated, then went on firmly. "There's one thing I haven't mentioned, Doctor. I'm bringing a sealed letter from Cromwell."

"Surely he wouldn't order an assault on Cuba."

"There's no better general in the field today. But one never knows, with these religious zealots. I *do* know that yet another ship will follow me in short order: the *Advance,* Abner Shaw the master. She's a ship of the line, one of the best in her class. There'll be troops aboard, and extra cannon. No one could say how many when we left Bristol."

"Perhaps it's only a force to defend the island."

"Let's hope that's the intention. The dons may think differently, when they hear of that extra sailing. They may even decide to strike before Eleuthera grows too strong."

"How much of this does Mistress Trevor know?"

"Only that the *Advance* is due at an early date. I haven't aired my opinions in her presence, and I hope you'll hold your tongue on this last item. Mistress Trevor's a woman of remarkable purpose. She's looking forward to a latter-day Utopia, unspoiled by greed or passion."

"She won't expect miracles, Captain."

Sperry nodded. "Granted, she has common sense to match her dream. Just don't cloud the picture in advance. Let her see Eleuthera as it really is, and form her own judgment. If this threat from Cuba's real, you can make plans for her safety later."

They were ready to leave the ship with the first light, a quiet departure that did not disturb the sleeping passengers—most of whom, exhausted by worry over their uncertain position, had sought their billets early to get what rest they could.

The wind had freshened, giving a sharp chop to the sea. Paul and his two-man crew needed all their skill to keep the shallop from smashing against the hull of the larger vessel. Anne came nimbly down the Jacob's ladder while they were still struggling with the jib. Paul saw she was wearing the same boy's clothes she had used to disguise herself in England. When she dropped into the stern sheets, the spots of color in her cheeks suggested that she remembered the intimacy of that ride from Salisbury.

"The captain said that skirts would be a nuisance on this voyage," she said. "I took him at his word."

"Hold fast until we clear the ship," Paul answered. "It's a bit tricky, in these cross-seas."

"I can take the tiller if you'll let me," she said quickly. "It's part of my training, you know."

Her hand had already closed above his on the helm: he saw at a glance that she knew what she was doing. Marco had just managed to break out the jib: the shallop steadied instantly in the chop, then glided free of the *Adventurer*. Already, it seemed entirely natural that Anne Trevor should be handling her, as easily as any man aboard.

"We'll swing around both ships before we set our course," said Paul. "I want Hood to see we're following orders."

With three pairs of hands at the mainsail, it was sheeted home in short order. The trim little vessel, with the bit in her teeth, bowled along smartly, to skirt the anchor chain of the *Falcon*. Viewed from this angle, the pirate ship was a dark cliff against the sunrise, her gun ports innocent of cannon, her sails still furled. It was only when the voyagers ran in her lee that Paul saw the crew was already at stations. Hood, standing at the rail to check the lashing of the towline, lifted a hand in salute when they danced past—but he, too, was intent on the business at hand.

"Shall we hold this tack?" asked Anne.

"We'll risk it for a while. I'd like to see a little of New Providence before we head for home."

Last evening, when he had approached the *Adventurer*, Paul had been careful to keep the ship between him and the land: until he was sure of Hood, he could not seem to spy on the pirate stronghold. This seemed a golden opportunity to assess its strength. Anne held a steady bead on the land, until the spout of waves on the first reef forced them to come about. As the mainsail shifted on the larboard tack, Paul saw that the buccaneers had chosen an ideal anchorage.

New Providence was now in clear view, a scant sea mile to the south. The island was much higher than Eleuthera, a chunky land mass that rose sharply from the water. Its harbor was formed by a long, palm-tufted sand bar that sheltered the roadstead on the north. Even at this distance, it was evident that the anchorage could be entered at either end, giving the pirates a maximum mobility for both attack and defense. The entrances were marked by wide swatches of blue water: there was no need to trace a dogleg channel here, no risk of grounding due to a sudden shift of wind.

Two ships were careened on the harbor side of the sand bar. They swarmed with sailors intent on their tasks of cleaning and scraping. On the island itself, a single watchtower lifted from the highest hill. Here, a lane had been cut through the dense piney woods that covered the slope, to permit easy access from the anchorage. There were no other signs of tenancy, save for a few barbecue pits along the shore. Hood had spoken truly when he declared that New Providence was only a rendezvous point, chosen for its location—which permitted swift strikes at any Spaniard who ventured in the Bahama Channel, or dared to penetrate the archipelago from the east.

"Shall we come about for another look?" asked Anne.

"I think not: the picture's complete now. We'll set our course and hope we can hold it. The wind's freshening a bit more than I like."

Anne's eyes were sparkling with excitement, but her hand on the tiller was steady. "To me, it's perfect sailing weather. I'll never thank you enough arriving when you did."

Paul's conscience urged him to admit that Silas had sent him and that (given his own choice) he would not have risked the disturbing intimacy of this small vessel. Today, his heart was too light to admit such dark thoughts. Disloyal though it might be, he wanted nothing to remind Anne that she was on her way to join his brother. . . . Fortunately, there was no time to say more. The business of setting the new tack, which would take them safely down the northern shore of New Providence, required the undivided attention of both helmsman and crew.

"We'll run south until there's deep water all around us," Paul said when he rejoined Anne in the stern. "Our first obstacle is a string of reefs to the east. We should be free of that danger in another hour—with room to spare when we beat upwind for Cupid's Cay."

"I've spent a good deal of time with Captain Sperry's charts," Anne said. "Shouldn't we bear more to the east to fetch Eleuthera?"

"We can't risk it yet. There's another string of reefs between the two islands. They could be dangerous if those line squalls come our way."

He nodded toward the dark weather marching across the broad sound that separated New Providence from Eleuthera. A little earlier, those smudges had centered on the southern horizon: now they had shifted to the northeast. Normally they would have moved on before the shallop could cross their path. At the distance, there was no way to judge their depth.

"Suppose we can't handle upwind?" Anne asked.

"In that case, we'll continue south and look for shelter on Cat Island. It isn't too far below Eleuthera, and we're equipped for camping."

The shallop heeled under a gust, sending a blanket of spindrift down the weather rail. Anne laughed exultantly as the bowsprit took a giddy dive, then steadied on course again. "I've waited a whole lifetime for this. The Bahamas are everything I hoped they'd be—so far."

Paul pretended to be busy with the chart. It was significant that Anne had made no mention of Silas as yet—but the sudden contraction of his heart was no less poignant. It was no help to tell himself that she would approve all he had done on Eleuthera—or that her presence, after these months of waiting, made his labors worth-while. At that moment, the success of the colony was only part of a bitter burden he had assumed for her sake—and must now relinquish.

"This may be our last chance to talk, Paul—"

He looked up from the map, aware that her voice had sobered. "What can we say, that we haven't said already?"

"I want to know everything."

"I had your letter from the *Dolphin*. I followed instructions and sent no answer. Didn't that say enough?"

"Only that Silas had been saved from his own folly. From what you told Captain Sperry last night, I gather the threat from New Providence has receded."

"Our leader will keep his word to Hood," said Paul, not too bitterly. "He'll have no option there."

"Then we *do* have a chance to survive?"

"An excellent chance—if we continue to keep our heads."

"I'll keep mine, Paul. Once I'm on Cupid's Cay, my adventuring's over." Again, she held the shallop tight to the wind, as the boom dipped to skim the sea. "I'll become a model wife, never fear. I've had training in that department too."

"I'm sure you will," he told her.

"How much longer do you stay on Eleuthera?"

"Sperry says there'll be a new doctor on the *Advance*. I'll sail back on the *Adventurer*."

"So soon, Paul?"

"Wasn't that part of our bargain?"

"Yes, now you mention it," she said gravely. "I've no right to detain you now."

"We both agreed it was the only way."

"So we did," said Anne, in the same grave tone. "Tell me all you've done on Eleuthera, Paul. Don't leave out a single fact." Her voice had steadied with the demand: he knew she had chosen the new topic deliberately.

"Didn't Silas describe our work? He sent back letters on the *Dolphin*."

Anne's eyes fixed on the dance of the bowsprit. "Silas made just one mention of the colony. Work, he informed me, was proceeding on the schedule he'd laid out. The rest of his letter was a detailed requisition for stores. He'll find Captain Sperry has most of them aboard."

Paul had expected this reaction from Silas: curiously enough, he felt no resentment. If the end product of these months was Anne's happiness, it scarcely mattered who received the credit. It was quite like Silas to accept even a brother's labors as a gift from Heaven.

"We've been incredibly lucky so far," he said. "Or shall I echo our leader, and pretend it's divine guidance?"

"Silas' greatest luck was in having you for a brother," said Anne. "Captain Sperry told me how you took hold when he was ill with the plague."

"I've done what I could," Paul admitted. "I've had expert help from Lebret, and many others, to make our settlement prosper. If you're satisfied, that's reward enough."

"Begin at the beginning, when you first stepped ashore," she begged. "And don't be modest."

Stirred from his self-pity by the warmth of her interest, he found he could laugh at the memory of those first taut days. "Silas wanted that honor," he warned. "He'll never forgive me for being first."

Anne's free hand dropped to cover his. "Never mind your brother now, Paul. This is your story—and I want to hear it all."

Taking her at her word, he told the history of Eleuthera from its beginning. There was no need to bear down on Silas' intransigence—or his acceptance of each item in the settlement's prosperity as his natural portion. Nor was there need to paint a too-rosy portrait. The facts of the narrative stood up without retouching. . . . When she stood on Cupid's Cay at last, Anne could find her father's hopes fulfilled. Paul could not promise the hope would endure: that was outside their bargain.

Anne did not speak for a long time after he had ended his report. Her eyes were still on the mad dance of the bowsprit: knowing she could not reveal her true feelings, he was not surprised when her first question bore no relation to the story he had just told.

"We've been on the same course since we left the *Adventurer*," she said quietly. "Shouldn't we come about?"

Paul ducked his head to peer beyond the sail. Canted at a dizzy angle as the shallop reeled off its larboard tack, the boom end seemed to cut the top of each roller. Far to the north, he could make out the fan of islets and palm-choked cays that still blocked a direct approach to Eleuthera from that quarter. The wind had freshened steadily, but the little vessel, with all her canvas drawing, continued to handle well in the white-flecked seas.

"We'll have to run south awhile longer," he said. "But for safety's sake, we'll shorten sail."

The maneuver was a dangerous one, but he risked leaving Anne at the tiller while he hastened to give Marco and Pronas a hand with the collapsing canvas. With a reef in the mainsail and the jib pulling well, the shallop righted promptly, with only an occasional heart-stopping dip at the height of a gust.

"How does she feel to you now?" he asked.

"Like a thoroughbred, fighting for her head. We mustn't let her run away, Paul."

"We won't," he promised. "Better let me have the tiller for now. In your place, I'd sit in the shade awhile. You're risking a fearful burn."

"I *want* to burn brown, like the rest of you. Wouldn't the elders approve?"

"I'm afraid not, my dear." Remembering the grub-pale complexions of the pilgrim women, he glanced at Anne's arms and shoulders. He saw that they were already deep-tanned, after her weeks at sea. When she felt his eyes, she rolled down both sleeves with a sigh.

"Apparently I've a great deal to learn," she said. "Let me find out the rest for myself: I won't burden you with further questions."

"The sun's a great healer, Anne. Silas has proved as much, in his own person. I've never seen him look better—or stronger. Perhaps he'll allow you to enjoy the same benefits."

Anne did not pursue the topic as she moved to the lee rail, and the shade of the mainsheet. "What would happen, if we held this course today and tomorrow? Would we fetch still another island?"

"The charts say there are hundreds more. Some are far larger than Eleuthera. Of course, we might miss them entirely and end in the arms of Spain."

"Consider the thought withdrawn, Paul. We can't run before the wind forever."

"That's true enough," he admitted. "We might encounter greater dangers than the dons—"

A shout from the bow brought Paul to his feet. Anchoring the tiller with his knees, he saw that Marco was pointing to the north. Elsewhere, the sky was bright blue. Here, it was blanketed in a white curtain that seemed to swallow the sea between as it moved south.

"It comes this way, *dottore*," said the Genoese. "A wind of gale force. Perhaps the *huracán*."

"Can we outrun it?"

"Only if we hold course. It would be madness to beat upwind now."

Paul shifted the helm to keep the shallop as close to the wind as safety would allow. The strategy was soon rewarded. The squall, howling into the southwest, and dragging skirts of rain behind it, was gone as soon as it had appeared, leaving a near-calm in its wake. This, Paul knew, was an ominous aftermath, suggesting that one of those strange blows (called *huracáns* by the dons) might be in the making before their eyes. Still imperfectly understood by navigators, the storms bore a relation to the tornado or the cyclone, since the gale moved in a long arc, with an area of dead calm at its heart.

The fear lessened when a second squall roared in from the northeast, preceded by a fusillade of thundercracks and a drenching rain that closed in on the shallop like a tent. So far, Paul perceived, this was only a severe gale. He could still take its full force on his quarter and run before it.

For the next hour, while Anne and his crew bailed for their lives, the little vessel staggered southward. Lapped in succeeding curtains of rain (which seemed to be one with the roar of the following waves) the voyagers could only pray their rough chart was accurate. There was no room for maneuver here, no option but an endless charge from hissing crest to green valley.

Even at the height of the blow, there was no show of fear aboard. Now and again, one of the crew moved to the stern sheets, to help Paul steady the tiller when the drag of a cross-sea threatened to turn the shallop broadside. As the day wore on, the squall lifted at last, and Paul was able to identify the silhouette of an island closing the eastern horizon. They had long since left Eleuthera astern. This, he felt sure, was the next land to the south. The colonists had sketched it on their charts—and named it Cat Island, because of its resemblance to a feline's claw.

Seen against a rain-washed sky that was beginning to grow murky with evening, the shoreline had a sinister look. It was scarred with white limestone outcrop that seemed to touch the water: to the south, the land dwindled into a mass of mangrove. It was not an encouraging prospect—but Paul knew he must probe for an anchorage while daylight lasted. They could not risk unknown waters in the dark.

He turned reassuringly to Anne. "We'll run for shore in another moment. There's bound to be a cove—or an inlet to the swamp."

"Can we tie up for the night?"

"It's the only safe procedure. We'll lose our canvas if we fight this wind much longer."

The gale had shifted rapidly in the last half-hour. The gauge showed it was now howling out of the open Atlantic, which meant the storm might well increase to hurricane force by morning. Low though the spine of Cat Island was, it broke the direct impact of the blast. Unfortunately, the shallop was hard to handle in the violent cross-eddies. After Paul had made sure that the coastline at this point was barren of shelter, he dared to run before the wind, while he ordered the mainsail lowered. Already, they had skirted more than half the island, with no break in the broth of white water that swirled about the coral heads.

"We'll try again, with the jib to hold course," he said. "If I remember, there's a beach below that next line of mangroves."

Pronas, at his command, had gone forward to make sure the jibstays were slotted home. Marco, spread-eagled on the forward thwarts, had anchored the Greek's ankles with both hands, to prevent his pitching overside. Dead ahead, they could see a cove of sorts, formed by a curving sandspit. The approach was perilous, hemmed as it was by coral spurs—but a lane of deep water was visible, and the wall of swamp to the south offered little hope of an anchorage.

"I'll run between the reefs," Paul said. "It's a tight fit, but we won't get another chance."

At that precise moment, as though a monster hand had stopped a bellows, the wind died to a murmur. The respite was brief. In a matter of seconds, another mighty blast, swiveling crazily from the west, boomed down on the shallop's stern. It was the first breath of the hurricane that had been in the making all that day, somewhere in the Atlantic. Striking thus without warning, it ballooned the jib with such force that the canvas was torn from its sockets.

The effect on the struggling vessel was cataclysmic. The sail, winging free like a maddened bird, lifted Pronas bodily from the foredeck: he was powerless to free himself, with both wrists twined in the jibstays. Marco, caught unaware by the blast, was also whipped free. For a split second, it was as though both men's bodies had served as the tail of a giant kite. Then, with a cannon-like boom, the jib tore free, dropping its human appendage into the sea.

The shallop, driving ahead on the crest of a following wave, passed over both struggling bodies in a twinkling: Paul's ears echoed to a double scream as the copper-shod keel ground down on his two-man crew. Powerless to control the madly bucking vessel, he felt his own answering cry choke in his throat. He had no way to rescue Marco and Pronas now—even if they had survived that grotesque tragedy.

For a moment more, the shallop rolled in a trough between two waves. Even in the bad light, the water was crystal-clear. Paul could see the outline of the reef ahead, waiting like a trap that needed only a touch to close its jaws. The next wave plummeted the boat into the yawning coral mouth.

The rudder was useless in that swirling surf. He fought back a moment more before he yielded to the force of wind and wave, driving the shallop deliberately on the reef, and whipping both arms round Anne's waist. When they fell together into the sea, he heard a rending crash behind them: it had needed but a single pounding wave to break the vessel's back.

Caught in the drag of that same wave, he found it impossible to swim. Anne was wrenched briefly from his grasp—and he gasped out a warning too late as a broken timber (whirling above them in the following sea) struck her a punishing blow. In another second, she was in his arms again, and he was treading water for his life.

He saw that she was unconscious. A trickle of blood at her temple suggested the blow had been less than mortal—though the form he clung to so desperately was inert enough. Already, she had swallowed enough water to choke her, unless he could reach land in time to empty her lungs.

The shore was visible when he lifted on the next crest—a sodden beach, backed by a wall of mangroves that had turned blue-black in the watery light. Each wave that roared over them was a push landward, though the undertow seemed to draw them back no less cruelly. His feet touched bottom before his strength could ebb. The cove was still shoulder-deep—but he found he could stand erect without losing his grip on Anne. A moment later, he had staggered into the shallows, barking his knee on a mass of coral, then falling for the last time in a gully between two dunes.

Sheltered at last from the gnawing wind, he felt a drowsy contentment invade his spirit, and fought hard against the urge to drop into oblivion: Anne was still in need of aid, if he meant to save her life. Standing above her, he lifted her with both hands pressed hard below her rib cage to empty her lungs. When he heard the cough that followed a rush of sea water at mouth and nostrils, he knew he had won a second contest with the elements. The cough told him she still lived: it had been a narrow escape, there in the debris of the shallop.

When he was sure that Anne's lungs were free of water, he stretched her full length on the sand, and unbuttoned her leather jerkin to admit still more air. There was a hint of sun in the west when he settled beside her, letting aching muscles relax in the blessed solidity of land. In a little while, he would rise to see how boat and shipmates had fared: he needed the breather before he stirred again.

Anne was still unconscious when Paul tottered to hands and knees to look seaward. Wave and wind commanded the reefs—but he could see that a remnant of the shallop clung to the coral spur where they had foundered. There was no sign of Marco or Pronas, and he realized with a sinking heart he must give them up for lost.

Getting unsteadily to his feet on the shoulder of the dune, he saw that the storm had shifted again to the east. Waves still pounded the shoals, but the cove was relatively calm. The spur where the shallop had grounded was now revealed a scant fifty yards offshore. Most of the planks had been washed free, but a portion of the stern was still wedged there firmly, including the locker beneath the sheets. Paul breathed deep as he waded into the boiling surge of the first oncoming wave and waited (with throbbing heart) for his strength to return. He knew he must swim to the spur before the next shift of the wind. Anne's survival and his own might well depend on the contents of that locker.

Short though the distance was, Paul was forced to wait almost an hour for the pounding of the waves to lessen. When he struck out for the coral spur the sun, burning through the clouds at afternoon's end, was painting prisms in the spray above the reefs.

It was a chilling experience to swim between the jaws of the shoal that had almost served as his tomb, to hoist his still-tired body to the spur, which now rose well above the restless waters. The shallop's stern, he saw, was undamaged. The doors of the locker opened easily, revealing its precious contents.

Paul had planned the compact bundles: they were meant to serve mapmakers like Silas, who were often forced to camp on remote beaches overnight. Both were swathed in waterproof cloth. One contained medical supplies, flint and steel, a two-bladed ax, a hand spade, and enough tools for emergency repairs on the shallop. The second waterproof was larger: it held blankets, a fish spear and tackle, a brace of *pistolas*, powder and shot, and enough hardtack, salt, and cooking gear to furnish two days of iron rations, including a flask of Giles' best French brandy.

When he had first planned these camping packs, Paul had never thought they might serve a pair of castaways. He could bless his foresight while he fashioned a float from loose timbers and guided his precious freight to the beach, just as the treacherous wind began to swing toward the west.

Anne still lay unconscious in the cleft of sand—but her even breathing suggested the blow she had suffered was not too serious. The sun had almost dried her clothing. Moving her carefully to make room for their makeshift shelter, he fashioned two camp beds, using the waterproofs as a base. He made her as comfortable as he could on one of them, with both blankets for her covering and his rolled-up coat as a pillow.

A grove of palms covered the landward slope of the dune. With two broken oars as ridgepoles, Paul cut a dozen fronds, which he wove into a rough thatch roof, supported by other poles, driven deep into the slope. If the rain returned, it would protect them until morning, when he could plan a sturdier shelter. Once he had built a backstop of driftwood to keep out the worst of the wind, they would pass the night snugly.

By this time the light was waning, and Paul's exertions, joined to the battle with the waves, had produced a raging thirst. He knew he would find water pocketed in the limestone outcrop of the island, but he could not risk leaving Anne now on such a search. The problem solved itself, when a visit to the beach revealed dozens of coconuts knocked down by the gale. The ax opened the tough outer sheath: a carpenter's awl pierced the eyes of the shaggy brown core. Each nut contained perhaps a half-pint of sweetish milk, and a white meat that satisfied the worst of his hunger. Survival already seemed assured, even if the two casta-ways were storm-stayed in their hut.

A fire was risky in the wind, but Paul decided to chance a small blaze: this was still the edge of the short winter season, and the nights held a hint of chill before morning. A fallen coco palm, split by the ax, yielded enough of its powdery inner lining to form tinder. Using dead twigs and guinea grass as a base, he scooped an open hearth in the sand before their shelter, built a tiny campfire of driftwood—and settled at last beside his com-panion to plan their next moves.

Exhausted as he was by their brush with death, and shaken by the loss of their two shipmates, he found that his brain refused to function, now that the basic needs of self-preservation had been satisfied. It was simpler to let his tired eyelids droop—to float in a half-world of drowiness that ushered him quickly into deep slumber.

He had not meant to sleep with the extent of Anne's injury still undiagnosed. A little later, shaken by her scream, he sat bolt upright—staring with dazed eyes at the fire, and uncertain for a moment of his whereabouts. It was Anne herself who brought him completely awake—flinging both arms about him and letting hysteria spend itself in a torrent of weeping.

Paul understood her breakdown well enough: he returned her embrace by instinct, murmuring what words of comfort he could find. Rousing from the stupor induced by the blow, unable to bridge the hiatus between the shallop's breakup and the dark present, Anne had felt sure (however briefly) that she was dead. Like any frightened child, she had groped toward human contact. When her lips sought his, it was part of the same compulsion.

He returned the kiss gently, and attempted to disengage himself from her straining arms. The effort seemed to increase her tears. This time, there was no mistaking the genesis of the passion that claimed her as their embrace deepened. Swept to the brink by his own long hunger, Paul found that he was returning her kiss with an ardor that could have but one sequel. . . . A pine knot exploded in the campfire, bathing their shelter in a ruddy glow—and he found he could fumble back to sanity. In that same breath, he was aware of rain on the roof, the high keening of the gale—and the fact that Anne, her own sanity restored, had gone from tears to laughter.

"I'm sorry—that was wrong of me. I had to be sure we were both alive."

"Do you believe it now?"

Her head remained on his shoulder—but he knew they were safe when she raised her face to his and brushed her lips across his cheek.

"What happened, Paul? Did you save me from drowning?"

"We saved one another. The surf brought us ashore."

"I struck my head in the wreckage—I remember that much. You must have carried me to the beach."

"You've been unconscious ever since. How does your head feel now?"

"It still aches—but I don't think I'm badly hurt. What of the sailors? Did they swim free?"

"I'm afraid not. The keel crashed down on them when we went out of control. We'll know for sure in the morning."

Anne let her head fall against him, and he could feel her body shake with sobs. This time, there was no panic in her tears. Only a deep sadness at a grotesque mishap that had cost two lives.

"We're alone, then?" she said at last.

"So it appears—but we'll be safe until daylight."

"Where did we come ashore?"

"On Cat Island—I'm sure of that much."

"Is the shallop a total loss?"

"All but the stern. I salvaged a few things from the reef." Paul moved to the fire to light a driftwood torch. "Let's have a look at that head wound."

Bad though the light was, he soon convinced himself that Anne's estimate of her injury was accurate. There was no sign of fracture below the wound, which had bruised the scalp without lacerating it. The bleeding seemed superficial: the headache could be soothed away by morning, with the aid of an opiate from his slender medical stores.

During the examination, he was careful to describe their present situation in its true light. While the wind held, they could only remain where they were. Even with transport, they could not risk beating across the channel that divided Cat Island from Eleuthera. It was enough for the present, to give thanks they still lived.

He felt a certain relief when he had finished his recital, the sense of a burden shared. With a less resourceful woman, he would have made light of their difficulties, shrugging off the threat of the storm and insisting they could soon cross to Eleuthera. Anne, who was made of sterner stuff, deserved a more accurate picture.

"Silas will think we've lost our lives."

"What else can he believe? The storm struck his island too."

He saw that she was shivering—and guessed it was not from cold. Moving to drape her shoulders with a blanket, he was careful not to prolong the gesture. Try as he might, he could not put down the memory of another shelter they had shared in England. Then and now, the world had seemed well lost beyond the circle of firelight.

"Perhaps I deserve this punishment for leaving my shipmates," said Anne. "Do you suppose the *Adventurer* rode out the gale?"

"The chances are good," said Paul. "Hood's obviously a past master at kedging, and it's only a short haul to his anchorage." He was splitting a coconut while he spoke, halving the core to offer Anne the thirst-slaking milk and the firm, fibrous meat. "It's time you took a little nourishment—and let the others solve their own problems."

The girl ate and drank with her eyes still on the fire: knowing what was troubling her, he did not break the silence. When she had finished a second coconut, he persuaded her to take a little brandy mixed with the milk, to which he had already added an opiate that would guarantee her sound sleep until daylight.

"How long can we last here, Paul?" she demanded.

"Forever, if need be. I've learned to live off the land—and the sea."

"You know what I mean. Are you afraid to answer?"

He cupped her chin in his palm, forcing her to meet his eyes. "Don't be ashamed at the discovery you made tonight. Passion has always been a part of man's nature. We must learn to control ours. The God you worship won't have it otherwise."

"Will you be strong for us both, then?"

"I don't go back on bargains, Anne. Nor do you."

"It wasn't a sin, then—what we almost did?"

"You were frightened—and I comforted you. Could I do less, when we escaped death together?"

The girl let her head rest against his shoulder: he knew she was weeping softly. The tears would wash away the last of her guilt, now they had renewed their bargain, and the sleeping draught would soon start to take effect.

"Only yesterday," she said, "I'd have blamed myself bitterly for that yielding. While it lasted, I wanted you—I won't deny it. All my teachings call that sinful. Lustful, even. Now you say it was natural, after the ordeal we shared—and I believe you. Is it the island magic, working on me already?"

Her voice trailed off, and he knew she had dropped into a slumber without dreams. Folding her in her nest of blankets, he sat for a long time at the opening of the shelter, listening to the howl of the gale—and damning himself for wishing the storm could go on forever.

The morning was overcast, the wind still high and steady from the north. When Anne wakened, Paul had already moved their stores to higher ground. Using the spear in a corner of the cove, he had captured a pair of plump sea trout, which he roasted over a second fire, built on a limestone hearth in the palm grove.

After they breakfasted, they turned beachcombers. Most of the wreckage from the shallop had been driven ashore. With Anne's aid, Paul dragged the flotsam high on the island's spine, where the storm could never reach it. Later, when he had drawn the nails, he hoped to construct a raft: the chore could wait until he had estimated their chances of crossing to Eleuthera, once the storm had abated. The most valuable item of salvage was the shallop's mainsail, which had tangled with the boom and drifted to the beach, trailing much of the cordage in its wake. It could serve as a roof for their next abode. Later, if he could mount a mast of some kind on the raft, it would speed their voyage.

He saw no trace of the two sailors, and judged that the bodies had drifted into the mangrove swamp. He was glad that Anne had been spared a grisly reminder of their loss.

During their morning's labors, the wind continued to pluck at their clothing with demon fingers, stinging their eyes with sand—and threatening, at the height of some gusts, to lift them clean off their feet. Wise in the perils of these Bahama gales, Paul soon taught Anne to cling to every scrap of cover. At midday, when the blow gave no sign of abating, he linked hands with her and set out to explore the beaches to the north.

Though he had done no more than skirt the approaches to Cat Island, Paul had seen that it was far smaller than Eleuthera. It lay well to the southeast of the larger island. The channel that divided them was a wide one, and he had needed upward of two hours to cross it in a sailing longboat on a previous exploring trip. This noon, when he had picked their way on a lee shore, and stood on the last sandspit, the desert of blue water to the north seemed an impassible gulf. Lashed by the full fury of the storm, pocked with wild eddies and leaping surf, the sight should have depressed him utterly. Instead, he felt his heart leap at the reprieve—and turned aside quickly, before Anne could catch his mood.

"I'm afraid you must endure my company a little longer," he told her. "We've no future as navigators with the weather in that quarter, even when the gale ends."

"What's our next move, then?"

"We must build a hut that's safe from wind and sea. This blow will bring more rain by nightfall."

They had already carried their stores (along with the mainsail, and such planks and spars as they would require) to the spot Paul had selected for home-building. So far as he could observe, it was the highest point on Cat Island, a limestone bluff with coco palms on both flanks and a cleft that would shelter them from bad weather. Once the canvas had been stretched on a sapling frame and lashed to pegs set in the porous stone, it was a simple matter to build walls around it, using a base of stout mangrove roots and weaving palm fronds into the pattern. When he had banked the walls with sand, Paul drove a series of willow withes into the earth, for added protection against the weather; the Lucayans themselves, he thought, could not have devised a stouter barrier.

Meanwhile, Anne had busied herself inside the framework of their dwelling. Eager to prove her own skill, she had improvised two mattresses of pine boughs and spread the blankets above them. She had also constructed a neat hearth in the sand outside, laid a pine-knot fire, and set out their meager household gear on a table made of salvaged planks. When Paul returned from the cove with the evening's catch (a five-pound trout, oysters from the mangrove roots, and four huge crabs he had netted in the shallows) she had built a bed of coals for broiling, and cut a palm-heart salad, garnished with the fruit of a mango that grew almost at their door.

"I told you I was trained to be a pioneer," she said proudly. "Do you believe me now?"

"Our house is your responsibility," he told her. "I'll make the raft my next task."

Anne glanced up at the cleft of sky between the limestone bluffs. The sun had fought through the driving clouds at noon, but rain scud had begun to set in with evening. They scarcely felt the wind in this nook—but they could hear its savage rhythm in the palm fronds below.

"Can't we explore all the island first?"

"My first duty is to deliver you to Silas," he told her. "What if the wind shifts tomorrow?"

"You said it was unlikely."

"If this weather holds, we'll make the best of things here. That's why it was important to have permanent shelter, and an adequate food supply. Now we're assured of survival, I must remember my mission—"

"—which can only end in good-by," she finished quickly.

"Don't think I *want* this to end."

"Nor do I, Paul."

"We must still think of Silas—and what he's suffering at this moment."

"If I know your brother, he's taken our disappearance as a sign of God's wrath, and has arranged the proper penance for the colony."

"Surely you're eager to shorten that ordeal—in all our interests."

"So you're testing my good intentions," said Anne. "Am I remiss in my duty, if I hope for a northeast wind tomorrow, and the day after?"

Paul saw that she had adopted a teasing tone deliberately, to cover her true feelings—and decided to play the game her way. While she was broiling the fish above the coals (and roasting the crabs in a dressing of palm leaves) he took a torch inside the shelter, to complete his final task of the day, the building of a yard-high fence down its middle. Constructed of pine stakes, and bound in a lashing of wild grapevine, it was an adequate barrier between the two couches, although a token one.

When he had bound the last stake, he squatted in the doorway of the hut, sharpening the ax blades on a whetstone while Anne moved from hearth to trestle table to serve up their repast. The dividing line, he told himself, was a necessary symbol. Merely by suspending his conscious memory (and the sense of duty that was now his constant companion) he could pretend they had been castaways of a year's standing, content with the turn of fortune that had brought them here.

"What are you building, Paul? I thought our house was finished."

"I think you'll find this a needed addition. It's ready for your approval."

Anne glanced into the interior of the hut as he raised the torch. In the flickering light, he saw her blush deeply. "No wall divided us last night," she said quietly. "We were immune to the devil's beckoning then. Why must we have a barrier now?"

"For just one reason, my dear. When I tell Silas I built us separate cabins on Cat Island, I'll be speaking truly."

Rain fell heavily in the night, but the shipwrecked couple slept well beneath their canvas shelter. With the dawn, there were scattered showers and the wind continued to boom from the north without ceasing. Their second day on Cat Island fell into an easy pattern, setting the tempo for the days to come. Like the others, it seemed over almost before it began—but Paul could have recited each event from memory.

Rising while Anne slept, he rekindled the fire, and made sure the supply of pine knots was adequate. Then, taking the fish spear and the bucket he had improvised from woven palm leaves, he followed the short cut to the beach to glean a breakfast from the sea. Mornings were spent in the scant piney woods, selecting dry logs for the raft and trimming them to the design he had sketched on the back of a ship's plank. Early afternoons (when the air filled with the promise of spring and the resin bubbled in the crosspoles of the hut) Paul resumed an excellent habit formed on Eleuthera, and rested from his labors in a two-hour siesta.

It was spent in drowsy talk with Anne—who had so far refused to adopt so Spanish a custom, and sat with her back to a coco palm, in open sunlight, letting her arms and shoulders burn a deep, rich brown. Silas (she had reasoned) could hardly object when she recounted the story of their hardships. Now that the healthy hue of her skin all but matched Paul's, she could feel a part of the Bahamas, though she had yet to set foot in her chosen home.

"In another month," he said, "you wouldn't dare expose yourself thus. Once the winter's really over here, you'd drop from sunstroke."

"If I were alone," she said, with a toss of her head, "I'd play Eve completely, and brown myself from head to toe. I'll grant you, that *would* be hard to explain—"

"Haven't you enough on your conscience?" he asked. "If I were half the man I pretend, I'd be splitting a pine log now, instead of lolling here. You've no right to detain me with such vanities."

"The logs are ready now, and the sail. You can lash them tomorrow—and the wind has yet to change."

"Tomorrow's a favorite word in these parts, I never hoped to hear it on a pilgrim's lips."

"I won't dare use it later, Paul. I'll walk with you to the woods directly. We can work a few hours more, at the day's end."

The raft he had planned would have a base of pine logs, trimmed to form a compact rectangle. He meant to balance it on both sides with still other logs, attached to the main raft by saplings or outriggers—a form of marine construction he had observed in the East, and a powerful steadier in rough waters. A long sweep, fashioned from another sapling (to which he had lashed one of the shallop's undamaged oar blades) would permit him to guide the raft's progress after a fashion. The squarish sail (hung from a mast he planned to step a little forward) would move the raft with a following wind. A southerly breeze would be imperative to assure their crossing of the channel. Limited maneuver would be possible—but any shift in the wind could only lead to disaster.

Working side by side with Anne, he had cleared a chute from pine grove to sea, down which the logs were worked, until they floated free. During lulls in the wind (when it was possible to move them without injury from the waves) they had ferried the logs along the coast, to beach them in the lee of the northern sandspit. It had been heavy work, and Paul had received more than one bruise for his pains—but it had seemed only sensible procedure. Had he risked building the raft on the spot, there would have been no way of moving it among the reefs that fringed the shore. On the sandspit, it could be assembled in a matter of hours, and launched at once in deep water.

The last log was ferried during the evening of their fourth day on the island. Anne helped with the moving, wading waist-deep among the coral outcrop, diving to escape injury when the long green rollers smashed down, and joining in Paul's cheer when their ungainly freight was brought ashore. Counting the outriggers, there were ten logs in all. Using loops of wild grapevine, the two castaways arranged them in the needed pattern, and Paul lashed them in place with the same tough lianas.

He had already brought mast and planking overland, and these were nailed in place to form a rough deck. Dusk was descending as this procedure was completed. He sent Anne to prepare their supper while he nailed down the outriggers and made sure that the whole raft was canted at the right angle, so that it would float free with only a thrust from the sweep. When the mast was stepped in place, his marine carpentry was ended. Once the sail was hoisted and the wind in the proper quarter, they could set sail for Eleuthera.

It was a solemn moment, and he faced up to it squarely while he followed the path Anne had taken to their home. That night, he mixed a coconut-milk punch to toast a happy voyage and went to his couch to sleep the sleep of exhaustion. When he wakened next morning, he was sure that he had heard sounds of weeping beyond the partition that divided his bed from Anne's— but there was no need to question her now. The breeze still blew strongly from the northeast, and his fellow castaway was humming as she moved to take their breakfast from the hearth.

He returned to the raft at once, to check on yesterday's labors and drive a few last nails. Dawdling over the work to make it last, wading beyond his depth in the shoaling water offshore, he admitted (past all doubting) that the long gale was beginning to exhaust its force at last, though the prevailing wind was still from the northeast. Reefs that had seemed merciless obstacles only yesterday were creamed with gentle surf; already, it was possible to estimate the extent of the long blue finger that pointed straight for his destination. Eleuthera itself (blotted from view until now by the steady rainfall) stood out against the sky like a solid cloud. While he had not yet dared to test the raft at sea, Paul was sure he could fetch the first headland in three hours' sailing, once fortune had granted him a southeast wind.

It would have been folly to attempt the voyage today. Shaking his fist at the sky (and praying, in the same breath, that there would be no immediate change in the weather) he followed the familiar beach trail one more time, and climbed the steep path to the bluff.

Despite his dawdling, it was not yet noon. There was no sign of Anne when he approached the hut, and the fire had died on the hearth. The mystery solved itself when he noticed the fragment of planking, propped between two stones on the trestle table. She had left a message there, scrawled with a bit of charcoal: *Bathing at Ocean Hole.*

They had discovered the spot on their first exploration—a circular limestone basin joined, in some mysterious fashion, to the sea itself. Salt-water ponds of this sort were common in the islands; when she returned from a morning's work on the raft, it was Anne's custom to bathe there. Today, aware that Paul might leave the sandspit early, she had warned him of her presence, lest he stumble on her unawares.

Or was the note an invitation to join her?

In his mind, he could see the pool as vividly as though he stood at its rim. He pictured her diving into its crystal heart, as visible as though she floated in air. He saw her poised on the limestone ledge below the water catch, letting her body brown in the sun, then cooling shoulders and breasts in the cascade of rain water from above. All his instincts shouted that her summons was deliberate, that they deserved this one flouting of Silas and his avenging deity before they set sail. The older, kinder gods would pardon them—and their secret would be safe, with no witness but the sun and sky.

His foot was on the path before reason could triumph over self. In that blinding flash of perception, the mist of passion lifted from his brain and he found the strength to master it. Now, at last, he could understand the torture Silas had suffered when he spied on Lili Porter. If his brother had won that battle, so could he. Dropping to his knees on the path, he whispered a short prayer of thanks for his deliverance. Silas' God would never accept that prayer, but he felt better for speaking it.

The respite was brief. He was cursing his conscience again— and splitting firewood viciously to take the edge from his frustration—when he heard Anne's voice from the bluff.

"Have you been here long, Paul?"

"Only a moment," he lied.

"The wind has dropped," she said. "There isn't a breath."

"Dead calms are rare here. It's sure to begin again by morning."

"Does that mean we can take off?"

He leaned on the ax handle and looked up at her silhouette, etched in cobalt as the sun poured down from a flawless sky. He was both angered and relieved to note she was fully clothed. Even now, the demon within him (chained though it was) had whispered that she might return naked as the first temptress.

"Your royal barge is ready, Mistress Trevor," he said. "The captain's prepared to put to sea."

"Thank Heaven we needn't leave at once. I've just learned why these islands deserve the name of Eden."

"Before or after the serpent?"

"Before, of course. Will you put down that ax and join me?"

He was still puzzled at the shining promise in her eyes when he climbed the bluff and followed her down the slope to the pool. "What did you find, Anne? Mermaids in the Ocean Hole?"

"Something even rarer. You must see to believe."

"Didn't you bathe at all today?"

"Only for a moment. I've been exploring in the mangrove swamp. We never did, you know."

"We couldn't, while the storm lasted."

"I managed to this morning, without drowning. There's high ground, after you cross the first slough."

Anne led the way at a half-run, refusing to answer further questions until they reached the tidal marsh, an arm of brackish water that seeped into the Atlantic between high-backed dunes. This was the entrance to the mangrove thickets that covered the southern reaches of Cat Island. So far, Paul had done no more than skirt it in search of oysters. Today, he lifted puzzled eyebrows when Anne laid a finger to her lips and moved confidently into the leafy maze.

For the first quarter-mile, walking was difficult, thanks to the mangrove roots, which spread in twisted arabesques from the bog —and seemed, at times, larger than the stunted, umbrella-shaped trees themselves. Beyond, the ground was almost dry. Anne laced fingers with Paul's, and repeated her warning signal. He found he was sharing her excitement, though he could not diagnose the cause.

"Where are we bound?"

"Don't talk! Don't even whisper!"

It was only when they glimpsed a shimmer of water ahead that Anne slowed her pace. Moving on tiptoe through the grass of the next hummock, she led him to the margin of a sedgy lake, then drew him down beside her in the green ambush.

"I had to share it," she told him, shaping the words with soundless lips. "Have you ever seen anything lovelier?"

The small lake was a nesting ground, its entire surface covered by a flock of incredibly graceful birds. Some of them were snow white, others pink as the sky at the first promise of dawn. All of the birds were waders—but, unlike such mournful breeds as the crane or heron, their stiltlike legs were part of their beauty, along with the curving necks and strange, dark bills. Many were guiding their young in tentative flights that soared briefly above the treetops, only to circle back to the nesting ground. A few still brooded above their eggs. Still others were engaged in an exquisite dance, a kind of minuet without music, which caused them to approach and withdraw from one another in a courting pattern older than time.

"What are they, Paul?"

"Guy Lebret might know. To me, they're a strange species."

As they continued their spellbound watch, one of the brooders rose high above the trees, where it hung suspended as an observer. The movement revealed a conical mound of earth, hollowed at the summit to contain a single white egg. There was time for only a glimpse. Another bird had already stalked to the nest; using its beak as gently as a mother touching a child, it shifted the egg in position, then settled over it.

"Which is the mother, Paul—and which the father?"

"Lebret says that many birds share in the nesting. Perhaps it doesn't matter."

High in the blue, the solitary observer gave a raucous, honking summons: it was the only jarring note in the picture. The effect on the colony was startling. Young and old alike, with a great whirring of wings, lifted at once from the lake. Flying in battalions, with the sentinel bird in the lead, they lifted high above the mangroves—all but the solitary nesters, who remained at their tasks. The young, Paul saw, had been well trained: the entire group soon formed into a series of long, rose-white files, with the elders in the van. Flying with the same fluid grace, spaced as precisely as figures in a Grecian frieze, they began to wing north. In a matter of moments, they were lost to view.

"That alone was worth leaving England to see," said Anne. She still whispered, as though the mangrove leaves above them were a church nave.

"Guy will be furious he missed it."

"Do you know why I brought you here?"

"To share a perfect moment," he said. "I'll always be grateful."

"It was more than that, Paul. Those birds were a portent."

"What do you mean?"

"A sign from nature—reminding us that the soul is greater than the body. Thank God I made the discovery in time."

"I still don't follow, Anne."

"Don't call me shameless—even though I deserve it. I left that message at the hut, hoping you'd follow me to the pool. I'd planned to have you take me there; I wanted that much from life, before I married Silas."

Anne moved to the lake's edge. One of the birds, startled by her footsteps, lifted from its nest with the familiar, raucous cry. She watched it with brooding eyes before she spoke again.

"I swam there a whole half-hour, waiting for you to join me: I said I'd only bathed for a moment, but I was lying. I was furious when you didn't appear; then I saw just how insane I'd been. That first night ashore, when I made you take me in your arms, you were strong enough to—save us both. I've no right to tempt you a second time, just because you love me." She turned to face him then, her eyes cleared of doubting, her chin proud. "You *do* love me—don't you, Paul?"

"That's hardly a secret, my dear."

"I love you too," said Anne. "I've loved you since that night in the snow. It was only today that I admitted it. Was I wrong to want you?"

"No, Anne."

"Do you see why I couldn't give in to that wanting? How unfair it would be—to us all?"

"Of course."

"While I waited at the pool, I'm afraid I didn't think too clearly. That's why I dressed in a rush, and ran into the swamp. For a while, I suppose, I was running from my own desires. Then, quite by chance, I stumbled on the lake—and saw this. Providence had saved me, just in time. Here was the proof."

"*Proof*, Anne?"

"A world that can create such beauty doesn't deserve our kind of sinning, Paul."

With a great effort, he kept back his own confession, the fact that he, too, had wrestled with desire and won in time. Anne had every right to exult in her victory. Nothing (he told himself) could be more upsetting to a woman than the discovery she had resisted temptation in vain. . . . Forcing a smile, he pressed her hand gently, then moved to the lake's edge to study the graceful balancing of the bird above them.

"Speaking of portents, we've just had another. When those

birds left their nesting ground, did you notice the *direction* of their flight?"

"They went north, didn't they?"

"Yes, taking advantage of a southerly wind. It's time we followed them."

By the time the castaways reached the sandspit, a strong breeze was blowing from the southeast. With six hours of daylight remaining, they lost no time in making their departure.

The raft floated buoyantly, once Paul had cut its mooring and shoved it down the steep cant of the beach. Anne took the sweep while he raised the sail on its makeshift mast. Having no suitable timber for a boom, they had left the canvas loose-footed: should the wind prove dangerous, the sail could be furled quickly by wrapping part of it around the mast.

Water had been put aboard in coconut shells, along with salted fish and the last of the hardtack. The blankets were rolled in their waterproofs, along with the ax and other tools. They had taken nothing else from their home on Cat Island.

With a compass to set his course, Paul called his first order to the steersman. Anne leaned hard on the sweep, bringing the raft before the wind; he did not need her cry of encouragement to realize it had answered the tiller well. Now they were really underway, it was evident their craft was seaworthy.

At this level, Eleuthera was no more than a vague shadow to the north: without his memory of other tentative explorations to guide him, Paul would have been hard-pressed to set a course. No more than twenty miles of water separated the two islands—but it was impossible to draw a direct bead at this point, because of the inevitable clusters of cays and reefs that lay between. The first leg of the voyage, as he had sketched it on the rough chart before him, would take them north by northeast, paralleling these treacherous barriers for a good part of the distance. Once they had reached close to the first headland, he would be in familiar waters again.

As he recalled, the coral barrier fell away sharply here, with plenty of sea room between reefs and land. It would be a simple matter to turn north by west at this point, following Eleuthera's southern beaches until the next headland was turned. At this point, the whole western sound would be open before them, with the settlement dead ahead: they would risk a direct crossing for the final lap of the voyage.

The whole venture depended on the following wind. In the next hour, he tested his sail thoroughly enough to risk lashing the lines and relieving Anne at the sweep. Though he could only guess at their velocity, he estimated their speed at three knots an hour. At that rate, they would draw their first real bead on their destination before sundown.

The voyage so far had been prosperous. With the wind behind them and a smooth sea running, they had breasted a thousand rollers without mishap. Now and again, the raft's nose had buried itself briefly, drenching the two sailors before it steadied. Such hardships were minor, when measured against their steady progress.

With no immediate risk of foundering, they could take pride in their ungainly craft—cheering each ponderous wallow, and laughing at the wild spirals of sea gulls that rose from the sandbanks at each disturbance of their repose. If Paul's own laughter was a trifle forced, he did not question the cause.

By midafternoon, the shadow to the north had changed to a green wedge of land, laced with powder-white beaches and the stains of winter-dry savannas. Anne had spelled Paul at the stern, while he studied his compass a second time to set their first true bearing. Taking the sweep from her hands, and lashing both lines, he motioned her forward of the sail.

"There's your new home, Anne. Your island of freedom. Sorry we've been so long in reaching it."

"You're *sure* it's Eleuthera, Paul?"

"Positive. I've sailed 'round that point a dozen times."

She moved forward for a closer view: he saw that her shoulders were drooping, and guessed that the moisture on her lashes was not caused by spray. While the land mass to the north had remained a near-mirage, she could pretend Paul's memory was false, that the gale had swept them into truly unknown waters. Now even that deception was denied her.

"Can we reach it by nightfall?"

"It's safer to stand off," he said. "We'll have a full moon an hour after sundown. We can sail by its light, if we keep beyond the reefs. The settlement's a good fifty miles to the north. So long as we have open water around us, and a fair wind, we should be within striking distance late tomorrow."

"Our adventure isn't quite ended, then?"

"Only the risky part. Praise Heaven *that's* behind us now."

Anne's eyes met his squarely. They had lost their hint of tears. Her last revolt against duty, it seemed, had been settled peaceably.

"What if the wind shifts?"

"We'll drive on the nearest shoal, and swim ashore. It's a fair journey afoot, but we'll make it."

Now the course was north by northwest, he knew the estimate was justified. Sailing before the wind into the open sound, he had feared the raft might be lost in the sea before he could shift direction. Now that they were running along the foot of Eleuthera, no real problems in navigation remained: a dozen cays and islets would offer a temporary haven while they awaited the rising moon.

The next two hours' sailing confirmed Paul's judgment: even the wind conspired in their favor, shifting a few points to the southeast to bear them down the channel that skirted the island beach. They were now perhaps a sea mile offshore, and tending steadily north. Their next main objective was the still-distant promontory. Paul did not risk an approach in the waning daylight. Just before the sun leveled with the horizon, he let the raft fall off to the west, using the last rays to pick an anchorage where they would wait for moonrise.

He chose the largest of a half-dozen cays, at the very edge of the channel. It was a spot he had used as a way station on trips with Lebret, a curve of sand bar with palms on its crest and a shelving bottom free of coral. He let the raft ground—and, with the sail furled and a cable lashed to the nearest palm bole, the voyagers took their first food since leaving Cat Island.

Somewhat belatedly, Paul realized he was faint with hunger. More than eight hours had elapsed since that departure.

"It's a poor captain who lets his crew starve," he told Anne. "Why didn't you mutiny?"

"Nothing was more important than a quick crossing," she said. "Can we see the settlement, once we're in the sound?"

"I'm afraid not. There's a great deal of bad water between, and many smaller cays."

"Does that mean we may not arrive tomorrow?"

"Only if the wind's in our favor. It's impossible to time this leg of the voyage."

Again, the prediction proved accurate. They were underway the moment the moon swam into view above Eleuthera. The silvery beams were a fair substitute for daylight, so long as the raft could stay in open water. Bowling north by northwest at their best speed, they continued to stand well offshore, rounding the blunt promontory in the last hour before moonset, and changing their course for the last time to draw a final (and tentative) bead on the still-invisible settlement.

Here, the water was treacherous with shoals—and the broad, nearly circular sound preceding the channel to Cupid's Cay was ill suited to navigation in that uncertain light. They sought a second haven between two sand bars, where only an occasional touch of the sweep was needed to hold their position.

With morning, Paul left the raft to go ashore on the nearer of the two bars. A survey of the waters to the north and east convinced him that this was indeed the backdoor of home. When the sun had risen in a cloudless sky, and the sweet southeastern breeze continued unabated, he could tell Anne, in all honesty, that the worst of the voyage was behind them.

When they set forth again the wind had freshened somewhat: it was a whippy day in open water, ideal for small-boat sailing but difficult for the more ponderous raft, since the meager spread of canvas was ill suited to balance the weight beneath it. For a space, Paul attempted to navigate under the propulsion of wind and wave alone, only to discover that the raft required the steadying factor of a sail to answer to its helm. Eventually, he was forced to abandon his original bead—which would have taken the raft directly across the sound, with the full strength of the breeze behind it.

Once he had run for the shelter of the land, there was no danger of losing the precious sail—but he was on a lee shore now, with the menace of submerged coral a constant threat. The wind, which had been friendly since the start of this strange journey, now turned fickle—speeding him down the coastline when its shape was in his favor, and driving him far too close when the land thrust westward. At such times, he was forced to sail offwind, a procedure which caused the raft to yaw perilously.

"Can't you find a break, Paul—and sail the lagoon?"

"We'll lose the wind altogether if we go closer. I'd rather chance shipwreck than give up now."

An hour before sunset, he picked out a lightning-blasted tree onshore that was one of the colony's outpost landmarks. At this point (had they dared to return to the open sound) Cupid's Cay was no more than four hours' sail. Should he drive the raft on coral and proceed afoot, it was still a good day's journey. Mangroves crowded the beach in this area, which meant a long detour inland.

Once more he risked a run for deep water—and held his own in the stiff breeze, to round the next swampy point. In the last glimmer of sunset, he picked out a still more welcome landmark, the first of the buoys that marked one of the channels to the harbor. The fact that the colonists had restored these markers was an augury that the *Adventurer* had cleared New Providence, and was now at anchor.

At that moment, the wind shifted toward the north, roiling the whole sound in whitecaps. Paul had hoped to run toward the buoy, and gain the anchorage by daylight. The change in the weather dashed that hope. Had their vessel been able to sail into the wind, he could have stood on and off with ease, until the rising moon had marked the bight that led to Cupid's Cay. With the raft laboring in the cross-chop, he could not risk losing his sail in open water. There was no choice but to run for land again, before the breeze turned to the east, making their position perilous indeed.

With the adverse wind, they were now retracing their course: for a moment it seemed certain that they would be forced to round the mangrove-point to the south, a defeat which would have wiped out most of the day's gains. Once they were in its shelter, Paul found he could sail into the wind after a fashion, bringing the raft within striking distance of the white ribbon of beach that gleamed in the fading light.

"Dive clear when I give the word, and head straight for land," he told Anne. "We're bound to break up in the next few moments." The raft yawed violently as a gust struck broadside. Anne moved to the sweep to add her weight to his own, steadying it for the run down the next roller.

"It's less than a half-mile now," he said. "There's enough light left to mark the reefs, and room to swim between. Just keep your head. We'll be ashore within the hour."

"Shouldn't you lead the way, Paul?"

"The captain's the last to leave his ship." He brought the raft close to the wind as he spoke, driving hard toward a break in the reef—and breathing more easily when they skimmed through, leaving one of the outriggers behind. With that wall of coral to break the worst of the rollers, he could count on smoother sailing in the lagoon.

The beach was in clear view now; there was a good quarter-mile of bright green water inshore to mark the limits of the outcrop. He could hardly hope to reach this far without mishap. The area between bristled with obstacles—and the wind, sweeping laterally in its rapid shift to the east, was driving the raft crabwise.

*"Abandon ship!"*

Anne dove cleanly with the order, striking the lagoon between two reefs. He held course until her head broke surface, a good twenty feet from the raft. Then, bringing the cranky vessel hard alee, he crashed down deliberately on the farther of the spurs. As he had planned, the raft wedged there firmly. Though it was canted at an angle that left it at the mercy of each oncoming roller, there was no immediate danger of a breakup. The timing was important, lest the two swimmers be injured by the debris in their progress to the beach.

There was no chance to salvage their stores. Paul paused just long enough to anchor the ax at his belt before he abandoned ship in turn. Anne was swimming strongly a hundred feet ahead, threading a careful course amid the coral masses that lay between her and clear water.

It was a good half-hour before they reached that translucent belt of green. Thanks to the girl's skill, he had no qualms for her safety—and hung back a little to the end, wishing the swim could be longer. When they entered the lazy inshore surf at last, he touched bottom slowly, offering his fellow castaway a hand.

Anne dashed the salt from her eyes, and declined his help.

"I'm not tired. Are we really here at last?"

"We've a fairish walk ahead. Sorry to bring you home by the back door."

Anne waded ashore, and shaded her eyes against the sunset to scan the curve of beach. "Cat Island was our home, Paul. I feel a stranger here."

"You'll belong in time."

"That's my task now, isn't it? I can hardly ask you to show me how. Your work is over when you've guided me to Cupid's Cay."

"We'll walk until our clothing's dry, then rest until moonrise," he said. "It's farther than it seemed from the sea—but we'll be there by morning."

They rested for an hour after darkness fell, on a sandhill that still held the sun's warmth. Paul gathered coconuts to slake their thirst. It seemed oddly appropriate that they should be ending their journey thus, barefoot and salt-caked, with only an ax to contend against the wilderness.

Once they had set out by moonlight, they made good progress, slowed on occasion by jungle growth at the water's edge. Twice, they swam round the obstruction to the next clear sweep of beach. Once, when the maze of reefs offshore made such procedure hazardous, Paul was forced to cut a path through the lianas. It was arduous work: an hour before daylight, he insisted they rest again. For all her young strength, he could see that Anne was beginning to tire at last.

He made no effort to waken her when the first stirring of birds announced the nearness of dawn. Landmarks were thick about him now: he knew the settlement was less than a mile away. If they approached before full light, they might be mistaken for marauders. . . . Anne's fingers had joined with his when she fell asleep. She rose obediently as he lifted her—and, for a last, bemused moment they stood facing the steel-gray promise of sunrise on the lagoon. There was no need to explain that he had prolonged the halt deliberately, or that Cupid's Cay was beyond the next point. Already, they could pick out the rigging of the *Adventurer* against the sky.

The settlement had not yet wakened when they threaded their way among the cabins. The hand ferry was berthed on Giles' beach. Beyond, at the stockade dock, a few fishermen were preparing to set forth. Busy with their gear, they did not notice the faint creak of the cable as Paul transported his brother's betrothed to the cay.

Neither of them had spoken on that last long walk. They paused now, on the porch of the surgery. Anne's hand fell upon his arm.

"Let me go on alone, Paul."

A splinter of sunlight, lancing through the palm-thatched roof, bathed her face in golden light. It was a picture he would remember always.

"Kiss me just once," she whispered.

Her eyes were misty when their lips parted, but her voice was strong with purpose. "He mustn't suspect we love each other, Paul. Please make sure of that."

She was gone before he could reply, running a little in her haste to overtake the fishermen before they could cast off. From the shelter of the porch, he saw the men turn incredulously—and heard their sudden cheer as they dropped their work to welcome her. He did not wait to watch them lead her through the stockade gate. Instead, he entered the surgery in haste, and closed the door behind him.

There was a stir in his bunk—and Paul found himself facing Guy Lebret. The naturalist had agreed to spell him here during his voyage to New Providence. Once he was awake, the Frenchman accepted his presence with aplomb.

"I told your brother you'd run to Cat Island ahead of the gale," he said. "I also assured him that you'd return in good time, with his bride in a reasonable state of repair."

"You might look a trifle more pleased," said Paul. It was not the greeting he had expected. There was something in Lebret's manner that put him on guard.

"I've my own way of praying, *mon vieux*: at the time, I asked God to spare you both. Since I don't put in such requests often, I felt this one would be answered."

"Say what's in your mind, man! Has there been sickness here?"

"Only a few minor cases. The health of our settlement is exceptional—and our new colonists have settled in like veterans. I can't say as much for our collective soul. *That's* desperately in need of your medicine."

"What has Silas done now?"

"You didn't come back a moment too soon, Paul. The elders have charged Lili Porter with witchcraft. She goes on trial two days from now—for her life."

# THE WITCHES' MARK

ONCE the first shock had subsided, Paul found that Lebret's story was logical enough. Hearing it in silence, he swore a great oath at the conclusion, and turned toward the door.

"Where are you bound, my friend?" asked the Frenchman.

"To have this out with Silas. He could have nipped the madness in the bud, and he did nothing. I want to know why."

"Shouldn't you talk first with Giles? *He* saw it all. I'm only repeating gossip."

Paul hesitated, with a hand on the latch. Angry though he was, he saw the wisdom in Lebret's suggestion. He would need all the facts before confronting Silas—and demanding the reasons behind this last, hideous proof of bigotry in action.

"Let's waken Giles now. If the elders are springing their trap day after tomorrow, we must move fast."

They found the innkeeper sprawled in his broad-beamed armchair on the tavern veranda. He was wide awake, despite the early hour. One glance at the usually placid moonface was all the warning Paul needed.

"I heard them cheering at the stockade," said Giles. "It wasn't hard to guess the reason. You might have returned sooner, Dr. Sutton."

"Guy's told me the essentials. Will you fill in the picture?"

"Does this mean you're on my side?"

"How can you ask?"

"It may be more than you can handle," said Giles. "Your brother's given orders for a trial. Lili's been accused in open meeting. As headman of his church, he's within his rights. We got fresh proof of that from our new settlers—the ones who came on the *Adventurer*. They're hanging witches—or what they claim to be witches—all over England."

"You know there are no such things as witches, Giles. So, damn him, does my brother—if he's in his right mind. Most of the colonists are intelligent enough to vote the elders down. They'll remember how Lili nursed them through the plague—"

"That was on the first voyage out, Doctor: it's a long time ago. Most of this second batch are Bible-backs. They give the Puritans a majority."

"He's right there," said Lebret. "I've just finished tallying their names. We've over three hundred colonists today. One hundred and ninety of 'em are Puritans." He turned to the innkeeper, with an explosive shrug. "Tell it from the start. You saw it all."

Giles lifted his mug of homemade cider, and drank deeply. "Remember the Welles brat, Doctor? The one called Patricia? You hadn't been gone two days when she began suffering from the vapors. Lebret dosed her with physic, but it didn't help. Whenever she had an audience—the bigger the better—she'd fall down and start squealing like a fresh-branded calf. Claimed she was seeing visions. So help me, the holier-than-thous believed her, to the last man. Insisted she stand up in church before the congregation and tell her story—" The innkeeper turned to Lebret with a snort of rage. "*You* heard that part yourself. Tell how it happened: I need a witness to believe my own story."

"She claimed she saw God on his throne," said the Frenchman. "Naturally, there were angels all about. Seven stars were shining above His head, and seven candlesticks burned before Him. The next vision was filled with strange and terrible beasts. In another, she stood before gates made of pearl that opened to save her—"

"How did the congregation take it?" asked Paul.

Giles shook his fist at the distant stockade. "So help me, they ate it up. At the time, I could half-understand why. Just listening to the girl's blather gave *me* the creeps."

"Did the elders accept her seizure as real?"

"Old Lambert said she'd been taken by the Spirit of God to point out our sins. He called it a warning of destruction, if we didn't repent straight-off."

"The Reverend Obadiah's a Bible student. Didn't he remind his flock that all these visions are described in the Book of Revelation? The Welles girl was either prompted by others—or putting on her own show to attract attention."

Giles and Lebret exchanged glances. "Now you mention it, Deborah Sikes said as much right after the service," the innkeeper muttered. "Welles' wife was so mad she fair spit in the poor girl's face. When my Lili stood between 'em, she tried to slap her. In the end, both girls tumbled her into a palmetto—"

"I took out a dozen spines in the surgery," said Lebret. "When that woman's rump's exposed, she looks more like a goose than ever."

"Never mind Mistress Welles' posterior," said Paul. "What's this to do with a charge of witchcraft?"

"You might call it a kind of overture to the main performance, Doctor," said Giles bitterly. "That same Sunday, at the big morning service, Obadiah was praying as usual—one of those poison-long orations, with no more intermission than a toothache. Like I expected, he asked the Lord to look after Patricia Welles, and show us ways to avoid damnation. Right then, the girl let out a shriek and fell to the floor in a faint. Then she began thrashing around—as though she was wrestling with someone we couldn't see. Old lady Welles ran out from her place in meeting, and took her daughter in her arms.

"'*What is it, Patricia?*' she yelled. '*Who's bewitched you?*'

"'*Lili!*' the brat yelled back. '*Lili Porter—the innkeeper's harlot!*'"

"Don't tell me they listened to such nonsense?"

"Froze in their tracks, every last one," said Giles. "They drank in each word—and loved it. How Lili came to the girl's bed at night and pinned her there. How she tried to scratch her, and pull out her hair. How the brat recited the Lord's Prayer to drive her off—"

"Surely they saw it was a trick—one the mother and daughter had rehearsed."

"Not when Obadiah himself thanked God for her deliverance," said Giles. "Not when Ralph Welles charged up to the pulpit and asked 'em to burn my Lili, then and there."

"Where was my brother?"

"At his preacher's right hand, same as always. He put a stop to that hullabaloo, before the meeting came to blows. But he still sided with Lambert and Welles. Once the church had calmed down, he said the canon law forced him to take action. A member of his flock had been accused of witchcraft. He had no choice but to put Lili on trial. The jury would decide if Patricia's vision was true or false."

Giles had spoken in a dead-calm tone that made his tidings all the heavier. It was the voice of a man who has abandoned hope, in the face of an authority too massive to resist. It seemed incredible that Silas Sutton, a disciple of the great Geoffrey Trevor, could have sunk to this plane—yet Silas' action had a perverted logic. It was part of his faith that the devil could use both man and woman as his mouthpiece: in the Puritans' lexicon, the word *witch* was printed in letters of fire—and any female convicted of such powers must be destroyed by hanging, or by flame. The fact that Silas had insisted on a trial for Lili was proof enough (in Silas' own book) of his fairness.

"What happened next? Where is Lili now?" Paul had spoken with his eyes on the harbor beach. Many of the colonists were up and about—and most of them had contrived to pass by the tavern area on their way to work. Without exception, they moved on after the briefest of pauses. It was already sadly evident that this was no time for an expression of opinion, or of loyalty.

"She's been locked in the jail to await trial," said the innkeeper.

Paul's eyes sought out the flat-roofed cabin at the extreme end of Cupid's Cay, a hundred yards beyond the stockade. It had been built on Silas' order, when the colony was founded: this was the first time it had been used. Paul saw that a guard was stumping in solemn circles around it. The glimpse of that bumpkin and his musket was too grotesque to be borne: he felt rage choke his throat as he strove to speak.

"Have you told me everything?"

"Not quite," said Giles, in the same dead voice. "While they were still outshouting one another at the Sunday service, Deborah Sikes spoke right up and called the Welles girl a liar. Deborah's been teaching the children in the stockade school. She said Patricia had cribbed the whole story from a book she kept in her desk—"

Paul turned sharply. "I remember such a book. It was in Silas' cabin on shipboard."

"We piled out to look for it," said Giles. "Of course it wasn't there. Jack Sikes insisted we search the Welles' cabin—with the same result."

"Obviously the brat has squirreled it away," said Lebret. "Anyone but Master Sutton would realize she'd used it as a primer—and an acting manual."

"As I remember," said Paul, "it shows what harm she could do with a charge of witchcraft."

"She's already proved that point," said Giles. "Next day she had a second fit at the schoolhouse, and called *Deborah* a witch."

"Surely no one believed that."

"You've been away less than a week, Paul," said Lebret. "But the lid's been lifted from Pandora's box, and the demons are loose. Hell-fire, a hot climate, and Englishmen make a bad mixture."

"Surely Silas has gone too far, if he's accepted this second charge."

Giles shrugged. "Deborah's been locked up with my girl during the past four days. Does that answer your question?"

"The hags in the stockade had reason to hate Lili," said Paul. "We can't dispute that. But Deborah had friends everywhere—"

"Not after she had the courage to speak up. Not when Welles, Lambert and company have added a hundred new Bible-backs to their ranks overnight. These new colonists aren't sure of their ground here, or their friends—but all of 'em know church law. If the girls are convicted, they'll vote for burning, to the last man."

"How many will fight to save Lili and Deborah, if it comes to blows?"

"Enough to make trouble," said Giles. "I'm not at all sure we'll win."

"A week ago, we had at least eighty Anglicans on the island. Don't tell me *all* of them have turned coward?"

"No, Paul," said Lebret. "But all of them know what Silas can do to their prospects. Saving your presence, Giles, the family men will hesitate to vote for Lili. Even the best of them aren't sure they *don't* believe in witches—"

"I'll see the girls now," said Paul. "Then I'll go to Silas. Until I know his stand, we can hardly make plans."

"You know it now, Paul," said Lebret. "He won't change."

"Then I must fight him all the way."

Giles got to his feet, swaying a trifle from a blend of weariness and drink. Never in his life had he seemed more raffish—or more harried. Picturing him as a witness at his daughter's trial, Paul felt his mind flinch from the image—and its impact on any Roundhead jury.

"Leave things as they are, Doctor," said the innkeeper thickly. "I've enough on my conscience, without setting brother against brother."

"Brother was set against brother long ago. The next move is mine."

A dozen voices called greetings to the doctor while he strode the length of Cupid's Cay but he answered none of them. At the entrance of the jail, the guard sprang to bar his path, his musket at the ready.

"Stand aside, David Brewster," Paul ordered. "This is a sick call."

There was something in his eyes that made the bumpkin step out of the doorframe. In another moment he had lifted the heavy crossbar and Lili was sobbing in his arms.

"I thought you'd never come back, Paul—"

"Steady does it, my dear. This business has gone far enough: I'll see to that."

THE WITCHES' MARK 219

The words, he knew, were braver than his manner. The windowless cabin already had the peculiar, airless stench of prisons the world over. Paul saw that it was empty of all furniture save for a pallet in the corner. The girl in his embrace seemed woefully thin. Deborah Sikes, who sat huddled in a corner like a rag bag, was in worse plight. It was apparent that the charge of witchcraft (and the dread penalty that hung over her) had broken her spirit. She did not even raise her head when Paul addressed her, and seemed unaware of his presence.

"Will it trouble Deborah if we talk?"

Lili cast a pitying glance at the other prisoner. "Nothing seems to reach her."

Paul knelt on the pallet and examined Jack Sikes' wife briefly. Deborah (though wasted from lack of food) was still sound physically: her illness was of the mind. When he had left the colony, the girl had been a bouncing young mother, ready with a joke and a cheering word for Puritan and Anglican alike. The fact she had changed so completely was a graphic illustration of the spirit that now gripped Eleuthera.

"Let's hope she'll recover when this is behind us," he whispered, as he led Lili away from the corner where her companion sat. "What can you tell me that I don't already know?"

"You've seen Father and Guy?"

"They gave me their side of the story. I'd like yours as well."

"There's little I can add. I've heard of these persecutions in England. I never thought *I'd* be a victim." Lili shivered, and pressed closer to the warmth of his embrace. "Now it's happened, I suppose I should have seen it coming. It's Mistress Welles' way of repaying me for those palmetto spines in her *derrière*. To say nothing of the jealousy that's tormented her—"

"Has Ralph Welles been molesting you?"

Lili tossed her head: in Paul's presence, she seemed to have recovered her aplomb. "Let's say he's been nerving himself to try. So far, he's been too timid to ask for what he wanted. You can't expect his wife to believe that."

"Why didn't you complain to Silas?"

"I'm afraid to speak to your brother directly, Paul: we've been over that. Besides, he wouldn't listen. He *wants* me to die at the stake. It isn't a pretty way to go. I'll kill myself before I let them take me."

"No one's going to hurt you, Lili. I'll see to that."

"How can you prevent them, now I've been accused? All the elders are on the Welles' side."

"I'm going to Silas now."

"He won't budge, Paul. He could have saved me when the Welles brat went into her trance. Instead, he had me locked up here, and ordered my trial."

"Does he fear you that much?"

"He fears himself," said Lili. "Most of all, he despises the weakness I've uncovered in that brassbound prison he calls his soul. He *knows* I could break the lock if he dared to face me alone. Letting me die as a witch is a cheap way out. Perhaps he honestly believes I am one—"

"All this may be true," Paul said carefully. "Silas *can't* have lost his sense of fairness. In England, he'd be within his rights to call this trial for witchcraft; he has the same privilege here. I'll guarantee it's run fairly, and so will he."

"How can we win a trial—with the evidence on his side?"

"You'll go before a jury. So will Deborah: that's part of the code. We'll insist it represent the whole colony—"

"Will you serve as my counsel, Paul?"

"Of course. I've lived between both worlds here. I'm sure our people will demand it."

"What if your brother refuses?"

"He won't dare. Either I defend you, or we'll break open this prison by force—"

"And be shot down from the stockade?"

"That's something else he wouldn't risk." Again, Paul heard his own voice proclaim a program of action invented on the spur of the moment. It was a time for improvisation, for an optimism that found no real backing in his heart. "Your jury will be chosen justly, and you'll get the best defense I can muster. Rely on that, at least."

"What if I'm convicted?"

He turned away shaken anew by the girl's calm acceptance of her plight. "We won't consider such matters now. Let's plot your defense. Two days isn't much time to prepare a brief."

"There's no doubt Patricia Welles was pretending," said Lili. "I'd swear on the Bible it's her mother's doing. It still can't be proved: the girl's too good an actress."

"You can swear Ralph Welles molested you."

"He didn't really—he only peeped at me. *I* can't say he was playing the voyeur—"

"I saw him myself one morning."

"They wouldn't believe you either, Paul. The whole colony thinks we're still lovers. They'd assume it was something we made up to shift the blame. Or they'd say it was proof positive of witchcraft—"

"In Heaven's name how?"

Lili sighed, and moved toward the door, as the guard's musket butt rapped out a warning the visit must end. "By his own account, Ralph Welles is one of the most virtuous husbands and fathers in our colony. It won't help my cause, if I say he was charmed into peeping at my nakedness. If I *did* see him on the beach, why didn't I report it sooner? And by what right did I swim in the surf, when swimming is forbidden here?"

Paul knew the reasoning was accurate. Similar charges had been made at other trials for witchcraft: some of them were listed in the book Patricia Welles had stolen. Here again, the burden of proof rested with the defense, since he had no clear evidence the book existed.

"We can make our plans later, when I've sounded Silas out," he said. Bit by bit, he could feel himself assuming the lawyer's measured tone for Lili's sake. "How are they treating you otherwise?"

"We're on a starvation diet, as you can see."

"I'll remedy that at once. I'll also insist that air vents be cut and cots brought in. Do they allow you exercise?"

Lili smiled faintly. "If they let us outside, Ralph Welles said we'd fly away on broomsticks. He wanted us both put in stocks—and almost won the point."

"I'll remember Master Welles when you're on trial," Paul promised her. "He can clear you if he's cornered—and so can the child. There *must* be ways of breaking them, if Silas will only listen—"

"I've told you what to expect of your brother," said Lili: her voice had lost none of the resignation that had chilled Paul from the beginning. "At this moment, he's found true peace of mind. So long as he truly believes I'm a witch, he's only performing a duty. Don't expect him to give up that armor easily."

"What if we prove he's mistaken, in open court?"

"Then he'll be reduced to a human being—with human desires. It's a hard line for a man who considers himself one cut below God."

His visit with Lili, Paul admitted, had told him nothing new—save for the girl's unerring instinct, which had pinned down Silas' true motives beyond all doubting.

Crossing the stockade to his brother's cabin, he considered throwing that motive in Silas' teeth—and rejected the impulse. The present visit had just one purpose, to learn if the leader of the Eleutherians had abandoned all pretense of justice. In that event, he would fight with other weapons.

The leader's cabin stood level with the blockhouse. From the window of the workroom, the visitor had a view of the harbor, above the sharp-toothed palisade. Informed that Silas had business aboard the *Adventurer*, Paul decided to await him here. The ship had anchored well inshore: he could see his brother clearly as the latter bustled about the deck, giving his final orders for the unloading.

Captain Sperry had returned from the pirates' careening ground with his hull in good order and his spirits high. Since he planned to sail within the week for Virginia and Massachusetts Bay, the settlers were busy with the cargo that would go aboard. A principal item was ten tons of brazilwood which was to go direct to the sister colony. The profits derived from the sale of this valuable cargo were earmarked as a gift to a college established in Massachusetts ten years ago and named after its principal sponsor, a church elder called John Harvard. It was quite like Silas (thought Paul) to feed the lamp of reason with one hand while dimming that same lamp on his own doorstep. . . . He was still brooding on the paradox when his brother stalked into the work-room.

"I know why you're here, of course," said Silas. "Let us not begin quarreling until I've expressed my gratitude."

"You've no cause to be grateful—if you refer to Anne. I promised to bring her here safely. I've done so—with a small interruption due to bad weather."

"Anne told me of your shipwreck, and your voyage from Cat Island. I must say you used your wits to preserve your life, and hers."

"Surely divine providence had a hand."

"I'd be a poor man of God to deny that," said Silas. He moved to the worktable, to add a new bill of lading to the stack that awaited his attention there. So far, his manner had been amaz-ingly tranquil. The eyes that had so often blazed like coals were benign today. So was the gentle voice that seemed to fend off argument in advance.

Remembering Lili's explanation of this change, Paul kept his temper. Until his brother had spoken his mind, he could hardly launch his own attack. "At least you two are reunited," he said. "I hoped Anne's presence here would teach you tolerance. Don't force me to conclude I'm mistaken."

Silas held up a soothing palm. "May we defer the subject of your visit a moment more? Let's finish first with Anne. I'm afraid her fate is rather more important—"

"I gathered her fate will be settled for all time, when she be-comes your wife."

"Read this, please, before you mock me again."

For a moment, Paul stared woodenly at the sheet of foolscap his brother had tossed across the table. Then, forcing his brain to cope with this new attack, he read it through. It was a brief but pointed note, signed by the great Cromwell himself, and ad-dressed, in glowing terms, to Brother Silas Sutton, "a defender of the faith." Cromwell began with a compliment to Silas' skill in converting an island wilderness to a bastion of England. It warned him that troops and ordnance were now en route to Eleuthera, aboard the British man-of-war *Advance*—but it added, in the strongest terms, that these re-enforcements were for defensive purposes only.

In no circumstances (Cromwell concluded) was Silas to consider a punitive war against the Havana: England's position, at the time, was too chancy to risk a challenge to Spain. Obviously, he must defend his island against all comers—including the Cuban Spaniards. Letters just received from Cromwell's agents in Madrid suggested that the dons (alarmed by the flourishing English settlement at the gateway to the Indies) were contemplating such an assault. Silas was advised to gird his loins for that attack. . . .

Paul tossed down the note with a shrug. "You guessed right, then—when you took my advice, and Captain Hood's. You'll be lucky if you can defend your present position. You'd have been destroyed if you'd moved against Cuba—"

"We won't discuss that now," said Silas. His voice was heavy with a resentment Paul knew too well: while the dour mood lasted, he seemed vastly more familiar. "I'll accept my role of colonizer, since Cromwell wills it thus. The crusade against Spain can come later."

"What's this to do with Anne?"

"I'm fearful for her safety, Paul."

"Cromwell's sending men and guns. Surely you can hold the island, with Hood to help you at sea—"

"I've every hope of repulsing the enemy," said Silas. "Until the issue's decided, I'd prefer to have Anne elsewhere."

"You'd send her back to England?"

"Not quite so far, perhaps. Captain Sperry will put into the Virginia colony on his return voyage. Anne might stay there awhile—"

"D'you think she'd leave your side at the first threat of danger?"

"Anne is not yet my wife," said Silas. "Already, I've reproached myself for bringing her here so soon."

"Eleuthera's her lifework too. Now she's here, she has the right to take part in its building."

"Not if I think otherwise. As governor, I can choose my colonists, and reject others. If I decide to deport Anne for her own protection, she must go."

"Without marriage?"

"Marriage can come later, when we've disposed of the papists. When I've united this region under one God, and made a true peace."

"In the colony, Silas—or in your own soul?"

"My soul is at rest: I've followed the Lord's will, and driven out sin where I found it. The fact remains we're facing parlous times. I've no wish to expose the woman I love to needless hardship—perhaps even to death."

Paul thought swiftly, as Silas continued to stare out at the harbor. For the first time, he could see that his brother was confused by the pace of events. Faced with a decision too big for his theology, he could only grope for a solution—and, though he was too proud to ask for Paul's help, it was obvious he expected that fraternal gesture to be made freely.

"What are you asking of me, Silas?"

"I hoped you'd endorse my view. There's a doctor on the *Advance:* your services will no longer be needed here. I want you to sail for Virginia with Anne, and make sure she's safely settled there. When this colony's established beyond all hazard, I'll send for her—"

"Forgive me, Silas—but that's too much to ask of any man."

"Even a blood brother? If you have my welfare at heart—"

"Anne's worth her salt: she'll stand by you here, no matter what the danger."

"I still demand that you do me this last favor."

Paul wavered for an instant, as he saw the chance for striking a bargain. Could he agree to squire Anne to Virginia, in return for the freedom of Lili Porter and Deborah Sikes? Once they were clear of the Bahamas, would he not have every right to court Anne in his own behalf—now that Silas (for all his strange, inverted reasoning) had refused to join his lot with hers?

It was a hard choice, but he made it instantly. Anne would refuse to leave Eleuthera now, no matter how Silas thundered— and Paul, on his side, could not abandon Lili and Deborah. One did not strike bargains with Silas Sutton—not when a witchcraft trial hung in the balance.

"I'm through with favors, Silas," he said. "I've brought Anne here safely. What she does hereafter is your affair and hers—and I'll have no part of it. Today, I've called on you for a more pressing reason."

"If you mean the trial I've ordered—"

"Why did you do it?"

"I had no choice. My people demanded justice."

"You could have stopped the uproar with a word. Why did you lock up two innocent women without cause?"

"They'll have a chance to prove their innocence in court," said Silas. "The matter is out of my hands until the trial."

"There's no way to stop it? Or should I say, restore this settlement to sanity?"

"None whatever, Paul."

"Will you permit me to serve as their counsel?"

The grimace that creased Silas' face was close to a smile. "I expected that request. You may take the case, if you insist. The women must have a defender in court. I doubt if another man on the island would step forward."

"Don't take your power too much for granted. You may be in for an unpleasant surprise."

"I've done no more than my duty."

"Can't you see this thing may destroy the colony?"

"Both women deserve to be tried, Paul. The charges against them are grave: if they're guilty, they'll be executed."

"On the word of a hysterical child and a jealous wife?"

"If that's a sneer at Mistress Welles, you're sadly mistaken."

"Can't you see the woman has used her daughter to get back at Lili?"

"Are you accusing Brother Welles and the Porter girl of improper conduct?"

"Bring him here. I'll call him a voyeur to his face."

"Such a charge is fantastic. Ralph Welles is one of the pillars of our congregation—"

"Outwardly, perhaps. I dislike quoting Scripture, Silas, but you'll remember the verses from Matthew: *'Whosoever looketh on a woman to lust after her hath committed adultery with her already in his heart.'* "

Silas turned away, and squared his massive shoulders: there was no flaw in his rocklike poise, but Paul knew the barb had sunk deep. He had aimed it deliberately—to prove, beyond all doubting, that his brother had lusted after Lili, as hotly as Ralph Welles. Lili, he perceived, had been right from the start. Tortured by desire, Silas had found no peace until the charge of witchcraft had offered an escape from his dilemma. By his lights, he had acted justly when he brought the two girls to trial. . . . Would he insist that it be conducted fairly?

"What you've just told me is hearsay," said Silas—and only the slight tremor in his voice betrayed him. "It's no charge you can make in court."

"Forget Charity Welles' motive. Pretend, if you like, that she didn't inspire her daughter. Would you call the child's babbling evidence?"

"The Lord has used children often as His mouthpiece. It's a fact you can't talk away."

"For the last time, will you stop this mockery of justice?"

"I couldn't if I wished. An accusation has been made according to canon law; a bill of indictment is being drawn today. If you'll call at the church house tomorrow, the clerk will give you a copy. I needn't tell you that the case against both women seems black as sin itself—"

"Meaning, of course, that they're guilty until proved innocent?"

"Mock me, Paul—if you must. I've done no wrong, and I stand by justice."

The battle was ended, and Silas had held his ground. Knowing they could never meet again save as enemies, Paul turned and left the cabin.

Anne, he learned, had gone to the Lamberts', where quarters had awaited her for the past week. He could think of no valid reason for stopping there. Now that he had announced himself as the prisoners' champion, he could hardly linger in the stockade.

Several cases awaited him in his sick bay—minor injuries, for the most part, with the new colonists supplying the victims. It was well after noon when he dismissed his last patient—and turned, in some annoyance, as a fresh shadow fell across the threshold. His anger vanished when he saw his latest caller was Anne herself.

"How did you escape so easily?" he asked.

"I'm here with Silas' permission," she said, hesitating but a moment in the doorframe before she stepped inside. With the light behind her, he was hard-put to recognize the fellow castaway who, only yesterday, had battled wind and wave beside him. The gown she wore (stiff with steel, and voluminous with petticoats) was almost matronly. Cut in the best Puritan tradition, it seemed a solemn masquerade, designed to remind him of the distance that now divided them.

"It's well known at the stockade that I'm skilled at nursing," she said. "I insisted I put that skill to use, in case you needed help in your surgery."

"Believe me, I've no need of assistants in that quarter—"

"I'm sure you don't," said Anne. With a single backward glance, she closed the door. "This was only a pretense, of course. Tell me what's happened since your departure. I can't believe my ears."

"How can you say that?" he asked harshly. "You're of the Puritan faith—isn't the witch hunt their favorite sport?"

"I don't deserve that, Paul. My father never condoned such practices. No more do I."

Their glances locked for a moment, while he fumbled for his self-control. "Don't mind what I say today," he told her. "As you must have heard by now, I've just declared war on Silas. Like it or not, you're in his camp. He insists these two poor girls be tried."

"Does that mean we must be enemies too?"

"There's no room for compromise, Anne. Situated as you are, how can I ask you to endorse my position?"

"Then it's true you plan to serve as defense counsel?"

"I felt it was my duty."

"Just as it's Silas' duty to order the trial—because a child is possessed of devils?"

"Do you believe such nonsense?"

"Not for a moment, Paul. I can't believe that Silas does."

"Have you talked this out with him?"

"I've scarcely seen him since I arrived. He sent me straight to my bed at Mistress Lambert's, and insisted I rest—after what he called my ordeal. I've heard the story of the trial through her. *She's* positive both prisoners will be convicted. Why did Silas allow their arrest?"

Paul hesitated. Burning though he was to reveal his brother's motives, he felt it was unfair to speak bluntly to Anne. This was no time to undermine her loyalty to Silas—shaken, as it already was, by the whisperings of Obadiah Lambert's spouse (a windy but accurate echo of her husband).

"Don't judge Silas too hastily," he said. "To my mind, this thing's a relic from the Dark Ages. To him, it's part of his function as a lay minister—and most of his flock agrees. In your place, I'd stand aside and let us fight our battle. He'll see it's fought fairly."

"Must it be fought at all? I'll beg him to reconsider."

"He's gone too far, Anne. Nothing will induce him to change his mind."

"There must be something I can do."

Again Paul hesitated as an inspiration came to him unasked. En route to his talk with Silas, he had paused at the blockhouse and given orders that both prisoners receive the regular colonists' ration: he had also ordered that the logs of their prison be cut below the eaves, to allow some passage of light and air. When he had stormed from Silas' presence, he had been too angry to ask if his orders had been obeyed. It might be good strategy to send Anne as his deputy.

"Would you care to visit the prisoners in my behalf?"

"I'll go gladly, Paul."

"Proper beds have been ordered for them, and a decent mid-day meal. Will you see if they've received them? It's your first chance to play Samaritan here: if *I* go, I'll be an object of suspicion."

"Have you any message?"

"Tell Lili I'm to serve as their defender—and I've no intention of losing my case."

Anne hesitated in the doorway. "Someone was with the prisoners when I left the stockade—a man named Zachary Daniels. Is the name familiar?"

Paul nodded grimly. Daniels was a crony of Obadiah Lambert's, a fat, bumptious fellow whose reputation for idling was well earned, thanks to his post as church archivist—a sinecure which permitted him to beg off from most hard labor.

"Did he state the purpose of his visit?"

"Only that he'd been sent by the Reverend Lambert to examine the prisoners. He seemed harmless enough."

"Let's hope you're right, Anne. Please come back, after you've made your own inspection. I'll be here."

Alone in the surgery, Paul found himself pondering Daniels' motives and liking them less by the moment. The visit had some connection with the charges Lambert was now compiling: Daniels, he knew, would use every trick to bring back the evidence the preacher desired. . . . The fellow had boasted often of his knowledge of witches and their ways.

In London, Paul had met others of his kind. One, a man named Matthew Hopkins (who bore the resounding title of Witch-Finder General), had been Daniels' image. Hopkins had won a ghoulish fame in England: he had found and identified witches in every shire, and collected handsome sums as his fee: only his enemies dared whisper that his victims were hand-picked, by persons in authority who could afford to pay him best. In the last few years, hundreds had been brought to trial on Hopkins' evidence—and the percentage of convictions had been frightening.

The witch-finder's methods were ingenious—and varied enough to bring in a full bag of culprits. One procedure was to strip the victim and prick the body with needles, to discover the so-called witches' mark, a portion of the skin insensitive to pain. During such tests, it was Hopkins' custom to force his suspect to sit bolt upright, with legs crossed tailor-fashion and arms extended upward. Since the pose was sometimes held for hours, numbness and near-paralysis were inevitable aftermaths—permitting the wielder of the needle to locate the "mark" at a spot of his own choosing.

The witches' mark was the most damning bit of evidence in Hopkins' book—but the man had other favorite tortures. Sometimes the thumb of a suspect's right hand was tied to his left toe with a stout cord. The body was then drawn through the nearest pond to test its buoyance. If it floated (as it always did, if the cord was held properly) Hopkins pronounced the suspect a witch or a wizard. (Since these creatures could fly at will, it was logical to assume they were unsinkable.)

It was also Hopkins' professed belief that a witch could change to an animal or an insect, leaving the human form as a carapace to dupe the unwary. For this reason, imprisoned suspects were spied on constantly by the guards to detect the presence of flies or spiders on their bodies. When such an insect was observed, a guard rushed in to kill it. If the creature died, it was labeled harmless. If it escaped, the migration of the witch's spirit was complete—and another proof of guilt established.

Still another bit of evidence was the victim's inability to weep, even when faced with proof of guilt. With her darkened mind, Deborah might well remain dry-eyed under Zachary Daniels' inquisition. Lili would hold back tears as a matter of pride. Paul wondered if this, too, would be held against them. . . . Or would the disciple of Matthew Hopkins use even cruder means to complete the indictment?

The question was answered, promptly enough, when Anne screamed Paul's name from the beach.

Running from the surgery to join her, he saw that she stood in the half-open jail door, trying to force the guard to stand aside. Heads had already appeared on the stockade: as he ran, Paul could hear the creak of the hand ferry, and guessed that other colonists were arriving posthaste. He did not pause to check the deployment of these hostile forces. The guard lowered his musket, just before Paul knocked it from his hand. No one stirred on the palisade when he charged into the jail, with Anne on his heels.

Deborah Sikes lay on the pallet, her clothing stripped down to the waist, her skin dotted with a hundred needle pricks. Despite the bad light, Paul saw that one of the punctures had been circled with red crayon to show the witches' mark. In a far corner, Lili Porter stood like a cat at bay. Her dress was ripped from one shoulder, the skin slashed with the same crayon—but she seemed otherwise unharmed.

"David Brewster held me at gun point," she said. "I couldn't save Deborah from the needle."

"Did Daniels mark you too?"

"Just once, Paul. I fetched him a clout he won't forget."

Anne had knelt at the pallet, to rearrange Deborah's torn clothing. Aware of a rising murmur outside, Paul stepped into the sunlight. His jaw hardened when he saw that Silas had appeared on the blockhouse roof and had spread both hands for silence—with all the fussy decorum of a headmaster facing a group of unruly schoolboys. By this time, more than a score of men had crossed from island to cay. Noting that most of them carried muskets, Paul knew they had understood the cause of Anne's scream.

"What does this disturbance mean?" Silas had spoken in his familiar voice of thunder. "Why aren't you people at your tasks? You're to approach the stockade only for divine service."

The murmur that answered him would have given most men pause but Silas did not waver. Before the hostile babble died, he leaped from palisade to beach, and approached the jail with wrathful, long-legged strides.

Anne had emerged to stand beside Paul. The guard, his back to the wall, fumbled with his musket and his lost dignity. Already, it was clear that the temper of the Anglicans was hair-triggered. Aware that something had gone amiss in the prison pen, they waited grimly for enlightenment.

Silas ignored their stares as he turned to vent his fury on the sentry—but Paul stepped between before his brother could speak.

"This is my doing, Silas. I'll answer your questions."

"Why is Mistress Trevor here?"

"You sent her to the surgery, to serve as my helper. I asked her to check on the health of the prisoners. Must she tell you what we found—or would you prefer to see it with your own eyes?"

A sob escaped Anne's lips as she took a step forward and faced Silas directly. Paul saw his face change at that wordless appeal, though he still refused to give ground.

"Show me what you mean, Paul. Don't stand behind a woman's skirt while you justify a breach of discipline."

"I'd already asked that the prisoners be properly fed, and given decent cots. Why were my orders ignored?"

Ralph Welles spoke up from the palisade. Tense though the situation was, Paul could not help smiling when he saw that the surveyor was careful to hide behind the porcine bulk of Zachary Daniels.

"There was no time, Brother Silas. The witch-finder's been with these women for the past hour."

"We're aware of that, Brother Welles," said Paul. "Allow me to exhibit his handiwork."

He could feel the crowd surge forward when he signaled to Lili, who moved into the open with an arm around Deborah Sikes. The innkeeper's daughter lifted her eyes defiantly to pick out Daniels on the palisade, and the witch-finder lost no time in diving behind the sentry walk. Lili's dress was still ripped away from her shoulder: she made no attempt to cover herself while she led her stunned companion to Paul.

"Show them what Zachary Daniels did to her, Dr. Sutton," she cried—and her voice was loud enough to carry to the farthest reaches of the palisades. "As you'll see, he tried to torture me— and failed. Tonight, he'll have a black eye for his pains—"

Paul drew down the tattered dress from Deborah's arm and shoulder, to exhibit the blood-pitted skin beneath. The rumble that rose from fifty male throats blended in a concerted roar. Paul stopped the impending rush with both hands extended.

"Stay where you are!" he cried. "I'm taking these girls to the sick bay. It's where they belong after such treatment—"

"On whose authority?" asked Silas.

"On my own—as doctor to this colony."

Silas had not left off staring since Lili emerged from the jail. He spoke with his gaze riveted—seemingly unaware of the peril his brother had just turned aside.

"Are you mad? This is mutiny."

"Not unless you force the issue," said Paul. "Promise there'll be no more of this persecution. I'll keep them safe until the trial."

"Don't let them go, Brother Silas!" shrieked Charity Welles. "They're witches. They'll only fly away." The woman had stepped into view on the palisade, both fists raised in malediction. Charity Welles had been ill named: there was no trace of forbearance in the pinched face that had just thrust into view among the spectators.

Silas recognized her with a nod.

"If they'd wished to fly away, Charity," he said, "I'm sure they'd have escaped long since. Apparently they're willing to stand trial. I've given my brother permission to defend them, and he's passed his word to keep them safe meanwhile. Shall we leave it at that—now that Brother Daniels has found the witches' marks?"

He had spoken in a voice drained of anger. No one stirred in the hostile grouping before the stockade. Silas' somber eyes turned again to Lili: he was studying her intently now, as though he could not get enough of staring. Turning to give the two prisoners what comfort he could, Paul saw that Lili was returning his brother's look defiantly. For the first time, he realized that her shoulder and half her bosom were still exposed, the deep-tanned flesh circled in red to mark Zachary Daniels' solitary pinprick.

"You heard your leader, Charity Welles," said Lili. "We're innocent of your charges, and we'll prove it. If there's a witch on this island, the court will find her."

"She accused me!" the woman screamed. "The devil speaks through her mouth!"

"We needn't prolong this," said Paul—addressing his brother directly. "Have we your permission to retire?"

"Go, by all means," said Silas. "We've had enough name-calling.

Keep these women in good health, and see they come to trial. They'll be judged fairly."

Paul signaled into the crowd, and Jack Sikes came forward to lift Deborah in his arms. At the wordless command, the group on the beach dispersed. Some followed Jack as he strode toward the sick bay. Others, with much head-shaking, began to move toward the hand ferry, and their interrupted tasks. . . . The crisis, it seemed, had been averted in time. Paul turned toward his brother, keeping his voice low.

"Thanks for small mercies, Silas."

Silas did not stir: his eyes had not left Lili.

"Take this woman from our sight," he said. "Save for her mark, she seems well enough. However, since you wish it, you may keep both witches in your surgery."

"Do you need help, Lili?" Paul asked.

"I'll walk alone," said the innkeeper's daughter. Her eyes matched Silas' glare: they held him fixed, while her hand lifted slowly, to close her torn bodice. Then, with head high, she followed Jack and Deborah.

# THE TRIAL

SILAS had set the time of the trial at eight o'clock, two days after Paul's return to Eleuthera. The place he had chosen was the church itself. It was also the general meeting-house, the only edifice on the island large enough to accommodate the colony under one roof.

Reviewing his notes for the last time at the desk in the surgery, Paul saw the people were beginning to move toward the stockade the moment their morning meal was finished: the creaking progress of the hand ferry had been constant for the past half-hour. In the sick bay, the two prisoners awaited his word to depart. Lili had donned the simplest (and sternest) garb—he had obtained the dress from Anne's own wardrobe, at the latter's suggestion. Deborah Sikes was still deep in stupor and was barely able to walk unaided. Her husband stood ready to help her on the short journey to the meetinghouse.

Paul closed the last of several tomes he had borrowed from Silas' workroom to prepare for his task. He had studied hard in the short time allotted, but was ready to admit that he was little wiser than before. In England, no established procedure had been set up for the investigation of those accused of witchcraft; as a consequence, trial methods varied widely. Indeed, Paul had soon realized that nearly all such trials (like the routine of accusation) were solemn farces: the accused were assumed to be in league with Satan—and argument advanced in their defense was judged to be a lie. Even positive proof that a person on trial had not been present at the scene of a crime could be ruled out—since it was generally believed that both witches and wizards could torment others by projecting their spirits through space.

It was a fearful task that awaited him. The stakes were the lives of two women, the adversaries an army of superstitions and primitive fears, some of them older than the spoken word. Paul had long since realized that formal preparation, in the strict legal sense, would be useless. He had decided to rely on the inspiration of the moment (and the mental plane of his adversaries) to see him through.

His heart was leaden as his spirits when he shepherded his small flock on the stroke of eight, and led them to their ordeal.

In the meetinghouse, every seat was occupied, and people were standing against the walls. After he had led Lili and Deborah to the defense table, Paul risked a look at the assembly while he pretended to sort his notes. He was hardly reassured by what he saw.

Most of the faces seemed noncommittal at first glance, but he could read indecision in a hundred eyes—and a refusal to accept commitment that was even more unsettling. It was true that the colony had rallied to the girls' defense after the incident at the jail. The hint of torture (represented by the unsavory person of Zachary Daniels) had brought a quick revulsion. Today, when both prisoners were decently clothed and bore no visible marks of suffering, some of the most indignant settlers had retreated to their original attitude of doubting. It was clear that they had come as spectators only. Only the hard core of ultrapious Puritans had condemned Lili and Deborah in advance—but most of the rest reserved judgment. Nearly all the newcomers were in this larger grouping. Fresh from England and the witch trials that had been one of the first legacies of civil war, these honest folk were careful to keep their faces impassive and their thoughts secret.

Anne, Paul noted, sat in the midst of the audience, between the wives of Obadiah Lambert and Adam Holborn, the leader of the second group of colonists. She gave him a quick smile as

she caught his glance, but no other sign of greeting. Aware of
the special ordeal she was suffering, he was careful to avert his
eyes.

At the front of the meetinghouse (in the area normally reserved
for the elders' benches) space had been cleared to accommodate
tables for defense and prosecution. Two pews awaited the un-
selected jury; the magistrates' table stood against the facing wall.
Ralph Welles—who, to the surprise of no one, had been selected
by the elders to serve as prosecutor—was in his place, shuffling
importantly through a sheaf of notes.

Silas occupied one of the two magistrates' chairs. The other
was still vacant. When Paul approached, he was deep in Obadiah
Lambert's bill of indictment. Paul had studied his own copy of
that preposterous document thoroughly: the fact that Silas was
reading it with attention seemed the worst of omens. He waited
(with what patience he could muster) until his brother had
turned the last leaf and gave him a belated nod of recognition.
Never had Silas' manner been more judicial—or more remote from
the everyday concerns of man.

"I promised you a fair trial for these women," he said. "Providing he's agreeable to us, you may name the second magistrate."

It was a handsome concession, and Paul was hard put to cover
his surprise. Letting his glance rove over the assembly, he settled
on Adam Holborn—a tall, gravely handsome man who had already won the colony's respect. Paul's own meetings with the
leader of the second group had convinced him Holborn was fair
enough, despite his Puritan persuasion.

He did not announce his preference at once. "I still demand
a jury," he told Silas.

"You may have one," said his brother. "Naturally, it must be
approved by the vote of the congregation."

Paul could have wished for a more direct method of selection—
but this was one of the first rulings in the Articles of the Adventurers, and he was too wise to protest.

"So far we agree," he said. "I choose Master Adam Holborn
as the second magistrate. The jury will be approved or rejected
by the people here assembled."

Holborn, he saw, was not too happy at the responsibility assigned him, but he moved to the empty chair on the wave of an approving murmur from the audience. Thinking the trial about to open, Paul returned to his table to examine his notes. When Obadiah Lambert rose from his place to stand behind the pulpit, he allowed a small groan to escape him. He had forgotten that no formal gathering could begin here without some statement from the presiding minister.

Lambert opened the great, gold-stamped Bible on the lectern and announced the text. It was from the third chapter of Zechariah:

*"And he showed me Joshua, the High Priest, standing before the angel of the Lord—and Satan standing at his right hand to resist him. And the Lord said unto Satan, 'The Lord rebuke thee, O Satan! Even the Lord that has chosen Jerusalem rebuke thee! Is not this a brand plucked out of the fire?'"*

The preacher closed the Bible and leaned over the pulpit to study each face in his congregation—pointedly ignoring the defense table, and the three figures seated there.

"Brethren," he intoned, "you have heard me read of the way Our Lord rebuked Satan. Elsewhere in the Holy Word you have read how he was ejected from Heaven with his accursed legions, filled with envy and malice against all the Lord's anointed—and seeking, by every way and means, to work for the ruination of mankind.

"Satan is a spirit. Hence, he strikes at the spiritual part of mankind, the most excellent part. Primarily disturbing and interrupting the animal and vital spirits, the Evil One also maliciously operates upon the soul by strange and frightful representations to the fancy. Sometimes he brings on violent torments of the body, through his agents—whom we call witches. Often he threatens to extinguish life, as he did in the case of this poor child before you—she who was so sorely afflicted by the two women whose guilt will this day be made plain."

Here was undue influence upon a potential jury, no less barefaced because it was wrapped in a traditional Bible reading. Paul caught Giles Porter's eye, and saw that the innkeeper was purple with anger at the unfair attack—but he made no move to interrupt. This, above all, was a moment when he was forced to tread softly. To most of these listeners, the minister spoke directly for God. Had Paul given this skulduggery its right name, Lambert would have accused him of unfairness against God himself.

"Not only does Satan vent his malice in diabolical operations on the soul," the preacher continued. "He also raises myths of darkness in the understanding, by which men are bereft of the very ability to distinguish right from wrong. All of us have seen evidence of these lower machinations of the Fiend—the vast body of sin with which mankind has always been burdened.

"The bodies and the souls of men and of women have always been liable to these invasions. No one who has observed such phenomena can have failed to see that conduct of the persons so afflicted—both in manner and in violence—cannot rationally proceed from any other cause. Satan thus exerts his malice immediately, by employing *some* of mankind to serve his ends, that his grand design may be undiscernible."

Lambert paused to let the weight of this murky rhetoric settle on his listeners—and, for the first time, let his eyes rest on the two prisoners at the defense table.

"We all know how Satan used the serpent in Eden, when he tempted the first man, through Eve, to eat of the forbidden fruit. Womankind is cursed with that primal weakness, an inability to resist such lures—hence, the greater proportion of witches are among them. Satan contracts with witches and wizards, that they shall be his instruments. It is but natural that all who serve him vigorously deny that service, lest they be recognized and shunned by those who love God.

"So far as we can guess at his administration of the kingdom of darkness, we believe that witches make witches. Once they become subjects of the Fiend, he may use them at his pleasure to affright and afflict others. No domain is safe from his entrance— for he can insinuate himself, through these vile beings who have the shape of true believers, into all levels of their society. At times, he can take on the shape of true saints and ministers— and, if it were possible to do so, he would deceive the very elect."

Lambert leaned down from his pulpit, spreading his wide-sleeved arms in an orator's gesture that embraced the whole meetinghouse. "Brethren, we know from the Holy Book that Satan is never more the Prince of Darkness than when he most resembles the Angel of Light. When he pretends to holiness, then does he most secretly—and, by consequence, most surely—undermine the very foundations of the soul. I charge all of you to remember that the devil works endlessly—yea, even in this very room. If we do not stamp out those who have subjected themselves unto him, others too must suffer hell's torments in the life to come.

"I say in the words of the prophet Micah to you, *'The Lord's voice crieth to the city and to the country also with an unusual and amazing loudness. He says, "Be sober, be vigilant, because your adversary the devil goeth about as a roaring lion, seeking whom among you he may distress, delude and devour."'* I charge you magistrates to be ever mindful of the presence of the Evil One. I charge you twelve—who will hear how he has taken these deluded women as his own—to armor your minds and hearts that you be not led astray."

A prayer followed this flaming exhortation. For once, it was blessedly brief. When it ended, the Reverend Obadiah, his face a patient mask, stepped down from his pulpit.

"Brother Silas, let the trial begin."

Henry Bellows, the sad-eyed clerk of the congregation, opened a ledger to keep a record of the proceedings. Paul and Ralph Welles had already risen to face the court. The fall of the leader's gavel demanded silence.

"Members of the Eleuthera colony," said Silas, "we are met together to perform a solemn duty—a full and fair inquiry into the activities of two of our number, who have been accused of leaguing with the devil. If found guilty, they will be punished according to the prescribed penalty for such guilt."

An almost visible shiver passed down the benches. Silas had not named the punishment. Every listener knew it was either death by hanging or burning at the stake, the latter being the usual method of destroying witches throughout the civilized world.

"As senior magistrate of the court," said Silas, "I have agreed that these women may be tried by a jury. The clerk of our congregation will read the names of those who have signified their willingness to serve."

Henry Bellows reached across the table for a second ledger, but Paul was on his feet before he could open it. He suspected that Silas had given the order without considering its implication. An immediate challenge was imperative.

"Do I understand that all the people of this colony have been told they may be called on to serve as jurors?"

"That is the purpose of the list, Doctor," said the clerk.

"I am a member of this colony—and I have not been told."

Guy Lebret spoke from the front bench. "Nor have I."

A dozen voices echoed the same objection, all over the church. Paul lifted his voice above the protests.

"Is this the fair trial you promised us? That book Henry Bellows is holding is a stockade register. Every man in it is of the Puritan faith."

Silas' face darkened as he turned toward the clerk. "Who compiled this list originally?"

"Brother Ralph Welles, I believe. The names were inscribed when our colony was founded."

Silas turned to the other magistrate. "Do you accept the list, Brother Holborn?"

"By no means," said Adam Holborn. There was a twinkle in his eye when he turned to Paul. "The objection by counsel seems a valid one. Any accused person, regardless of his crime, is entitled to be tried by a jury of his peers—not by members of a sect, however holy."

"Even when the crime is against God?" asked Obadiah Lambert.

"Even then, Brother Obadiah," said Holborn. "These charges concern the whole colony. If they are true, our very existence is threatened by the Evil One—as you so eloquently stated from the pulpit. Certainly we must pass judgment as a group, if we are to call ourselves a self-governing body. Don't you agree, Brother Silas?"

Silas hesitated, and his mouth hardened into a familiar mold. It was clear to Paul that he had never really paused to question the jury list.

"Do you feel that our jurors should include Anglicans as well as Puritans?"

"How else can their verdicts be of value?" Holborn's glance strayed along the crowded benches. "The entire colony is assembled here. Would you care to put the matter to a vote?"

"We need hardly vote on a point of law," said Silas drily. "I'll yield to the defense, in the interests of complete justice. The clerk will list every able-bodied man in the colony on separate slips of paper. The names will be mixed in a bowl and drawn at random. Is the method agreeable to both lawyers?"

Paul glanced at Ralph Welles, who had settled between his wife and daughter. The surveyor's arms were folded, and his face and neck had turned red as a turkey cock's—but he bowed his head in angry consent. His weather-vane mind (trained to turn with the prevailing wind) had sensed his error.

"I'll need time to prepare such a listing," said Henry Bellows. "Some of our new arrivals are not yet registered as settlers."

"In that case, we'll adjourn court until tomorrow," said Silas. He spoke generally, addressing the gathering. Once again, he had the air of a schoolmaster who has permitted an annoying change in class routine, but will condone no other lapses. "All of you have tasks to perform, I'm sure. I suggest you go about them."

Paul had gone into the trial expecting a bitter contest from the outset. In its way, the adjournment was an anticlimax. He knew that even Lili's spirits were drooping after he had led her back to the sick bay, with Deborah and Jack Sikes behind them. Fortunately for his own peace of mind, there were enough tasks to occupy his time until evening—when Lebret stopped by to give his own impression of the proceedings.

"The law's a sluggish beast," said the Frenchman. "Never prod its behind, once it's in motion. All in all, I think you came out better than Welles today."

"At least we've a chance for an impartial jury—if any jury on Eleuthera can be impartial."

"I've been taking opinions all over the settlement," said Lebret. "Granted, most of the colony is cautious—but there's sentiment in the girls' favor. The Welleses aren't the most popular family on the island. A good many people think they settled on the main to spy on the Anglicans."

"How many accept Patricia's story?"

"The child's a born troublemaker—there are no two opinions on that. Unfortunately, many honest men actually believe in witches—and their power to influence others. It's too bad neither of us actually saw the girl when she claimed to be possessed. Time after time, I was told it changed people's blood to water—"

"They swallowed her story, then?"

"I'm afraid there's no doubt of it."

"I'm positive she planned the performance—and that her information on witches, such as it is, came from the book she stole from Deborah Sikes' schoolroom. But I haven't a shred of proof, unless I can find the book."

"Did you mention it to Silas, when you asked him to release the girls?"

Paul shook his head. "I intended to. I'm sure he had the book in his cabin on the *Adventurer*. It seemed a waste of breath, when I saw there was no way I could break through. He'd have closed his mind to that argument as well."

"I'm not sure that's the case," said the Frenchman. "Call Master Sutton what you will, he's doing his utmost to conduct this case within the limits of canon law. If he suspected the Welles girl of play-acting, I'm sure he'd change sides—"

"You're forgetting that Silas *wants* to brand Lili as a witch."

Lebret stood in the surgery window to look out at the dusk-dimmed harbor. Lights had winked on around the tavern, as the colonists began their preparations for the evening meal. The Frenchman shook a fist at Welles' cabin, in clear view on the slope above the ferry landing. Something in the gesture made Paul look up sharply. He had sensed from the first that Lebret was the bearer of news—which he would reveal in his own way.

"What if the book were found?" asked the Frenchman. "Would it win your case?"

"At the moment, I'm not sure. There's no doubt it would help." Paul gave a shrug of exasperation. "Why ask the question? It's obvious the thing's been lost or destroyed."

"Don't be too sure of that."

"You searched the Welles cabin and found nothing."

"Perhaps we didn't search well enough."

"Stop playing cat-and-mouse, Guy. If you've a lead, let's hear it."

"Don't get your hopes up, Paul. What I've learned today may come to nothing—but when the trial adjourned today, your brother asked me to take *la petite Anne* on a tour of the fruit orchard. I stopped there to do some pruning. She returned alone, to make calls in the settlement. When I returned, I was surprised to find her waiting at the hand ferry. Her first impulse had been to come to you direct—but she didn't want tongues to wag."

Paul went to his worktable, to prepare the opiate that would insure Deborah Sikes a night's repose. Like so many of his race, the Frenchman had an orderly mind: he believed in telling a story from the beginning.

"Do I gather that Mistress Trevor has made you her messenger?"

"She wished me to say she was much impressed by your efforts in your clients' behalf. She's praying you'll win your case."

"Is that all?"

"By no means," said Lebret. "As I remarked, she can't speak out openly in your behalf. However, she *did* witness something she wished you to hear without delay. Just before dusk, she was passing the Welles' cabin, and observed their *enfant terrible* playing in the yard—"

Paul kept his eyes on the posset he had just drained from mortar to glass. The impulse to seize his friend's throat and shake out this morsel of news was powerful—but he knew Lebret could not be hurried.

"Today, as usual, Patricia Welles was playing alone," said the naturalist. "She has no friends, for excellent reasons. So far as Mistress Trevor could tell, she was attempting to free her doll from a witch's spell with prayer and incantation. When her efforts failed, she climbed into a swing her father had hung from a cedar limb—and consulted something hidden in the trunk. Mistress Trevor is sure it was a book."

Paul felt his heart leap as he turned on Lebret: he could contain his impatience no longer. "Why, in Heaven's name, didn't you tell me this at once?"

"Because it was not yet dark, *mon brave*. You can hardly be seen when you investigate this hiding place in the cedar."

"What if it's only a toy?"

"The thing we're seeking is legitimate evidence in this case, and it's still missing. Cover that shirt with a cloak and follow me. I've a candle-lantern outside. If we're stopped en route, we're heading for the barnyard, to see if our sow has farrowed."

Crossing on the hand ferry with Paul at his side, Lebret waved affably to the usual group of drinkers on the tavern porch. The way to the pigsty led past the doorstep of the Welles' abode: Paul noted that the family was about to settle at its supper table in the kitchen. The naturalist had chosen his moment wisely. Ralph Welles was famous for his lengthy blessings at every meal —all of them delivered full-voice, so that his reputation for piety would reach neighbors' ears.

"You've time, Paul—but not too much. Slip into the yard, and see what you can find. I'll wait in the barn."

It was an easy matter to vault the fence that marked the limits of Welles' landhold. The low-limbed cedar, and the rope swing the surveyor had hung there for his daughter, stood out clearly against the stars. Mounting the seat, and reaching toward the tree trunk from Patricia's estimated height, Paul found her hiding place immediately, above the first fork—a hollow formed by the pruning of a dead branch.

Eager though he was to prove Lebret's story, he hesitated a moment before plunging his hand inside. This, after all, was part of a child's secret world, and he felt a keen sense of shame at being here. In the cabin just beyond, Ralph Welles continued to give thanks to God, in a ringing voice that shook the palm-thatched roof—joined now by the voices of his wife and daughter,

as the family chanted a Bible text in unison. . . . Patricia Welles
(thought Paul) was a demon who had never really been young;
her parents were a brace of hypocrites cast in a standard mold.
He thrust his arm elbow-deep into the hollow, and let his fingers
close on the object concealed there.

Two minutes later (forcing himself to proceed at a normal pace
in the darkness) he had turned the corner of the path and entered
Lebret's barn. The naturalist had hung his lantern above the pen
that held the new-farrowed sow. She was contentedly suckling
her brood, and Lebret had just completed his count.

"An appropriate place for a conspirator's meeting," he said.
"Bring your discovery into the open. We are unobserved."

They looked together at the fat volume in Paul's hand, and
the gold lettering on its spine. Though he had known the title in
advance, Paul could feel a weight lift from his mind.

"*Witch-finding*, by Matthew Hopkins," he read. "She *did* steal
it from the schoolroom, just as Deborah said."

"Hide it carefully, before she steals it again," said Lebret. "Once
she finds it's missing, she'll know who was playing in her swing.
I will thank *la petite Anne* in your behalf—since you must keep
your distance until the trial's over."


The second day in the meetinghouse began much like the first.
Henry Bellows, his fingers ink-stained from his long labor, had
inscribed the names of all male members of the colony on separate
slips. At Silas' order, they were mixed in a huge copper bowl on
the magistrate's table—after both Welles and Paul had checked
them against the village register and agreed the listings were complete. The clerk then drew a name at random—and the process of
impaneling the jury began.

The first man drawn was one John Skeffington, a Londoner of
the Anglican faith who had been the final colonist to join the
first voyage of the *Adventurer*. Welles challenged him as an individual of doubtful piety. A wrangle between the two lawyers
ended in a careful examination of the Articles of the Eleutherian
Adventurers, which were read into the court record in their en-
tirety. To his surprise, Paul saw that Silas was now prepared to

enforce the provisions of those articles to the letter—including the sections referring to religious intolerance.

"In the colony on Massachusetts Bay," he said, addressing the whole gathering in his dry schoolmaster tone, "only those professing the Puritan faith are listed on the church rolls and allowed to vote as citizens of the settlement. No like provision applies here. Master Holborn agrees that it would be impossible to insist on such a stricture in this trial and remain true to our charter. As your spiritual leader, I regret that this provision does not exist. I must still insist that all of you be granted the privilege, and the responsibility, of jury service."

"Would you permit a known atheist in the jury box?" Welles demanded indignantly.

"He, too, would have his rights under the law," said Holborn.

"If the court please," said Welles. "Such provisions are an affront against God."

"You may challenge John Skeffington if you wish," said Silas. "That, too, is your privilege under our law. Each counsel may have six direct challenges, and six for cause."

Welles permitted the Londoner to enter the box, reserving his objections for other names that might prove really dangerous to his case. On his side, Paul was careful to conceal his satisfaction at a ruling that was to become part of history—the living proof that a New World colony could function as an assembly of equals, not only in opportunity but in justice, regardless of religious beliefs. . . . The fact that this trial itself was, by its very nature, a mockery of justice could not obscure the victory.

After the last objection had been exhausted, the assembly of the twelve jurors was quickly completed. The distribution was not evenly divided between members of the two major faiths, since eight of the twelve names drawn from the bowl were Puritans. However, by hoarding his challenges, Paul had managed to keep hard-core elders from the box. No matter how limited their horizons, he felt the twelve men he faced were honest. But he could not keep down a shiver of dread at their respectful attention when Ralph Welles rose to address them.

"Your Honors the magistrates and gentlemen of the jury," said the surveyor. "We are here today to stamp out—at its genesis—the intrusion of Satan. I stand before you with proof positive that witches exist in our colony; I will cite evidence that these evil creatures are his favorite method of perverting mankind. Let them flourish here, and Eleuthera will become an abomination that cries out for the vengeance of Jehovah. Burn them from our midst, exorcise them on our doorstep, and we will go on prospering as God's chosen warriors.

"I anticipate that the counsel for these two wretched defendants, being a man of science, will attempt to bemuse your minds concerning the very existence of witches. To refute such assaults on your reason before they are made, let me present the testimony of persons who—you must agree—cannot possibly be in error concerning the presence of the Evil One in human form. I refer you first to the account given by Martin Luther of his intimacy with the devil during his confinement in the castle of Wurtburg:

"'*Among other things they brought me hazel-nuts which I put into a box and sometimes did crack and eat. In the night-time the devil came and took the nuts out of the box and cracked them against the bedposts, making a very great noise and rumbling about my bed. When afterwards I began to slumber, then he kept up such a racket and rumbling on the chamber stairs as if many barrels had been tumbled down.*'"

Welles put down the document from which he had been quoting, and took up another. "I am sure that none of you, including counsel for the defense, would dare to accuse Martin Luther of falsehoods. I will now quote a second authority—no less a personage than Bishop Jewel, in a communication to the late Queen Elizabeth:

"'*It may please your Grace to understand that witches and sorcerers within these last four years are marvelously increased within our realm. Your Grace's subjects pine away even unto death. Their color fadeth, their flesh rotteth, their speech is benumbed, their senses are bereft. I pray God they never practice further upon the subject.*'

"Thus we have it, on the word of two unimpeachable authorities, that the devil does exist on earth—that he can use human beings as his agents. That you may know the range of activities he manifests in his use of human beings as witches, I will give you the eight classes into which they have been divided, according to the best authority of English witch-finders. These are the diviner, gypsy or fortunetelling witch; the star-gazing, prognosticating witch; the chanting, canting, or calculated witch who works by signs and numbers; the veneficial or poisoning witch; the conjuring witch; the gastronomic witch; the magical speculative or arted witch; and the outright necromancer."

The prosecutor had rolled these Gothic categories on his tongue —and the reference to the cult of English witch-finding had not been lost on Paul. Fresh from his own perusal of Matthew Hopkins, he had already recognized the source of Welles' catalogue.

"I must tell you further," said the surveyor, "that the devil affixes his mark to the bodies of those in alliance with him—and that the point where this mark is made becomes callous and dead. Both the accused have been subjected to expert scrutiny in this matter. Both have been found afflicted with the witches' mark, as it is universally called.

"Let me also remind you that witches can take the shape of most known animals and insects. We will prove that lizards of various kinds were seen consorting with the accused, as well as flies and spiders. While they were imprisoned, some of these creatures were attacked and killed by the guards, showing they were innocent. More often than not, the vermin escaped, indicating that they were imps, sent out by these women to do mischief elsewhere.

"It is also well known that a witch may cause grievous injury at a distance, when her sight falls upon a victim. At such times, she can so plague and torture him as to cause severe pain and even danger of life. We will demonstrate this power as inescapable evidence of guilt in the accused. It is believed that an impalpable fluid darts from the eye of the witch and penetrates the brain of the victim. Only when the afflicted person is brought near the witch and the latter is forced to touch him is the malignant fluid drawn off and the victim freed from his sickness."

Welles picked up yet another paper from his table, and flourished it before the jurors. "I will close my remarks with a final quotation, from England's own King James regarding another well-known idiosyncrasy of witches:

*"'In a secret murder, if the dead carcass be handled thereafter by the murderer, it will gush blood—as if the blood were crying to the heavens for revenge. So it appears that God hath appointed that water shall refuse to receive them in her bosom that have shaken off the sacred water of baptism and willfully refused the benefit thereof. Their eyes are unable to shed tears, threaten and torture them as you please—albeit the womankind especially be otherwise able to shed tears at every like occasion when they will, though it were dissimblingly as crocodiles.'*

"Not even the defending counsel in this trial can refute the testimony of so pious a ruler as King James. Look into the faces of these women, members of the jury, and ask if you have ever seen them weep. They are dry-eyed now, as they await your verdict. They will be dry-eyed on the pyre that consumes them."

Welles bowed to the court and sat down. A rapt silence had spread over the assembly. There was no doubt that the listeners had been impressed by his bill of particulars—and Paul saw that the twelve jurors, responding to the infection, were just as deeply troubled.

"Does counsel for the defense wish to address the court?" asked Silas.

Paul spoke without rising—hoping that a casual pose would make its own contrast to the brimstone Welles had served up so prodigally.

"The statements made by the prosecutor are too vague to be worthy of an answer at this time," he said. "If he will dare to make more specific charges in his examination, I propose to give him the lie direct. It is also my intention to prove that the accusations made against these two women rise from the jealous and malignant feelings of certain persons who have reason to hate them because of weaknesses of their own, which they dare not acknowledge publicly. Further, I intend to prove these facts from the transgressors' own mouths, on the witness stand."

The surveyor, Paul observed, had gone rigid as the import of this threat reached his brain—and the glare that Charity Welles fastened upon him was added evidence that his suspicions were justified. Silas frowned from the bench, and Paul could only wonder if his brother had half-guessed his intent.

"Let the accused be brought to the bar," said the senior magistrate.

The two armed guards in the doorway moved forward to act as bailiffs. At Silas' nod, chairs were brought from the side aisles and placed before the magistrates' table. Lili and Deborah rose to take their places there, a move which brought them face to face with both spectators and jury box. A low, sighing murmur ran through the assembly, like the breath of icy air that precedes a storm.

On the front bench (where she sat in her role of complainant) Patricia Welles leaned forward to watch the tableau with dancing eyes. Never had this twelve-year-old child seemed a more unfortunate fusion of her parents. Her face combined her mother's high, ascetic cheekbones and martyr's mouth with the father's ferret eyes and long nose that twitched in moments of stress. Yet Patricia lacked her mother's shrewish temper and her father's posturing. Paul was sure that her intelligence far exceeded theirs. He had long since measured the malignancy of her spirit.

Lili faced her inquisitors bravely at the bar of justice. Her arm was tucked firmly through Deborah's: the other girl stared vacantly before her, and stumbled before she could reach one of the two chairs reserved for the accused. Welles was already on his feet, with a sheaf of notes spread fanwise in one hand. This was the bill of indictment, and it was his privilege to recite it to the accused.

Paul made no protest while the familiar list was read into the record. It included the original charge of witchcraft, the prosecutor's contention that the defendants had consorted openly with the devil and practiced ungodly rites in "the plantations of Eleuthera." It stated further that both women had grievously afflicted one Patricia Welles, that they had caused pestilences and storms to be visited upon the colony, and brought in various devils in the shape of lizards, spiders, and newts. The list was long. Paul hoped it would numb the jurors' minds with its absurdity—and bring an inevitable revulsion.

When Welles had finally ended his arraignment, he turned first to Deborah. Like all cowards, he had begun with the weaker adversary.

"Deborah Sikes, what evil spirit have you served?"

The girl stared at him dully and made no reply.

"Answer—or your silence is witness against you. What contracts have you made with the devil?"

Deborah spoke then, after a fashion—but the words emerged in a meaningless jumble. This, Welles shouted to the jury, was itself a proof of guilt. Only a disciple of Beelzebub would dare to speak in jargon at such a moment.

"Why did you torment the child who sits facing you?"

Paul got to his feet at last, and pounded the defense table with his fist. "This badgering is as cruel as it is futile. All of you know this woman's mind has been clouded by her misfortune—and that Ralph Welles, more than any other, is her persecutor."

"I am not on trial here," cried the surveyor.

"You may be, when the verdict is announced."

"What do you mean by that, Doctor?" asked Adam Holborn.

"If the court please, Ralph Welles is one of the main accusers in these proceedings," said Paul. "He is also the prosecutor. In any other court, his presence at the bar would be a perversion of justice. Later, I intend to show why this same Ralph Welles is so anxious to destroy these two women. At that time, I will ask both jury and congregation to decide who is more worthy of punishment."

Silas' gavel had already fallen. "Defense counsel will save remarks of this nature for his closing argument," he said. "The prosecutor cannot be denied the right to develop evidence before the court. Brother Welles will proceed."

"Why did you torment this child, Deborah Sikes?" the surveyor demanded.

Deborah stared at him blankly. "What child?" she asked quietly. It was the first coherent utterance.

"My daughter Patricia, who sits opposite you."

Deborah turned in her chair to face Patricia Welles. As their eyes met, the girl screamed and fell writhing to the floor. It was a convincing imitation of a seizure. Paul noted the rolling eyeballs, the traces of froth at the lips, the convulsive muscle spasms and grinding teeth. Most marked of all were the jerking and thumping of the body—though Patricia had been careful to fall in the open, where she was in no danger of injuring herself by contact with chair or table.

Welles addressed Paul directly for the first time. "Look upon the child, Dr. Sutton. Tell me what you see."

"I see nothing that I have not already observed in other young females. Hysteria is a well-recognized medical condition, with standard symptoms. This is not the first girl who can mimic it at will."

Patricia (and this, too, was expected) let out another howl as he spoke, muffling the effect of his words on the jury. She now seemed to be wrestling with a phantom assailant, identified as the spirit of Deborah Sikes—and, from time to time, as Lili. People were standing on every bench to witness the demonstration. The frightened silence told Paul they believed it to be genuine.

The attack ended, as sharply as it began. Patricia Welles sat up in her mother's arms, and rubbed her eyes—as though she were rousing from normal slumber.

"What happened?"

"You were bewitched, my dear," said Charity Welles.

"Come closer, Patricia," said her father. "Touch this woman, and the evil will be withdrawn from you."

At first Patricia drew back—then, at her mother's prodding, rose to her feet and approached Deborah on fearful tiptoe. This time, Paul stood back with folded arms, making no attempt to brand this mummery with its proper label. Deborah was staring at the child as though she did not recognize her. As Patricia put out a tentative hand, she addressed her directly.

"It's Patricia: I know you now. You were always my best student."

It was the girl's cue to feign terror, and she seized it promptly. "Witch!" she howled. "This woman is a witch!"

Deborah spoke as though she had not heard. "But you told so many lies!"

"The prisoners have no right to vilify a witness," said Welles.

"The prosecutor wishes to reveal all evidence," Paul countered. "So do the magistrates. These are the first intelligible words the accused has spoken. I demand they be recorded."

Silas pounded his table for silence. His face was somber—but it was evident that Paul's protest had won.

"Let the accused speak," he ordered. "It will be entered by the clerk."

"Why did you always tell lies, Patricia?" Deborah asked. Her voice was mild enough.

"*Witch!*" Patricia screamed. "*This woman is a witch!*" The child had redoubled the volume of her screaming—yet, for the first time, her shrill voice seemed to rebound from a wall of silence. Paul cast a glance at the spectators before he turned to the jury box. Every eye was fixed on Deborah Sikes—for the moment, Patricia was ignored, and pouting visibly at the change of interest.

She stood close to Deborah: obeying a sudden inspiration, Paul lifted the prisoner's hand and put it on the girl's arm. According to the accepted belief, the touch of a witch was enough to withdraw the so-called evil eye. As Paul had hoped, Patricia forgot the rules, topping her second accusation with another seizure, quite as violent as the first.

"The devil's influence has been withdrawn," he said quietly—letting his voice carry to the jury box, and no farther. "You may compose your muscles, Patricia—and your eyeballs."

He had been careful to stand between the child and the jurors, so that he could meet her eyes directly, without witnesses. Caught for the first time in her subterfuge, Patricia recovered promptly—but the look she flung at Paul was distilled from pure venom. Charity Welles, sensing the setback, had already risen from the front bench.

"Look how quickly the evil has left her!" she screeched. "That proves Deborah Sikes is a witch."

"It proves your daughter is a dissembler," Paul countered—but the taunt was lost in the babel that filled the meetinghouse. Silas gaveled furiously for silence, and nodded to Adam Holborn. As usage demanded, it was the assistant magistrate's right to ask the next question.

"Does the spirit of the Fiend afflict you now, Patricia?"

"No, Brother Holborn," said the girl sweetly. "As the doctor said, Deborah Sikes has taken it away."

Every eye was on Deborah, who had subsided into another stupor after her brief moment of lucidity. To Paul, it was a familiar phenomenon in patients who had lost their senses. The spectators (he realized this, all too keenly) would take it as a fresh proof of Deborah's guilt—since it had coincided, all too neatly, with Patricia's apparent recovery of sanity.

"Look upon this woman," said the assistant magistrate. "Are you sure she is the one who tormented you?"

"She visits me often," said Patricia. "Sometimes she appears out of the darkness. Sometimes, she rides through my bedroom window on a broom. Always, she laughs like a madwoman. Often she's content with spoiling my night's rest, and says nothing. Then she tells me I must swear by the book to follow the Evil One—"

"What book?" asked Adam Holborn.

"She did not say. I thought she meant the Bible."

John Skeffington leaned forward in the jury box. "Would a sorceress ask her victim to swear by Holy Writ?" he asked. "I thought the devil feared the Scriptures."

Paul saw that Patricia had sensed her mistake. "I never saw the book, Master Skeffington," she said. "It could have been any of a hundred in the schoolroom."

The juror leaned back, with a satisfied nod. At another time, Paul might even have admired the quickness of the child's wits, if not her skill in lying. Already, it was evident she would stop at nothing to convince the court her accusation was valid. Her own motive was clear. Deborah had caught her lying in the schoolroom (probably on several occasions) and had lectured her before the other children. This was Patricia's notion of revenge.

Ralph Welles had waited respectfully during the exchange. There was no mistaking the depth of his satisfaction when he faced the bench.

"I believe the fact that the defendant Deborah Sikes is a practicing witch has been established beyond reasonable doubt," he said. "I will now interrogate the second prisoner, Lili Porter, on similar lines."

"Do you wish to cross-examine, Doctor?" asked Adam Holborn.

"I have nothing to say at this time," Paul announced coldly: once more, he was trying hard to balance an austere delivery against the surveyor's rolling periods. "At the proper moment, I'll make my defense for both the accused. May I serve notice on the court that I intend to call Patricia Welles as a witness for the defense?"

"For the *defense,* Dr. Sutton?"

"Precisely—to testify under oath concerning these charges, with a view to establishing both defendants' innocence."

The murmur that swept the assembly was Paul's reward. So was Ralph Welles' bellow of protest.

"A child should not be sworn in a court of law!"

"If a child cannot be sworn," said Paul. "then her testimony cannot have weight to condemn an accused. Why object to her examination under oath—unless she's lying?"

The surveyor, scrambling to emerge from the pit into which he had so obligingly stumbled, harangued the bench a moment more in a futile effort to excuse his daughter from the witness chair. Holburn turned a flint-hard face to his pleadings—and Silas himself apparently perceived the logic of the point Paul had raised. After a whispered conference with Holborn, he addressed the prosecutor testily.

"Take care, Brother Welles, lest you protest too much," he said. "Any witness in a court must take the oath. Since Patricia is the complainant, she may be cross-examined now—or called later by the defense."

Paul watched the child narrowly during the exchange: as he had feared, she did not turn a hair at the ruling. On the contrary, she seemed happy at the suggestion that her performance might be prolonged. There was no escaping the conviction that she would gladly add perjury to her other sins, if it would secure a conviction.

There was a slight delay while Deborah was returned to her place at the defense table. Paul bent over her for a moment, fearing the ordeal had proved too much for her. He drew a real breath of relief when he saw the girl's color was returning, though she seemed no less oblivious of her surroundings. Her collapse at this moment would have been a setback for the defense—since the jury would have interpreted it as a trick to win their sympathy.

"The second defendant will now be questioned," said Adam Holborn. "Lili Porter, face the magistrates."

The innkeeper's daughter, who had risen to make sure of Deborah's recovery, returned with perfect composure to her witness chair. As Welles launched into a recital of the charges he had already leveled at Deborah, she fixed him with a look of contempt that soon alerted the assembly. Here, obviously, was no inert target an enemy could strike at will. The surveyor himself seemed aware of the change. When he put down the bill of indictment, his tone was almost civil.

"Lili Porter, what evil spirits have been your familiars?"

"None," said Lili calmly.

"When did you make your contract with the devil?"

"Never."

"Why did you torment and injure this child?"

"I didn't harm your precious Patricia," said Lili. "She dislikes me and is making this up. Deborah has already called her a liar—"

"I will ask the questions here," Welles roared. "Confine yourself to the answers."

"I was only telling you the facts," said Lili. "Ask any child in Deborah's class. Your daughter's the most inspired liar on Eleuthera."

"Your punishment will be all the worse if you are scornful!"

"What's worse than burning? That's what your wife wants for me, isn't it?"

The gavel hammered the bench, stilling the gasp of the crowd —and Silas ordered Lili to answer the questions without comment. His voice was taut as he addressed the girl directly: while they faced one another across the silent courtroom, Paul could believe they were the only adversaries that mattered. His own role of defender seemed puny indeed, when measured against Lili's self-reliance—and Ralph Welles, for all his bluster, was reduced to the merest pip-squeak.

"The clerk will repeat the last question," said Silas. "The accused will answer directly, without appealing to the emotions of this gathering."

"*Why did you torment and injure this child?*" read Henry Bellows.

"I did neither."

"Do you deny you're the devil's agent?" asked Welles.

"I deny it absolutely. Patricia has not been harmed, except in her imagination."

"How can you deny you've used witchcraft, in the face of this evidence?"

"I've heard no evidence of witchcraft."

Welles tossed up his hands and turned to the bench. "Let her confront the child then," he said. "It's the only way her guilt can be established."

Paul turned in his chair at the defense table to study Patricia, who was already tensing herself for a second seizure.

"Will you face the complainant, prisoner?" Welles demanded.

"I will not," said Lili. "She'll only pretend to have another fit. Why waste the court's time?"

"You've been warned, Lili Porter," said Silas. Again, his voice was oddly constricted, as though the words had been forced through unwilling lips. "Obey the prosecutor, and look upon the child."

Lili glanced at Paul—who nodded an endorsement, but quickly closed his eyes to indicate she should do likewise. As she turned toward Patricia, he saw that Lili had grasped his intent. Her eyes were tightly shut when she faced the front bench—but the child, unaware of the stratagem, had already begun her bout with Satan. The people of the congregation (whom Lili was now facing) were aware of the closed eyes—and the fact that Patricia's howls and gyrations were, if anything, more frenzied than before.

"Let the jury note that the defendant closed her eyes and did not look at the accuser," Paul cried. "Doesn't this prove the child is play-acting?"

Prone on the floor boards, working into the climax of her fit, Patricia could hardly help hearing the charge. She quieted at once —and rose on one elbow to glance toward her mother in a silent plea for instructions. Lifting on tiptoe, Paul signaled to Lili to open her eyes. Again, the innkeeper's daughter took her cue and leaned forward in the witness chair, to stare down at the recumbent brat.

"Please note as well that the accused is now looking directly at the accuser with no ill effects," said Paul. "I submit it as additional proof of her mendacity."

Patricia had already sensed the trap and thrown herself into a supreme frenzy to escape it—half-stunning herself as she crashed at last into a table leg, and babbling defiances to the imaginary fiend who was overpowering her. Leaning with folded arms against a corner of the jury box, Paul studied the twelve men on whom Lili and Deborah depended for their lives. He could read shock and incredulity on most of the tight-lipped faces—but even now, could not be sure his object lesson had found its mark.

Ralph Welles was beside the witness, his voice an odd blend of wheedling and bluster.

"Touch the child!" he commanded Lili. "Withdraw the evil from her soul!"

Patricia was still on the floor—howling as a splinter pierced her leg. Paul sprang forward before Lili could move, and grasped the child's arm. Since Patricia was face down, she could not see who touched her—but she quieted instantly, letting her head fall forward like a dreamer released from nightmare.

"What happened? I feel as if something had left me."

"Only this," said Paul—and bent to pluck out the splinter.

Patricia let out a last, despairing scream, as she realized Lili had not left the witness chair. "*He* bewitched me, Father! The doctor bewitched me!"

"If anyone bewitched you, it was yourself," said Paul.

It was a full moment before the magistrates, shouting for order,

could quiet the courtroom. It was time enough for Welles to recover his aplomb. Helping his daughter to her feet, he made no
attempt to disguise the hate in the glance he shot toward the
defense table.

"The doctor was close to the witch," he told the jury. "Her
power was withdrawn through him."

Paul shrugged, and resumed his seat. He had hoped the evidence would speak for itself. In any court but this, Welles' fumble
at an explanation would have been greeted with laughter. Here,
so great was the influence of Silas' black-browed stare, the remark
was received in silence. Paul saw that both congregation and jury
(steeped in the dark night of superstition) still refused to make
up its collective mind. . . . Perhaps it was enough, for now, if
they remained open to conviction.

Welles, making a great show of consulting his notes, kept Lili
in the chair a moment more without questioning her further. After
a grudging dismissal, he called the first of an hour-long procession
of witnesses. Puritans to the last man, their testimony seemed
cut from the same brassbound pattern. All of them spoke of various ills (from sprains to bad dreams) which they attributed to
witchcraft. In every instant, either Lili or Deborah was identified
as the devil's agent. Zachary Daniels was sworn, and described
his search for the witches mark—which each of the girls was forced
to exhibit to the jury, still circled with the red chalk of the finder.

Paul let the dreary procession pass the bench without interruption. So far, he could detect no sign of ennui in the jury box,
but he trusted that revulsion was growing behind those twelve
iron masks: as good men and true, the jurors could hardly relax
their decorum while the surveyor and his well-coached minions
droned on. There was no doubt that the congregation itself
(inured though it was to the prolix sermons of its ministers) was
growing restless at the plethora of witnesses, and the sameness
of their avowals.

Welles seemed aware of this in time, for he dismissed his final
spokesmen somewhat brusquely. However, his smug assurance
seemed restored when he sat down at last. Paul could hardly deny

the man had proved his case completely, according to the methods set down in Matthew Hopkins' *Witch-Finding*. Honest though they were, the jurors might well subscribe to the same dogma. He could not even be sure he had convinced them that Patricia Welles was a born dissembler.

What the defendants' case lacked (he made the admission grimly) was solid evidence in their favor to match the mouthings of the prosecutor. By the logic of the Puritan creed, a witch bore the burden of her guilt to court, until some powerful voice spoke in her behalf. It was not enough to question the credibility of the complainant: Lili and Deborah needed a sponsor, a witness for the defense whose voice the jurors would respect.

Paul rose from the defense table and looked hard at Silas, aware that his brother had drawn deeper within himself as the trial proceeded. Was it too much to hope that the leader's fairness, his natural intelligence (indeed, his whole long training at the feet of Geoffrey Trevor) had rebelled at last? Had he risen above his blind reliance in the tenets of his religion, to admit (in his own soul) that what Ralph Welles had called witchcraft in Lili Porter had another, shorter name?

The whole case could turn on Silas' change of mind—assuming, of course, that a change was taking place before his eyes, that Silas' tortured, almost furtive manner was a true harbinger. It was a desperate gamble at best to hope that his brother had descended from the mountaintop. He could not risk it without consulting Lili.

"With the court's permission," he said, "defense requires a brief recess before proceeding with its case."

Silas roused from his private world, and turned to confer with Holborn. "Will the presentation be a lengthy one?"

"On the contrary. Unlike the prosecutor, I'll be brief. Only three witnesses will be called, and I will dispense with opening remarks. The people of this colony may return to their tasks in good time."

Silas whispered again with Holborn, then rose from the bench. "A quarter-hour recess is granted: the court will be cleared for that interval."

He stalked from the church house without glancing to right

and left. Watching him go, Paul knew that his brother (no less than the congregation at large) had welcomed the intermission. In another moment, the room was empty, save for the three figures at the defense table. Welles had made a show of lingering, only to beat a retreat at a sign from the bailiffs.

Moving to close the meetinghouse door, Paul felt his heart contract as a new spasm of fear assailed him. The jury, marching as one man to the room reserved for its deliberations, had seemed more funereal than ever—and he had sought in vain for a single friendly eye in the assembly, save for the group that surrounded Giles and Lebret.

Lili had not stirred from the defense table. From the beginning, she had sat with Deborah's hand in hers, comforting the huddled figure as best she could.

"Have we lost, Paul?" she asked quietly. "Don't soften the blow for me."

"I think I've shaken them," he said.

"I watched the jury go out," said Lili. "They seemed like twelve monuments to your brother's faith. Why should *they* be shaken?"

"Surely they realized the brat is lying."

"Perhaps they did, Paul—in their hearts. She's still the daughter of a church elder: Deborah and I are only a brace of pagans. I can't blame them for closing ranks."

"We've four Anglicans on the jury."

"And eight Puritans. Our own people must live with the herd. Why should they risk their future?"

"They'll vote for us if we can find an advocate."

"Who'd dare to speak in our favor, outside my father's friends? *They'd* be suspect in advance."

"I can name one candidate," said Paul. "If my guess is accurate, he can save our case."

"*Silas?*"

"He was troubled when he watched Patricia. I believe he's shocked by Ralph Welles' conduct of the case. When the court returns, I'm going to put the brat on the stand, and do my best to expose her. I've a special trick in reserve, in case she balks.

Her father comes next, as a classic example of a Peeping Tom. Then I'll call Silas as our final witness—and demand he give this whole evil business its proper name."

"Would he turn against his own people?"

"I think so, Lili, if he realizes just how far bigotry has driven him—and how wrong he was to call this trial."

Lili did not speak for a moment. Deborah had begun to weep uncontrollably, and she drew the girl's head down to her shoulder. "I think she half-understands what we're saying, Paul. Perhaps that's all the answer we need."

"You agree with my strategy?"

"If you're sure it's the only way."

"Men tend to run in packs, as you just remarked. At the moment, the pack's against us. Only its leader can turn it in the right direction."

"Suppose your brother's unchanged? As a magistrate, he can refuse to testify."

Paul dropped his voice to a whisper, and glanced at the closed door. Outside, he could hear the buzz of voices, and knew the congregation was growing impatient at the delay. He did not dare guess whether this was a good augury—or a bad one. Some of those listeners were on his side, reluctant though they were to show their sentiments. The bitter truism remained: most crowds were many-headed beasts, thirsting for the kill.

"If you're convicted," he said, "they won't impose sentence until tomorrow. Your father has hidden arms for fifty men in the tavern. If need be, he'll rescue you tonight, and take you to New Providence."

"You gave your word to deliver us to Silas."

"Only while the trial lasted," said Paul grimly. "What happens thereafter is on his own head."

The congregation took its place with much whispered converse. Paul rose and waited patiently for the noise to subside. Even when the last murmur had stilled, he hesitated a moment more before addressing the bench. It was an orator's trick and he used it without shame. After the skulduggery of Ralph Welles, any subterfuge was justified.

"I have said I will question just three witnesses," he announced. "If need arises, I may call a fourth. There will be no opening address. The prosecutor's own conduct, with its emphasis on superstition instead of fact, will—in the end—assist the defendants far more than any eloquence on my part. If my defense seems unorthodox to the bench, I claim its indulgence. The lives of two innocent females are at stake—and the evidence will be extracted in the interests of truth and justice."

"Can you name your witnesses now?" asked Silas.

"I would prefer to name them in order," said Paul. "Will Patricia Welles take the stand?"

The brat flounced up to be sworn as though she had anticipated the summons.

"Let me begin by reminding you that you are under oath," Paul told her. "Remember, too, that the future of two immortal souls depends on your telling the truth. Do you understand that fully?"

"I understand, Doctor." Patricia had assumed a model pose, with both hands primly folded.

"Do you still say that Lili Porter and Deborah Sikes have afflicted you in the guise of witches?"

"They have, Doctor."

"On how many occasions?"

"So many I have lost track of them," said Patricia, in a tone that managed to be both solemn and childishly airy. "I have wrestled with the devil often, and with his familiar spirits. They visit me at night, and demand I do evil deeds for them."

"Have you seen the devil himself?"

"Never, Doctor. He always sends the spirits of Lili and Deborah to afflict me."

"How do you know it's the devil who sends these spirits, as you call them?"

"Everyone knows the devil sends witches, Doctor. The Reverend Obadiah has told us so a score of times, in this meetinghouse. Whole books have been written on the subject."

"Have you read such books?"

"No, sir. But I have heard of them."

"Don't forget you are under oath, Patricia. You're sure you have never read a book on witchcraft?"

"No, Doctor. My parents do not think such reading is fit for a young girl."

"Yet you have a wide knowledge of witches."

"Only because I have been afflicted by them."

Paul returned to his table, and took out Matthew Hopkins' tome, which he had hidden in a stack of manuscript. Concealing the volume in the skirts of his coat, he returned to the witness chair.

"I ask you once again: You have never read a book on witch-craft?"

There was a flicker of doubt in the child's eyes. "Never, Doctor."

"I ask if you have ever seen this book, Patricia." He had whisked Hopkins' *Witch-Finding* into view. Now he brandished it, for all the room to see.

The ferret-snout was twitching, but the girl herself seemed rock-calm.

"May I look at it closer, Doctor?"

Paul opened the book under that twitching nose, and held it steady while the child scanned the title page. It was then passed on to the bench, and handed to Henry Bellows to be introduced as an exhibit in evidence.

"Does this refresh your memory, Patricia? Have you read this book?"

"Indeed no, sir. But I do remember seeing it."

"Will you tell us when and where?"

"In our cabin. Father was reading the book when he was preparing his case."

"And you never opened it?"

"No, Doctor. I wouldn't dare."

Paul turned to the magistrates. "With the permission of the bench, I will ask this child to step down for a moment. I mentioned an emergency witness just now, whom I would call if need arose. I hope she's prepared to testify at this time."

Silas nodded and Patricia left the chair to sit beside her mother. Her face remained a righteous mask. Obviously, she felt she had emerged the victor in this first bout of lying.

"I call Mistress Anne Trevor," said Paul.

He was pleased to see his brother's jaw drop. For a moment, he thought Silas would forbid the summons, but there was no sound from the bench when Anne (blushing a little under the universal stare) approached the stand. She took the oath in a firm voice: it was evident that she understood the reason behind her summons.

Paul came to the point without preamble. "Mistress Trevor, will you tell the court exactly where you saw the book that now lies on the clerk's table?"

"It was last evening, in the yard of the Welles' cabin," said Anne. "I'd just left the fruit orchard, and taken the lane that runs beside their fence. Patricia was playing with her doll, in the shade of a cedar tree. While I watched, she mounted a swing that hung from a lower branch, and took the book from a hollow just below it."

"The same book Master Bellows is holding now?"

"I'm sure it was the same. I recognize both the lettering and the binding."

"What did she do with the book?"

"She glanced at its pages for a moment. Then she returned it to the hiding place, and went back to her doll."

"That is all, Mistress Trevor." Paul glanced quickly at Welles, expecting a cross-examination: the identification of *Witch-Finding* had been something less than conclusive, according to the usual rules of evidence. But the surveyor, with a glassy stare, made no motion to approach the stand. Evidently he had anticipated the sequence of events in his own mind—and feared another attack would not advance his cause.

"Patricia, will you return to the witness chair?"

During the questioning of Anne Trevor, Paul had kept a close eye on the brat. So far as he could tell, there had been no exchange with Charity Welles. His heart sank when Patricia approached with her aplomb unshaken. Already, it was evident the Welles family had learned of the disappearance of *Witch-Finding* and had prepared a rebuttal.

"You've heard Mistress Trevor," he said. "We've been told she saw you consult this book—which you withdrew from its hiding place in a hollow tree. Do you wish to change your testimony?"

"No, Dr. Sutton."

"Do you deny the charge?"

"I *did* hide the book in the tree. I admit it, freely."

"Do you deny reading it?"

"Yes, Doctor." This time, the girl's eyes sought the magistrates' bench, in silent protest. "I have told you that my parents forbade such reading."

"Mistress Trevor has just testified you stood on the swing to consult this book."

"The lady's mistaken," said Patricia calmly. "I climbed the swing to make sure the book I'd stolen from our cabin was still in its hiding place."

"Did you say *stolen?*"

"Father borrowed it from the school library to prepare his case. That was the first time I saw it. Yesterday I moved the book outside the house, to the tree hollow. I hoped the witches couldn't find it there. I was afraid that such a book would draw evil from those two women and afflict me all the more."

The girl had not raised her voice during this amazing recital: an outside observer would have believed her story instantly. The whispers that swept the congregation were an ominous portent: intent on pinning the charge of perjury on Patricia, Paul had found an opponent who could think even faster. . . . Seeing that he must change his tactics (or risk losing the jury) he determined on a fresh approach, one that had been in his mind since the opening of the trial. He had seen the trick performed often in the East, by fakirs in the bazaars—who used volunteers from their audiences. In some ways, it seemed a rather shabby dodge—but the child had forced his hand.

As a doctor, he suspected the trick was based on a trance

created in the subject's mind, despite its aura of the occult; as a spectator, he had felt his scalp prickle at the alleged magician's dominance of his victim, who spoke and acted as the fakir wished. The method for inducing the trance was simple: it required only a burning candle and a performer skilled in the Oriental art, which Paul himself had practiced often to quiet excited patients. It was the candle that had inspired him today, since Patricia had spoken originally of a vision involving stars and seven-branched candlesticks. Silas might forbid the experiment in court—but that, too, was a risk he could not avoid. He put down his notes, and strode toward the pulpit, where a dozen candles stood in their pewter sconces.

"With the court's permission," he said, "I will bring light to the defense table, as a preliminary to further questioning of the witness."

Guy Lebret rose at his nod. Between them, they brought seven sconces to the defense table, arranging them roughly to simulate the famous candlestick mentioned in the Book of Revelation, which Patricia had plagiarized so glibly in her first vision. Working against time, he could feel the disapproval on the bench—but neither magistrate spoke until Lebret had lighted the last candle and returned to his place in the audience.

"What is the purpose of this, Doctor?" asked Adam Holborn.

"My preparations may seem elaborate," said Paul, "but they have a direct bearing on my defense. To be precise, on a vision Patricia Welles experienced in this meetinghouse."

Silas, he observed, sat ramrod-stiff with his eyes fixed on space. He seemed lost in a vision of his own, but Paul was positive he had missed nothing. Patricia, still in the witness chair, was staring eagerly at the seven candles. It was the precise reaction he had hoped to stir in that volatile mind.

"Do you recall your first vision, Patricia?" he asked gently.

"Yes, Doctor."

"Did it include a seven-branched candlestick?"

"There was much more. God on his throne, a sky filled with angels and stars—"

"And fearsome beasts that threatened you?"

"Yes, Doctor."

"It was after this vision that you first claimed to be afflicted by witches?"

"Yes. It was the beginning of all the evil that has visited Eleuthera."

Holborn broke in sharply. "Do you intend to re-create the conditions under which this child was first subjected to sorcery?"

"I hope to do more than that, sir," Paul answered. "If Patricia is indeed tormented as she claims, I plan to exorcise her demons, here and now."

Ralph Welles rose from his place. "Will the court permit this outrage, gentlemen? I must protest, in the strongest terms."

"On what grounds?" asked Holborn.

"This is necromancy—in itself a form of witchcraft."

"The whole colony is assembled here," said Paul. "Let it be my witness. If it thinks I've practiced sorcery, I'll call myself a wizard and stand trial with Lili and Deborah."

The challenge was a bold one, but Paul sensed that it had swung the balance in his favor, even before Holborn (after a whispered conference with Silas) overruled Welles' objection. He plunged at once into his gamble, while his ears still rang with the congregation's gasp at his willingness to risk his own life for the defendants.

"Patricia, I want you to continue to look steadily at those seven candle flames. In a moment, I'll ask you some questions. Try, if you can, to concentrate upon them, to recapture your vision. Between us, we may drive this threat of witchcraft from our colony."

"I'll do what I can, Doctor," said the brat. Moving a step closer to the witness chair, Paul saw that she was eager to participate in this dramatic demonstration and delighted with her leading role.

"Look directly at the flames," he urged. "Build a picture in your mind of the seven-branched candlestick in your vision. Think of nothing else—"

"Nothing else, Doctor," the child echoed dutifully.

Paul dropped his voice to a confidential purr: it was the precise note the fakirs had struck. "Do you see the candle flames clearly?"

"Quite clearly, Doctor."

"As clearly as they shone in your vision? Could these be the same candlesticks?"

"They could, Doctor." The child, he noted triumphantly, had already risen to the bait, echoing his words as dutifully as the volunteers in the bazaar.

"Think only of those seven flames," he whispered. "They are the light of reason. They will banish the darkness which has descended on Eleuthera."

Patricia had settled deep in the witness chair. Her eyes were riveted on the seven spots of light that glowed (like yellow stars) in the shadowed meetinghouse. Like all bad performers, she was enjoying her own performance enormously. At the same time, there was no mistaking the trance that was settling on those staring eyes.

"The candles burn brightly," said Paul. "The flames are steady in the darkness. Hold your mind upon their light—and God will reveal to you the light of truth. You *are* a seeker after truth, aren't you, Patricia?"

"Yes, Doctor."

Already, her voice seemed faint and far away: he could see that the trance-inducing effect of his own eyes and voice had done its work. Behind him, the courtroom seemed lapped in a trance of its own. He stole a glance at Ralph Welles—and saw that the prosecutor could not nerve himself to interrupt.

"I'm going to lift your right hand, Patricia. Hold it high, and repeat what I'm about to say."

The child did not resist as he lifted her right hand above her head. When he released his grip, the arm remained fixed, without so much as a quiver. This, too, was part of the fakir's technique. Until he wished, his victim was frozen, no matter how strained his posture.

"*I, Patricia Welles, swear I will speak only the truth before God.*"

Patricia repeated the words in a drowned whisper. Paul's heart leaped as he saw her eyelids were drooping.

"If you feel sleepy, you may close your eyes."

When the child's lids had closed, he grasped her arm and brought it slowly to her side. As he had expected, it felt immobile as stone.

"You hated Deborah Sikes, didn't you, Patricia?" he asked, lifting his voice so the room could hear.

"I always hated her."

"Why?"

"She accused me of lying before others."

"Did you tell lies?"

"Yes, Doctor."

"For what reason?"

"To get the best of people. To make myself first."

"Is that why you called Deborah a witch? Because she exposed you as a liar to the other children?"

"Yes."

"She never really afflicted you?"

"No. I made that up because I hated her."

A low sigh escaped the congregation. Paul glanced again at Welles. The surveyor had turned white, but it was clear that he dared not break in.

"And Lili Porter? Why did you name *her* as a witch?"

"Mother said she made men lust after her. She deserved burning at the stake."

"Was that your only reason for saying she afflicted you?"

"Yes."

"When did you first decide to accuse her and Deborah?"

"When I read the book."

"What book?"

"The one I stole from the schoolroom, and hid in the tree."

"The book called *Witch-Finding*, by Matthew Hopkins?"

"Yes. It told what people say when they accuse other people of sorcery. I showed it to Mother. She made me practice for two days, before I spoke up in meeting."

"Then your whole story was invented?"

"Yes."

"Why did you tell this lie, Patricia?"

"I wanted people to look up to me. I wanted to be a witch-finder too, like Master Hopkins."

"I think you've told me quite enough," Paul said. In a space of minutes, he had tricked the child into betraying herself as a monster: he found he could close his heart to pity. "I'll blow out the candles now. You'll stop feeling sleepy. All this will be like a dream."

He had spoken the last words in the same measured tone: the silence held while he moved to the defense table. Lili's hand closed on his in a grateful pressure as he blew out the candle flames, one by one—then clapped his palms together as the fakirs had done, to signal the spell had lifted. Patricia responded promptly, sitting upright in the chair and opening her eyes.

"Are you awake, Patricia?"

"Of course I'm awake," the child said sharply.

Paul turned to the court. "I have no more questions. The witness may be excused." He sat down beside his clients, while Lebret busied himself returning the seven sconces to the pulpit.

Patricia stared hopefully at the bench. With no memory of her revelations, she obviously felt cheated. Silas returned the girl's stare for a long, thoughtful moment. He seemed on the point of speech, then shook his head slowly, as though he was unable to take in what he had just heard.

Adam Holborn leaned forward. "The court will question the witness," he said. "Patricia, do you still believe that Lili Porter and Deborah Sikes are witches?"

"Yes, Master Holborn. They afflicted me as I have stated."

"You did not make up the story, with your mother's help—using a book called *Witch-Finding* as your model?"

"No, Master Holborn. I hid the book in the tree. I didn't dare open it."

"No one told you to speak out against these two women?"

"No one. They afflicted me—and I told of it, so they could not afflict others."

Welles approached the bench. Paul saw he had recovered his wits.

"If the court please—"

Silas regarded him heavily, as a man might regard a stranger who has interrupted his thoughts without warning. "Is this objection in order?" he asked Holborn.

"I'll grant it's a bit tardy," said the assistant. "Brother Welles must still be heard."

"I demand that this travesty of justice be stricken from the record!" the surveyor shouted.

"Your daughter has told the court two conflicting stories," said Holborn. "Obviously, only one of them is accurate."

"What she just said is the truth. She has already so testified under oath. The other is a sorcerer's trick—"

Patricia had listened attentively to the interchange: Paul saw that she had grasped her dilemma perfectly. In a flash, she opened her mouth on a hair-raising howl of terror, and flung herself into the arms of Charity Welles.

*"Save me, Mother! The doctor's a wizard!"*

"I demand a ruling on that charge," Paul said instantly. He had spoken just in time: Charity Welles, rocking her daughter in her arms, had begun to rend the air with her screams. The invective she flung at Paul was well-nigh unintelligible—but it was evident she was asking that he, too, be tried for witchcraft.

He knew that Charity's ranting would get no response. However limited their perceptions, the congregation was intelligent enough to choose between Patricia's trance and outright sorcery. The fact they believed in the existence of sorcerers was still a mark against him. He had not really shaken the girl's story.

It was true that Patricia had confessed her deception—and the doubt planted in the jury's mind was considerable. And yet (so stubborn is the human will) that same jury would continue to cling to its first premise. An innocent child, in its view, had been doubly harassed, first by evil spirits, then by the defense counsel himself. Patricia had spoken in a trance—and the method was suspect. Lili and Deborah would not be saved by words drawn from the complainant's mouth.

Silas spoke from the bench. "No ruling is possible, in these circumstances," he said. "The girl has told two stories, one of which is false. It is not within the province of magistrates to choose between them. That is the jury's function."

The statement, just though it was by Puritan canons, struck like a hammer on Paul's brain. He had seen how deeply Silas had been shaken by Patricia's ruse; he had hoped his brother would forget himself (and his present office) long enough to speak his mind.

"I still insist the statements made under sorcery be stricken," Ralph Welles shouted.

"The prosecutor will restrain his temper," said Holborn sternly. "The bench has already ruled that Patricia's entire testimony is part of the record. Counsel for the defense may proceed."

Paul accepted the small victory for what it was worth. "I will call just two more witnesses," he said. "Then I will rest our case. The first is Ralph Welles."

The surveyor argued against the summons with all the fustian eloquence he could muster. In the end, he went sulkily to the chair. Paul fired his first question abruptly, hoping to catch Welles off balance.

"Your daughter has stated she accused Lili Porter of witchcraft —at her mother's behest—because 'men lusted after her.' Is the statement accurate?"

"It's an outright lie."

"You accuse Patricia of falsehood?"

"She spoke thus after you'd cast a spell upon her. It was you, lying through her mouth."

"Did your wife tell the child to name Lili because of jealousy?"

"Jealousy?"

"Isn't it true that *you* desired Lili?"

"The question's infamous. I refuse to answer it."

From the back bench, a guffaw cut the silence like a knife. It was the first show of mirth in the courtroom, and Silas gaveled it down, so viciously that the magistrate's table shook under the blow.

"Two women's lives are at stake here," he said. "I'll clear the court, if there's so much as a whisper hereafter. Answer the question, Brother Welles."

The surveyor had paled visibly, and sweat pearled his forehead. Across the room, Charity Welles watched him through slitted lids, her daughter's blubbering forgotten. Paul knew that the whole room had felt the bitterness in the woman's eyes. In its way, that look had done more for his case than Patricia's skein of lies.

"Speak up, Ralph Welles," said Silas—and the look he fastened on the witness matched the woman's in hatred. "Your silence is a bad augury."

"I must beg the court's indulgence," said the surveyor. "The intent of the question escapes me."

"The clerk will repeat it."

*"Isn't it true that you desired Lili?"* read Henry Bellows.

"I deny the allegation," said Welles. "If Lili Porter made that charge, she lies."

"Is it not true that you followed her to the beach on several occasions?" Paul asked. "Didn't you spy on her from the bushes, like a Peeping Tom?"

"That too is a falsehood."

"She observed you more than once. Shall I call her to the stand to put the charge on the record?"

"What use is the testimony of a witch?" Welles was stammering badly now. "I beg the court's protection. If she said that, the devil spoke through her lips to blacken my character."

"The testimony of an accused witch is not acceptable here," said Adam Holborn. "Counsel for the defense is aware of that. Does he have other witnesses to this alleged sinning?"

Paul shook his head. It would be a waste of effort to question Welles further. The surveyor's reputation as a timid satyr was established in the colony (the guffaw had told him that). He could hardly ask the man's neighbors to say as much under oath.

"I've finished with this witness," he said. "Unless, of course, he's willing to go into a trance like his daughter. It might be even more revealing."

"You'll practice no spells on me!" said Welles, in a shaky voice.

"In that case, you may step down."

"One moment, please," said Holborn. "Brother Welles, do you deny under oath that there's been wrong-doing between you and Lili Porter?"

"I do deny it," said the surveyor. "Under oath, and before God." He left the box with dignity—but Paul noted that he was careful to avoid his wife's eyes when he took his seat at the prosecutor's table.

Silas had not moved a muscle since his last ruling: his glance turned now to Welles, and his powerful hands flexed and closed, as though he were strangling an enemy. It was the moment Paul had awaited, and feared, since the trial began. The weight of the evidence, he told himself, was in favor of the defendants—if the jury would open its mind to reason. Yet even now his whole case seemed to float in a fog of doubting, superstition and outright bigotry. The evil mist had filled the courtroom all through the long day. A breath of sanity was needed to dispel it, an appeal not even Puritan minds could resist.

Silas, and Silas alone, could save Lili and Deborah now.

"If the court please," he said, "I will call the final witness for the defense—my brother, Silas Sutton." He crossed the courtroom in the stunned silence that followed his request, and stared hard at Ralph Welles. "I'm sure that even the prosecutor will find his veracity beyond question."

Welles had been busy adjusting his self-righteous mask after his ordeal on the stand: it was a moment before the import of Paul's strategy could penetrate his brain. He seemed to reel a little as he got to his feet—and gripped the table for support. The protest he forced out was a doleful squeak.

"It's an insult to this congregation that its leader should be forced to testify."

"No coercion is involved," said Paul. "I ask for a ruling from the bench. As senior magistrate, it's my brother's right to refuse."

Silas rose from his place, and spoke with his eyes on space. They were strangely vacant, now he had made his decision.

"I've just remarked that the lives of two women are at stake here," he said. "The clerk will swear me. I'm prepared to answer any question."

Paul was careful to stand aside while his brother took the witness chair. A volume lay open on the defense table, and he consulted it carefully: it was the last item he intended to read into the record. As he finished, he stole a glance at Anne. He knew she had sensed his purpose, even more quickly than Welles: his eyes begged a silent pardon before he faced the court. He could hear the congregation stir behind him, and realized it was again growing restless at the delay. Every eye was on Silas, who continued to stare vacantly into space.

At the magistrates' table, where Adam Holborn now presided alone, the gavel pounded for silence.

"You may question the witness, Doctor."

Paul held the book open as he advanced to the clerk's side. "With the court's approval, I will first read a short passage to the jury, and ask that the clerk transcribe it. Numerous authorities have been cited during this trial. Mine is the opinion of a minister of the Puritan faith. I think you will find it apropos of the single question I will then ask the witness."

"Approval granted," said Holborn.

" 'It is possible for the soul to rise to such a height,' " Paul read, " 'and to become so divine, that no witchcraft can have power upon the body that houses it. It is only when the bodily life is too deeply awakened that it draws the intellect, the flower and summit of the soul, into a conspiracy with it. Then, and then only, are we subject to the obnoxious assault of evil. It cannot be said too often that magic and sorcery are founded only in this lower or mundane sphere. Both are powerless to injure the man who is truly free from their blandishments.'

" 'Such men exist as saints among us; such men, by their lives and actions, enkindle the divine fire on earth. Their power is great enough to lift them above all love of corporeity, all sympathy with the frail flesh. Living as they do above the fate of this inferior world, their minds are adorned with a special majesty that beats back all enchantments. In their presence, the Fiend *himself trembles—hating the light which issues from them as a beacon contrary and repugnant to his own dark nature.'"*

Paul closed the book, and faced the jury. He could see they were impressed—and somewhat puzzled as to his purpose.

"These words describe the most unreal of beings, the saint on earth," he said. "To my mind, they also apply to a man whose dedication to a cause has always transcended self—the man who now occupies the witness chair. Silas Sutton may not be quite a saint. But no man among you can deny that his devotion to his faith and to this colony is absolute. Eleuthera has become the crowning achievement of his life. All of us know that he has tried to govern us justly from the beginning. I am sure he will agree that his conduct must be above reproach—and that witchcraft should have no power over him."

Paul put the book aside. The stage was set for the attack he could avoid no longer.

"Silas Sutton, my question is simply this. Has the defendant Lili Porter influenced *you* for good or for evil? And if this be true, was such influence due to witchcraft, or to lusts to which the body is heir?"

Silas' face was stone, and it did not change by a flicker. Only the sudden fire in his eyes betrayed the pain the question had caused him. Never had Paul felt closer to Silas than at this moment—and never more deeply saddened. On the one hand, he felt sure, was his brother's unsatisfied desire, a purely carnal impulse which he could no longer deny honestly. On the other was the impulse that had caused him to permit this trial—and a natural reluctance to admit his error.

Whatever the decision, it could only bring suffering in its wake —either to his own rocklike integrity, or to the innocent women he had sought so grimly to condemn. . . . Knowing Silas as he did, feeling the brief but genuine surge of empathy that united them, Paul could predict his answer in advance. His brother's intolerance had always been matched by his honesty. This was his supreme testing.

"Do you wish the question repeated?"

"No," said Silas. He had risen with the words—and his voice

was low and oddly intimate, as though they stood alone in the meetinghouse. The effort was enough to break the bond that had held them in such tenuous intimacy. When he spoke again, Silas had shaken off his lethargy as though it had never been—and his words had a clarion ring.

"Before God and these people, I confess that I too have been tempted in regard to the defendant Lili Porter. And I confess my firm conviction that the attraction was purely carnal, with no regard to witchcraft or possession by demons."

There was a gasp from the crowd, a murmur that just escaped turning into a cheer. At the prosecutor's table, Ralph Welles seemed to shrivel in his chair. With that simple statement, the leader of the Eleutherians had blasted his case beyond repair— and damned him as a liar.

"The defense rests," said Paul. "There will be no closing statement. My brother has just supplied it."

"If the court please," said Silas, "I have more to tell the people of this colony. The evidence presented by the prosecutor in this case is not worthy of the name. It shows clearly that a lying child was not only allowed to create mischief—but was encouraged in it by her own parents. The fault here is great. In the mother, who encouraged the child to build her evil fancies; in the father, who exploited and perverted them in his efforts to sway this jury—"

His eyes were on Lili Porter now, and he faltered briefly before he continued, his voice taut with passion.

"It goes without saying that the greatest sin was my own. As your leader, I should have seen through this evil plot. There was no need of this day in court to convince me that devils have been conjured up where none existed. Jesus taught us to forgive and have compassion for the frailties of others. I had forgotten that lesson, to the peril of my soul. Out of my own frailty and sin, I have allowed matters to go to the point where the unity of my settlement and my people is threatened. I say to you of the jury— and you of the congregation—that I believe the charges against these two women are false. I believe that they should go free."

He stepped from the witness stand as he spoke—and, for a moment, seemed about to leave the meetinghouse. Then, obeying an afterthought, he turned again to face the bench and the congregation.

"Master Holborn will conclude this trial," he said. "I must be alone awhile—to pray that I may lead you more wisely in future."

He did not meet Lili's eyes again when he strode toward the outer door—and, though his glance brushed Anne Trevor in passing, he seemed unaware of her presence as he left the church house.

The balance of the trial was a formality. Adam Holborn made no attempt to charge the jury, since Silas had already performed that function. The eight Puritans and four Anglicans in the box (their minds swept clean of doubting by their leader's words) voted for acquittal without even leaving the meetinghouse.

Decorum was thrown to the winds when the verdict was announced. The crowd that surged forward to congratulate Paul and the defendants included both sects and it was hard to know which was noisier in its joy. He could understand the relief well enough, now the strain was over. With a few sorry exceptions, these were good people at heart. The fact they had yielded to dread of the occult was easy to condone, now they had been saved from the consequences of that all too human lapse.

Accepting the handshaking and the backslapping, the bearlike hug that Giles Porter bestowed upon him, the kiss that Lili considered his due, Paul found he was standing like a rock in the swirling gaiety that surrounded him. He had won his case—and the winning had preserved two lives—but the triumph was like ashes on his tongue. He had had a final glimpse of Silas' face, just before his brother stalked from the church house—and the torment he saw there told its own story.

Knowing the unbending conscience that drove him, Paul could not believe Silas would be content with the public confession of his guilt. When he had seen Anne leave the church a moment later by the side door, he had guessed that she shared his views. He could not blame her for refusing to join the crowd that surrounded him—but her departure had stung, no less keenly.

Worst of all was the realization that he must continue to walk a chalk line, no less carefully than his brother's promised bride. There was no way, even now, to comfort her in her loneliness— while she waited for Silas to finish this last, desperate battle for his soul.

# THE ATONEMENT

IT was the first night since the trial that Deborah Sikes had slept without opiates.

Calling at her cabin after his morning sick list was cleared, Paul found her seated on her side porch, in the shade of a flowering flame vine, with her husband on the stoop below. Jack Sikes held his wife's hand soothingly between his own. With each passing day, the shadows that had darkened her mind were lifting, though she spoke only in snatches.

"I do think she's on the mend, Doctor," said Jack. "This morning when she wakened, she asked for the child as naturally as though she'd never been away. When I said we'd boarded Prudence until we could start housekeeping again, she didn't turn a hair."

The girl on the porch (she was still little more than that, despite her ordeal) offered no resistance when Paul turned back one eyelid to examine the sclera and tested the pulse at her wrist. This morning, her heartbeat was steady—and the serene look she gave him (unwinking though it was) seemed an augury of happier times. When Jack returned with his wife's luncheon, and fed her as he would a child, Paul could tell himself that there was genuine hope—providing the young husband's patience and understanding did not falter.

"Walk down the path a bit," he whispered. "Deborah won't

mind, if she sees you aren't leaving. I'd like to discuss the case with you."

Jack was glowing with good spirits when Paul had finished his diagnosis. "When will she really come out of the fog, Doctor?"

"She's emerging now. I can't set a time limit for her illness. She's suffered a hard blow to her pride—a spot that hurts most."

"Doesn't she realize she's been acquitted?"

"Not yet, I'm afraid. When she does, we'll hope your troubles are over." Paul hesitated over the next question, aware he could defer it no longer. "How does the colony feel about my brother, Jack? I want the truth—so don't spare me."

The yeoman hesitated, but only for a fraction. "The truth is, sir, his stock's gone up after that confession in court. Asking your pardon, but he's proved himself a man, just like the rest of us. Before that, you couldn't help feeling he was God's deputy on earth. The sort who has all one needs to be a leader, except the common touch."

"How do *you* feel, Jack? After all, his mistake hurt you the most."

"All of us make mistakes," said the yeoman. "I don't doubt he honestly thought Deborah and Lili were witches, when he gave orders for the trial. In his place, I don't suppose I'd have acted otherwise. He might have gone on believing just that, if it hadn't been for your defense—"

"I can't take too much credit there," said Paul. "It isn't an easy thing to see your own kinsman humbled—even though he deserves the lesson. Will the settlement take him back as its leader?"

"Master Sutton never gave up the post, Doctor. All he did was sail off for another spell of map-making."

Their glances met, and Paul could read Jack Sikes' unspoken thought. It was now three days since the ending of the trial: during that time, Silas had been absent from the colony on business of his own. Ostensibly, he had gone to camp on the northern shore of the island, to fill in the last section of the map that had been his special project from the beginning.

Adam Holborn (who had been left in charge) had accepted this excuse without blinking. Silas had taken the sailing skiff, loaded it with his usual camping gear, and departed immediately after his statement from the witness chair had closed the trial. Save for Holborn, and a brief visit with Anne Trevor, he had spoken to no one. It would have been natural for the colonists to assume this abrupt departure was a form of abdication. It cheered Paul mightily to learn that the people of Eleuthera had taken a more charitable view.

"Why did he leave, Doctor?" asked Jack.

"So far, I can only wonder."

"To make peace with himself—and God?"

"That's as good a guess as any," said Paul.

"I wish he'd held back awhile," said Jack. "I meant to go to him that same day—to tell him there were no hard feelings on my side. Still, I can't blame him for wanting to be alone a bit: it took courage to make that sort of confession."

"So it did. Even my brother's worst enemies will admit he's a brave man."

"Asking your pardon again, sir—but there were two people fighting each other on that witness stand. One was your brother: *he's* a person we'd all like to know better. The other was the preacher's shell he'd lived in all his life, like a hermit crab. It's my opinion the best man won."

"The fight isn't over, Jack."

"Can you help him win it, Doctor?"

"Silas stopped taking my advice long ago. He'll win his own way, or not at all. Meanwhile, it's good to hear he has the people's confidence."

"You can count on that, sir." Jack turned toward his cabin, where Deborah still sat beneath the flame vine, her tranquil eyes fixed on space. Having stated his views, he seemed anxious to break away. "Could I go to the orchard this afternoon? The trees need pruning badly."

"You can't leave your wife alone. I'll stop at the tavern and ask Lili to sit with her."

Jack's wide-open stare had been candid enough—now, he hesitated visibly before he spoke again. "Lili isn't on hand just now. She's left us too—in a sailing dinghy."

"How did you learn this, Jack?"

"Early yesterday, before the rest of us were up, she stopped here and asked me to help her with the sail. I thought nothing of it at first. She'd gone out before, to catch her father's breakfast—"

"Perhaps she's returned by now."

"I think not, Doctor. She expected to be gone overnight. Perhaps even longer."

"What more did she say?"

"Only that she'd consider it a favor if I kept her departure a secret. I could tell just one person—you. And then, only if you asked for her."

"I hope you'll keep that promise, Jack."

"You can trust me there, Doctor."

They exchanged a last, troubled look as Paul turned away. "I hardly think she'll come to any harm—if she's only stayed away overnight," he said.

"Do you have any idea where she's bound, sir?"

"I think we both know that," said Paul steadily. "There's no need to question her motives. Let's leave the rest to her—and hope she's done right."

Since the trial, Paul had been at great pains to keep clear of Anne Trevor. Anne, for her part, had stayed within the stockade, setting her face resolutely against the glances that followed her. After this talk with Jack, Paul saw that he must risk a meeting.

He meant to keep Lili's secret if he could: there was no need to trouble Anne with conjecture. At the same time, he could no longer afford to remain in the dark as to his brother's motives. Anne had spoken to Silas, just before the latter's departure. He would ask her to tell him what she could.

Their meeting was arranged through Guy Lebret—who, by a happy chance, was planning to take Anne on a shell-hunting expedition that afternoon, in one of the inlets that scalloped the island's narrow waist. On his return, the Frenchman would stand guard at Spyglass Bluff, a shoulder of land where the colonists had erected a watchtower to cover the northern approaches to

Eleuthera. Paul had told Lebret he would ascend the bluff in mid-afternoon, to relieve the current watchman. When the naturalist arrived in turn, it would be logical to bring Anne to the tower, if only for the view. . . .

"What do you hope to discover?" Lebret asked.

"At the moment, I'm fumbling in the dark. She may be able to explain why Silas left so suddenly."

"You know that answer now."

"Not all of it. Perhaps we can help him between us."

"Your brother is already beyond your help—and Anne Trevor's."

Paul kept his face blank. Lebret (who knew everything) might well have heard of Lili's absence—and guessed the cause. "They say confession's good for the soul," he remarked.

"To some men, yes. Others, like your brother, may find confession a near-mortal blow. To such men, the acknowledgment of a weakness can destroy their most precious illusion—the belief in their own omnipotence."

"Can't he survive that admission?"

"I'm not sure," said Lebret. "One thing is evident: he's gone to North Cove to search for his lost pride."

"He may return a better man—now he's admitted he almost destroyed Lili and Deborah."

"Forgive me if I still wonder."

"Why can't he find his pride again? His prestige in the colony was never higher—"

"He's made Holborn his deputy," said the Frenchman. "It's my guess he'll be a long time returning. Have you forgotten that Mistress Trevor witnessed the whole trial—including his avowal of guilt? How can he face her again, until he's conquered his demon too? Not even Silas Sutton could wrestle *that* enemy in public."

"He'll win the bout, Guy."

The Frenchman spread his hands in a gesture of dismissal. "We've said enough, Paul. The outcome's best left to God."

"Your God—or my brother's?"

"My God would have forgiven him long ago," said Lebret.

They had talked on the beach, where the hand ferry waited to

transport the naturalist to Cupid's Cay. In the end, the Frenchman had gone to conduct Anne on the shell hunt. Paul (with a
heavy heart, and a foreboding he could share with no one) had
turned into the path that led to Spyglass Bluff. . . .

The lookout on duty was happy to surrender his post at the
doctor's hail. The observation platform (lashed to the trunks of
three tall pines) commanded the finest view on Eleuthera. The
colonists had erected a semaphore here, to transmit instant warn-
ings to the stockade: there was a bench for the lookout, and a
tripod for the ponderous Dutch telescope, trained at all times on
the open sea to the north. Paul climbed to the platform with a
sigh of resignation: he already knew what the glass would find.

Yesterday, and the day before, when he had guessed that Silas
would make his bivouac in North Cove, he had swept that coastline with the glass. His brother's camp was in plain view, among
the hills that formed the outpost wedge of the island—a white
speck of tent, a brownish wedge that was the sailing skiff. . . .
Today, the tent was gone, and a sailing dinghy had replaced
the skiff on the beach. The changed pattern told its own story.
Lili Porter had made contact with the man of God—and Silas had
fled the challenge.

While Paul watched, a figure emerged from the underbrush
that half-concealed the campsite and raised the dinghy's sail. In
another moment, the feather-light craft had slipped into deep
water and caught the breeze. It was too far to know if the sailor
was man or woman when the dinghy turned the northern cape
of Eleuthera.

One other detail had changed, and Paul noted it with a puzzled
frown. The buoys that marked the treacherous ship channel to
the north, left in place to assist the imminent departure of the
Adventurer, had vanished from the blue plain of the sound. Paul
could only conclude that Silas had cut them last night, for reasons
of his own: needing a focus for his misgivings, he cursed the last
lookout for not reporting their absence.

He was still wondering at his brother's action when he observed
Anne and Lebret on the steep trail to the bluff. He descended
to ground level to greet them.

"I won't pretend this visit is unexpected," he told Anne.

"It was good of you to arrange the meeting, Paul. I was about to send for you."

One glance at her strained, white face was warning enough. He could never tell her that Silas' camp was now deserted—or that Lili Porter had just left North Cove.

"Shall we walk to the beach?" he asked.

"If you like. I'll wait for you below the bluff."

Lebret, poised on the lookout ladder, lifted one hand in debonair farewell as Anne descended the path. There was no haste in her withdrawal—but it was apparent that she was unwilling to linger on the bluff, which was in plain view of the settlement.

"Anything particular I should know, Paul?"

"Only that Silas has broken camp—and the buoy markers are gone."

"I'll signal the stockade at once," said the naturalist. "D'you think Silas took them?"

"Who else?"

"What was your brother's motive?"

"Perhaps he'll reveal that when he returns," said Paul. He knew he had spoken tartly—and avoided his friend's level glance.

"Don't be too sure he's returning," said the naturalist. "If he spent last night with Lili, he may need a wider horizon for his repentance."

"Who told you he was with Lili?"

"I've known for some time that she followed him to North Cove," said Lebret. "So have you."

"There's no need to jump to conclusions, Guy."

"Only two conclusions are possible. Either your brother's initiated in the rites of Venus—or he's departed with his virtue."

"Must you be so explicit?"

"I don't call it too bad an estimate," said the Frenchman. "Considering his training, it's quite possible that Silas escaped in good time." He ran nimbly up the ladder, pausing a dozen rungs from the ground. "Obviously, my opinions are my own: you needn't share them. Nor would I mention them to *la petite* Anne: she has enough burdens."

"We can agree on that," said Paul—and took the path to the beach. Anne, he observed, had entered a gully between the dunes: he overtook her just as she was mounting the seaward slope. Without a word, she put her hand in his. It was a gesture of trust, and he accepted it in kind while they proceeded toward the boom of the surf.

"Tell me what you can," he said. "It may clear the air."

"There's little you don't already know, I suppose." Anne's lips were set in a thin line, her eyes heavy with unshed tears. "You saw how Silas left the meetinghouse. I'm sure you could guess where he was bound—and why."

"Did you blame him too much?"

"No, Paul. Being Silas, how could he behave otherwise? What I minded most was his refusal to let me share his suffering. I couldn't reach him, even when he came to say good-by—"

Paul turned toward the roar of waves on the beach, unwilling to face Anne's grief. She wept quietly for a moment: when she spoke again, he knew she had put tears behind her.

"I'm telling this badly, Paul," she said. "It's a simple enough story. Silas has convinced himself that he's sinned deeply. Not just because he desired another woman when he was—promised to me. What really troubled him was the way his desire had blinded him to justice. Without the trial, he said, he could have sent those two women to their death. How could God forgive him—ever?"

Paul nodded, without trusting himself to speak: he could see his brother's gesture of abnegation, all too clearly.

"He told me he must go into the wilderness like St. Paul, until he found absolution. He planned to camp in one of the northern coves—to pray and fast there, until he was fit to ask God's help again."

"Did you try to dissuade him?"

"I used every argument I could think of. I said the colony had accepted his confession in the spirit he offered it. I assured him that no real damage had been done, now that Lili and Deborah were free. But he refused to listen. You know how easily he can close his mind."

"Did he set a time limit on his absence?"

"No—but he asked me to release him from our engagement."

Paul's heart gave a great bound. "You refused, of course."

"I said I wouldn't hear of it—that I'd stand by until his torment was ended. I might as well have spoken to a blank wall: I could almost hear my voice echo. I realize now he'd made up his mind about me long ago."

"I can't believe that, Anne."

"He said it wasn't just the trial. Even before I set foot on Eleuthera, he'd planned to send me away—because of the threat from Cuba."

Again, Paul nodded mutely. He remembered his quarrel with Silas on the day of Anne's arrival. It was quite like his brother to rationalize the proddings of this guilt.

"He insisted I go to Virginia on the *Adventurer*," said Anne. "If I wished to hold him to our engagement, he'd honor his promise later, when he felt himself worthy. For the present, he wouldn't have me in the stockade. Not with this storm brewing in Cuba."

"Was that his only reason for asking you to leave?"

Anne drew in her breath sharply, but she was still in control of her voice. "No, Paul. Before he was done, he mentioned the girl too."

"Did he say he loved her?"

"He said it had nothing to do with love. It was more like a fire you can't put out, like a starving man's need for food. He said he'd fought that need ever since he'd left Bristol. That it was something he couldn't expect me to understand. How could I explain I understood him perfectly? *I'd* learned on Cat Island what that hunger meant—and how to control it."

Paul kept his eyes on the Atlantic. The pound of the surf, under the lash of a heavy offshore wind, could not match the thud of his pulses. "It's you he loves, Anne," he said. "He's trying to spare you all he can."

"He said that too. He told me he couldn't ask me to remain here to witness his atonement. The question of Lili would remain, even when he'd made peace with his conscience. So long as he'd thought of her as a witch, he could consign her to the stake—since witches have no souls. *Now*, if God pardoned him, it was his duty to save her too."

"So we're back where we started?"

"We've come full circle," said Anne. "There's one small difference—Silas has admitted he's no more than human."

"Human enough to love you."

"What good is that kind of love?" she cried. "This talk of prayer in the wilderness is only an evasion: Silas is running away from a desire he can't control. The girl has followed him, to prove that running's useless."

"Who told you she followed him?"

"Night before last I couldn't sleep," said Anne. Her voice was quite steady now, and empty of anger. "I went to the palisade to wait for the dawn. She was taking off in a sailing dinghy, with Jack Sikes' help. I could guess where she was bound."

Once more, Paul gave up the hope of deceit: Anne's clear-eyed wisdom was immune to falsehood. "At least Silas made no attempt to mislead you," he reminded her.

"I'd forgive him his desire, if he needed *me* a little," Anne said. "What I can't pardon is this plan to send me away. Never in my life have I felt so unwanted—and so useless."

"Will he go through with that plan?"

"Adam Holborn told me as much this morning. Silas left orders that I'm to be put aboard the *Adventurer*."

"When does she sail?"

"The moment the *Advance* arrives from England." Anne managed a wan smile. "I haven't told you everything. According to Master Holborn, you're to come with me—and make sure I'm settled safely in Jamestown."

"For a man obsessed, my brother's thought of everything."

"I won't leave Eleuthera now, Paul. Nor will you."

"How can we help him, if he can't help himself?"

It was a question that had no answer: he could only take her in his arms, letting his kisses give her what comfort they could. Like all their mutual surrenders, the respite was brief. Anne's

breathing was stormy—but she had broken from his arms before
the double boom of the cannon sounded from the harbor.

"What does it mean, Paul?"

"Guy's sighted an enemy vessel. It's our call to quarters."

During his first days on the island, Paul had imagined that
iron summons a hundred times. Later (with the stockade built,
and each man in the settlement trained to spring to its defense),
the threat had taken the dim shape of nightmare. The alliance
with New Providence had driven it still deeper. . . . Today, as
he took his place in the force that would defend Eleuthera, Paul
found he was strangely calm.

Lebret confirmed his first suspicion when they met in the
blockhouse, to confer with the elders and Adam Holborn. Two
hours before sunset, he had sighted a vessel off the northern cape
—a man-of-war, to judge by her size. Even without the red-and-
gold banner at her forepeak, he would have known her for a
Spaniard by the looming silhouette of her sterncastle. Captain
Sperry, who had hurried to the lookout to verify the report, estimated that she was of at least four hundred tons burden, and
capable of transporting five hundred men at arms.

At the moment the enemy was standing well offshore on the
Atlantic side: it appeared that he was unfamiliar with the coastline of Eleuthera and was still uncertain of his approach. But
there was little doubt he meant to force a landing. Lebret had
counted a half-dozen longboats at each rail—and the pikes and
morions of the invaders had been a steel forest amidships. The
landing would come—once the heavy surf had died. After the
enemy had established his beachhead, he would take whatever
losses the colonists' fire could inflict, then push on across the
island's spine, to lay siege to the stockade. . . . Facing that conclusion squarely, the council of war agreed the situation was
critical, but not hopeless.

Sperry was positive that the boarding party, whatever its size,
would come ashore on the Atlantic side, in the narrow midsection
of Eleuthera. Lacking a chart to the western bight, the geography
of the island made that choice mandatory. To the south, the

densely wooded shores (broken by a series of mangrove swamps) was clearly unsuitable. To the north, the island was cross-cut by sloughs, which made operations by land impractical. An attack must be mounted in force: no commander worthy of his rank would risk an assault in depth without an adequate beachhead.

Thanks to Silas' maps (now virtually complete) it was evident that the dons must secure their first toe hold in the area bounded by Spyglass Bluff and the first mangrove thicket to the south. This stretch of beach was less than three miles in length, all of it backed by a series of high, steep dunes. True, breaks in the coral reef would permit a strike at several points. A mobile defense could still meet the landing with all its available strength, discourage it with massed volleys from the dunes—and, if the enemy persisted, withdraw to the stockade to face the war of attrition that would follow.

"How long can we last, Monsieur Lebret?" Holborn asked.

"Three months, perhaps. We've planned for a siege from the day we stepped ashore."

"The *Advance* is due within the week. She's a warship, with a garrison force aboard. Not strong enough to win a land engagement, I fear—but she could harry the enemy from the sea, since he'll have no anchorage."

"Shouldn't we send word to Captain Hood?" asked Paul.

"You'd accept aid from a pirate?"

"My brother was willing, Master Holborn."

The deputy leader shrugged. "Apparently we've little choice in the matter. How soon can we dispatch a messenger?"

"Not before tomorrow," said Sperry. "No small craft could reach New Providence in this wind."

"The gale isn't an unmixed curse. At least it will keep our beaches safe until tomorrow." Holborn looked round the table at his lieutenants. The set of his jaw, his low-voiced speech, had heartened each man in the room. "It's agreed, then—that we'll fight at the water's edge? Or would you gentlemen prefer to retire to the stockade now, and stand there?"

The vote for action on the dunes was unanimous: this, too, seemed a good omen to Paul. The colonists had hastened to move

their families to the shelter of the palisades, but there had been
hardly a flicker of fear. Men were still laboring in the fields as
the day ended—and the keening wind from the Atlantic promised
safety until morning.

"Perhaps we should scout our battleground while it's still light,
and mark out the best defense posts," Holborn suggested. "I'm
asking Monsieur Lebret to share command with me. You, Doctor,
will set up a field station in the safest spot we can find. Captain
Sperry will defend his ship—"

"My crew will fight beside the colonists," the seadog rumbled.
"We've taken our own vote on that."

"We can use your help," said Holborn gratefully. "It's your
privilege to slip your cables tonight, if you think you can get
away."

"There's no navigating that channel by dark," said the captain.
"It'll be too late tomorrow. Those *caballeros* would like nothing
better than running us down. We're in this land war together,
Master Holborn—and let's hope the enemy doesn't reach our
harbor. We can hold the stockade a long time—but I'm afraid
he'd make short work of the *Adventurer*."

The path that crossed the island from west to east had never
been shorter—and the low, pine-clad hills had never seemed
more vulnerable. Ralph Welles (a bad intriguer but a competent
surveyor) had proved that over a mile of land separated the
western bight from the open sea—but it seemed a matter of
minutes before they stood on the crest of the highest dune, to
survey their chances. Because of the peculiar shape of these wind-
molded sandhills, it was apparent that an armed force could
fight from almost any point, with the seaward slope of the dunes
as a natural defense. Even with both feet ashore, an enemy would
find the strip of beach rough going.

It was agreed that the settlers would divide their forces equally,
massing at the far ends of the shoreline, with Holborn's command
post on a high dune between. When the dons had selected their
beachhead, the two forces would unite to oppose them—spacing
their fire power to pepper the longboats as they entered the surf,
then using a final, punishing volley at close range. It was a logical

battle plan: had the colonists possessed twice their present force, it could have resulted in victory. As the odds stood, Paul realized it could be no more than a holding action—and a risky one, once the Spaniards had beached their whole strength.

Long after the others had returned to the stockade, he stood on the seaward slope of the dunes to watch the green-gold aftermath of sunset. The enemy vessel had sailed nearer in the twilight. It seemed one with the encroaching shadows, a bat-shape that floated between sea and sky. A random shot, belched without warning from a gun port, sent up a geyser of sand as the ball buried itself nearby. Paul felt it prudent to retreat—though the gunner could hardly have noted his silhouette in the gloom. This was not the moment to stand brooding on the future—and there was work to do in the surgery.

Instruments and supplies had been packed that afternoon for transport to the blockhouse, and willing hands had carried most of them to his new headquarters. Tomorrow, when he joined the troops in the field, he would use only the portable case of a field surgeon. It stood ready on his worktable: he lighted a candle to check its contents.

It was only when the reflection of the flame struck the far wall that he realized he was not alone. His visitor was Lili Porter.

"You might tell me I'm welcome," she said.

In the uncertain light, she seemed absurdly small, and oddly defenseless. She was wearing the garb she always used on her fishing excursions: nankeen trousers cut short at the knee, a sailor's blouse, and a scarlet bandanna to protect her hair from the salt. With a familiar gesture, she untied the kerchief and let her dark locks tumble about her shoulders. The gesture restored the girl he knew so well—the *gamine* who would never lose her zest for life's surprises, or the ability to withstand its shocks.

"I hoped you'd return sooner," he said. "Did you have luck with your fishing?"

"I brought back two baskets. They're salting them now at the stockade."

"Is that the story you're telling?"

Lili shrugged. "It will do for now, I think."

"How did you explain last night's absence?"

"I lost the wind at Four Mile Slough, and camped there until morning."

"Sure you didn't sail a bit farther?"

"It isn't like you to doubt my word."

"It isn't like you to lie. I happen to know you were at North Cove with Silas. So does Guy Lebret. So, I fear, does Anne Trevor."

"None of them questioned me when I returned," said Lili. "Why must you?"

"Silas is my brother. He left the colony to escape you."

"Silas went to North Cove to escape himself," said Lili. "It's too large a task for any man."

"This is a poor moment for sophistry."

Lili rose from the chair and touched his shoulder lightly before she perched on the worktable. The candle flame, striking high lights from her copper-dark skin, gave her face an exotic starkness. At the moment, she might have passed for the sorceress Patricia Welles had described so glibly.

"I didn't mean to hold you off, *chéri*," she said. "Only for a little while—until you realize I'm not so black as I'm painted."

"Do you still deny you passed a night at North Cove?"

"Not if you'll keep the secret."

"Did you drive Silas away?"

Lili shook her head. "Far from it. An hour before dawn this morning, he set out for New Providence in the sailing skiff."

*"New Providence?"*

"To warn Captain Hood that a Spanish man-of-war was standing off Eleuthera."

"How do you know this?"

"We made the discovery together, Paul. I wanted to go with him. He insisted I return and warn the colony."

Paul controlled his impatience. This, after all, was Lili's moment: she had chosen to confront him deliberately, and she would tell her story in her own fashion. At least, it was a relief to know his brother's whereabouts.

"Why did you follow him, Lili? To prove you're stronger than his will?"

"He proved that for us both, in open court." The girl's full red lips curved into the Lilith smile Paul knew so well. "Until he admitted I was only a *human* witch, he was one of the few men I ever really hated. After he'd spoken up, I saw how badly I'd misjudged him. I wanted to thank him for saving Deborah and me. I wanted even more to say how sorry I was for—hating him."

"Were those your own reasons?"

"Word of honor, Paul. Believe that much, or I'll tell you nothing more."

"I believe you, Lili."

"It was dark when I reached North Cove. I couldn't sail back before morning." Lili was in deadly earnest now. "I *did* want to make peace with Silas Sutton—but it went deeper than that. There was a force drawing me toward him: it was as though your brother was a magnet and I a helpless scrap of steel. He'd proved himself a man in court. I couldn't rest until I was sure of it."

"*That* I can understand perfectly," said Paul.

"Don't be a cynic tonight," she cried. "Try to see your brother as I saw him."

"I'm trying hard."

"When I sailed into the cove, he was at his campfire: he didn't notice me until I'd beached the dinghy. I thought he'd be furious —but he seemed to take my arrival for granted. 'You're just in time for supper,' he said. 'Will you share a fish with me, and some hardtack? It's all I have to offer.' Then he handed me ashore, as though I were some kind of princess.

"It was like a dream. Even after we'd shared his meal. I couldn't believe it was happening. His voice was different—quiet and gentle. I might have been a child he knew he must humor. He didn't ask me why I'd come all that distance. He only said he was glad—because having me here beside him tonight would save time for us both. So far, he hadn't dared ask the Lord to forgive him for all the harm he'd done me. Now, if I'd kneel beside him, he'd ask God's help for us both.

"He must have prayed for hours, Paul. At first, I tried to shut out his voice. Then, don't ask me how, I found myself listening. After that, I lost track of time. I remember the campfire had burned itself out when I heard a second voice, repeating the words of the prayer. All at once, I realized it was my own. It was the first time I'd prayed since my mother died—"

The scene, to Paul, was now unbearably vivid. All the trappings were present: the last, dying flicker of the campfire, the two panting voices, the swaying bodies, converging in the fevered embrace that had been inevitable from the beginning. Lili's voice shattered the image, like a pebble dropped in the mirrored surface of a pool.

"You think we made love, don't you? You're sure that's why I followed him. I won't pretend the idea never crossed my mind. But it didn't happen."

"Will you take your oath on that?"

"I won't say it *couldn't* have happened, without the interruption. Silas called it a sign from Heaven. I'm inclined to believe him."

"What interruption?"

"Six Spaniards in a longboat, rowing in from the darkness. I couldn't have been more startled if a brood of angels had dropped out of the nearest cloud. They didn't see or hear us. The sound of their oarlocks gave us warning."

"Spaniards from the man-of-war?"

"So we learned. Right then, we couldn't stop to think: we had to scramble for our lives. The fire was out, as I've said. We pulled both boats into the mangroves before they could notice them. As it turned out, we were in no real danger—they were rowing toward a sandspit on the western rim of the cove. Once they'd grounded the longboat, they set about making supper there.

"Silas told me to hide in the scrub while he went to spy on them, but I wouldn't let him go alone. It was child's play to creep up on their fire without being noticed: *they* didn't think there was a human being within twenty miles. And it was lucky I stayed close to Silas: They were talking in Spanish, of course—and he needed a translator.

"Their ship was well offshore, too far for us to notice in the dark. They'd beaten up from Cuba against the wind. Tomorrow, they planned to run down our coast. Meanwhile, the longboat had come ashore to pick out landmarks. They had to make sure this island was Eleuthera—"

Paul nodded: Silas had been right when he called that nocturnal visit a sign from Heaven.

"They'd sailed well to the west the day before," said Lili. "They didn't dare approach the bight, because of the reefs. The longboat's task was to explore the coastline to the east, to see if there was a passage. From what they said, they weren't too hopeful—but they set off at once, the moment they'd finished eating.

"We still had an hour before dawn. Silas had the sail on his skiff before they'd cleared the harbor mouth. He told me he'd take up the channel markers, in case they retraced their course. Then he'd cross the sound to New Providence. With the east wind, he hoped to reach it before the day ended.

"I asked to go along, but he wouldn't hear of it. He said I must hurry to the stockade and report to Adam Holborn." Now that she had poured out her news, Lili seemed almost composed. "We even arranged a story to—protect us both. I was to say we met at sea, off the channel reefs, that he'd told me he was getting help from Hood. Now Mistress Trevor can have her nuptials—and your brother will come to the altar a stainless bridegroom."

"Providing we aren't all dead this time tomorrow," said Paul.

Lili tossed her head, and got down from the worktable. "If God didn't mean us to win, why did we overhear the enemy at North Cove? Why has there been a gale since noon? With a west wind, the sea would be flat and the Spaniards could be ashore by now. Tomorrow, when we join forces with Hood, they'll be cut to pieces on the beach—"

"Will that be God's work too?"

"War is man's work," said Lili. "The Lord can still take sides."

Eleuthera's small army left the stockade with the first light. Marching by squads, it climbed the landward side of the Atlantic dunes—aware, even at the early hour, that the roar of the surf had diminished to a gentler rhythm, now that the wind had veered. All that long morning, the Spanish vessel continued to sail an easy triangular course offshore. At high noon, with the surf flattened to a lazy ground swell, the man-of-war made the first truly aggressive move, running straight for land, then dropping her mainsail outside a wide opening in the coral.

A scant quarter-hour later (hove to less than a mile offshore) the Spaniards put their first longboat into the Atlantic.

Crouched at the crest of the dune that served as Holborn's command post, using a tuft of bay grape as cover, Paul studied the vessel through the glass. He saw that the men-at-arms pouring overside knew their trade. So did the officers giving orders at the rope ladders—and the captain who paced the poop deck with the air of a man executing a routine maneuver. Judging by the overloaded boats, he intended to sweep the field in his first thrust, by sheer weight of numbers. The boom of a single cannon, the scream of the round shot that winged above the sandhills to shear off the top of a coco palm, was only a contemptuous footnote to that intention.

"They must know we'll fight for the beach," said Holborn. "Why do they advertise their intentions so openly?"

"Perhaps they're asking us to show the white flag now."

"They'll regret the request in a few more moments."

"Shouldn't we be joining forces with Lebret?"

"I've just given the order, Doctor. It seems they plan to run the surf directly below us. That's a point in our favor."

Paul nodded a silent agreement. It had been a long wait behind the dunes. The colonists, seeking what shade they could find, had been parched by the merciless beat of the sun. It was a relief to know the action would be joined at last.

"I'll pass out water-and-rum when the men are at their posts," he said. "They've earned a nip of courage, after this wait."

"Is your field station ready?"

"Captain Sperry gave me two of his quartermasters to serve as stretcher bearers: I've enlisted Jack Sikes as my assistant—he's a cool man in a crisis. We'll set up quarters at the foot of this dune, so you can pass down your orders—assuming this will be the center of our line."

"There's no doubt of it now," said Holborn. "See how tightly they're moving inshore? They'll fan out before they reach the surf, of course—but this will be their own center." He pointed to a mound of driftwood on the narrow strip of beach below. "My guess is their shore commander will use that spot as his head-quarters. Let's hope he makes a good target."

The longboats, unreal as long-legged beetles when they had left their mother ship, were now alarmingly close to the beach. There was a sailor at each oar, an arrangement that gave the fighting men aboard a chance to save their wind. It was a clear indication that the boats would return to the ship, to bring in fresh troops: so far, only a third of the enemy force was com-mitted.

Moving swiftly in the screen of dunes, Lebret's command ar-rived from the south to take its assigned post as Holborn's right wing. The leader's own forces had already settled in the gun pits they had scooped out that morning. Whispered jokes were ex-changed as these marksmen drew their first tentative beads on the meeting place of sea and shore: the maneuver had been executed in a space of minutes.

Paul (who was no stranger to combat) could feel panic choke his throat as the first longboat swam into musket range. Jack Sikes, creeping on hands and knees to the crest of the dune, an-nounced in a husky whisper that the last of the rum-and-water ration had been distributed.

"It's been a hot morning, Doctor. Looks like we'll have a still hotter afternoon—"

Holborn lifted his hat on his sword's point. It was the signal for his best marksmen to fire at will, and a score of muskets barked down the length of the dunes. Timed to catch the long-boats as they began to run the surf (a commitment that did not permit them to row out of range) the first volley was effective. When the smoke lifted, Paul saw that a dozen men had slumped in the thwarts. One of the steersmen had tumbled overside, and his boat (yawing violently in a trough between two waves) would have foundered had not the nearest soldier grasped the sweep. In another boat, a tangle of splintered oars, slowing the drive toward the beach in the midst of a breaking wave, brought the slender vessel broadside. Burdened as it was, it capsized instantly, tumbling other men to their death, as they sank like so many stones in their armor.

The other boats ran ashore unhurt, save for a few bullet holes: the soldiers piled into the shallows with disciplined ease while the oarsmen reversed their blades for the return run. Holborn held back his signal until the enemy was massed at the water's edge. The second volley, delivered at close range, was truly lethal. Paul counted over fifty dead, and half as many wounded, before the sorely harried dons could reform their lines and begin to return the fire.

There was no time to witness the next phase of the attack: as field surgeon, he had more pressing duties. Hearing the first call for stretcher bearers, he scrambled downhill to his post, ready to salvage what lives he could among the defenders. From this point, the battle would come to him in snatches.

The first wave of the attack did not quite attain the crests of the dunes. Forced to take what cover they could find, probing for a break in the rain of lead that swept the narrow beaches, the enemy pressed on relentlessly for a while, inching into the gullies in desperate efforts to turn the colonists' flank—then retreating to exchange shots uphill, at an ever-elusive target.

In the next half-hour, the contest had assumed a rough pattern. On their side, the dons had established a rough half-moon of beachhead, taking shelter in improvised trenches, buttressed by driftwood and foundered palmetto logs. Directed by their field commander (a roly-poly officer in full armor, who seemed immune to bullets) they had staked out a tentative foothold on several of the smaller dunes, without daring to risk a movement on the landward side. Their losses had been formidable, but far from decisive. In the colonists' ranks, casualties had been slight. At midafternoon, they continued to reload red-hot muskets—and since they were still firing downhill, had pinned the bulk of the enemy force to the water's edge.

Paul, working at the base of Holborn's dune, had picked up these details from his own wounded. Most of them were routine cases: a grazed skull, a bullet through the chest, and a shattered hip were the worst, plus the inevitable minor hurts that are the product of every war, regardless of the battlefield. Several men had been injured at the powder magazine, when a cannon shot, shattering the trunk of a pine tree nearby, had sprayed the area with flying splinters. Two of these cases had died under his knife: Jack reported that three more lay dead beside their muskets. . . . The slightly injured had been returned to the stockade. Others were bedded well to the rear, in the shade of a palm grove.

When Paul was able to lift his eyes at last, to survey the field as a whole, he realized that the fighting had reached a temporary lull, broken only by sporadic gunshots from the dunes.

"I'm going to have a look, Jack," he said. "Call if I'm needed."

A little later, spread-eagled once again in the sand beside Holborn, he parted the tuft of bay grape and studied the extent of the enemy beachhead. At this height, it was easy to count heads. The sand was thickly sown with bodies, but it was obvious that the survivors (craftily dug in, and too cautious to attract more than an occasional shot) were now numbered by the hundreds. The second wave had come ashore while he labored in his field surgery. The third was forming aboard the mother ship, awaiting their officer's word to drop into the bullet-scarred longboats.

The sun was still high, he noted: it was barely two hours since the beginning of hostilities. The shape of the coming battle was clear. Already, the men on the beachhead outnumbered the colonists two to one. When that third and final wave had come ashore, there would be a general charge that could only end in the defenders' rout.

"Should we withdraw now, Master Holborn? It'll be rough going if they overrun us."

The leader shook his head. "Give me a half-hour more, and we'll save the day," he said. "The wind's held steady from the west: it's bringing us help from New Providence."

"The *Falcon*?"

"She was sighted from the lookout, on the stroke of two."

"Can we pass the word down the lines?"

"I couldn't risk it, Doctor. It would only start a cheer, and give us away." Holborn glared down at the thick ranks of the invaders. "One hard rush could destroy us in our tracks—if they knew our true strength."

"Will you get that half-hour?"

"Look out to sea. Four of their longboats have been smashed so far: they'll need two trips to bring their full strength ashore. It could make the difference."

Paul's heart raced as he let his thoughts close on that calm appraisal. His brother, it seemed, had reached the pirates' careening ground in good time: Captain Jeremy Hood (flairing to the hated scent of Spain) had lost no time in keeping his promise. At the moment, their lives depended on his skill in tracing the channel to the bight. The fate of the enemy would be sealed if the colonists could hold their ground until his arrival. A retreat to the stockade at this time could bring, at best, only a partial victory, since the surprise element would be lost. A glance at Adam Holborn told him that the deputy leader was prepared to gamble.

"How do we stand on ammunition?"

"Fresh powder kegs have come from the cay. We've two dozen rounds per man—"

From the beach, a single musket cracked the stillness, bringing a bellow of pain from a nearby dune. Rising on hands and knees, Paul saw his stretcher bearers move into action.

"Tell me what happened when it's over," he said. "It seems my breather had ended."

His newest patient, Paul learned, was Giles Porter. The innkeeper had been hit in the thigh. The wound was bleeding profusely. It did not seem too dangerous after the probe had extracted the bullet—though Paul saw that prompt action was needed to tie off a severed artery near the femur.

Giles was half-conscious when the stretcher bearers (staggering under their mountainous burden) dropped him at the field station. At Paul's direction, he stretched out dutifully on the improvised operating table, sucked at a whiskey jug while the scalpel made its first deep strokes, and fainted dead away at the rasp of knife on bone. . . . The business of ligating the damaged vessel was an exacting one, demanding the utmost concentration on the surgeon's part. While he worked, Paul was dimly conscious of a clash of steel on the dune above, and realized that hand-to-hand combat had begun at last. If the sandhills were overrun, the field station would be exposed to enemy fire. Knowing the fighting habits of the dons, he would be a sitting target before his task was ended.

Whipcord ligatures finally closed the artery. In the act of reaching for a dressing, Paul was aware of a full-throated cheer, rising and falling like surf along the battle line. Giles had shown signs of returning life in the final stages of the operation. Now, as Jack Sikes released an iron grip on his leg, the innkeeper opened his eyes and reached again for the jug.

"That must be our friends from New Providence, Doctor."

"You knew they were coming?"

"It was only a rumor, but it spread fast."

The query had already been answered. The buccaneers, bursting from the piney woods in a fast-running wedge, had broken into detachments to pour down to the beach through every available cleft in the dunes. Each man was armed to the teeth—and they were firing as they ran. The headlong charge, intent on its main objective, skirted the field station without a pause. At the same moment, a pair of Spaniards (shielded from view in a brush-choked gully) charged downhill to dispatch the doctor and his helper.

They were armed only with cutlasses, and each bore the marks of battle: Paul guessed that they had broken free of the general melee in time, and meant to inflict what damage they could before they were hunted down. There was no time for conscious planning in the face of that deadly attack. Intent on saving his patient, Paul snatched up one of the cutlasses left by his own wounded, tossed a second blade to Jack, and rushed to meet the nearer of his adversaries.

From the first clash of steel, it was a hopelessly unequal contest. Paul had never been an accomplished swordsman: well-muscled though he was, he made a poor match for the Spaniard's iron wrist and fury-laden strokes. Fighting blindly, without daring to check on Giles, he knew only that he had lured his attacker to a stretch of level grass that made a fair dueling ground . . . His ears rang with a high, keening scream, as Jack Sikes' own duel ended—but he dared not turn to discover who had won.

Locking guards, he met the enemy eye to eye, only to lose ground on the thrust that freed the two blades. The recoil had sent him reeling into a palmetto clump. Unable to judge his footing, he felt his heel catch in a projecting root. He righted himself in time to dodge a murderous stroke that could have split head and shoulders, had it landed fairly. There was a flash of steel, as the Spaniard locked guards a second time, twisting the cutlass from his hand with practiced ease.

Unarmed and dodging for his life, he went down on hands and knees among the palmettos. He heard the Spaniard's shout, caught the flash of sun on steel: for an endless interval, the man's body seemed to hang in space above him, but the death blow did not fall. Instead, Paul heard the bark of a *pistola* from his field station—and realized that Giles, rising painfully on an elbow, had just shot his adversary through the back. He rolled aside, before his would-be assassin pitched head foremost into the scrub.

"Sorry for the delay, Doctor," said Giles. "I couldn't risk a shot earlier, for fear of hitting you."

Jack Sikes, who had just cut down his own man, helped Paul to his feet. Their belated involvement in the battle had ended in a matter of minutes. In that interval (to judge by the roar of cheers from the beach) the contest had been decided beyond dispute. Leaving Jack to finish the whiskey with Giles, Paul scrambled back to the command post where Captain Jeremy Hood knelt side by side with Holborn to survey the prospect below.

Intent on the finale of the battle, the pirate gave Paul the briefest of nods. "Sorry I couldn't hold your brother back," he said. "As you'll observe, he insisted on leading our charge."

Save for a last pocket of resistance at the sea's edge, the field was already won for England. The enemy dead lay in windrows, knocked down by the combined cross fire of colonists and buccaneer: the latter still ranged among the tumbled bodies, dispatching the wounded without mercy. In the surf, three of the longboats had wallowed out of gun range: the men at the oars (a corporal's guard for each boat) were rowing for their lives. The other boats had been scuttled in the shallows, and their crews cut down at the thwarts. Only a fragment of the enemy force had escaped the trap. Their frantic haste to reach the mother ship set a final seal on the debacle.

Paul's eyes found Silas last of all, half-hidden as he was by the driftwood mound that had been the enemy's strong point. His brother was stripped to the waist, his great torso crisscrossed with a red map of wounds. Dead lay all about him, clubbed down by the musket he still held aloft. Among them was the Spanish commander, sprawled at his feet with a crushed skull.

"A crusader to the end," said Hood. "Go to him, if you wish. He's done with fighting."

Paul shouted his brother's name as he ran down the seaward slope. Silas lifted his head slowly, letting the musket drop to the beach. His eyes blinked in the glare of the westering sun. Then, without a sound, he collapsed among his fallen enemies.

He was not yet dead when Paul knelt beside him—but each of several wounds he had received (in that reckless dash into the Spanish line) was clearly mortal. When he spoke, his voice was entirely tranquil.

"Have we won?"

"Completely—thanks to you."

"It's only the first battle, Paul. There'll be many others."

"We'll win them too."

"Not you and I."

"Other Englishmen, then. The Bahamas will never be part of Spain."

"They'll still be disputed ground," said Silas. "I want you to take Anne out of it."

"Now? When we've won?"

"Now, Paul. To the Virginia colony—if she wishes to stay in the New World. She'll be safe there." Silas' even voice had not wavered, though his eyes had taken on the glaze that precedes death. "I want you both to be happy—in a way I never could. It's my last wish. Promise you'll fulfill it."

"I promise, Silas."

"Tell her I didn't mean to disappoint her. I wanted to give her a Paradise on earth. I see now it existed only in my mind. I wanted to love her—but earth-bound love was beyond me."

"Must I tell her that?"

"There's no need. She knows it already. Will you forgive me too?"

"There's nothing to forgive."

Silas' breath escaped in a long sigh. Paul bent forward sharply, positive that he was gone. When his brother spoke again, his voice was less than a whisper.

"Last night at North Cove, I asked God to absolve me. I meant to be His messenger on earth. I failed in that—but I could still save Eleuthera. It's my atonement, Paul. I think I've earned my right to Heaven."

The last word was almost lost as Silas' head lolled forward. After a moment, Paul lowered his brother's body to the sand. The red-and-gold flag of Spain, its staff splintered, lay across the driftwood mound. He lifted the banner to cover the body, before he turned back to his field station, and his task of aiding the living.

"He died content," Paul said. "He lived out his legend. Few men have done as much."

"Are you sure you've told me everything?"

"Everything that matters, Anne. He was a great man, as well as a brave one. In the end, he even learned to rise above self. I won't say the lesson came too late."

They stood together on the beach of Cupid's Cay, watching the last stores go aboard the *Adventurer*. Two days had passed since the repulse of the Spaniards, and Captain Sperry planned to put to sea with the morning tide.

Across the harbor, the *Advance* rode at anchor, her gun ports gleaming in the sun. She had come down the channel only yesterday, with fresh cannon for the ramparts, fresh troops to guard them—and a hundred new colonists to swell the population of Eleuthera. Hours before, the *Falcon* had left that same berth, confident she could run down the Spanish man-of-war and bring it to heel without further loss of blood. . . . It was hard to believe that so short a time had elapsed since the battle—and harder still to face the fact that some thirty Englishmen had died on the Atlantic beach in defense of Eleuthera.

Anne and Paul had just returned from the funeral of those thirty heroes. They had knelt with the other colonists while Obadiah Lambert had said a prayer for them all—standing above Silas' grave, the last to be closed. The Spanish dead would be buried later, in a mass trench among the dunes; their own chaplain would say the proper prayer above it. He was one of the few prisoners the buccaneers had taken. Captain Hood felt that he would have a certain value as a hostage, and he would be sent to New Providence in good time. . . .

"Must we go to Virginia, Paul?"

He looked up from his own deep well of grief, and took Anne's hand. "I promised him, my dear. We can't go back on my word. You've made your contribution here—and so have I. There'll be work to do in Virginia, a place of honor for us both. You can rely on that."

"You're right, of course," she said. "It was his dying wish: I was selfish to question it."

"They're bound to have other battles, and other heartbreaks, before the Bahamas are part of England. Hood won't always be an ally: a pirate's a fair-weather friend at best. The dons may come back for revenge. Adam Holborn and his successors can fight those wars. We deserve this voyage to Virginia."

"Shall we go aboard now, Paul?"

"In a few more moments. I must say good-by to Lili."

Anne looked across the harbor. He saw she had turned deliberately, lest he note the shadow of pain that had darkened her eyes.

"Go to her by all means," she said. "She's been a good friend—to us all."

"That's true enough," said Paul. "Even when she joined Silas at North Cove. I'm glad you understand that, Anne. Few women would."

When he left Anne on the beach, he hurried toward the hand ferry without looking back. His other good-bys had already been spoken—to Adam Holborn, to the young doctor who had just taken his place in the sick bay, to Giles Porter (recovering there from his wound), to Guy Lebret (who would stay on awhile at Eleuthera, to complete his tome on the Bahamas). He had put off this meeting with Lili to the end—since he had dreaded it more than he cared to admit. He could not close the record otherwise.

He found her in the empty tavern, packing the last of her father's trunks. The Porters had learned the *Advance* would sail direct for Bristol, and had changed ships at the last moment. Giles' nephew (who had managed the Feathers in his absence) would arrive on the next ship to take over here. He would farm the choice acres held by the innkeeper as an original settler on Eleuthera.

Paul closed the door and leaned against it, without advertising his presence. An unanswered question still cried out for utterance. He hoped he could find the words to phrase it.

When Lili sensed his presence and faced him, they spoke for a while of other matters—knowing in advance that evasion was futile. Only an hour ago, they had knelt together at Silas' grave. His brother had paid a high price for eternal rest. Paul would find no rest on earth until he knew the details of that payment.

"Say what you're thinking," she demanded at last.

"Silas had paid for the sin of pride. He'd risen above desire. There was no need for him to die."

"No need *we* would accept, Paul," said Lili quietly. "The need was real enough. He'd been courting death since he laid eyes on me in Bristol."

"If his desire was so great, why didn't he take you at North Cove?"

"He couldn't, Paul—don't you see why? His love of God was greater than the needs of the flesh."

"Wasn't it enough to rise above temptation?"

"Your brother had lusted in his heart," said Lili. "It was more than he could bear. All his life, he'd been above the battle. Here on Eleuthera, he found he was a man, with a man's passion. Death was the only atonement that had meaning."

"What if you'd never met, Lili? Suppose he'd given Anne his name, as he'd intended. Could they have made a marriage?"

"I think not. That was part of his torture—knowing he could never be a true husband. Silas Sutton wasn't meant for marriage. Or for any real happiness—"

"What was his purpose, then? His life wish?"

"To be a saint on earth," said Lili. "It's a noble aim. Who are we to censure him, if he fell short?"

"Are you sorry now that you followed him to North Cove?"

"No, Paul. When I followed him, I pitied his loneliness—"

"All of us are lonely. *I've* been lonely, all my days."

"Not as Silas Sutton was lonely. I'd have given myself to him freely, if I'd thought it would help. How could I tell him that life is worth living, if you'll meet it halfway? He'd already fixed his sights on Heaven. *His* only love was death."

Lili was weeping when he kissed her good-by. He knew that her tears were for the infinite stupidity of man, faced with the riches of the world.

"We've prayed at your brother's grave," she said. "Take Anne to Virginia, as he asked. Marry her there—and give her the life you've both earned. He'd have wanted that—for you both. And shed no more tears for Silas Sutton, now he's left you. Like all martyrs, he's where he belongs."

Paul stood awhile on the tavern porch, for a last look at Eleuthera. Lili's wisdom, as always, had sprung from the earth on which her feet were so firmly planted. Today, she had spoken in the tongues of angels.

*Silas was right to send us to Virginia,* he thought. *We could never live here with today's memory between us.*

In a different country (he told himself) his brother's memory would be forever green. Other men would die in the Bahamas, before Silas' paradise was a reality. . . . Sailing north with Anne on the morrow, he could say they had written a vital page in its

history. No matter how the ending read, the name of Silas Sutton
would have a place of honor, on a more exalted role than the
Eleutherian Adventurers.

When he crossed to Cupid's Cay, his heart was afire with the
future. On the beach, below the Puritans' stockade, his bride was
waiting.